Four Steps to the Perfect Revenge

OTHER TITLES BY LILIAN MONROE

The Four Groomsmen of the Wedpocalypse

Conquest
Craving

Manhattan Billionaires

Big Bossy Mistake
Big Bossy Trouble
Big Bossy Problem
Big Bossy Surprise

The Heart's Cove Hotties Series

Dirty Little Midlife Crisis
Dirty Little Midlife Mess
Dirty Little Midlife Mistake
Dirty Little Midlife Disaster
Dirty Little Midlife Debacle
Dirty Little Midlife Secret
Dirty Little Midlife Dilemma
Dirty Little Midlife Drama
Dirty Little Midlife (fake) Date

The We Shouldn't Series
(Brother's Best Friend Romance)

Shouldn't Want You
Can't Have You
Don't Need You
Won't Miss You

The Protector Series

His Vow
His Oath
His Word

The Love/Hate Series

Hate at First Sight
Loathe at First Sight
Despise at First Sight

The Unexpected Series (Surprise Pregnancy)

Knocked Up by the CEO
Knocked Up by the Single Dad
Knocked Up ... Again!
Knocked Up by the Billionaire's Son

Four Steps to the Perfect Revenge

A romantic comedy

LILIAN MONROE

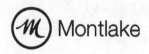 Montlake

Published by Montlake, Seattle

www.apub.com

Amazon, the Amazon logo, and Montlake are trademarks of Amazon.com, Inc., or its affiliates.

ISBN-13: 9781662518508 (paperback)
ISBN-13: 9781662518515 (digital)

Cover design by Letitia Hasser
Cover photography by Regina Wamba of ReginaWamba.com
Cover image: © Runrun2 / Shutterstock

Printed in the United States of America

Four Steps
to the
Perfect
Revenge

STEP ONE: FINDING AN ACCOMPLICE

CHAPTER 1

Ellie Davis needed muscle. Ideally, she'd find great, ambulant slabs of it attached to a frame that didn't ask too many questions.

"What are we doing here again?"

Ellie scowled at the scrawny blonde woman crouching in the bushes beside her. Wynn Howard had been Ellie's best friend since the first day of first grade, but she was not made for sitting in foliage under a steady, gray drizzle. Wynn pulled a leaf off the bush and hunkered down under her black rain jacket, a grumpy tortoise uninterested in important covert operations. "I'm hungry."

"You're a terrible accomplice is what you are." Ellie turned back to the fence looming ten feet away, pushing a branch aside so she could see what she was up against. The fence was timber and about eight feet tall. It had a gate secured with a metal chain and a solid padlock. Ellie knew it was solid because she'd failed to slice through it earlier with the only tool at her disposal. The bolt cutters in her hands were slick with water, the red duct tape wrapped around the handles warm beneath her fingers. "As to what we're doing, we're getting Louie so I can get off this island for good."

"Oh, come on, Ellie. You're not serious about that, are you? Where are you going to go?"

"I'll figure it out once I'm on the mainland." She'd crash on her sister's couch, cuddle her dog, and move on from this place.

Wynn let out an exasperated noise, peeking around the side of her hood to meet Ellie's gaze. "It was *one* mug shot. Your mom has, like, a hundred mug shots from the seventies and eighties. It's practically a family tradition. Your grandmother was *proud* of you."

Ah, yes. The illustrious family legacy. How could Ellie forget? She'd lived in the shadow of her parents' misspent youths her entire life. Her mood grew darker than the oppressive cloud cover draped over her head. "Is this supposed to be convincing me to stay on this stupid island? Because it isn't working, Wynn."

"Fernley is your home."

"*That* was my home." She pointed the bolt cutters at the cedar shingle roof poking above the nearby trees. "Now it's the building I'd burn down if I had any desire to commit arson."

Wynn lifted her head, pushing the hood of her rain jacket back an inch so she could stare at the house through the scraggly fir trees. She seemed to mull over Ellie's words, tearing the leaf in her hands into teeny, tiny pieces. Then she glanced at Ellie and gave her a thoughtful look. "Your mom got arrested for arson once, right? Didn't she burn down the mayor's house when she was fifteen?"

Ellie didn't dignify that with a response. She'd worked hard to rise above her parents' reputations so the people on this island would give her a chance. She'd built a business, put everything she had into gaining the respect of her peers. And now—

But never mind that. Ellie had only one thing to do before she could be free of this place. Her dog was behind that fence, and she wasn't leaving the island unless Louie was by her side.

Six months. *Six months* was how long she'd spent trying to get Louie back the right way, the legal way. She wasn't waiting one minute longer.

With one last look left and right, Ellie dashed to the padlocked gate and tried her might against the chain once more. Her first attempt hadn't yielded any results, but now she was desperate. Desperate women were dangerous—and effective.

The chain holding the gate closed was thick, galvanized steel, and it didn't even dent in the jaws of her stupid bolt cutters. Fergus O'Hara had sold them to her out of the trunk of his car in exchange for an extortionate three hundred dollars, and he'd been a damn liar about how sharp they were. The patina of rust and the duct-taped handles should have been her first and second clues as to their effectiveness, but Ellie hadn't had many options in the bolt cutter department. Buying new ones at the hardware store moments before breaking and entering would have won her another mug shot and a second lifetime's worth of humiliation.

She squeezed until her muscles gave out.

The chain held, clinking gently against the timber fence, laughing at her. She scowled.

If she were staying on the island, Ellie would give Fergus a piece of her mind. These bolt cutters might not get through steel, but they'd probably work on human toes—and other body parts. Luckily for Fergus, she'd be on the next ferry out of here when he rolled out of bed at the start of the next century.

Grunting and growling with effort, Ellie put all her weight into squeezing the handles one more time. She needed to break this chain, *needed* to get Louie out of there . . .

She fell back, panting. Stumbling forward again, she wiped raindrops from her eyes to see if the chain was any closer to yielding.

Nothing. Not even a scratch on the metal link she'd thrown all her weight into snapping.

"I'm going to kill him," Ellie grumped. "*Best bolt cutters on the island*, my ass."

The thick padlock shackle didn't yield to Ellie's efforts any more than the chain did, so she resorted to whacking it with the pointy end of her useless tool like it was some kind of felonious version of a strongman carnival game, where the prize was not getting arrested. Or, more accurately, not getting arrested *again*. The sound of metal hitting metal echoed around the forest, sending a nearby bird flapping in outrage.

"Let me try." Wynn held out her hand, pink nail polish perfect as always.

"Your arms are twigs."

Wynn pursed her lips. "I've been working out, Ellie. Plus, it's about technique more than brute strength."

Ellie wasn't so sure about that, but she handed the cutters over.

After a short struggle, Wynn let out a frustrated huff and started whacking the padlock too. Once she'd exhausted herself, she let the bolt cutters dangle from her fingertips and met Ellie's gaze. "We need someone with lots of brute strength. Technique is not important."

Ellie snorted, slipping the bolt cutters into her backpack before hiking it up on her shoulders and clipping the chest strap. She frowned at the chain, then backed up a few steps and studied the top of the fence.

"Um . . . Ellie?" Wynn took a step closer. "You're not going to—"

Ellie took off at a sprint, channeling her inner Jackie Chan as she lifted her leg to try to propel herself up the fence with a powerful kick. She'd never run up a vertical surface before, but today was her day. She leaped, hanging in the air as time stopped around her. Then her fingers brushed the top of the fence and slipped off, and she landed on her back on a bed of wet ferns.

Note to self: ferns do not provide for a soft landing. Especially when her backpack was full of lumpy tools and sharp edges.

Groaning, she clutched her tailbone. The chain knocked merrily against its gate while the muddy imprint of her shoe stared back from the surface of the fence, taunting her.

So far, Ellie's career as a criminal had been pathetic. She wasn't even living up to the family name she'd tried so hard to outrun.

Wynn appeared above Ellie's head, hand extended. Accepting her friend's help, Ellie clambered to her feet and set her jaw.

"I can jump that fence. Then I'll grab Louie and go out through the front."

"The front is padlocked too," Wynn pointed out.

"I'll go through the house."

"What about the alarm? I'm sure the code has been changed since you moved out. And you know it probably connects directly to Sheriff Jackson's phone. He'll be here within minutes if it goes off."

Damn Wynn and her stupid, faultless logic. Ellie stared at the barrier separating her from her dog. "So I'll jump the fence, grab Louie, then . . . then . . ."

"I'll give you a boost," Wynn suggested; "then you pull me over with you, and we can lift Louie back over together. He'll be fine jumping down from the top. Then I can boost you over again, you pull me up, and hey presto, we're gone without a trace."

Ellie grinned. "This is why I keep you around, Wynnie. That's genius."

"You keep me around because everyone else thinks you're a crazy person who's going to snap and attack them with a baseball bat."

Ellie would never live that mug shot down. "Low blow, Wynn."

Wynn grinned and scampered away. She knelt near the fence and braided her fingers together, lifting her head awkwardly so she could see Ellie under the hood of her rain jacket. "Ready."

Ellie blew out a breath and joined Wynn at the fence. A moment later, propelled by Wynn, she pulled herself up onto the top of the timber fence, swinging one leg over to straddle it. The fence had a flat piece of two-by-four across the top, just above the foot-tall privacy lattice. It was wide enough to sit on but not exactly comfortable.

Wynn cheered. "See? I'm strong." She jerked her chin toward the yard. "Any sign of Louie?"

Ellie scanned the space. It was just as she remembered. A hot tub sat dormant near the back door, on the left side of the big deck. The fire bowl at the bottom of the deck's steps was filled with wet ash and charred wood, surrounded by concrete pavers and new patio chairs. Green, lush grass was edged with weeds and the carcasses of last year's flowers. New blooms wouldn't get planted this year because Ellie didn't live here anymore, not that she was bitter about it or anything. And on the far side of the yard, a yellow doghouse with a red roof shone like a beacon of light in an otherwise soggy, dismal world.

A snout poked out of the opening, followed by Louie's black-and-white head. Her happy, loving, beautiful, smart, loyal border collie.

"He's here," she breathed, unbelievably relieved. "He's okay." Even though he'd been left outside in the rain. From the reconnaissance Ellie had done over the past six months, her ex-fiancé kept Louie outside almost all the time. The dog was fed and watered and had a comfortable doghouse, but Louie deserved better. That he'd been banished from the house was enough to make Ellie's blood boil, but now wasn't the time to get angry. Now was the time to get even—and get out.

"Good. Help me up." Wynn extended her arms. "Let's be quick. We've wasted enough time. Jason will probably be home soon."

"In and out," Ellie confirmed. Seeing her ex-fiancé while she was trespassing in his yard was not on her agenda for the afternoon. He'd probably have the police cuffing her in no time, and one item on her rap sheet was more than enough for a lifetime.

She tried to reach Wynn's hand by bending to the side, using her thighs to anchor her to the top of the fence. Even at full stretch, their hands were still a foot and a half apart. Wynn made a pitiful jump and didn't come close to grabbing Ellie's outstretched arm.

"Um. Hold on." Ellie braced her hands on the top of the fence and lay flat across it, letting her legs dangle down. The timber was slippery and wet, and it dug in uncomfortably at her chest and hip.

A whine from the far end of the yard caught her attention. Louie was out of his house, watching her. He barked once, tail wagging so hard it whacked the yellow corner of the doghouse in a steady *whump-whump-whump.*

"Hey, buddy," Ellie called out, throat tight. "I'm coming for you."

Louie barked again, tongue lolling, then came bounding across the yard toward her. He jumped up on the fence, his front paws a few inches below her dangling foot. He snuffled and yipped, then dropped down and zoomed in a circle on the lawn, overcome with doggy joy.

"Good to see you too, Louie."

The dog panted, then yawned and sat down, watching her. He'd wait patiently, because he was a good boy—and he could probably smell the treats she'd stashed in her backpack. They were Louie's favorite, homemade by the local veterinarian. She doubted her ex had gone out of his way to buy them, which meant Louie had suffered six months without.

Ellie blinked hard to clear her eyes, then returned her attention to Wynn. They had to both get over this fence and somehow get Louie and each other back out again, and time was running out. Tears would only slow her down.

She clung to the fence with her knees and extended her arm down, wiggling her fingers. "Try now. We should be able to reach."

Wynn stepped up to the fence and reached up, stretching onto her tiptoes—

"Yes!" Ellie wrapped her hand around Wynn's wrist. Their skin was slick from the rain, but that shouldn't be a problem for a simple lift. All Ellie had to do was haul Wynn up high enough that her friend could pull herself the rest of the way.

Easy-peasy.

"Jump on three, Wynnie. One, two, thr—"

Wynn jumped early, a half second before Ellie could brace herself against her friend's weight. She immediately pitched to the side, scrabbling to grab the slick wood with her opposite hand.

But it was too late.

Between Wynn's hard yank, the awkward position on top of the fence, the weight of the backpack shifting, and the water drenching absolutely everything, Ellie slipped off the top of the fence and came crashing down on top of Wynn.

The ferns failed to soften their landing once more. Wynn cried out in pain, Ellie groaned, and they writhed around on the wet forest floor like beached whales until they could untangle their limbs and sit up.

"Argh!" Ellie slapped the ground with both hands. Frustration singed her chest, burning against the inside of her rib cage. She just wanted her dog back. Was that too much to ask? Louie wasn't even supposed to be here. All his papers had Ellie's name on them. Every vet visit, every toy, every treat, every kibble had been bought with Ellie's money.

Jason had no right to keep him, but he was the heir to the Brownlow fortune. He was the director of the Brownlow Foundation, a stupid, celebrated charity that purported to fight for environmental sustainability on the island. She'd glimpsed some of the paperwork, and she knew that the upper echelons of Fernley society donated *generously* to the cause. Yet, in addition to the charity, Jason was building a luxury resort next door to Ellie's parents' property, which involved clear-cutting a huge swath of virgin forest.

Nobody seemed to notice this obvious conflict of interests. The only uproar was from people like her parents who had no political or economic weight to throw around.

Jason, on the other hand, had the whole damn island in the palm of his hand—including Sheriff Jackson, who'd refused to intervene when she'd complained about Louie. The dog was a civil matter, the sheriff had said. Nothing he could do.

Yeah, right.

After Ellie's arrest, the sheriff had given her the runaround for *five months* before recently admitting that he wouldn't help her get her dog back. The Brownlow-nosing jerk. (The first month after her arrest had been spent wallowing. It was a bad time. Ellie preferred not to think about it.)

Well, Ellie was done relying on other people. She wiped her eyes to clear the raindrops and the tears of anger that clung to her lashes. She'd cry when she was on the mainland with Louie by her side, once she was off this island and away from these people. She looked at Wynn. "You want to try again?"

Wynn leaned against the fence, using her hands to gingerly lift her calf. She winced, then met Ellie's gaze. "I don't think I can, Ellie. Something's wrong with my ankle."

CHAPTER 2

The two women hobbled away from Jason Brownlow's tacky imitation of a cabin that was really just an ostentatious mansion—Ellie could say that now because she didn't live there anymore—and made it to the cover of the thicker trees that surrounded her ex-fiancé's property. She was glad to be away from that place. It had been a charming old log cabin once upon a time, built about a hundred years ago by a logging magnate who had settled on the island, but Jason had expanded and renovated it until it was unrecognizable. The house had lost most of its charm in the process, and Ellie had never really felt at home there.

Wynn had an arm around Ellie's shoulders as they hopped along the narrow trail that led straight south. Ellie tromped through tall, wet grass and shrubbery beside Wynn, trying not to let tree branches whack them in the face any more often than necessary.

Wynn panted, her fingers clinging to Ellie's neck hard enough to hurt. "Are you sure Lionel will help us? He never does anything for anybody unless he's getting paid."

Ellie tightened her grip on Wynn's waist to try to carry more of her weight. "So I'll pay him."

Wynn huffed. "With what money, Ellie? You just told me this morning that your savings are disappearing into thin air. Let's just go to the car."

"The car is stashed down an overgrown logging road, and it took us nearly an hour to scramble from there to Jason's house. It would take triple that time to get back at this pace, and you're already exhausted. Lionel will help."

Wynn grumbled but kept hopping down the trail. After a few more yards, she accidentally stumbled onto her sore ankle and cried out. Ellie stopped, helping Wynn under the boughs of a nearby conifer to shield her from the worst of the rain. "Let's rest a bit," she said, worried but trying not to show it. It was still a long way to Lionel's house, and Wynn was looking pale. Ellie never should have brought her on this stupid mission. If Ellie was going to screw up her life, she should do it on her own. There was no need to bring everyone else down along with her.

She was the one who'd been blinded by Jason's status and money. She was the one who'd dated the man, who'd nearly married him. What did that say about Ellie's judgment? How could anyone trust her to make good decisions? How could Ellie trust herself?

Asking Wynn to come along today was just another mistake to add to the ever-growing list.

She hadn't even managed to get her dog. With no way to get him over the fence, they'd had to abandon the plan and leave Louie behind—after tossing a few treats over the fence for him, of course. But it wasn't enough. She needed to get Louie back soon; otherwise, she'd snap. Again.

Not to mention the rain seemed to be getting heavier, and it was getting darker by the minute. Everything sucked.

Wynn leaned a hand on a tree trunk. She caught her breath, and once the pain had cleared from her expression, she asked, "How are your parents' sheep doing? Have they recovered from whatever was making them sick?"

Ellie knew Wynn was just trying to distract herself from the long, painful walk ahead of them, so she shook her head and said, "They lost

Curly last week. Still no idea what's wrong. My dad's really cut up about it. Blames himself, I think."

Her parents owned about a dozen sheep, bought from shepherds who'd bred them for meat and wool. When they became too old to be productive, Ellie's parents took the elderly ruminants home and tried to provide a healthy, happy sheep retirement on their small acreage. And now their beloved sheep were ill and dying.

Wynn made a sympathetic noise. "Sorry, Ellie."

"We'll figure it out," Ellie said with more conviction than she felt. Her parents' sheep had been getting sick for a few weeks now. They were irritable and twitchy, ate constantly, and were increasingly colicky and bloated. As much as Ellie hated the reputation she'd inherited, she loved her parents, and her parents loved their sheep. It killed her to see them worried over their animals. Now that Ellie's business had imploded because of her own stupid mistakes, she couldn't even give them any money to hire a vet—and she was living with her parents again (at the tender age of thirty), so she was an extra drain on their meager resources.

Everything really, really sucked.

"Ready to keep going?" she asked, not wanting to scratch at old scabs. "We'll lose the light soon."

Wynn straightened. "Yeah. Let's go."

Fernley Island was roughly ten miles long and seven miles wide, generally oblong shaped, and had a permanent population of five thousand people that more than doubled in the summer months, when tourists abounded. It was a lush, forested island near the San Juans, nudged up close to the Canadian border. The island was blanketed in ferns, mosses, oaks, firs, madrone, and hemlocks, and it was home to various species of birds, squirrels, deer, and the odd black bear that made the swim from nearby islands. It rained a lot.

The air smelled fresh and earthy in the early spring, the lush natural surroundings slowly preparing to explode into summer. The island was its own little ecosystem, moving at its own pace, with its own quirks.

One of those quirks was Lionel Hartford. The sixty-two-year-old had more in common with an oak burl than most of the other island residents, in that he was probably pretty nice on the inside but you'd have to cut him open with a chain saw to find out. Lionel lived alone in an old shack next to a humble marina that now boasted an impressively rickety pier, where he spent his days fixing boats and avoiding people.

Lionel's cabin came into view, the Salish Sea a cold, gray expanse beyond. Ellie blew out a breath, her arm and shoulder aching from half carrying Wynn, her tailbone still protesting from its earlier mistreatment. Lionel would have those wonderful inventions called chairs and a roof. She'd pay him in solid gold for the pleasure of using them.

They'd crashed through the underbrush for a few more paces when Ellie froze.

"What?" Wynn complained, wobbling on her one good leg. "Why'd you stop? We're so close."

"Shh," Ellie hissed, crouching down. She pushed a prickly fir branch out of the way to get a clearer view and let out a curse under her breath.

Wynn crowded closer, eyes widening. "Who's that?" she mouthed.

Ellie's lips pinched, her eyes narrowing. It wasn't unusual to see strangers on the island at this time of the year. It was a bit early for the hordes of tourists, sure, but not unheard of. However, tourists didn't wander to Lionel's house by accident—it was too far off the beaten track—and tourists definitely didn't hunch over the front window with a crowbar in their hands.

The stranger was male. He had a green poncho thrown over his broad shoulders, making his proportions look absolutely gargantuan. He had to be over six feet tall, with dark hair poking out below the black beanie covering his head. He strained at the window, wrapping huge hands around one end of the crowbar as he tried to pry it open.

Ellie slowly replaced the branch and faced Wynn. "I think he's trying to break into Lionel's house."

Wynn's gray eyes widened. "What do we do? Do we call the police?"

"And wait hours for them to show up?" Lionel Hartford definitely didn't have Sheriff Jackson on speed dial. Lionel's bank account had too few zeroes.

Wynn peeked around a tree trunk. "He has the screen out of its frame now. He's starting on the window."

Oh no, he didn't. Lionel didn't deserve this. Sure, he was a grouch and a cheapskate. He never did anything unless you promised to pay him for the trouble. He wasn't exactly neighborly, and he didn't have friends. But Lionel kept to himself. He never hurt anyone. Ellie was so sick of people like Lionel getting the short end of the stick when others—like her wealthy, arrogant ex-fiancé—could stomp on whomever they pleased on their way to the top.

It wasn't fair. It wasn't right. These people didn't get to steal dogs and rob old men.

She slipped her backpack off and slowly, gently unzipped it. The sound of the rain muffled their movements, but she checked on the stranger once more as she touched the red tape that covered the handles of her trusty bolt cutters. They might not be good at slicing, but they worked just fine for whacking.

The man fiddled with the window frame. He was almost in. A few more minutes, and he'd be robbing Lionel blind.

"What are you doing?" Wynn asked, gripping Ellie's jacket.

"Stay here." Ellie ducked around her friend and circled the copse of trees they'd been hiding behind. Her heart thumped. Her skin was clammy, but she felt hot all over.

Whoever this guy was, he wasn't going to steal from Lionel. No way. Ellie wouldn't stand for it. She might be leaving the island soon, but she had integrity, damn it.

She gritted her teeth and tightened her hold on the bolt cutter handles. She eased around the trunk of an oak and avoided the ferns growing at its base. There he was, struggling to open the window, twenty feet away, asking to get bonked on the head with a pair of overpriced shears. She'd bonk him good. She'd bonk him so hard he'd regret ever setting foot on this island and intending to do harm. Nobody came to Fernley and robbed people like Lionel. Not on Ellie's watch.

As her blood pounded harder, Ellie began to run. She must have made some kind of noise, because at the very last moment, when she'd brought the bolt cutters up above her head with the intention of smashing them over the criminal's skull, he half turned toward her and let out a surprised yell.

Too late, asshole.

Ellie brought the bolt cutters down in a double-handed smash. The stranger dodged at the last moment, so the cutters ricocheted off his thick head and bashed against his shoulder. Ellie screeched and brought them back up. Her second hit glanced off his forearm as he blocked.

"What are you—"

He grunted as Ellie crashed into his middle, tackling him to the ground. He landed with a groan, long limbs sprawling out on impact.

Ha! Score one for the good guys.

"Lionel!" Ellie screeched. "Lionel! I got him!"

She let out a low *oof* as the man flipped her onto her back. The bolt cutters slipped from her grip, tumbling just beyond her reach, and she kicked her assailant to give herself time to grab them again. His heavy body landed on top of hers, a hot hand manacling her wrist before she could get a good grip on her weapon. He reached above them and tossed the bolt cutters into the nearby bushes.

"What are you *doing*?" he shouted, pinning her down with his hips. His weight was immense. What a turd. His poncho flapped, trapping Ellie's limbs further.

Ellie writhed and shrieked. "Get off me! I won't let you do it!" She got a hand free and tugged his earlobe, causing him to jerk away and cry out in pain. Ellie used his moment of distraction to wriggle out from under him. She crawl-sprinted to the bushes, seeing a hint of red beneath a leaf. Inches away from the weapon, a hand wrapped around her ankle and yanked her back. She landed on her stomach with a grunt, then slid through the mud and grass and dead leaves on her way back to the stranger, screaming the whole way.

He flipped her over and grabbed her wrists, pinning them above her head. His tree-trunk-size thighs held her lower body down. She bucked and struggled, but he was too strong. She was caught, and he was still conscious.

Damn him and his stupid gigantic body. If his skull wasn't so thick, he'd have been apprehended by now. Would *nothing* go right today?

Finally accepting the reality of the situation, Ellie stopped moving and glared. The stranger panted above her, a trickle of blood dripping from his temple down to the neckline of his poncho. His eyes flashed with terrible menace. His chest heaved. He was covered in dirt and rain and blood, and he was furious.

"What the hell is wrong with you?" he demanded, tightening his hold on her wrists.

"Me? What the hell is wrong with *me*?" she scoffed, incredulous. "You're the one breaking into Lionel's house."

"Breaking in—" He bit off the words and glared at her. "Who are you?"

His eyes were milk chocolate brown, dotted with little specks of green. He'd lost his beanie at some point in the tussle, and his dark hair clung to his head and temples in messy, wet curls. The rain grew heavier, pelting down on them both as they glared at each other.

The last time she'd been in this position, Ellie had been naked and still infatuated with her cheating prick of an ex-fiancé. The memory was unwelcome.

Ellie's arms ached from being held above her head, and the rest of her body was very unhappy with her. Not that she'd let it show. She stuck her jaw out at him and narrowed her eyes. "I could ask you the same thing. Where's Lionel? Why were you trying to rob him?"

His lips went slack. They were pale pink and framed by his dark stubble. "Rob him? Why would I rob him?"

"You tell me. And get off me!" She bucked her hips against his for emphasis.

He grunted and shifted away slightly, eyes narrowing. "I don't know if I should. Are you going to attack me again?"

Oh, for crying out loud. She struggled against him. "I was—protecting—*oof*—Lionel!"

"Ellie," a scratchy voice said from the house's front doorway, causing both Ellie and the stranger to freeze. "I see you're getting in trouble, as usual."

Wow. Rude. It was literally one mug shot, and the police hadn't even pressed charges.

The screen door squeaked as Lionel opened it. "And you've met my nephew."

Lionel's nephew. Ellie collapsed onto the ground and closed her eyes, waiting for the now-familiar humiliation to wash over her. It stung, but she was used to it. At least the only witnesses were Lionel, Wynn, and this brute.

"Who's that over there?" Lionel continued. "Someone's hiding in the bushes."

"That's Wynn," Ellie said, eyes still closed. The nephew hadn't moved from his position on top of her. At least he was warm, even though he was ginormous and rude. "She's hurt. We need help."

Lionel grunted, and the screen door banged as he went back inside.

Ellie finally opened her eyes. "You can let go of me now," she said through gritted teeth.

"You promise not to attack me?"

"Like it would do much damage. Your skull is too thick."

He snorted and heaved himself off her. Rain soaked Ellie's front as she sat up in the mud, exhausted and sore and embarrassed. So, basically, business as usual in Ellie Davis's world.

Wynn hopped around a tree trunk, carrying the backpack. Ellie got to her feet and went to help her friend over to the porch, where the nephew stood holding the door open. They shuffled through, dripping leaves and water and dirt all over the foyer floor. Lionel tossed old towels at their faces, which Ellie failed to catch before impact. She stumbled back into something large and warm, scrambling forward again when she realized it was the nephew's chest.

She'd had quite enough of his chest in her personal space, thankyouverymuch.

There was an awkward shuffle in the foyer while everyone removed boots and jackets, dried themselves, and made their way inside.

Lionel sat in an armchair, carving a piece of wood into a spoonlike shape, ignoring everyone. His cabin was mainly one big room topped with exposed timber rafters holding up the tin roof, with two doors leading to the single bathroom and the bedroom. Knotty pine floorboards spread beneath their feet over the entire space, carrying all the mismatched, worn furniture. A door at the back of the cabin opened onto a small wooded trail that ended at the workshop by the pier, where Lionel spent most of his time.

Wynn sat down on a wobbly chair at the scarred wooden kitchen table. She let out a huff and closed her eyes for a beat, then lifted her ankle onto another chair with obvious effort.

Ellie bit her lip as she watched her friend, then glanced at Lionel. "Do you have any ice? Wynn's ankle is injured."

Lionel grunted.

"Thanks," Ellie said, crossing to the kitchen. An ancient bag of peas waited for her inside the freezer, which she wrapped in one of the towels they'd use to dry themselves and then placed on Wynn's ankle. She ignored the colossal man leaning against the kitchen counter with his arms crossed over his chest, even though she could tell he was watching her. She would *not* apologize for her actions. She'd acted completely reasonably, based on the information at hand. Anyone in her position would have attacked him. Anyone!

Little bits of wood shavings fell to the floor beside Lionel. He ran a wrinkled thumb over the curved edge of his spoon, then went back to carving with his knife. Silence settled over the room, thick and oppressive.

Finally, Ellie huffed. She glanced at the man in the kitchen. "I thought you were breaking in. That's why I hit you with the bolt cutters."

"Is that supposed to be an apology?"

"Obviously not," she shot back. "It's an explanation."

He'd wiped the cut on his temple when they entered the house, but it was bleeding again. A tiny, infinitesimal seed of guilt sprouted in Ellie's heart. She squashed it.

"You were prying the window open with a crowbar," she continued. "What was I supposed to think?"

Lionel grunted. Everyone turned to look at him. He kept whittling in silence.

"The window is jammed," the man finally said. "I was trying to get it open so the bathroom would air out."

"Gross," Ellie said.

"No," the man said, straightening. "Not—it was just damp from the steam from the shower. Could grow mold."

Ellie stared at him. "It's raining outside. How would that help the dampness inside?"

He gritted his teeth, glaring at her. "Lionel said it was jammed. I offered to help."

This was ridiculous. Ellie just wanted to move on and get Wynn to the island's medical center. "Fine."

"Fine," he replied.

She narrowed her eyes. "I'm not sorry."

"Neither am I."

Ellie shrugged. "Good."

"So we agree."

"We do."

"Wonderful."

"Great."

Wynn cleared her throat. Ellie snapped back to herself and gave her friend an apologetic glance. Wynn rolled her eyes.

Ellie turned to Lionel. "Could you possibly drive us to the medical center? Wynn might need an x-ray."

Lionel pointed his knife at the cell phone on the kitchen counter. The cell phone was plugged in, covered in a sturdy black case. "App," he said.

Ellie huffed. "Really, Lionel? Wynn is hurt."

Lionel said nothing.

Ellie took a deep breath, willing herself to find every scrap of patience left inside her battered body. "Can't I just give you some cash? It's a ten-minute drive."

Lionel paused, lifting his hazel eyes to meet Ellie's. "App," he repeated.

The nephew frowned. "What's going on?"

"Lionel insists on using a stupid app to do any stupid favors for anyone," Ellie grumbled, walking to the backpack Wynn had dropped by the front door. Her phone was in a plastic bag at the bottom of the pack, thankfully still operational. "He thinks the FBI Financial Crimes Division is going to burst through the door at any minute and slap cuffs on him."

"Dunno about the FBI," Lionel said, angling the spoon toward the lamp to inspect one of the curves, "but if the IRS sees legitimate income, they won't ask any uncomfortable questions."

"I'm sure the IRS and the FBI and every other alphabet government agency are just waiting for a boat mechanic on Fernley Island to slip up," Ellie deadpanned. "They'll raid this place any minute."

Lionel grunted.

The nephew looked baffled. She wondered how long it would take him to figure out that half the people on this island lived in deep suspicion of the government and did all they could to remain off grid. The other half were richer than God, and the government didn't bother with them either.

Ellie navigated to the OddJobs application, used her face to log in to her account, then tapped the tile for a new job. The app allowed her to either post the job to the public or send it to a specific profile, so she found Lionel's profile and sent the job request to him with what she thought was a more than generous price, considering it was a short drive and Wynn was injured, and any decent person would stop carving their stupid spoon and help her without question.

Deep breaths.

Lionel's phone dinged. Everyone turned to look at it. Lionel shifted his gaze to his nephew and waited. His nephew pushed himself off the kitchen counter, unplugged the phone, and moved his tree-trunk-size legs across the room to bring it to his uncle. Lionel unlocked the phone, tapped it with his index finger a couple of times, then put it down on the arm of his chair.

Ellie's phone buzzed. She looked at it and let out an exasperated noise. "Lionel, you refused the job!"

"I'm busy," he said, returning to his wooden spoon.

"I'll just call my sister," Wynn said. "It's fine."

The nephew ripped a paper towel and pressed it to his bleeding head. "I'll drive you," he said. "I should get back to the hotel anyway, and the medical center is nearby." He walked over to Ellie and Wynn and stuck out his hand. "I'm Hugh, by the way. Nice to meet you."

Ellie stared at his palm for a beat (it was predictably large). "No one likes a liar, Hugh."

Then she shook his hand and introduced herself.

CHAPTER 3

Hugh had never sat beside a human-size hand grenade until he got behind the wheel with Ellie in the passenger seat. She vibrated with tension, her face only softening whenever she'd glance in the back seat of his rental car to make sure Wynn was okay.

She was one of those people who never seemed to sit still. Slim and tall enough to reach his shoulder, she wore her rain jacket and muddy sneakers like a well-worn uniform. Her brown hair was pulled back in a ponytail, revealing high cheekbones and almond-shaped eyes of dark, glittering blue. Her nose had a little hook on the tip, and her lips were a touch small for her face while still being perfectly formed. Hugh hadn't been able to stop looking at her from the moment he'd had her pinned on the ground outside his uncle's house. He couldn't decide if it was because she was so striking or because she had the energy of a carpet viper about to attack.

"You want to call your mom, Wynnie?" Ellie asked quietly as Hugh turned onto the paved road that intersected Lionel's long gravel driveway.

"No, it's okay," Wynn said. "My sister's working today, and it's probably better to figure out what's wrong with my ankle before freaking anyone out. I just texted Jane that we were on the way."

Ellie nodded and turned back toward the front.

Hugh cleared his throat. "How did you hurt your ankle?"

There was a suspiciously long pause. Wynn finally said, "I, um, fell."

Hugh glanced in the rearview mirror for a moment but had to return his eyes to the winding road. Trees grew straight and tall on either side of the hilly landscape, with gentle curves and hairpin turns providing very poor visibility, especially in the rain.

When they turned onto the slightly wider main road that ran north–south along the length of the island, Ellie spoke. "I didn't know Lionel had any family," she said. "Are you close?"

Hugh appreciated her attempt at polite conversation, but he had no desire to tell her anything about his messed-up family tree. The truth was, until yesterday, he hadn't seen Lionel in over twenty years. Today, he'd gone outside to fix the window because he'd grown tired of the silence in Lionel's house, and he'd wanted to clear his head. Soon his business on the island would be done, and he'd leave. Whether or not he rekindled his relationship with the elderly boat mechanic wasn't meant to be a priority.

Still, Lionel was family. Hugh had never had an uncle; maybe it was simple curiosity that had brought him to Lionel's door.

He'd left the heat and sun of Arizona for this gloomy island. So far, the only thing he'd succeeded in doing was getting drenched while being bashed on the head with a pair of bolt cutters.

"Uh, no, we're not close," he finally replied, tapping the button for his seat warmer. He clicked Ellie's seat warmer on too, half expecting her to make a sarcastic comment about it. She said nothing, so he continued, "I haven't seen Lionel since I was a kid," he admitted. "He and my dad had a falling out, and we stopped visiting."

"Is your dad on the island too?" Ellie snuggled into her seat a bit, evidently feeling the warmth starting to permeate through the leather. This pleased Hugh, which was odd. He didn't know why he should care.

He frowned. "My dad's dead," he answered.

"Oh," Ellie said, turning to look at him. "I'm sorry."

He shrugged. "Don't be. I'm not." Then, because he learned this was something people asked, he added, "Massive heart attack. Came out of nowhere." Or so he'd heard when the lawyer had called with the news.

Ellie nodded and said nothing. He liked that she didn't try to fill the silence.

They drove without speaking until he'd crossed the town limits into Carlisle, the main town on the island and the location of the single ferry terminal that served the Fernley population. The town was set on a hillside that sloped down toward the water, giving most homes and businesses a view of the harbor. The medical center was near the top of the hill, its helipad and helicopter silent atop the two-story building.

The sliding glass doors opened as they drove up, and a woman in scrubs walked out with a wheelchair, then stopped under the awning and put her hands on her hips. "There's my sister," Wynn said.

"She doesn't look happy," Ellie noted.

"Maybe you should stay in the car, Ellie," Wynn answered.

Ellie just snorted and unclipped her seat belt as soon as Hugh put the car in park. They both jumped out and helped Wynn into the chair, while her sister clicked her tongue.

"What have you gotten her into now, Ellie? Can't you just be responsible, for once?"

"I'm always responsible, Jane," Ellie replied, and it had the rhythm of an old argument. "I ran my own business for years and didn't have a single complaint, until . . ."

Hugh glanced over when she didn't finish the sentence.

Ellie waved a hand. "Well, whatever. That's not important."

Jane didn't look impressed as she checked that Wynn was comfortable in the wheelchair. "I'll take it from here."

Wynn gave Ellie a tired smile. "See you tomorrow?"

"Of course," Ellie replied, ignoring Jane's death glare. "You sure you don't want me to stay?"

Wynn gave her a loaded look and tipped her head toward her sister. Ellie snorted and stepped back. Then Wynn looked at Hugh. "Thanks for the lift."

"Anytime."

"Careful what you promise around that one," Jane mumbled darkly, meaning Ellie.

Ellie looked like she wanted to say something, but she clenched her jaw and held her tongue. Hugh felt the undercurrents of history in the air around them and knew he was an outsider. For the first time since he'd arrived on Fernley, he wished he wasn't.

As Jane wheeled her away, Wynn's hand appeared above her sister's shoulder, waving goodbye.

Ellie slumped, then took a deep breath and met Hugh's gaze. "Well, thanks. I'll just grab my bag and be out of your hair. Sorry about the"— she pointed at his head, which felt like it was bleeding again—"you know."

"You need a ride somewhere?" Hugh heard himself ask, even though he should probably let Ellie go cause chaos wherever she was headed next. He jabbed his thumb over his shoulder at the waiting car. "I might as well drive you wherever you need to go."

Ellie opened her mouth, and Hugh knew she was about to refuse. It was for the best. She was obviously unhinged, and Hugh had paperwork to review. His business on the island had started with the news of his inheritance, and he was neck deep in deeds and half-finished deals. The sooner he got it over with, the sooner he could leave. He didn't have time to play taxi for a woman who tore through the world with the destructive capacity of an F5 tornado.

Then her phone buzzed. She dug it out of her pocket and gasped, head jerking up to meet Hugh's eyes. "The trail cam just went off," she said, like that was supposed to make sense to him. "Someone just drove up to my parents' back field."

"Um," Hugh said. "Okay . . . ?"

"That's where the sheep have been grazing," she enunciated, like he was some kind of idiot.

He was not an idiot, and he also didn't know why the hell this woman was telling him about her parents' sheep.

She was already at the car, sliding into her seat and gripping the door. She gaped at him. "Come *on*, Hugh! Drive, drive, drive! I'm going to get this asshole before he kills any more of our animals."

This was a terrible idea. Going anywhere with Ellie would end with injury, arrest, or death. But the alternative was going back to his hotel room, ordering room service, and flicking through the details of the inheritance he'd never expected to get, no matter what his father had promised before he died. Lionel had shed no light as to what kind of person his father had really been. The paperwork hadn't told him much more.

If he read everything for the hundredth time, he might figure out why he'd come here in the first place instead of leaving it to his lawyers. He might put pen to paper and finish this mess so he could be done with the island—and his father. He could get out of the rain, get warm and dry, and have a good feed.

Or he could see what was up with Ellie's parents' sheep.

Hugh got into the car and drove.

Ellie led him to the very northern tip of the island, a fifteen-minute drive from Carlisle. The roads became narrower, the houses smaller and farther apart, and the trees denser, except when they opened up to reveal the angry sea beyond. He recognized the area from his drive out here yesterday.

"Take that road," she said, pointing to a small gap in the trees that definitely didn't qualify as a road. It consisted of two gravel-filled tracks with overgrown grass in the middle. "We'll sneak up on him from the back gate."

"Tell me again what this is about," he said, navigating onto the track, hoping the rental car's undercarriage came away unscathed.

"My parents' sheep have been getting sick, and Mom and Dad didn't believe me when I said someone was messing with them, so I installed trail cameras near the grazing pastures."

"You think someone's killing your parents' sheep?" Hugh frowned, gripping the steering wheel tight as the trees crowded closer.

"I know they are. Sheep don't just get sick for no reason. Well, I mean. Usually. Maybe." Ellie rolled down her window and tucked her side mirror in, nodding for him to do the same. "It gets pretty narrow up ahead," she informed him.

Wonderful. He'd known this was a terrible idea. Now he just had to add "property damage" to his list of Ellie-induced consequences.

Hugh tucked in the mirror and followed the road for a few minutes, then parked where Ellie indicated in a small circular clearing that obviously acted as a turning area, finally pointing the car back toward the exit. It was dark out now, with the rain coming down in a steady mist. He zipped up his jacket and rounded the car to join Ellie on the other side, watching her clip her backpack strap across her chest.

"I'll take it from here," she said, pointing to the car. "You should go back to town."

Like hell he would.

He clenched his jaw and said nothing.

Ellie looked at him, shrugged, then ducked between the trees, not looking back to see if Hugh would follow.

CHAPTER 4

It had been a long day fraught with insult and injury, and Ellie was sick of losing. Whoever this intruder was, she wasn't going to let him get away. She *knew* something weird had been going on with the sheep. Her parents were way too trusting. They'd thought she was crazy when she said it could have been someone acting maliciously.

But on this island? Anything was possible.

Once again, Ellie found herself tromping through a wet forest, except this time her partner was about twice Wynn's height and weight, and he was surprisingly silent on his feet. She could feel his presence at her back, and it was oddly comforting. That wasn't good. She was turning into her parents, trusting every stranger who did her half a favor. She knew what happened when she trusted people; they hurt her, then she humiliated herself, and she was forced to run away with her tail tucked between her legs.

Trust was nothing more than a steel-jawed trap waiting for an unsuspecting foot. Ellie had learned that the hard way, had the limp to prove it.

Pushing Hugh out of her mind, she crouched low at the sight of a white-paneled pickup truck parked at her parents' back gate. This guy wasn't even trying to hide. He was brazen about it, tailgate wide open, hauling heavy bags back and forth to the gate. Ellie squinted, but in the dark and with the misty rain, she couldn't make out who it was.

Hugh crouched beside her, his biceps brushing hers. She could feel the warmth of his body, so she shifted away half an inch. "What's the plan?" he asked.

"I'm going in."

"Wait—"

Ellie took off. The sheep killer was on the opposite side of the truck, so she'd have cover until she was on top of him. This time, when she tried to channel her inner action movie hero, she succeeded. She jumped onto the truck's hood and slid across on her butt in an impressively smooth motion. It was glorious. She flew off the other side of the hood, aiming to land in a pivot, ready to attack.

Unfortunately, that's where her action movie dreams ended. She overshot the pivot landing and got her feet twisted around each other. She went stumbling into a nearby tree and bashed her head against its trunk, landing in a wet, dazed heap on the mossy ground.

"Ugh," she groaned, sitting up.

"Ellie?" a voice called out by the truck. "Is that you?"

Then, like a ghost, Hugh came circling around the back of the truck. He reached the sheep killer and banded his arms around him, throwing him to the ground in some sort of judo twist. In an instant, Hugh was on top of him, tying the intruder's wrists together with a length of twine he must have gathered along the way. The whole thing took about three seconds.

The man screamed and struggled. Ellie stood, wobbling.

Hugh kept his knee on the man's back and looked up to where Ellie was regaining her balance. "You okay? You hit the tree pretty hard."

Oh, so he saw that. Great. "I'm fine," she said.

"Ellie, what the heck?" The man on the ground grunted and squirmed.

Anger rushed through her like a blaze in dry grass. She stomped to the side of the truck, pulled out her phone, and turned on the flashlight—then froze.

"*Spencer?*"

"Ellie! This guy just tackled me and tied me up!" He wriggled on the ground, not unlike Ellie an hour or so earlier. At least this evening wasn't a total bust; if Ellie ever needed someone thrown to the ground and hog-tied, she knew who to call.

"Spence, what are you doing here?" She waved her hands at Hugh to get him to lift his knee off Spencer's back. She helped Spencer to his feet, untied his wrists, and got him to lean against the side of the truck, shining the flashlight in his face. "Well? Tell me."

Spencer Wisneski was five foot eight with a protruding belly and shaggy blond hair beginning to streak with silver. He was in his mid-forties, and he'd worked at the ferry terminal since the dawn of time. He had a fascination with boats that had started in early childhood and hadn't ebbed with age. He was a friendly, happy man who would go out of his way to free insects into the wild without hurting them. Louie loved him. There was literally no reason for Spencer to be here, in the dark, at her parents' back gate, unloading burlap sacks packed full of some unknown substance.

"Ellie, back up," Hugh said. "I don't want him to hurt you."

"Hurt her?" Spencer's big blue eyes grew even wider. "Why would I hurt Ellie?"

"Spencer," Ellie said sharply. "What are you *doing* here?"

"I'm—I'm feeding the sheep?" Spencer's voice was small, tentative.

Ellie reared back and glanced at Hugh. Hugh loomed in the darkness, positioning himself between the two of them like some sort of hero. Good for him. Little did he know, the only person Spencer was likely to hurt was . . . well, no one. None of this made sense. She found one of the bags by the gate and tore it open to see its contents.

"Milkweed," she said, shining the light inside the bag. "At least I think it is." She touched a few of the pink-and-white flowers, frowning. She'd have to ask her dad to be sure, but she knew they tried to eradicate the plant whenever they found it where the sheep grazed. She turned back to Spencer, shining the light in his eyes. "What the heck are you doing with bags and bags of milkweed?"

"Feeding the sheep," Spencer said, sounding befuddled. "It's good for them. Extra nutrients."

"Spencer, milkweed is poisonous to sheep."

Spencer blinked again and again. "No." He shook his head. "No, it's not. It's good for them! It has vitamins!" He was getting agitated, and Hugh put a hand on his shoulder to keep him from jumping forward. "It makes them stronger! They're old, so they need more vitamins. The wool . . . it . . . it . . ."

Ellie's head pounded. She hoped she didn't have a concussion. There was a bump on the side of her head that would turn into an impressive goose egg if she didn't get ice on it sometime soon. Today had battered her body far beyond its limits, and it wasn't even over.

The misty rain grew heavier. Exhaustion hit her like a plank of wood across the temple. She was cold, and wet, and hurt, and hungry, and so tired she didn't know if she'd ever recover.

Spencer was still protesting, and Hugh . . . well, Ellie had no idea what Hugh was thinking. He probably thought she was insane. Maybe he was right.

Then Spencer said something that penetrated Ellie's swirling thoughts. "Jason said it was good for them. He said he wanted to help you after everything you'd been through. He told me he was doing you and your family a favor, and it was the least he could do. I thought that was pretty decent of him, you know? So I said I'd help."

Ellie's blood ran cold. She flicked the flashlight off and let her eyes adjust to the darkness, sucking in long, deep breaths to get herself under control before she spoke. "Jason Brownlow told you to spread milkweed over my parents' pastures?" Her voice was menacing, and the dark outline of both men leaned away from her.

"Ellie," Hugh said slowly, "hold on now. Let's take a breath."

"I'm breathing." She inhaled for emphasis. "See? Lungs are functional. Everything works. Everything is fine except the fact that my ex-fiancé tried to *kill my parents' animals!*" The last words came out as a shriek. Her hands were clenched so hard she knew she'd have half moon–shaped indents in her palms. She let out a shrill scream and kicked the bag of milkweed, sending little pink flowers spilling onto the ground.

This was beyond comprehension. This was so messed up she didn't even have words for it. All she knew was getting Louie back wasn't enough. Taking her dog and leaving the island was no longer an acceptable solution to the problem of Jason Brownlow and his smarmy, stupid face.

Ellie wanted revenge. She wanted to surgically dissect Jason's life piece by piece, destroying every bit of it along the way. She wanted *him* to run off the island with his tail between his legs. She wanted to see him cry and beg for forgiveness.

A shift happened within her, something terrible and final. Jason could mess with Ellie. He could destroy her business, her reputation, and her life. He could cheat on her at her own damn engagement party, then get her arrested when she snapped. He could walk away from the whole thing without even a blemish on his character, but he could not—*could not*—hurt Ellie's parents.

"Ellie, I didn't know," Spencer blubbered. "I thought it was good for them. He said . . . he said . . . it was supposed to be a secret. Oh *no!* I wasn't supposed to tell you, and now . . . now . . ."

Determination settled over Ellie like a second skin. She straightened, not caring about the rain or the milkweed or Hugh Hartford and what he thought of her.

"Come on, Spence," she finally said. "Come inside. I'm sure there's dinner enough for you, and you can tell us exactly what happened." She turned to Hugh. "Do you need help finding your way out?"

He watched her for a beat, his face shadowed. She had no idea what he was thinking, and she didn't care. He'd probably be gone from the island within a few days anyway. He wasn't from Fernley; he wouldn't understand her even if he had a thousand years to try.

Finally, Hugh shook his head. "I'll be fine," he said, and he waited until Ellie and Spencer were behind the gate before disappearing through the trees in the direction of his car.

CHAPTER 5

Ellie inhaled the familiar scent of patchouli and tried to exhale her worries. It didn't work. She stared at the decades-old char mark in the center of her parents' kitchen table, tracing its outline with her gaze. When Ellie was about six or seven, her father had put a hot pot down directly on the timber table, scorching it. Her mother had cried.

Now the black crescent moon in the middle of the table was as much part of the house as the family photos in every room, or the old tapestry her parents had bought in Morocco hanging on the wall, or the mismatched collection of mugs sitting on the open shelves.

She took the bag of ice off her head and probed at the lump that had grown there after her skull had lost its battle with the tree. It hurt.

"Ellie, honey," her mother, Helen, said. "Say something."

Spencer had begged for forgiveness, accepted a bowlful of beef-and-lentil stew served with Dad's homemade sourdough for dinner, then allowed Ellie's dad, Claude, to walk him back to his truck. Now Claude was back, sitting at the opposite end of the oval table, with Ellie's mother and grandmother on either side.

They were all staring at her.

She lifted her gaze from the burned wood and met her mother's eyes. "My ex-fiancé has been killing my parents' sheep. What would you like me to say?"

"Now, Ellie-Belly," Dad said, lifting his palms. "We don't know that Jason meant to kill the sheep. Maybe there's some explanation."

"Oh, there's an explanation, all right," Ellie said, pointing to the corkboard on the wall where the family pinned mail, grocery lists, and reminders. A flyer for the Brownlow Foundation Gala gleamed in the low light, gilded letters on a black background looking completely out of place in her parents' colorful, homey kitchen. Ellie had helped him plan the event, where he was expecting his yearly influx of generous donations. She'd been surprised when the invitation for her parents had arrived in the mail, considering everything that had happened between them and the fact that they hadn't paid for a table at the gala.

But along with the invitation, there was an offer to buy part of Ellie's parents' land.

"Jason is trying to pressure you to sell your land so he can build an enormous resort across the waterfront. The land he owns east of us wasn't enough, so he's made a deal with the investors who own the land on the other side of your property. Do you see what I'm saying? He's wanted to buy the waterfront part of your property ever since he started planning this resort project. He used to ask me about your coastline all the time, and I always told him you'd never sell, but he kept asking and asking. He knows that too many vet bills and a failing flock would put huge financial pressure on us, especially now that my work has dried up. The man is *evil*."

Grandma Mabel grunted. "Never liked him." Her nimbus of curly white hair was particularly wild tonight, because she'd run her wrinkled fingers through it a thousand times while listening to Spencer's story. There were spots of color high on her cheeks, and her blue eyes were as outraged as Ellie had ever seen. "He's always been a sniveling little bastard. Same as his father, and his father before him."

"Mom," Helen chided.

"What?" Mabel leaned back and crossed her arms. "You can't trust a man with a family history like Jason Brownlow's. I'm tellin' ya—no integrity."

Ellie ground her teeth. If only she'd realized that before she let herself be seduced by her ex, she could have saved herself and her family a lot of heartache. She was ashamed of herself, ashamed of how much she'd enjoyed the lifestyle and status Jason had provided. She should have seen him for who and what he was.

"I'm going to call Daphne," Helen said, pushing her chair back, presumably to go get her phone.

"No," Ellie said, grabbing her mother's hand. "Please, let me handle this."

Daphne was Ellie's older sister. She lived in Seattle, and she was mostly insulated from the dramas of Fernley Island. Daphne had warned Ellie about Jason. She'd said that he was a jerk, that he'd use her, and that he'd break her heart. Daphne was smart like that. She'd gone to college and had a good job. She had a mortgage and a fiancé of her own. She hadn't ruined her life the way Ellie had. The thought of her older sister hearing about this fresh drama was too much to bear. Not until Ellie had had a chance to fix it.

Ellie had to handle this on her own.

"Ellie, you have that look in your eyes," Dad said, his chair creaking as he leaned forward, "and I don't like it."

"What look?" Ellie knew the look he was talking about.

"The look that means you're about to do something stupid."

"I don't do stupid things."

Grandma Mabel laughed, then shrugged at Ellie's answering scowl. "What?" Mabel asked, the picture of innocence. "It was funny. Were you not joking, Ellie-Belly?"

No, she hadn't been joking. The chill that penetrated to Ellie's marrow hadn't melted away. She still wanted to ruin Jason's life. She met her father's gaze. "The first thing I need to do is figure out if what Spencer said was true. If Jason really did try to hurt your animals, then I'll find a way to make him pay."

An uncomfortable silence settled over the four of them. "Maybe we should call the police," Mom said. "We can get Spencer to give a statement."

"And then what?" Ellie protested. "Sheriff Jackson will laugh in our faces. You should have seen everyone at the station when they let me go after they arrested me. It's like they expected me to be back. And they were so impressed that Jason was being magnanimous about not pressing charges. You know the Brownlows have had the police in their pocket for a hundred years."

Grandma Mabel grunted in agreement.

"Helen," Claude said gently. "We can't go to the police without actual evidence. They'll just dismiss Spencer outright, even if he gives a statement. You know people won't take him seriously. Not if it's his word against Jason's."

"Well, I don't want Ellie to go all vigilante on us," Helen protested. "That didn't work out so well the first time, did it?"

Oh, that was rich, coming from her mother. Maybe Helen had amnesia, and she'd forgotten her life from age fourteen to age thirty, and that's why she was being so preachy and overcautious.

Or maybe she just cares about you, a voice in Ellie's head whispered.

Ellie pushed her chair back and stood. "I need some air." She stalked out of the kitchen, stabbed her feet into rubber boots, and went outside. The rain had abated, but the scent of it hung heavy in the air. She wandered down along the nearest pasture's fence until the field gave way to trees. They were sparse in this area of her parents' land, with a wide path leading to a bubbling creek. The creek eventually became a misty waterfall as it spilled into the sea, part of the mere couple of dozen yards her parents owned along the water. The land had been in her father's family for generations. Now it was part of Ellie's DNA.

And Jason was threatening it. Threatening her family.

She walked in the darkness, inhaling the earthy scent of the forest, wrestling with everything that had happened today. She missed her dog.

Ellie brooded for a while, throwing a few pine cones into the stream to watch them disappear as they were swept away. Then she heard shuffling footsteps approach behind her. Grandma Mabel's white head appeared between the trees, a thermos dangling from her fingertips.

"Thought you might want something to warm you up while you sulk," Mabel said, coming to stand next to Ellie.

"I'm not sulking," Ellie sulked. "I'm plotting."

Her grandmother cackled. "Attagirl." She popped the top off the thermos and poured a mugful of hot toddy, boozy tea with lemon and honey. She passed the cup to Ellie, then took a sip from the thermos itself. "What sort of plan have you come up with?"

"Nothing concrete. Mostly just fantasies of separating Jason's head from his body."

More laughter from her grandmother, which made Ellie's shoulders relax. She drank more hot liquid, letting the alcohol warm her down to her toes.

"We need proof," Mabel finally said. "Otherwise it's just conjecture, and we'll never be believed."

"Sounds like you know that for a fact."

A bitter huff. Mabel watched the stream disappear through the trees and let out a sigh. "I was young when Jason's grandfather took over their logging company. He wanted to clear-cut the entire island and nearly succeeded. I saw an ugly side to him. Mercenary. He'd lie and cheat and steal just to get his way, and anytime scandal erupted around him, he'd magically come out unscathed. Somehow, even though the Brownlows had pushed for clear-cutting, now they're seen as environmental champions. They wash their history so clean, there's hardly any of it left except in the minds of old, doddering fools like me." She paused, her eyes pointed toward the distant coastline that Jason coveted. "This luxury resort project stinks, Ellie. Like something rotten."

Ellie thought of the way Jason strutted around Carlisle like he owned it. How he acted like he was royalty, not just another citizen of the island who happened to have more money than most. He was so entitled, so arrogant. She'd been so blind.

Ellie glanced at her grandmother's shadowed face, then said, "Why didn't you tell me you disliked Jason? Why didn't you warn me about him?"

Mabel finished the last of the hot toddy and screwed the cup back on the thermos. She sighed, then finally met Ellie's gaze. "You were in love, Ellie, and I hoped I was wrong."

"Was that love?" Ellie threw one last pine cone down the stream and shook her head. "I don't know, Grandma. When I think about the three years I spent with Jason, I don't recognize myself."

The truth was, she still didn't recognize herself. She was completely untethered, lost in a roiling sea of anger, betrayal, and humiliation. Six months ago, her engagement had ended, and her life had imploded.

She'd been so sure of Jason. So sure her life was on the right track. To be so utterly wrong about it all had rocked Ellie to her core. How could she trust her own judgment after that? What was she supposed to do with her life when she didn't trust herself to make good decisions?

Now, at least, she had something to point her rage at. She had a goal that was bigger than her own ego: she had to protect her family, because no one else would. That, she could cling to. Revenge made sense when she sought it for the people she loved.

They walked back to the house in time to find Claude flicking through his bookcase full of old records. "Aha!" He pulled out a familiar record and beamed as Ellie kicked off her boots. "Just in time, Ellie-Belly. We're about to listen to a good one."

Ellie smiled. With reverent hands, Claude dropped the needle on the record, and Joe Cocker's "Feelin' Alright" started playing through their wood-paneled sound system. Claude danced his way over to Helen, pulling her up to her feet as he shimmied his shoulders. Soon, he was singing lead while Ellie's mom belted out the backing vocals, the two of them wrapped up in their own love, their own world.

It made Ellie's heart hurt. She'd been so stupid to think she could have that too.

"Night, everyone," she mumbled, then slipped off to her room so she could ache in peace.

CHAPTER 6

Hugh found the survey stake that marked the edge of his father's land buried in a bed of moss. Except it wasn't his father's land any longer, was it? It was his now, all fifty-two acres of it, including the half-mile-long stretch of waterfront.

Technically, his father's company had owned the land, but the only asset the company had was the land on Fernley, which had previously been leased to various farmers and shepherds over the years. Now Hugh owned the company and its land, just like his father had promised.

Hugh hadn't believed it until he'd seen his name on the papers.

He walked downhill until the trees thinned, the land falling steeply into the cold, crashing waters below. A staircase of weather-beaten timber descended to a private beach, although you couldn't pay Hugh to take a swim in those waters. Even with the sun shining, there was a chill in the air he wasn't used to.

With his feet firmly planted on his father's legacy, Hugh couldn't wipe the oily feeling from his skin. He wanted to be gone from here. Hated that he'd come to Fernley in the first place.

After all these years, his father had finally succeeded in buying Hugh's attention, and Hugh hated himself for taking the payment.

He walked back along the coast toward his car. When he got to the flat patch of gravel where he'd parked, another car pulled up beside his, the blond man behind the wheel lifting two fingers in a casual greeting.

The man exited the car with a roll of architects' drawings under his arm. "You must be Hugh!" he boomed, his mouth spreading into a wide smile full of straight, white teeth. "Good to finally meet you. Your father spoke very highly of you."

Hugh doubted that. He doubted his father had ever mentioned him at all. Alexander Hartford had been content to leave Hugh in peace up until about three years ago. What could Alex possibly have had to say about Hugh? That he'd tried to reconcile with his estranged son and failed?

Maybe Alex had played the martyr, and Jason had heard some sentimental lies about his trials as a father. That would be just like him, to try to garner sympathy for himself from the wounds he'd inflicted upon others.

Gritting his teeth, Hugh nodded at Jason and ignored the mention of the other man. "Nice to put a face to the name."

Jason Brownlow was taller than he had expected, with a firm handshake and perfectly tousled dirty-blond hair. He wore dark jeans, a long-sleeved plaid shirt, and a puffy down vest paired with sturdy work boots, like the perfect poster boy for Pacific Northwest Casual Workwear Chic. He clapped Hugh on the back, then guided them both to his car, where he unrolled the large sheets of paper on the hood.

"Here it is," Jason said, placing his phone down on one side of the unrolled drawings and his wallet on the other. Despite their weight holding the papers down, the corners still curled inward. "The Fernley Luxury Resort and Spa." He slid his hand over the drawings. "Three hundred rooms. A heated pool. Tennis courts. New marina with kayak rental and boat tours for whale watching. We're planning on dredging out the coastline so we can create a sheltered bay for swimming and water sports. Your father was very excited about an additional marina, where we could have guests moor their yachts." He grinned, then swept his arm toward the Salish Sea. "And the view!"

With the sun shining on a blue sea and the skies clear, the view was indeed worthy of a postcard. In the distance, the ragged coastline of the San Juan Islands dotted the horizon to the north. For the first time since he'd arrived on the island, Hugh could see the appeal of this place. It was rugged, beautiful, and so lush it made him want to buy a down vest of his own, just to fit in with the locals. The more time he spent here, the less he missed the heat. The air here tasted sweeter than it did back home.

"What do you think?" Jason grinned. "Pretty special, huh? Construction of phases one and two should take two years, and we have enough interest that we'll be cash flow positive within six months. You're sitting on a gold mine here, Hugh. All you have to do is sign the contract, and we can get started."

Jason's pitch was pretty slick, Hugh had to admit. He had rendered drawings of the proposed resort in three dimensions, along with floor plans and elevations. Hugh and his lawyer had reviewed the contract and the financial documents before Hugh arrived on Fernley, and everything had looked aboveboard: in exchange for the use of his land, Hugh would become a part owner of the new resort. While reviewing the maps and surveys, Hugh had also noticed that the best access road was on his land. Jason hadn't said so, but Hugh knew his land was a crucial piece of the plan. Without his access road, the construction of the resort would be orders of magnitude more difficult.

Still, he was getting a good deal. The forecasted profits in the proposal documents promised that once he signed the contract, Hugh would likely never have to work again. Seeing the land in person was even more convincing.

Except for one thing.

"I met the neighbors yesterday," Hugh said, jerking his chin toward the property line he'd just walked. "One of them, at least. According to the drawings, the resort spans all three properties, correct? Mine, the Davises', and yours. Have you secured their consent as well?"

"Oh, Claude and Helen?" Jason's smile widened but got a little wooden around the edges. "We're in talks about acquiring their waterfront. Very advanced talks. It's a done deal, basically. Phase one of the project will be the main hotel, which is entirely on your father's— apologies, *your*—land, and phase two will be the spa building, tennis courts, and outbuildings, which will extend through the nearest property line, past the Davises' place, and over to my land. Phase three is the dredging and marina, which we're projecting will commence in eighteen months, just before the completion of the first two phases."

"I met Ellie, actually," Hugh said, keeping his voice casual. He glanced at Jason and caught the tail end of a fleeting expression, a hardness in his eyes that hadn't been there before. "I drove her home."

Jason let out a snort, shaking his head. "Stay away from her," he warned. "She's batshit crazy."

Based on her skill with a pair of bolt cutters, Hugh didn't exactly *dis*agree with Jason's assessment, but he didn't like the other man's tone. "Oh?"

"I was engaged to her, if you can believe it. Thank God I got out before we tied the knot, is all I can say."

"She didn't seem that bad. A bit intense, maybe."

Jason snorted. He grabbed his phone and let the architects' drawings spring into a neat cylinder without the weight of the device holding them down. After pulling up a photo on the screen, he tilted it to show Hugh. "Does this look like 'not that bad' to you?"

A photo of Ellie stared back at him, but not the Ellie he'd met yesterday. The mug shot was about as flattering as any other mug shot he'd seen, a white background with black lines denoting her height. Her brown hair was wild and messy, hanging in greasy hanks on either side of her face. Her forehead was red and swollen. Her eyes betrayed a burning, boiling fury that instinctively made him want to lean away.

He looked at Jason, who nodded at him.

"I'm telling you, Hugh. Better to give her a wide berth. But never mind the Davises. What I want to know is when we can expect the signed contract back from you."

"My lawyer is still reviewing the financials," Hugh hedged. It was a lie; his legal team had given him the green light to sign the contract at his leisure. He was one swoop of the pen away from making himself a very rich man.

With the money this deal would provide, Hugh would be able to buy the music studio where he'd worked for the past twelve years before it was dismantled. He'd be able to start his business, start his life. His mother's mortgage would get paid, and she wouldn't be living under the weight of ever-increasing living costs. She'd actually get to retire. Hugh would be able to give her that. Everything he'd ever wanted was just on the other side of a bit of ink on a bit of paper.

And it disgusted him.

It felt like his father paying him off once and for all. Hugh had told himself he'd accept the inheritance, sign the deal, and throw a middle finger up at his father's memory. At least he'd get something from the old man, right? He'd be an idiot not to take the money and make a better life for himself and his mother.

He'd also be a hypocrite, who, deep down, might be exactly like his father after all. Someone who put money above integrity, above morality. Someone whose idea of right and wrong depended on the weight of a purse of gold in his hand.

He needed the money; he hated the money.

He wasn't going to walk away from it.

But.

But how could he sign on to a lifelong business partnership with this man, when he'd stood in the rain and heard accusations about him poisoning an innocent family's sheep? How could he go through with the deal without knowing more about what he was getting into?

His conscience had protested before. Now it howled.

Asking Lionel about his family history had been about as productive as asking a lump of moss. Three years ago, when Alex had called Hugh out of nowhere the first time, he'd talked about this land. He'd promised it would belong to Hugh one day.

Hugh had put as much stock in that promise as he had the rest of them. He never trusted a word out of his father's mouth.

But now Hugh was here, and he wanted to find . . . he didn't even know what he wanted to find! Ever since his father had walked away from him two decades ago, he'd felt incomplete. Adrift. Angry.

Coming here was supposed to give him answers to questions he didn't even know how to ask, but now all he was finding were more questions.

Had Jason poisoned Ellie's parents' sheep? Was Ellie as crazy as Jason said? Did he want to entangle himself with these people and their drama? Had he been wrong to rebuff his father's attempts at reconciliation? Was he wrong to accept this inheritance, even if it changed his and his mother's lives?

"Your father was happy with the deal," Jason said, interrupting Hugh's thoughts. "He was going to sign, before . . ."

Hugh tore his gaze away from the glittering sea and met Jason's gaze. "Before he died," he finished.

Jason had the good sense to look embarrassed. "I'm sorry for your loss, by the way."

Hugh nodded. "Thanks. I'll get back to you when I hear from my lawyer."

"Of course. Oh! And before I forget, you'll come to the Brownlow Foundation Gala next week, right? I emailed you the invitation a couple of weeks ago." At Hugh's expression, Jason lifted his palms. "No pressure to donate when you're there. It's just a free meal on me, to celebrate our partnership. A lot of the other investors will be there as well. I'd like to introduce you to everyone."

"All right," Hugh said, unconvinced. He shook the other man's hand, even though he didn't want to, then got in his car and drove away.

After turning off his property and onto the road, he passed the little gravel-strewn gap in the trees that he'd navigated in the dark and the rain last night, and he wondered if Ellie was home.

Then the phone rang. Lionel's name flashed on the car's center touch screen. He pressed the button to answer, taking the call through the car's system. "Yeah?"

"Got a job for you." Lionel's gruff voice sounded odd through the car's speakers. "You remember Ellie Davis, the girl from yesterday?"

How could he forget? "Yeah."

"Her car's battery is flat. She needs a jump. Just came through on the app, but I've got two motors to tune up and I can't spare the time. Figured you're just fartin' around town all day, might as well make yourself useful."

Hugh snorted. "Right. It's not like I have anything else to do while I'm here."

"Exactly," Lionel answered, and Hugh knew he was being deliberately obtuse. He suspected the old man had a soft spot for Ellie, but Lionel's soft spots were well concealed beneath a thick layer of quiet surliness. "I'll send you the location. She said she has jumper cables, so all you have to do is find her."

The call disconnected, and Hugh drummed his fingers on the steering wheel. Looked like he'd be seeing Ellie again today. He touched the scab on the side of his head and wondered if he should pick up a first aid kit on the way to her location, just in case. Who knew what injuries would occur when he saw her this time?

Hugh found Ellie halfway up a steep, overgrown road that didn't look fit for modern vehicles. Branches scraped the sides of his car as he crawled up the hill, gravel kicking up to attack his car's undercarriage once again. The road widened slightly, leaving enough room for two vehicles. Ellie sat on the back bumper of a red Toyota Corolla hatchback that looked a couple of decades old, at least. She stood as he approached, frowning, then gestured for him to park beside her car.

She wore tight light-wash jeans and a loose white tee that was tucked in at the front. Her long brown hair fell around her shoulders, something shining and golden dangling from her ears. Dappled sunlight danced on her hair and skin as she moved to face him. Her mouth was set in a thin line, her blue eyes looking paler in this light than they had last night. Hugh remembered the feel of her body beneath his, how she'd hissed and bucked like a furious, soaked cat. He'd been too angry about her attack to think about anything other than making sure she didn't injure either of them, but now he could admit that he'd like to feel her body against his again. Preferably out of the rain and mud.

She was a beautiful woman. An angry, short-tempered, fearsome, beautiful woman. At the sight of her, a tightness in Hugh's chest unknotted. He parked the car and watched her twist her hair into a messy bun on top of her head using some sort of female voodoo that took two seconds flat to complete. Sunlight glanced off her cheekbones, her collarbones, her lips.

When he exited his car, she had her hands on her hips. "Where's Lionel?"

"Had a couple of motors to fix," Hugh answered. "He sent me."

"Fine." She popped the hood of her car and gestured for him to do the same. She'd obviously dealt with a dead car battery before, because she had the jumper cables clipped on correctly within moments. She jerked her head at Hugh's car. "Turn it on."

He did, then slipped out to let it run for a few minutes to charge the battery. Glancing around, he asked, "What's your car doing here, anyway?"

"Wouldn't you like to know?"

He glanced at her, at the shape of her lower body in those jeans. "Um. Yes?"

"Lionel doesn't usually talk when he does these jobs for me." She picked up a piece of gravel and threw it at a tree. "It's one of the reasons I hire him so often."

Hugh laughed. She glanced at him, looking startled, then let her lips curve into a slight smile.

Hugh picked up his own piece of gravel and tossed it into the forest, missing the trunk he'd been aiming at. "Did you find out what happened with Spencer? What was he doing at your place last night?"

Ellie huffed. "Exactly what he said when we first caught him. He was sprinkling common milkweed over the field. Apparently Jason Brownlow put him up to it, saying it was good for the sheep. And because Spencer is a total sweetheart who loves animals, he was more than happy to help. He'd done it three times so far, over the course of the past month and a half. Spence had no idea he was hurting the sheep, and when he found out, he wouldn't stop crying. It was awful."

"And you believe him?"

Ellie gave him a sharp look. "Why wouldn't I?"

Hugh shrugged. "From what I understand, the Brownlows are well respected around here."

Ellie snorted. "Yeah. Right." Her lips pinched, and she looked away from him. "Let me try my car. Maybe the battery's got enough juice." She slipped behind the wheel of her little red hatchback, turned the key, and started the car. She slipped back out again and unclipped the cables, looping them over her arm before tossing them in the trunk of her car. She nodded to Hugh. "Thanks." Then she got in her car and drove off.

Hugh watched her leave, feeling as conflicted as ever about the business deal waiting for his signature.

And, oddly, he felt equally disappointed that he hadn't needed that first aid kit after all.

CHAPTER 7

Ellie had two problems. The first was the lock on Jason's house, and the second was the alarm. If she was going to find evidence of his wrongdoings, her best bet was to get inside his study, that room that she hadn't dared to enter even when she lived in the house with him.

With a bit of luck, Ellie would be able to infiltrate the house, find evidence, then snag Louie and be out before Jason ever knew she'd been there. Sure, her first attempt at breaking and entering had ended with Wynn in the hospital, but this was different.

This time, she was going in through the front door. All she needed to figure out was how.

Still, as she drove, she found herself thinking of Hugh Hartford. He'd let her clip the jumper cables without trying to muscle his way in, which she appreciated. Jason had always treated her like an idiot. Her ex would have questioned her every move and made her doubt herself. Hugh just watched her with those light-brown eyes of his, causing her stomach to tighten.

Now that she was away from him, she felt like she could breathe again. The last thing she needed was a man, especially a blow-in from off-island. Ellie needed to focus on the task at hand. She needed to get her dog back and destroy her ex's life. Jumping into bed with another man was not a good idea. He might be big and brawny and have a nice laugh, but Hugh would only get in the way of what Ellie had to do.

What was she even talking about? Getting in bed with him wasn't even on the table. She'd skipped about a million steps between "attack him with a pair of bolt cutters" and "get naked together." Her brain was short-circuiting. It was probably the pressure of the last few months and the horror of her discovery last night. There was too much going on, and Ellie wasn't thinking straight.

Best to stay away from Lionel's nephew.

Ellie drove to Carlisle, avoiding the street where her old business's office was. Avoiding that road meant she had to make a long loop around town, but it was worth it to prevent the twinge of pain in her heart at the sight of the sign hanging above the door, the dark windows, the memories of everything she'd lost.

She'd been a good event planner while it lasted, but the pride of her achievements was overshadowed by their unfortunate ending. Any goodwill, any respect she'd gained had been obliterated, and she couldn't bear to be reminded of it. Not right now, when she needed to stay focused.

Ellie parked outside the Sunrise Diner, a 1950s-style eatery that served breakfast all day. The diner was near the ferry terminal, halfway up a gentle incline on the main drag through town. It overlooked the water, with its crying gulls and brown clumps of seaweed clinging to the rocky shore. The air smelled of the sea, rain, and boat fuel. Ellie would miss it when she left.

A horn blasted long and loud, and Ellie watched the morning ferry depart. It pulled away from the pier in a froth of white water, with workers in fluorescent safety vests scurrying around both on the shore and on the ferry. Cars glittered on the main deck in six neat rows, with a few walk-on passengers milling about near the stern of the ship, waving to their loved ones on the shore. More passengers climbed the stairs onto the sundeck at the bow. Ellie was supposed to be on that ferry with

Louie by her side. She should've been sitting in her car, drinking one of the overpriced coffees from the terminal café, unwrapping a gigantic white-chocolate-and-raspberry muffin that she'd eat for breakfast. She would've wandered over to the edge of the vessel's deck and watched the prow slice through the water. She would've rubbed Louie behind the ears and spent the hour-and-a-bit journey planning her next steps, her new life.

But that was before she'd found out what Jason had done. Now she had to make a new plan.

She entered the Sunrise Diner and scanned the space. Wynn was waiting for her in the teal-and-pink corner booth, her white mug full of coffee and her laptop in front of her. Her leg was propped up on the booth's seat, black-rimmed glasses perched on the end of her nose. She was working, which was no great surprise. Wynn was a graphic designer who also worked part time at the sign shop on the island. She was always busy.

She smiled. "Hi, Ellie."

"How's the ankle?"

"Same as last night. Still badly sprained."

Ellie winced. "Sorry, Wynnie."

"Worth it. Especially after what you told me." She scowled. "I can't believe Jason would ask Spencer to do that."

Ellie had called Wynn last night and updated her about the goings-on. Wynn had been suitably outraged, and her friend's reaction had helped calm Ellie down.

Now, Ellie slouched in the booth and let her head fall back. "I feel all cold inside, Wynn. I want to kill him."

"At least we know you look decent in a mug shot."

Ellie snorted and gave her friend a flat look. "That mug shot made me a laughingstock. I look terrible in it."

"I don't know," Wynn said, tilting her head from side to side. "I think it gave you street cred with the tinfoil-hat-wearing radicals on the island."

"Great," Ellie replied with an eye roll. "Just what I've always wanted."

Tracey, the longtime waitress and part owner at the Sunrise Diner, walked up to the table and topped up Wynn's coffee. Her black hair was coiled in tight ringlets that were streaked with gray, and she was comfortably soft all over. She gave great hugs. "What can I get for you, sweetheart?"

Ellie didn't have to look at the menu. "A coffee and scrambled eggs on wheat toast, please. And hash browns on the side."

"Comin' right up." Tracey ambled away. She was one of the only people who still treated Ellie the same, even after everything that had happened. There were no side-eyes, no snarky words, no turned-up noses. Tracey was as constant as the rain on Fernley. She was one of the reasons the diner had survived so long.

The door banged open behind them, and Ellie heard her grandmother's voice. "I'm telling you, Harry, Mary O'Hara puts cyanide in her blackberry pie. Why else would it taste so bad and make me want to drop dead?"

Harry—Harriet—let out a bark of laughter. "Wouldn't that make it taste like almonds? Seems to me it'd be an improvement."

"Wouldn't feed it to a cat," a third voice grumped. That was Greta, the third white-haired dragon in Mabel's troupe.

The elderly ladies stopped in front of Wynn and Ellie. Mabel looked at Ellie. "What do you say, Ellie? Would you eat Mary O'Hara's blackberry pie?"

"Didn't she win the Fernley Com-Pie-Tition last year?" Ellie asked. The island's pie-baking contest happened annually and had grown incredibly popular of late. "Her blackberry pie can't be that bad."

"Everyone knows she bought the judges off," Harry cut in, thumping her butterfly-patterned cane on the vinyl floor.

"It was a travesty," Greta agreed. "Rhonda Roberts should have won, hands down. Classic apple pie with that lattice top and jammy filling. It was perfect. Perfect! That bit of sugar on top?" She looked at Mabel and clicked her tongue. "Robbed."

"I heard Mary O'Hara had an affair with Irving Matthews, and that's why he gave her the trophy," Wynn interjected, slurping her coffee.

"Wouldn't put it past her," Mabel said. "Maybe he was judging a different kind of pie."

Ellie gagged. "Gross, Grandma."

Mabel laughed. "What are you doing here, anyway? Shouldn't you be out causing trouble?" There was that word again—"trouble." But when Mabel said it, it didn't sound like an insult.

"Trying to figure out how," Ellie admitted.

"Why? What's going on?" Harry hip-checked Ellie deeper into the booth and took a seat. "What trouble are you looking for? You want to get arrested again?"

Ellie arched a brow. "No, not particularly."

"Oh, don't be boring," Greta said, pulling up a chair. "Spill."

Ellie pursed her lips. Telling the island's white-haired gossip brigade about her less-than-lawful plans wasn't exactly a good idea. Still . . . "Hypothetically speaking," she started, "if you needed to get inside someone's house, and you didn't have a key, and you didn't want them to know you'd been in their house, how would you do it?"

"Back door," Harry answered.

"Say it's locked."

"Window," Mabel said, miming a jab of her elbow.

"Say they're alarmed."

"Housekeeper," Greta said, snagging the coffee Tracey had put down on the table before it could make it to Ellie. She dumped three sugars in it and stirred, oblivious to the wide-eyed look Ellie gave her, then exchanged with Wynn.

"The housekeeper would have the new alarm code," Ellie said quietly, accepting the plate of eggs Tracey handed her over everyone's heads.

Greta's spoon clinked against the white porcelain. Tracey returned with more mugs and poured everyone coffee, jotting down the old ladies' food orders. When she walked away, Ellie stared at the dark brew in her mug, heart thumping.

"Uh-oh," Wynn said.

"What?" Ellie lifted her gaze.

"You have that look in your eyes."

Ellie frowned. "What look?"

Mabel cackled. "Like you're about to do something stupid. Have you got a getaway driver, at least?"

"Oh, to be young," Harry said wistfully. "I'd come along if I could, but my legs don't work so well anymore."

"Neither do your eyes," Greta cut in, "or your ears."

"My ears and eyes work just fine, you old hag," Harry answered, scowling at her friend. "I can see that mole on your face has three big hairs growing out of it from all the way over here."

Greta harrumphed and drank her coffee.

Ellie glanced at Wynn, then down at her cast. "No," she said, answering her grandmother's question. "I don't have a getaway driver."

"Better find one," Mabel said, sipping her cream-and-sugar-laden coffee. "Always have an escape strategy. Otherwise, you risk getting caught."

The two other old ladies nodded sagely, like they knew that from experience. Hell, they probably did. The way Mabel had laughed and laughed at Ellie's first mug shot was a clue. Also the fact that she'd called it a *first mug shot*.

Maybe, despite her best efforts, this apple had fallen exactly where destiny had ordained. Ellie was her mother's daughter, who was her mother's daughter too. Maybe it was time Ellie stopped fighting it and started embracing her family's legacy.

She was a troublemaker. She did stupid things—and she was amazing at it.

Plus, Mabel was right. Ellie was going to need a getaway driver and a decent plan of action. She scarfed down her food, then made her excuses to leave. Before anything else could happen, Ellie had a housekeeper to bribe and an alarm code to acquire.

The old dragons were busy eating and drinking, so Ellie was trapped in the booth. She checked her shoes to make sure they were clean, then climbed over the back of the booth to get out. Then she froze, straddling the two vinyl-upholstered seats, her head bumping the hanging light fixture that ran the whole length of the diner—because in the open doorway, Hugh Hartford stood, watching her with an amused twinkle in his eyes.

Mabel whistled. "Well, isn't *he* a tall drink of water?"

Hugh wondered if Ellie ever did things the way normal people did. He doubted it, which made him stop and stare, just to find out why she was straddling two booth seats. As he watched, she climbed over the seat, straightened her spine, and pranced to the waitress's station to grab a spray bottle.

He approached as she squirted some disinfectant on the booth and wiped it clean. Trying to stay away from her was like resisting the pull of gravity. His feet carried him forward without conscious input from his brain.

She clutched her spray bottle like a queen with her scepter and gave him a curt nod. "Hugh."

"Ellie." He watched her walk all the way back to the waitress's station to drop the spray bottle. Her ass still looked fantastic in those jeans.

"Oh, they *know* each other!" an excited voice said in a not-so-hushed whisper. An elderly woman pushed her chair back and studied him openly. "Look at his eyes, Harry. Aren't they gorgeous?"

Two more white heads popped up over the side of the booth and stared at him.

Ellie turned and scowled at the old women. "Grandma, please."

"Ellie, don't be rude. Introduce us!"

"I don't have time for this," she mumbled, but she still grabbed Hugh's elbow and dragged him to the table. Her hand was warm through the thin fabric of his long-sleeve tee. Dropping his elbow, Ellie used the same hand to sweep in front of his body like she was a model on *The Price Is Right* and he was a solid cherrywood bedroom suite. "This is Hugh, Lionel's nephew. He jumped my car battery this morning."

"And he drove us to the medical center," Wynn added.

Hugh blinked. He'd been so busy staring at Ellie that he hadn't even noticed the slight blonde woman sitting with her ankle propped up on the booth. "How's the foot?" he asked.

"Still attached," Wynn answered with a shrug.

"Hugh, this is my grandma Mabel and her friends Harry and Greta. Try to stay out of touching distance. It's for your own safety."

"Oh, please," Mabel said with a click of her tongue, then immediately jumped up and grabbed him by the biceps. She gave them a little squeeze, then looked over her shoulder and said, "Very muscular, ladies. His arms feel nice and solid."

"I wasn't aware Lionel had a nephew," one of the other ladies said—Greta, Hugh thought. She sipped her coffee and stared at Hugh with a gimlet eye. "What's your father's name?"

"Alexander. He was older than Lionel and already away at college when my grandparents and uncle moved to Fernley, so he never actually lived on the island."

"Oh, of course!" Mabel patted his arm. "Alex Hartford. I remember. He used to come visit in the summer. How is he?"

"He passed away, Grandma," Ellie interjected, "and I'm sure Hugh doesn't feel like being interrogated about it. Now stop fondling him."

"What, you gettin' jealous?"

Ellie's cheeks turned pink. "I have to go. Hugh, I'd recommend choosing another dining establishment unless you want to have your entire family history extracted and subsequently passed around the island like breaking news."

Hugh grinned. "I'm just here to pick up lunch for my uncle and me, so I think I'm safe."

"You'd be surprised," Ellie answered darkly, then said goodbye to the group and walked out the door. Hugh watched her leave, and when he turned back to the table to make excuses of his own, he found Wynn and all three elderly ladies staring at him *very* intently.

"I, uh, have to go," he stammered. "Nice to meet you."

Mabel smiled and patted his chest a few times. "Nice to meet you too, dear. Take care."

CHAPTER 8

On the northwest side of the island, where the oceanic wind and rain battered the Fernley coast for three hundred–odd days a year, was the Blue Skies Trailer Park, named by a very optimistic person who hadn't been on Fernley Island very long.

The second double-wide trailer from the front gate was militantly neat and belonged to Gemma McMorton. Beside the trailer was a van branded with a cartoon image of a mop and bucket, proclaiming it the property of the "Tidy Galz Cleaning Service."

Gemma was home. Perfect. Ellie parked her car next to the van and got out.

A small child came tearing around the corner carrying an enormous water gun. The kid was wearing yellow shorts and nothing else, and he came to a skidding stop at the sight of the unfamiliar vehicle. Then his little mug took on a suspicious expression, and he lowered the gun to point it at Ellie's chest.

"Wait, I—"

The kid fired. Ellie screeched, jumping behind her car as the child cackled and chased her. They circled the vehicle three times before the trailer's door banged open and Gemma's voice boomed. "Cory. Stop that! Didn't I tell you not to spray visitors? Get over here so I can call your mother!"

The kid took off at a sprint, his bare feet clearly unbothered by the gravel beneath them. Ellie watched him leave, wiping water droplets from her face. Even on a sunny day, she managed to end up soaked.

"Sorry about that, Ellie," Gemma said. "What brings you around?"

"You mind if we talk inside?" The walls had ears here, and it was bad enough that Mabel's posse knew where she was.

Gemma's eyes narrowed. "Sure." She opened the door for Ellie and stepped in after her.

The interior of the mobile home was similar to the outside, in that it was sparkling clean while being worn enough to look like it needed a full renovation. The carpet was a thick brown shag, and the walls had yellowed over time. The kitchen / living room was furnished with a beat-up sofa covered in a worn slipcover, a Formica table and four chairs, and an old La-Z-Boy recliner pointed at the television. Gemma gestured to the table and chairs, and Ellie took a seat.

She tapped her fingernails on the tabletop and gathered her thoughts. Here went nothing. "Are you still cleaning Jason Brownlow's house?"

Gemma's eyes narrowed as she pulled out her own chair. "Who's asking?"

"A concerned citizen."

Gemma snorted. "Not a jilted ex-lover?"

"Yes or no, Gemma. You still cleaning his place?"

Gemma sat down and leaned back, crossing her arms. The truth was, Gemma was a little scary. Over six feet tall, with an athletic build, she was physically intimidating, but that's not why people heeded her. It was because she'd look at them the way she looked at Ellie right then, like she could read every thought rushing through Ellie's mind, and none of them impressed her. She supported her entire family with her cleaning business, including that little boy Cory, her nephew, who lived next door. Gemma McMorton took no shit, and people mostly stayed out of her way.

Ellie felt a strange bit of kinship with Gemma, mostly because both of them had fought the weight of their families' reputations and started their own successful businesses. The only difference was Gemma's life and business hadn't imploded, while Ellie's had—and in spectacular fashion.

The woman pulled out a pack of cigarettes from her purse and lit one before sliding open the nearest window with her other hand. She watched Ellie through the smoke she exhaled toward the opening. "You got a lot of nerve coming here, demanding answers," she finally rasped.

Ellie deflated. "I know. I'm sorry."

"Why do you want to know about Jason?"

"I really can't tell you, Gemma. The less you know, the better."

Gemma watched her. Ellie couldn't read the expression in the other woman's eyes, so all she could do was try to look as earnest as she felt. She was rewarded when Gemma nodded and said, "Yeah, I'm still cleaning his place."

Ellie chose her words carefully. "Yesterday, I found out that Jason was trying to mess with my family in a big way. I need to get into his house to see if I can find evidence. In order to do that, I need the code to his security alarm."

Gemma ashed her cigarette into the ashtray in the center of the table. "Evidence of what?"

"Of him being a piece of shit."

The woman laughed. "You really need evidence? You were engaged to the guy, weren't you? Isn't that enough?"

Ellie flattened her palms on the table. "I want to ruin his life, Gemma. I need evidence of what he did so I can expose him to the entire island."

Gemma hummed. "You're asking me to betray one of my biggest clients and put my entire livelihood in jeopardy, Ellie."

Ellie met the other woman's gaze. "No one will know you gave me the code. No one will even know I was there. I promise."

Gemma was silent.

Desperation scratched sharp claws along Ellie's skin. She needed that code to get inside Jason's house, or she'd never find proof that he was behind the milkweed. She'd never get to ruin his life the way he'd ruined hers. Her parents would be vulnerable to his next schemes, to the power of his name and his money.

"I think he poisoned my parents' animals, Gemma," she finally said in a hushed voice. "I think he tricked Spencer into doing the dirty work, and I need proof."

Gemma's gaze sharpened. "Spencer Wisneski?"

Ellie nodded.

Gemma crushed her cigarette into the ashtray, then immediately got up and cleaned the whole thing out. She dried the now-clean ashtray and replaced it on the table with a thunk. "Spencer never hurt anyone, and he doesn't deserve to be dragged into any of this. I'll give you the code, Ellie."

Ellie's heart soared.

"But you gotta do something for me first."

Gemma led Ellie to the far end of the Blue Skies Trailer Park, out the gate, and down a beaten dirt path to a nearby property. Ellie's heart thumped. She knew this property. She was familiar with the tall, craggy coastline and the tidy house that overlooked it. Its white clapboard siding was pristine, the asphalt roof shingles sparkling under the sun. New green shoots of flowers were starting to poke their heads above the rich, dark earth that lined the back of the house.

A dead tree had been felled and chopped into cylindrical sections that littered the lawn in a haphazard fashion, as if a giant had shaken them up and scattered them like a throw of dice.

Ellie looked at Gemma. Gemma looked at Ellie.

"I'm not following," Ellie admitted.

"Mary O'Hara said I could have this wood as long as I chopped it and took it away myself. She gave me until the end of the week to do it, or she's putting it up for free on the island's social media page. I don't have time to do it myself, and with the van full of cleaning supplies, I'll have to cart it all back to my trailer in wheelbarrows."

"So if I chop this wood, you'll give me the alarm code for Jason's house?"

"Chop it, carry it to my trailer, and stack it in the shed."

Ellie looked at the rounds of wood. They were at least a foot in diameter and half that again in length. They must've weighed a ton, and there were dozens of them.

"Chopping all this will take hours," Ellie said.

Gemma shrugged, glancing at her nails in a move that was a bit too casual. She really wanted this wood. "If you want that code, these are my terms."

Ellie sighed. She didn't have time for this. Jason was wandering around the island, killing innocent sheep. She needed to get into his house, find some dirt on him, grab her dog, and get out before word of the milkweed spread. Because it would spread; of that, she had no doubt. Secrets didn't exist for long on Fernley. Her own mug shot had circulated the island within hours. A piece of gossip like potential sheep poisoning would get out, and then it would be too late to act. Jason would know she was onto him, and he'd cover his tracks. He'd smooth over the rumors and somehow manage to make her look bad. The only advantage she had was his ignorance. Against a man who had a blemish-free reputation and an overflowing bank account, Ellie could use every meager advantage she could find.

"Can't I just pay you for the code?" Ellie asked, desperate.

"My trailer, my parents', and my sister's all have wood-burning stoves. This firewood will keep us all warm for two winters, at least. You'd have to give me at least two thousand dollars to make it worth my while."

Ellie planted her hands on her hips, shifting her gaze from Gemma's bulldog expression to the scattered chunks of tree trunk. She didn't have two thousand bucks.

Did she have any other options?

She could try the old alarm code in case Jason hadn't changed it after they broke up—and risk being caught. Any other attempt to enter the house would result in her arrest and humiliation.

She needed that code.

"Damn it, Gemma."

"So, you'll do it?"

"I'm not doing it alone," she grumbled, pulling out her phone. The OddJobs app loaded quickly, and she typed out a quick description of what she needed. She quoted a price and posted the job—publicly, this time. She wasn't risking Lionel foisting his nephew on her again. This job was going on the open market.

"If no one answers this post, I'll head home and get an axe. You think Fergus would help, seeing as this is in his mom's backyard?"

Gemma just snorted. "Fergus? Doubt it. And even if he showed up, Mary wouldn't want her precious boy doing any manual labor."

When Ellie's phone dinged, she grimaced at Lionel's name on the screen. He'd accepted the job and sent her a message to say he was on his way. He'd better show up himself. She didn't feel like dealing with Hugh. It was hard enough figuring out how to ruin Jason's life. She didn't need some stranger judging her for her perfectly reasonable (if less than legal) plans.

Plus, her body seemed to have a mind of its own when Hugh was around. Her stomach did that weird tilting, tightening thing whenever he met her gaze. She'd actually *blushed* earlier at the diner when Mabel asked if she was jealous.

Ellie needed to stay focused on the task at hand. She didn't have time for Hugh Hartford.

"I'll go talk to Mary," Ellie told Gemma. "I need to ask her if we can chop here or if she wants us to do it elsewhere."

Gemma nodded, looking pleased. She had gotten a couple of years' worth of firewood for free, after all. And maybe Jason's reputation wasn't as spotless as Ellie had previously thought. Maybe other people on this island wanted to stick it to him as much as Ellie did.

The two women walked around the small bungalow to the front door, knocked, and waited for the door to open. A moment later, it swung open to reveal Mary O'Hara. She was in her early sixties, but she could pass for ten years younger. She wore a pastel-yellow top and matching skirt with a baby-blue sweater loosely tied around her shoulders. Her hair was wrapped in her usual French twist, and her ears were adorned with smooth pearl studs. When she saw Ellie on her doorstep, her lips pursed. She looked like someone who had just discovered she'd accidentally stepped in dog poo while wearing her favorite designer shoes.

Ellie was used to it, but it still stung. Her mug shot had circulated, along with the story of its inception, and noses had turned up in unison. Mary O'Hara wasn't exactly in the upper tiers of Fernley society, but she was clinging to every coattail she could—which was honestly hilarious, considering what a deadbeat her son had turned out to be. But Fergus's failure to launch meant Mary had had to try extra hard to distance herself from riffraff like trailer park dwellers such as Gemma or—*shudder*—someone with the last name Davis.

In the end, Mary decided to ignore Ellie's existence entirely. She turned to Gemma. "What do you want?"

"Hi, Mrs. O'Hara," Ellie started sweetly, ignoring the snub and deciding to be the bigger person for once. "I was hoping to help Gemma with that firewood out back, and I wondered if we could do the chopping on your property. It would make it much easier to carry away."

Mrs. O'Hara's lips turned down. "That'll make a mess, won't it? Kindling and shards everywhere."

"We'll clean it up," Ellie promised. "We'll be out of your hair by this afternoon."

"No," the older woman replied. "I'd really rather you do the work elsewhere."

Ellie sighed. Being the bigger person was overrated. She should have stuck to being the very small, very petty person, and she could have covered Mary's yard in splinters to her black heart's content. "All right. As soon as the truck gets here, we'll get the wood off your lawn."

Mary nodded sharply. "Good." Her gaze shifted over Ellie's shoulder as the sound of an engine approached. "Who's going to help you?"

Ellie turned to watch the vehicle turn down the driveway to Mary's house. "Oh, that's Lionel Hart—"

Ugh. Oh no.

Lionel's old pickup truck slowed to a stop, the engine cut off, and both the passenger door and driver's side door opened. Lionel exited the driver's side.

"Who's *that*?" Mary asked quietly.

Gemma made a noise, like she was also wondering about the answer to that question.

Ellie's mood darkened. "That's Lionel's nephew, Hugh."

Hugh shut the pickup door, his gaze cutting to Ellie's. There were a lot of things in his eyes. Curiosity, amusement, maybe even interest. Then he looked at her shirt, and his eyebrow twitched the tiniest bit.

Ellie looked down. She was still pretty damp from Cory's attack, and her T-shirt hadn't exactly survived unscathed. Wonderful. Just once—just *one time*—she'd like to not look like a total idiot in front of Hugh.

Hugh turned to the bed of the pickup truck and grabbed a big axe out of the toolbox attached to the side. He held it across his broad chest, turning to face the three women watching him. Paul Bunyan, eat your heart out.

Ellie felt flustered and frustrated, so she squared her shoulders and stepped off the porch.

"Hi, Lionel," she said, pointedly ignoring the looming figure beside the old man. Yes, she was doing the exact thing Mary O'Hara had done, which she'd hated. No, she wasn't going to think about why. "Thanks for coming."

"This job is about firewood?" Lionel asked, his lined face looking unimpressed.

"Yeah. Gemma needs it."

"What's that got to do with you?"

Ellie frowned at the old man. "You accepted the job, Lionel, which you didn't have to do. I'm paying you to be here and chop wood, not to ask questions."

He huffed and glanced at his nephew, then back at Ellie. "Hugh'll be doing most of the chopping."

Ellie shrugged. "Fine. We'll have to load the wood rounds into the truck and chop them elsewhere. Mrs. O'Hara doesn't want the mess, so—"

"Oh, don't be silly, Ellie!" Mary came floating down the three porch steps and beamed at Hugh. "It would be much more convenient for these boys to chop on site, wouldn't it? I don't want to make more work for everyone."

Ellie stared at her. Gemma appeared beside Ellie, smoothing and resmoothing her hair down as she blinked at Hugh like she'd never seen a real-life man before.

Everyone had lost their minds. This island must have mercury in the water supply, because every single resident was loony. Hugh was handsome, sure, but he wasn't worthy of this kind of admiration.

Was he?

Ellie finally looked at him again up close and tried to be objective. The sun shone on his sable hair, his stubble-lined jaw strong and square as he stood there groping his axe. He did look very strapping and manly; she'd give him that. But he still annoyed her.

"Come, come," Mrs. O'Hara insisted. "I'll bring you around. It's so warm out today; I'll make some lemonade for you and bring it out. Hugh, was it? How long have you been on Fernley? Has anyone shown you around yet? There are some absolutely lovely spots on the island, but you need a local to show them to you." She hooked a hand around Hugh's elbow and dragged him toward the side of the house.

"Just got here a couple of days ago," Hugh replied, neatly avoiding the rest of Mrs. O'Hara's speech. "It's a beautiful place."

Ellie fell back beside Lionel and hissed, "Why'd you have to bring him, Lionel? I thought I was hiring you."

"I'm too old for that kind of hard work," Lionel admitted. "I've chopped enough wood to last a lifetime."

Exasperated, Ellie stared at him. "So let someone else accept the job! I posted it publicly. You didn't need to take it."

Lionel hobbled on, squinting against the sunlight as they emerged in the backyard. "Need the money to declare on my tax return. Don't want those IRS freaks sniffin' around, asking questions. Boat repairs have picked up lately, so I need to make sure nothing looks fishy. People pay cash, I take it. Don't necessarily want to tell no one about it, though."

Ellie rolled her eyes.

"Here we are!" Mrs. O'Hara beamed at Hugh and presented her wood. "Ready for a big, strong young man to chop it up."

Hugh glanced at Ellie and looked like he wanted to laugh. Ellie wanted the earth to open up and swallow her whole.

Then again, why did she want that? Why did she care what Hugh thought?

"Start with this one." Lionel pointed to a nearby log, and Hugh obliged. He placed it on top of another, wider and flatter piece, unclipped the leather sheath protecting the head of the axe, and got in position.

Everyone stood and watched the wonder that was Hugh's body in motion. The big log split with a loud crack, two neat halves falling apart.

Gemma let out a breath. "Well," she said, then stopped, her hand clutched at her breast.

As loath as she was to admit it, Ellie knew exactly what Gemma meant.

Hugh put the head of the axe down and leaned its shaft against his leg. He wore a long-sleeve tee, and he spent a few focused moments rolling its sleeves up to the elbow. His broad hands worked the fabric, exposing inch by tawny inch of muscled forearm. Then he gave his arms a little shake and combed the fingers of both hands through his hair. For a beautiful, breathless second, a sliver of abdominal skin was exposed between the waistband of his jeans and the hem of his top.

Beside Ellie, Gemma let out a tiny puff of breath.

Oblivious, Hugh picked the axe up again and continued the show. He grabbed an entire half of the split log in a single large hand—seriously, *how*—put it back up on his makeshift chopping platform, and swung.

He did it again, and again, and again, bringing the axe down onto those innocent pieces of wood until sweat dampened his shirt and ran down his temples. Then Mary appeared with fresh lemonade and fawned over him while Ellie stepped in for a while, chopping nowhere nearly as efficiently as Hugh had.

"You want me to take over?" Hugh asked quietly a few moments later as Ellie tried to catch her breath, leaning on the axe's handle. "It's harder than it looks."

"I know. That's why I hired Lionel to do it."

Hugh glanced at Lionel, who was snoozing on one of Mary's deck chairs, and grinned. "I think we both got swindled. We were finishing lunch when he saw the notification. Didn't even tell me where we were going, just said he got a job and needed me to help."

"More like he needed you to do all the grunt work."

Hugh laughed, and Ellie was temporarily thunderstruck. He was truly a handsome man, with his wide smile, long, lean dimples, and gleaming dark hair. Then she shook herself. Soon, she'd turn into Mary O'Hara and start making him cold drinks every five minutes. Pathetic. It's not like a guy who looked like Hugh would ever be interested in someone like her. She'd deluded herself into thinking that handsome, charming, successful Jason had actually cared about her; she wasn't going to make that mistake again.

"I don't mind helping him out," Hugh admitted, glancing at his uncle. "I didn't really know my dad all that well. Lionel's the only uncle I've got, so I figured it might be worth getting to know each other."

Well, that was admirable, she supposed. "Any luck so far?"

Hugh grimaced. "The most Lionel's spoken to me was when he gave me his lunch order."

It was Ellie's turn to laugh and Hugh's turn to stare. Embarrassed by his gaze, she lifted the axe to hand it to him. When he took it from her grasp, his fingers brushed hers. His skin was warm and rough, and the touch sent little lightning bugs flitting through Ellie's veins. She truly needed to get a grip on herself. This was getting ridiculous.

She backed away and let Hugh get to work.

Ellie carted the split logs to the pickup truck while Hugh chopped. They made quick work of it as Gemma, Lionel, and Mrs. O'Hara watched on from the deck.

When Ellie returned from one of her trips to the pickup truck, she found Mary O'Hara on her back deck, calling everyone to partake in her award-winning blackberry pie. Ellie caught herself staring as Hugh stalked across the lawn toward the deck, his shirt clinging to his chest, his cheeks flushed from exertion.

He was magnificent. Watching him move mesmerized and enthralled her, and for a moment, all she could do was stare. Jason didn't move like that, in a way that commanded attention. He didn't suck the air out of Ellie's lungs. She had to blink and look away to gather herself, because for the past hour, she'd forgotten why exactly she was here.

She was here to get the code for the security alarm that protected her ex-fiancé's house. She was here to get her dog back. She was here to set in motion her plans of revenge. Now she was drooling over a man who would probably be gone from the island in a matter of days. It was absurd and distracting, and Ellie had to pull herself together.

Mrs. O'Hara dished out pieces of pie, giving Hugh a particularly large slice. Ellie dug into hers and immediately regretted taking such a big bite. It tasted bitter and awful, and the filling was full of some sort of grit. The bottom crust of the pie was soggy, giving the whole pie an off-putting slimy, gritty texture. Harry was right; cyanide would be an improvement. She scanned the space for a napkin or a bush she could use to dispose of the bite, to no avail. In her search, she met Hugh's gaze as he chewed a bite, looking frozen and horrified.

"What do you think? The secret is the warm spices and the fact that the blackberries are straight from my garden." She pointed to the vast prickly bushes that lined the far end of the yard. "First place in the Fernley Com-Pie-Tition. I'm hoping to take the title two years in a row."

Ellie suspected Irving Matthews was hoping for the same. She didn't want to imagine what Mary had done to him to get this pie the first-place ribbon in the island's pie-baking contest. Ellie finally swallowed her bite and, as politely as she could, set her plate down. "I'm watching my figure," she explained when Mrs. O'Hara gave her a questioning glance.

"That's smart, Ellie," the older woman said. "I noticed you were getting a little porky after Jason Brownlow left you."

Everyone froze.

Ellie stared at Mrs. O'Hara, letting the words sink in. A little porky . . . after *he* left *her?* Outrage went off like a flare inside her, warning of impending doom. She was so *sick* of people judging her for the breakdown of her engagement. Jason *cheated* on her! *At her own engagement party!*

Hugh finally swallowed his bite with what looked like immense effort. "I think Ellie's body is perfect," he offered, and when everyone turned to gape at him, he stuffed another big bite of near-inedible blackberry pie into his mouth. He glanced at Ellie, but whatever he saw in her expression made him look away.

Ellie's anger evaporated. She sat there, stunned, unable to process his comment. No one had ever called her perfect before. She stood. "I'm going to get back to work."

By the time they'd finished chopping and loading the wood, it was well into the afternoon, and Ellie knew she wouldn't get to search Jason's house until the following day, when her ex was at work. She tossed the last chopped log into Lionel's pickup truck and sighed, not wanting to walk all the way back to Gemma's trailer. She'd chopped only about 10 percent of the wood, but her body was sore. Truthfully, it hadn't recovered from the battering she'd given it yesterday.

"You want a lift?" Hugh asked, opening the passenger door. His brows were drawn low over his eyes, and it almost looked like he was worried for her. But that would be ridiculous. He was probably just anxious to get done with this job so he could move on with his life.

Ellie glanced at the truck's small cab. It had one long bench, which meant she'd be sandwiched between Lionel and his nephew for the duration of the ride back to the Blue Skies Trailer Park. Gemma had already walked back an hour or so ago, wanting to start dinner and clear out the shed for her new firewood.

She really should just walk back and avoid any and all physical contact with Hugh. But she was tired.

"Okay," she finally agreed.

To her surprise, Hugh slid into the truck before her, which meant she had no choice but to get in after him. The bench seat was upholstered in red leather piped with white, and it matched the red dash and fuzzy white ceiling. The truck was very Lionel: old and weird and inexplicably charming. To Ellie, at least.

She climbed in, pressing her side against Hugh's as she pulled the door closed. It was a tight squeeze. Hugh's bulk pressed her hard against the door until he lifted his arm and slung it over the back of the bench to give them more room—which also meant his arm was around Ellie's shoulders. He was warm, and he smelled faintly of sweat, but not in a bad way. Ellie's head swam.

Lionel started the truck, then turned it around and drove to the trailer park. It rumbled and bounced, and Ellie's eyelids grew heavy. It wasn't her fault; Hugh was so warm, and his arm was comfortably heavy against her shoulders.

She jerked awake when the truck stopped, wiping drool from the corner of her lips. Hugh reached across her body to open the door, steadying her shoulders with his other hand. For an instant, she was entirely wrapped in his arms, and she didn't hate it. Not even a little bit.

Ellie really, *really* needed to get out of this truck. Sliding out, she took a big gulping breath of fresh air. She waved as Gemma exited her trailer and showed them to the attached shed that would house the wood. Then it was a long slog of transferring the firewood into the shed until every stick and scrap of kindling was out of the truck and in Gemma's possession.

Finally, the other woman presented Ellie with a folded piece of paper. She held Ellie's eyes. "Anyone finds out about this, and I'll kill you."

Ellie believed her. She nodded. "No one will know."

Gemma dipped her chin, then let her home's door slam as she went back inside.

Turning, Ellie caught Lionel before he closed the door to his truck. "Hey, Lionel," she called out. "You busy tomorrow?"

The old man closed the door, then rolled the window down. He leaned his arm against the frame and frowned at her. "Depends."

She walked over, ignoring the way Hugh stared at her through the open window. "I'm going to need a lift. Probably an hour or two of work. You'll mostly be waiting."

Lionel grunted and jerked his chin to her car, still parked next to Gemma's van. "What's wrong with your car?"

"Well, I guess I don't really need a lift so much as I need a driver." A getaway driver, to be precise. She smiled her best, most innocent smile. "So, are you busy?"

"Book it on the app," Lionel grunted, putting the car in gear.

Ellie stepped back to give him room to drive away, then called out, "Hey, Lionel!"

The old man turned to look at her, brows raised.

She spread her arms. "You think I'm getting porky?"

Light glimmered in Lionel's hazel eyes. "Ask my nephew," he replied. Then he drove off.

Hugh let the wind ruffle his hair as his uncle drove back toward his home, the temperature dropping quickly as the sun went down. After so many hours of hard work, the cool air felt like heaven on his skin. He'd been overheated since the short drive from Mrs. O'Hara's house back to Gemma's mobile home, the memory of Ellie's head against his shoulders a reminder of how rare it had been for him to hold a woman in his arms. That kind of intimacy—a drowsy head snuggled on his chest—wasn't something he'd ever appreciated or sought out. He'd never been one for relationships. Not since he'd watched his parents' marriage implode. His father's actions had broken some deep slab of trust inside him, a fracture that had never quite healed.

He turned to look at his uncle and asked, "Were you close with my dad growing up?"

Lionel glanced at him briefly. His uncle had long gray hair that was tied in a low ponytail that curled at the ends. He had thick, bushy eyebrows and bright hazel eyes that missed nothing. His hand kneaded the steering wheel as he considered Hugh's question. "Close enough," he finally replied. "I was younger. Looked up to him."

"What about later, as adults?"

Lionel shrugged. "Didn't like what he did to your mother. Told him so. He didn't like me telling him so. That was pretty much the end of that. We didn't speak for twenty years; then I got the call that he'd died."

That sounded a lot like Hugh's relationship with his father, except for the few pathetic attempts Alex had made to reach out in the past few years. For all intents and purposes, Hugh's father hadn't been part of his life for twenty years either. He leaned his elbow on the open window frame. "Oh."

"Wasn't right, what he did."

Hugh's throat felt tight. It was still impossible for him to speak about his father's betrayal, to put words to the wound that had shaped his entire life. "No," he finally answered. "It wasn't."

It also wasn't right that Hugh would profit from his father's estate. That was as good as condoning what Alex had done. But shouldn't he and his mother get *something*? Couldn't he call it reparations, or restitution, and be done with it?

They drove in silence until Lionel parked the car outside his cabin, right beside Hugh's waiting rental car. Before they got out, Hugh worked up the courage to ask, "What do you think about this resort? The deal my dad was working on with Jason Brownlow."

Lionel opened his door and slid out. "None of my business." The door slammed, and Hugh was alone.

Hugh watched Lionel disappear into his home, then slowly got out and made his way to his own car. His uncle wouldn't help him make any decisions about the Fernley Luxury Resort and Spa, that was for sure.

He should just sign it and leave this island. He should wash his hands of this place, these people. No pointless moralizing could justify turning his back on his and his mother's financial stability. No matter how dirty he felt about it, it would be worse to refuse the inheritance and sink the deal.

But his father had made a fool of him, made him feel gullible and small. That wasn't going to happen again—especially not because of someone like Jason Brownlow. Hugh would get to the bottom of whatever was going on before making a decision. He'd make sure that when he signed those papers and green-lit the construction of Fernley's first luxury resort, it wouldn't be a place built on lies and deception, the way his parents' marriage had been. The way his relationship with his father had been.

Everyone lied, but he wasn't going to get caught out again.

STEP TWO: RECON

CHAPTER 9

Ellie wasn't even surprised when it was Hugh who picked her up the next day instead of Lionel. She opened the front door of her parents' house, saw him looming on the doorstep, and sighed. "Come on in," she said. "I'm almost ready."

"Who's there?" her mother called out from the kitchen.

"Lionel's nephew," Ellie answered. She gestured to the couch and darted back to her room to grab her backpack full of supplies. Today was the day she'd find evidence of Jason's crimes. Today was the first step in her plan to ruin his life.

Today was the day she'd take Louie home.

Dressed in jeans, a black tank top, and a dark-green cardigan her mother had knitted from their own sheep's wool, with her hair out of her face in a high ponytail, Ellie was ready to break and enter. For real, this time. And no one was going to get injured or arrested. Hopefully.

She checked her backpack one last time but still had the nagging feeling she'd forgotten something. She probably hadn't, but the feeling remained, so she grabbed her usual cross-body purse and emptied its contents—a hair tie, expired lip gloss, ancient lip balm, hand sanitizer, a piece of gum squished flat in its wrapper, spare tampons, a few dollar bills, and faded receipts, among other treasures—into the small pocket at the front of the pack. Her hands trembled slightly, which was probably a bad sign. Ignoring her trepidation, Ellie slung the bag over her shoulder, the weight of it comforting against her back.

Go time.

But when she emerged from her bedroom, she found that the go-time memo hadn't reached the living room. Both her parents were fawning over Hugh, offering him hot drinks and peppering him with questions. Her mother was placing a mug of steaming tea on a coaster, while her father flicked through records on the shelf, evidently looking for the perfect soundtrack to their inquisition.

"And what did you do in Arizona?" Her mother spun the mug so the handle faced Hugh.

"I managed a small recording studio," he told her. "Mostly for independent artists, some freelance narrators, that kind of thing. I helped an old friend of my mom's start it when he had dreams of being a big-shot producer. He lost interest pretty quickly, but I loved being in the control room."

Ellie's father spun around to face Hugh, his expression betraying true, undying love. "You built the studio yourself?"

Hugh nodded. "Studied audio engineering in college. The owner didn't know much about the equipment he needed, so I helped design and build it. We had some reasonably big names come through to record demos and EPs, but now the owner wants to sell it. It's slowed down in the past few years, and the upkeep is expensive."

"Will you be able to keep working there if they sell it?" Helen asked, perching herself on the edge of the nearest armchair. She smiled at Hugh, and it was her win-friends-and-influence-people smile. Ellie needed to extract him quickly before this devolved any further.

"Maybe," Hugh answered, "but I've always wanted to have my own place. I'd love to buy him out, but we'll see." For a moment, bitterness seemed to flash across his expression. Then he smiled at Ellie's parents. "Been working there twelve years, so I've learned a lot about the management side of things. I think I'd be able to run my own studio. Just need to find the right space."

"Of course you'd be able to, honey," Helen told him.

Ellie's father looked like he wanted to drop to his knees and profess his everlasting love.

Hugh cemented himself as Claude's new best friend when he pointed to the speakers placed on stands on either side of the record player. "Are those Spendor BC1s? Beautiful-sounding speakers. They don't make 'em like they used to."

"Couldn't agree more." Ellie's father turned back to the wall of records, flicking feverishly now. "Let's have a listen. I want your opinion on my setup. I feel like it's a little bit heavy on the bass, but I'm not sure—"

"We have to go," Ellie interjected, grabbing Hugh's arm and hauling him up off the couch. This was a herculean task, because Hugh was very heavy and the couch's springs were permanently depressed from decades of use. "Sorry, Dad. Maybe next time." There wouldn't be a next time. She needed to get Hugh out of here before her parents adopted him as their long-lost son, or arranged her betrothal to him, or some other horrible fate she hadn't foreseen. Why was he still on the island, anyway? Why was he *here*?

Hugh arched a brow but allowed himself to be led out of the room. "Nice to meet you both. Thank you for the tea."

"Be safe, you two!" Helen called out.

Ellie shut the door more firmly than strictly necessary and glared at Hugh. "What was that about?"

He reared back. "What was what about?"

Ellie wasn't quite sure. All she knew was that having Hugh in her space, charming her parents . . . it didn't feel right. It was too much. Her parents were the kindest people on the planet. They'd fall in love with Hugh—and he'd break their hearts.

"Never mind," she grumped, stomping to his rental car. She slid into the passenger seat and watched Hugh fold his long body into the space behind the wheel.

He turned the key in the ignition, then glanced at Ellie. "Where to? The OddJobs post just said, 'vehicle needed for hauling of supplies.'"

Well, she couldn't exactly write, "Getaway driver needed for criminal activity," could she?

"Take a left at the gate," she said. "Head for Lionel's."

Once they were on the road, Hugh tapped the screen and put on a playlist entitled "Drive Tunes." The Doobie Brothers' "Listen to the Music" came on, and Ellie thanked her lucky stars she'd extracted Hugh from her parents' house before her father discovered Hugh's taste in music. She'd never have gotten him out if they'd started talking about rock and soul and the glory of the 1970s.

Despite herself, her fingers started tapping to the beat against the door. It was a great song, after all. Some of the tension in her shoulders dissolved.

When they got close to their destination, Ellie turned down the volume and directed Hugh to a side street on the far side of Jason's property.

On the way there, they passed a black SUV with dark-tinted windows, a vehicle Ellie didn't recognize. Her heart pounded. She peered through the windshield, trying to identify the driver, but they crossed each other too quickly. She glanced out the back window. The license plate didn't look familiar either. Her skin prickled.

That was a bad sign.

Or (and this was more likely) Ellie was just paranoid because she was about to break into her ex-fiancé's house to gather evidence she wasn't even sure existed.

"Everything okay?" Hugh asked.

"Yeah. Thought I recognized that car," she lied. "Take the next right, drive to the end where the picnic table is, and turn around. I'll show you where to park."

After her conversation with her grandmother at the diner, she'd realized that her original plan with Wynn had been flawed. She'd been so focused on hiding her car that she hadn't considered her exit strategy. But she could learn from her mistakes. The car—and Hugh—would remain nearby, concealed from the main road while being mere moments away from a clean escape. She could sprint over and hop in, and they'd be gone in less than a minute.

When they found the spot she'd chosen, she told Hugh to park. "Okay," she said, checking her backpack for the final time to make sure everything was there. "I'll be back in half an hour or so. Keep the noise down. I don't want anyone to find you. If anyone asks what you're doing, just say you went for a walk along the Fernley Coastal Trail, then drive away, hang a right, and take the next left. Park behind the run-down lean-to. I'll find you."

"Wait, what?" Hugh sat up straighter. "Where are you going?"

"Do you understand, Hugh? Stay here unless someone sees you. If they do, go to the lean-to. I'll find you either way."

"Hold on," he said, putting a hand on her forearm. "I want to know what you're doing."

"What I'm doing is not your concern," she answered, her voice hard. "I hired you to drive."

Hugh gritted his teeth. His hand was still on her forearm, the heat of it sinking into her skin. They stared at each other for a second. Two.

"You're going to get yourself hurt," Hugh finally said through clenched teeth. "Whatever you're doing, you shouldn't be alone."

Ellie blinked, then shook off his hand. "Stay in the car."

She slipped out, scanned the forest, and gently closed the door. Then she threw her backpack over her shoulders and set out on the road to Jason Brownlow's destruction.

Hugh watched Ellie disappear into the trees, his body a coiled spring. It was wrong. She shouldn't be going out there on her own.

He'd only met her two days ago, but Hugh knew that whatever Ellie had planned for today had a high likelihood of ending in disaster. The human-size hand grenade had suddenly lost its pin, and he'd watched it disappear in the lush foliage.

He gripped the steering wheel and looked at the empty road ahead of him. In his rearview mirror, he saw nothing but green and brown and distant gray. The sky was overcast but not oppressive. A bird twittered in a nearby tree. He wanted to scream.

The logical thing to do would be to drive away and tell Lionel to shove his OddJobs bookings up his wrinkled old ass. Hugh was on the island to make a business deal. He was supposed to be checking all the particulars of the new resort—which were looking less and less attractive the more he learned—not following some deranged woman on her harebrained schemes.

But Ellie had looked so determined. He could almost sense the edges of her fraying, like she was one sharp tug away from unraveling completely.

He shouldn't care. He really, really shouldn't. He barely knew her. Getting involved with Ellie Davis could spell disaster for his entire life. The deal might not be as squeaky clean as he'd originally thought, but he didn't have to know every detail. He was already crossing a line by accepting this postmortem gift from his father. Who cared if Jason was also a piece of shit? He'd been working with Alex Hartford, after all.

Hugh should just sign the papers and book a spot on the next ferry out of here. If anything blew up, he wanted to be well away from the blast radius. His lawyers had okayed everything. The deal was done. Just sign it, leave, and forget about elderly sheep getting sick and a slightly sleazy business partner. He'd get on the ferry, drop off his rental car on the mainland, and take a flight back to the heat of his home state. He'd buy the recording studio and pay his mom's mortgage. Life would go on, and his father would be a distant, painful memory he'd be careful not to prod. He'd never come back to Fernley Island. There would be no need.

Yes, he would always hate himself a little bit for taking the money. But his mother would live out the rest of her life with the dignity his father had stolen from her. Hugh would be able to fulfill his only ambition and spend his life helping people make music.

Driving away from here and leaving Ellie to her madness was the smart thing to do. The logical thing. The lucrative thing.

"Oh, screw it," he muttered and unclipped his seat belt. He stepped out of his car onto a bed of gravel and pine needles and followed Ellie into the forest.

CHAPTER 10

Ellie crouched at the front door and unrolled her mother's old lock-picks. She'd found them over a year ago in an ancient trunk pushed into the corner of their garage and had felt the urge to take them. Her now-reformed mother would have disapproved, so Ellie hadn't mentioned her find.

The problem was the only lock she'd managed to practice on was the doorknob to the bathroom in her home. It had been laughably easy to pick. Jason's front door was another beast.

She squinted at the lock and sat back on her heels, then chose the two instruments she thought would work best. They slid into the lock, and she was feeling for the telltale notches, when—

"What the hell are you doing?"

Yelping, Ellie fell back on her butt and tumbled down the front porch. Hugh stood over her, staring at her with thunder in his eyes. She scrambled up and glared right back. "I told you to stay in the car."

"You're breaking into someone's *house*."

"I'm breaking into the house I used to live in," she corrected. "And I'm not going to steal anything." Probably.

"Ellie." His voice was deep, menacing. The sound of her name on his lips sent a thunderbolt cracking through her sternum.

She set her jaw. "Hugh, you have two choices. You can walk away right now, or you can help me."

"No. There's a third choice. You can walk away too. Whatever this is, it isn't worth it."

"How the hell would you know?" The question hissed through her lips. "Leave me alone, Hugh. Go back to the car and drive away. I'll be fine. Your services are no longer required."

His jaw worked as he ground his teeth, glaring at her, which was— wow—very scary. She snorted and turned back to the door, gathering up the lockpicks that she'd scattered over the welcome mat.

"Ellie, stop."

Fat chance. She worked the thin pick into the lock and closed her eyes so she could focus. "Tell me if you hear a car coming," she told him.

Even with her eyes closed, she could feel Hugh's anger vibrating behind her. It was like standing a bit too close to a bonfire. Her eyebrows would get singed right off if she turned around to face him again.

The lock should have caught by now. She wiggled the instruments, then let out a frustrated noise. Clawing at her pocket, she pulled out her phone and started tapping the screen.

Hugh peered over her shoulder. "Are you looking up a YouTube video on how to pick a lock? Seriously?"

"You got any better suggestions?"

"Yeah, how about we turn around and go home?"

"You can do that, Hugh. It's not an option for me."

He was silent for a beat. Then he crouched next to her so his eyes were level with hers. In this light, the green specks in his irises looked particularly bright. "Ellie," he said softly, "whatever's going on, I promise you breaking into this house isn't worth it."

When he looked at her like that, it made something deep in her heart ache. That voice—low and soft and caring—sounded so unlike anything she'd heard from a man before. What would it be like to have someone speak to her like that on a regular basis? What would it feel like to be supported, respected, loved?

Then Hugh went ahead and ruined it by asking, "This is Jason's house, right? Your ex? Is this about the mug shot? It really wasn't that bad, Ellie. Why not just let it go?"

Like a flash, her anger detonated. So Hugh had seen the mug shot. Of course he had. It was practically a rule upon arrival on the island. Step One: Disembark from the Ferry. Step Two: Witness Ellie Davis's Humiliation. She felt the hot spill of fury spreading through her chest, poisoning her veins. Her breaths grew shallow, and she gulped to try to control herself.

Another man, trying to tell her what was best for her. Another man, minimizing her feelings. Another man, reminding her of her shame.

How long had it taken her to be charmed by Hugh? She'd known him, what, three, four seconds? She'd preened when he'd called her "perfect" and fallen fast asleep when he put his arm around her. Apparently, for Ellie, that was enough to start thinking a man was trustworthy.

Had she learned *nothing* from Jason's betrayal? What could have possibly convinced her that Hugh was different?

Angry at herself for being hurt, Ellie stood to face him. Hugh straightened, crossing his arms. She glared at him, and he glared right back. *Ugh!*

She couldn't let it stand. She had to speak. "Jason asked me to marry him, then cheated on me at our engagement party," she said, her voice cold. "I found him in a conference room at the Fernley Hotel with his pants around his ankles, balls deep in his pretty, blonde fundraising manager. So yes, Hugh, I snapped. I took a baseball bat out of the trunk of my car, and I tried to smash the hood of his vehicle. I wanted to go Carrie Underwood on his ass, and I wanted it to feel good. Then the bat rebounded and hit me in the face."

She admitted the most embarrassing part of the whole ordeal and waited for the familiar smirk to grace his lips. People loved telling and retelling the story. Not only had she snapped and become the proverbial Crazy Ex-Girlfriend, but she hadn't even succeeded. She'd been a long-lost Stooge, a funny story to tell around the dinner table in every house on Fernley. Hugh would be like everyone else. He'd let her writhe around in the embarrassment of it all.

But Hugh just stared back, his expression unreadable.

She could have stopped there, but she wanted him to know. To understand. She wanted to kill any bit of attraction that existed between them. The hurt, vindictive, self-destructive part of Ellie wanted him to look at her with that smug, derisive expression she'd learned to despise. If he stared at her with disdain like everyone else did, it would destroy any confusing feelings that had started to sprout inside her.

She needed him to be just like everyone else, just like Jason. Then she could turn her back on him and focus on what she needed to do. Everyone else on this island had judged her and found her unworthy. It was easier to lump Hugh in with the rest of them and move on.

"I was arrested, spent a night in jail, and the charges were dropped. Do you understand?" Ellie asked, growing more frustrated by his lack of reaction. "I hit myself in the face with a baseball bat, and I got arrested for it. There wasn't even a dent on his car. They found me passed out on the ground with a bat in my hands and a lump on my forehead."

They stood in front of each other, mere inches between them. Hugh let out a breath, his gaze flicking between her eyes. "He was a piece of shit for doing that to you."

She opened her mouth to snap something snarky at him—then his words sank in. Ellie blinked, then backed off.

It surprised her how sincere Hugh sounded. Maybe he'd been cheated on too. Maybe he understood a little of how Ellie felt. Her anger morphed into something softer. The righteousness she'd clung to suddenly turned murky. She wasn't sure what she felt anymore. She wasn't sure what she wanted Hugh to think either.

That's why, when his palm slid over her cheek, she didn't push him off. A cool spring breeze swept over her skin, and she let Hugh tilt her face up. His thumb swept over her cheekbone as he stepped closer, holding her like she was made of glass. "I've never met anyone like you, Ellie."

"If that's supposed to be a compliment, it needs a lot of work," she replied, her voice a little shaky, "because that can mean a lot of things."

His grin was devastating. Ellie's stomach fisted into a hot, hard ball, her legs suddenly unsteady. She stood on her ex-fiancé's front stoop with lockpicks scattered at her feet and felt a flutter in her chest. Hugh's hand was warm and rough against her skin, his eyes intent on hers.

As his smile faded, he dipped his head—and kissed her.

She should have seen it coming, but it still startled Ellie so much that she nearly lost her balance. Clinging onto his arms (which were as solid as Mabel had said), she parted her lips and kissed him back. Blame it on the bizarreness of the situation, or the strength of his arms as they wrapped around her, or the way his scent made her head spin.

Whatever it was, Ellie fell into the sensation of Hugh Hartford's kiss and realized she'd never experienced anything like it before. He swept his tongue against hers and banded an arm around her back. He pinned her to his body and let out a rough groan as he deepened the kiss, like he wanted to memorize the feel of her in his arms. His stubble abraded, his lips plundered, and Ellie lost herself in it all.

Ellie's hands roamed, sliding up his shoulders to tangle into the curling locks of hair at his nape. She breathed him in, forgetting everything that had come before and everything that would come after. The only thing that mattered was the feeling of this man kissing her like she was the only woman he'd ever wanted. It was addictive. Ellie had never had a man kiss her like this. She'd never felt the world stop while her own body kept spinning. She'd never had her mind go so quiet.

Then a seagull squawked, and Ellie's brain finally came online again. She pulled away from Hugh, wide eyed, breathing heavily.

Hugh watched her, chest heaving, his lips glistening in the overcast light.

"What the hell was that?" Ellie demanded.

His brows dropped. "Don't pretend you didn't participate, Ellie."

Well, he had her there. She glowered. "You're just trying to distract me from picking this lock."

"You think the only reason I kissed you is to stop you from breaking into Brownlow's house?"

"What other reason could there be?" The words exploded out of her. She held up her palms when Hugh looked like he would speak. "You know what? Forget it. Seriously. Forget that ever happened."

Not that Ellie ever would. She was pretty sure Hugh had just ruined kissing for her forever. Vision swimming, she crouched to gather her lockpicks again, sucking in deep breaths to compose herself.

Hugh stepped away, and she heard him exhale heavily. Glancing over her shoulder, she spied him scrubbing his face with both palms. Then he dropped his arms and turned back to face her. "I'm sorry. I shouldn't have done that."

"No, you shouldn't have," Ellie answered, intending to banish him from the porch so he would stop muddling her brain. She needed to get inside this house, and the longer they stayed on this stoop, the more likely it was that someone would find them and her whole stupid plan would go down the toilet. Plus, he was distracting.

But then Hugh tilted his head toward the door and said, "I still don't think this is the best plan. There has to be another way. No matter what your ex did to you, Ellie, you can't break into his house."

Any question of Hugh understanding her vanished. He didn't get it. He probably never would. Ellie shook her head and dropped her gaze to Hugh's collarbones. It was easier than looking at his eyes, and the last thing she wanted him to see was the bitter disappointment churning in her gut.

Why should she be disappointed, when she continued to make mistake after mistake? Kissing a man and thinking it meant more was just more of the same for Ellie. She'd dated Jason and thought he valued her, and she'd accepted his proposal, thinking they had a future.

Ellie's hurt was her own fault. Her expectations were too high, and her ability to judge people's character was too low. No wonder she'd become a laughingstock.

"Ellie," Hugh said softly. "Talk to me."

She met his gaze. "He took my dog. Did you know that?"

A line appeared between Hugh's brows. "Your dog?"

Ellie pinched her lips, nodding. "Yeah. He's in the backyard. I'm taking him home with me today. Been waiting six months to do it."

Once she had Louie—and once she'd found a way to make Jason pay—she'd get on the ferry and get gone. Sheriff Jackson and Jason could try to steal her dog from across the Salish Sea if they wanted. It wasn't going to stop Ellie.

"Why six months?" Hugh asked.

"After I got arrested, the first thing I did was come here to grab Louie and take him home. Jason laughed in my face. Told me to go to the cops if I wanted Louie back so badly."

"Did you? Go to the cops?"

"Of course I did!" Ellie let out a bitter huff. "Over and over again, no matter how humiliating it was to go back to the police station and beg. I brought ownership papers, printed out all my receipts from the vet, even showed them my online orders for dog kibble, as if any of that would make a difference. The other night, when we met—"

"When you bashed me on the head with a pair of bolt cutters."

Ellie had to fight the urge to grin. What was it about this guy that made her want to smile? He was just like Jason! He was horrible!

But he stared at her with his eyebrow raised and a grin playing around his lips, and she had to admit he wasn't horrible at all.

"When I defended Lionel against a dangerous intruder," she amended, and Hugh laughed, "I was trying to get Louie back. Wynn hurt her ankle attempting to climb the backyard fence."

Understanding lit Hugh's eyes. He nodded.

With a deep breath, she continued: "I hated Jason for cheating on me on that day, in that way. I hated him for taking my dog. I hated him for acting like a gracious overlord for not having me thrown in jail for longer than a night. But this?" She pointed at the front door. "This has nothing to do with me. This has to do with Jason using an innocent man like Spencer Wisneski to hurt my parents. This is my last Hail Mary, my last chance to stop my ex-fiancé from steamrolling the entire island into doing his bidding. I *have* to do this. I have to stop him."

If she stopped Jason, if she proved beyond a doubt that *he* was the one who should be shunned from polite society on Fernley, then maybe she could walk around the island with her head held high.

Hugh dropped his gaze, bringing his hand up to rub his forehead. He let out a long breath. "I'm sorry that happened to you. But we can stop him some other way. We can . . ." He drifted off, sighing heavily. "I . . ." He clicked his tongue, shaking his head.

Ellie had no idea what that meant. Suddenly, she felt exhausted. When she spoke next, her voice was dull. "There is no 'we,' Hugh. Thank you for your sympathy. The kiss was great, but we will not be doing it again. You can leave now." She crouched down and propped her phone on the doorframe, then pressed play on the YouTube video.

Hugh walked over and paused the video, grabbing her hand and squeezing it gently. "Ellie, I can . . ." He clenched his jaw like he was biting back words. "There are *legal* ways of making Jason pay."

This man would never understand her. He'd never understand this island. The Brownlows might as well *be* the law around here. She shook him off, set her jaw, and pressed play on the YouTube video. She skipped the long, drawn-out introduction where the person on the screen tried to sell her ten thousand different products. Finally, she listened to the tips on how to pick this particular lock. Her tools weren't quite right, she discovered, but there should be a way to do it—

"Why didn't you practice this ahead of time?" Hugh asked, standing now, watching her. The man just would not go away.

She glanced over her shoulder. "Why are you still here?"

"Because if you're doing this, I'm going to do it with you."

"That's the stupidest thing I've ever heard." Even though it did make her feel slightly fuzzy around the edges.

"Yeah? What does that make you?"

"Ooh, good one," she said, then returned her attention to the video. It froze, then got stuck buffering for long enough that Ellie grunted in frustration and clicked it off. She stuffed the phone back in her pocket and glared at the lock. Reinserting her lockpicks, she tried once more.

Nothing.

Hugh just stood there, looming.

Ellie's lips felt oversensitive. She really, really wished he hadn't kissed her, and she especially wished he hadn't been all noble and sweet and understanding when she told him about Jason and Louie and the arrest. "Can you just, like, turn around and look at the trees or something? I can't do this with you breathing down my neck."

"Looks like you can't do it at all. Why are all of your tools rusty?" He picked up one of the lockpicks and inspected the tip. "Did you get them at the same store as those bolt cutters you attacked me with?"

"Oh, I get it," she said, snatching the lockpick back.

"Get what?"

"You're trying to annoy me so much I'll give up and leave with you. Talking didn't work. Trying to distract me with sex didn't work, so now you're trying this. Very clever. Keep trying, buddy." She knelt in front of the lock again and set her shoulders. Maybe she should call Mabel, or even her mother. They could probably walk her through how to do this—but it would also involve them in her schemes. She wanted to give them every bit of deniability she could.

But she was also getting desperate.

Pulling her phone out again, she found her grandmother's number and dialed. "Hi, Grandma," she said when the old woman answered.

"Ellie-Belly! What are you up to? Your mother told me you had a very special visitor this morning! Are you still with him? What's he wearing?"

Ellie tamped down her frustration. "Um, yeah, I'm still with him." She glanced over her shoulder. "He's wearing jeans and a fleecy kind of top, one of those ones with the quarter zip they sell at the outdoor store on Fifth Street," she said as casually as she could, which made Hugh look at her like she was crazy (again). While her grandmother cooed in appreciation, Ellie asked, "Hey, have you ever picked a dead bolt lock? I feel the pins in the lock, but I can't get past one of them. It's almost like there's a magnet or something. Do you know what I'm talking about?"

There was a very short, very pointed pause. "Ellie . . . ," Mabel said. "Yes, but—"

Hugh plucked the phone out of her hand and clicked to end the call, still staring at her like she was insane, which was honestly getting kind of rude. If he thought she was such a lunatic, why had he kissed her?

Then Hugh took a step forward so his shin brushed her back. He leaned over and grabbed one of the decorative rocks by the front door. He flipped the rock over toward Ellie, revealing a silver key tucked into a slot designed to hold it.

Huh. How about that?

When he stood and took a step back, still holding the key-concealing rock, cold rushed in everywhere he'd touched. Ellie frowned, not liking that feeling one bit. Her body was a runaway train, and she was clinging on for dear life.

Stupid kiss. Stupid her for indulging in it.

She gathered her lockpicks and bundled them up, stuffing them in the main pocket of her backpack before standing up. Planting her hands on her hips, she faced her accomplice. "How long have you known that key was there?"

He shrugged. "Since I walked up and found you trying to pick the lock. All these fake rocks look the same, and my mom used to have one when I was a kid."

"Aren't you clever," she grumbled, reaching for the rock.

He pulled it away from her, holding it high above his head. "Didn't you say you lived here? How did you not know the key was there?"

Ellie glared. "That fake rock is new. I've never seen it before."

Hugh held her gaze, still holding the rock aloft. "Promise me we aren't going to steal anything."

God, she hated this man. "I promise we aren't going to steal anything," she repeated dutifully.

"Promise me if I tell you we need to go, you'll listen and leave right away."

"This is *my* operation."

He looked at the key, then at the lock, then at her. One dark eyebrow arched pointedly. "Doesn't look like your operation from where I'm standing."

Gah! She really, really hated him. She should have pushed him off as soon as he'd touched her cheek, but no, she'd actually *kissed* him. What the *hell* was wrong with her?

But he had the key to the front door, so Ellie took a deep breath. "We'll be in and out, Hugh. I just need proof to corroborate that Jason was the one behind the milkweed poisoning."

Hugh watched her for a beat, then shook his head. "I can't believe I'm doing this. It's going to fuck up my entire life."

"There's still time to walk away," she said hopefully.

His jaw set, he pried the key from its plastic home. "Nice try. In and out, Ellie. That's the deal." Then he handed her the key to Jason Brownlow's front door.

CHAPTER 11

Hugh watched Ellie retrieve a little scrap of paper from one of the many pockets of her backpack. He was in the process of making a monumental mistake, and he couldn't stop himself.

He was almost certain Brownlow was behind the milkweed incident, because he knew about the plans for the resort. They needed that entire strip of waterfront land, including the twenty or thirty yards that belonged to the Davises between his property and Brownlow's. He'd pored over the survey reports and put two and two together last night, at the same time as he'd looked up the public arrest records about Ellie.

He wondered if Brownlow's relationship with her had been a scam from the beginning. Had Brownlow entered into a relationship with Ellie for those few yards of land? To try to get leverage over her parents? He hoped not, for Ellie's sake. He couldn't abide cheaters, and the thought of Ellie enduring that kind of mistreatment made him want to punch a hole through a wall.

He should never have kissed her.

It's just . . . she'd been standing there, looking so hurt and determined and strong, and it had been too much to bear. He'd had to touch her cheek just to feel the warmth of her skin against his palm. But once he'd done that, well, trying to stop himself from kissing her was like trying to stop the tide from going out by sheer force of will. He hadn't expected it to feel like *that*, though, for his body to turn electric from one instant to the next.

But now he was here, and he knew he should have never stepped across the threshold behind her.

All he had to do was tell Ellie that he could blow up the resort deal simply by not signing it, and they could leave without committing any more crimes. They could close the door, replace the key under the fake rock, and walk away.

That would ruin Jason's plans, which would satisfy Ellie and protect her parents. Game over.

But he wouldn't get his recording studio. His mother wouldn't get her house paid off. Not yet, at least. He'd have to stay on the island and decide what to do with the land, and who knew how long that would take?

Plus, if he told Ellie about the land, he'd have to tell her about his father. He'd have to admit that he'd taken the inheritance, allowing his old wounds to be washed clean with his father's money. What would she think of him then?

Ellie didn't weigh a purse of gold in her palm and let it affect her opinions of right and wrong. She was better than that.

Hugh also didn't know the extent of his father's involvement. Had he known about the underhanded pressure Brownlow was exerting on his neighbors? Had he cared? Did it matter?

Hugh found himself needing to find the same proof that Ellie wanted, some undeniable scrap of evidence that would either exon-erate his father or condemn him. Wasn't it worth the risk to find out whether or not Alex Hartford had been rotten all the way through? If his father supported bullying a nice family and murdering innocent animals, Hugh could wash his hands of the man forever. He'd find some other way to help his mother and fund his studio.

He knew the chances of finding any evidence were slim, but he had to try. If he told Ellie about his land and his participation in the resort deal now, he'd lose this chance to find out the truth.

So he entered the house behind her and watched her key in the code scribbled on her scrap of paper. He shut the front door with one final glance to make sure they were still alone. When he turned the dead bolt, it slid home with a thunk that rattled his bones.

The alarm panel beeped twice, and a steady green light came on. Ellie blew out a breath. "Thank you, Gemma," she huffed under her breath. "This way," she said louder, striding down the hallway ahead of Hugh. "We're going to search the study, but I just need to do one thing first."

Hugh followed her through the house and out the back door, where a dog came bounding toward her. Ellie dropped to her knees and wrapped her arms around the pup, laughing and scrubbing his fur as the dog climbed all over her, his tail wagging furiously.

"Hi, boy," Ellie cooed. "Hi, Louie. Yes, I'm here. I'm back. It's good to see you too." She spun her bag around and pulled out a treat, beaming as her dog munched it down. Her eyes were glassy as she met Hugh's gaze.

Hugh felt a twinge of guilt. In that moment, he discovered that it wasn't only his desire to find out about his father's involvement in the sheep poisonings that had held his tongue. He was also afraid that once Ellie found out about the land, she'd never speak to him again.

Hugh came forward and knelt, holding his hand out for the dog to sniff. Once Louie was satisfied with the introductions, the dog moved closer to demand head scratches, which Hugh happily provided.

"Cute dog," he said, smiling.

"He's the best." Ellie looked more relaxed than he'd ever seen her. She ran a hand down Louie's back, then smiled as the dog turned in a circle and flopped at her feet. She rubbed his belly and watched him close his eyes in canine contentment.

"I have to go inside now," she told the dog, "but I'll be back to get you in a few minutes, and then I can finally get you out of here."

The dog's tail thumped on the concrete, and they stood, then returned indoors. Ellie gave one last glance to the dog through the glass, then turned back toward the house with a deep breath. "Okay," she said, and she set off down the hallway once more.

The office was locked, but this time, Ellie managed to pick the lock within seconds. She grunted as the door swung open soundlessly, then wrapped up her tools again. "See? I'm not an idiot."

"I never said you were."

She gave him a flat look. "It was implied in the grand reveal of the fake rock. Very heavy handed, Hugh, I have to say. You could use a little more finesse the next time you want to make me feel stupid."

His lips twitched. "That wasn't the goal. I just wasn't sure how else to make you listen."

"Words, Hugh. You could have used words." She entered the study, and he watched the way she moved for a moment before following. She was determined, dangerous, and more than a little addictive. No, finding out the extent of his father's involvement wasn't the only reason he was here with her.

"You take that side of the room," she said, waving him toward a filing cabinet. "I'll start at the desk."

On top of the cabinet was a folder with plans for the resort. He glanced over his shoulder to see Ellie occupied at the desk and gently moved the plans aside, not wanting her to ask any uncomfortable questions. His own identity wasn't on these documents yet, but it would be easy enough to figure out who owned the land now that his father had died. The deed had his father's holding company on it, but the company's ownership was on the public record.

If he spent much more time with Ellie, Hugh knew he'd have to own up to the truth and face Ellie's judgment. Though now that they were in the midst of committing a felony, it probably wasn't the right time.

He cleared his throat. "What are we looking for?"

"Um." Ellie opened a drawer and rifled through stationery. "Invoices for bags of common milkweed? Emails with evil plots for killing sheep written in them? Magazine cutouts of fluffy white lambs with big red Xs on their faces?" She glanced at him, brows arched. "I don't know, Hugh. We probably won't find anything. In case you haven't noticed, I have no idea what I'm doing."

"High risk, low reward," he said, "like all the best operations."

"I know I just said you should use your words, but I was wrong. You should use fewer words. Like, zero."

Hugh couldn't stop the smile from tugging at his lips. He opened the top drawer of the filing cabinet and started flicking through the folders inside, keeping one eye on Ellie.

She slammed the drawer shut and sat down at the desk, then flipped open the laptop. Hugh watched her wiggle her fingers above the keyboard before typing a password on the screen. A little triumphant grin graced her lips when the laptop granted her access.

"He didn't change his password after you broke up?" Hugh asked.

"His password is 'password123,' which is about as safe as a key under a fake rock."

"And yet, he has an alarm system." Then Hugh had a horrible thought. "Cameras? Are we being recorded?"

Ellie shook her head, her eyes on the screen. "Jason hated the idea of being on camera. He figured the alarm system would be enough to keep the home insurance company happy. He used to say that if someone wanted to steal his TV, they were more than welcome. No one would steal from the Brownlows, though."

Hugh nodded and moved to the second drawer of the filing cabinet. More paperwork, along with a little lockbox (unlocked) that contained a wedding band and a woman's engagement ring. He glanced at Ellie, then closed the lockbox back up. The paperwork was all related to his charity, the Brownlow Foundation, detailing donations and disbursements. He flicked through it quickly and closed the drawer. No fluffy sheep with red *Xs* on their faces in here.

Ellie huffed. "Wow. Apparently, Jason was having an affair for two years before I found him in the conference room. And it was all right here in his email. He wasn't even trying to hide it. Pictures and everything!" Her voice was artificially light. She gave Hugh a grimace of a smile.

"Looks like you dodged a bullet," he replied.

"If this is dodging the bullet, I don't want to know what getting hit feels like," she mumbled, then tapped a few keys on the computer and shut the top. "This is pointless. I searched the words 'milkweed' and 'sheep,' and nothing came up. Wait—let me look up my parents' names."

Hugh leafed through some papers, seeing nothing. He glanced at Ellie again.

"A memo to invite them to the gala. Some survey plans from the island archives. Spencer, maybe? Wisneski? Hmm . . . nope." She clicked her tongue, scrubbing her face with both hands. "What the hell am I doing? Let's just get Louie and get out of here. You were right, okay? Happy? This was a stupid idea. I shouldn't have come here. Let's go."

"Okay." Hugh opened the bottom drawer of the filing cabinet. It contained a small gym bag. The bag was obviously old, with the plastic lettering peeling off, the fabric stained in spots. The handles were patched with tape. Behind him, Ellie stood, pushed the chair in, and grabbed her backpack from where she'd placed it on the floor.

With his foot, Hugh started to push the drawer closed—then hesitated. It was a strange place for a gym bag. And the bag itself didn't really fit with its surroundings. It was too old, too worn. Curiosity niggled, and he bent over to pull the drawer open again. He unzipped the bag. His eyes bugged. "Holy—"

CHAPTER 12

Ellie stared at the bag of cash for a good minute, minute and a half. Hugh stood beside her, his arm brushing hers, his presence disconcerting and comforting all at once.

The money was rolled up into thick bundles held together by rubber bands. She'd never seen so much money in one place. She didn't even know how you would *get* so much money together in one place. Finally getting over the shock, Ellie picked one up and flicked the corner of the bills. "How much do you think is in here?"

Hugh inhaled deeply. "What's one bundle . . . five grand?"

The roll in her hands was made up of twenty-dollar bills. She flicked the corner of the bills, trying to get a rough estimate of how many bills were in a roll. "Five grand seems like a lot. That would be two hundred and fifty twenty-dollar bills. Maybe two grand?"

He scanned the bag. "There are at least a hundred bundles in there. Is there any reason for Jason to keep two hundred grand in cash in the bottom of his filing cabinet?"

Ellie couldn't think of one. She tossed the roll of cash back into the gym bag and watched it tumble against the others. "It didn't come from the bank, that's for sure. It would be stacked and wrapped in labeled paper, not rolled with dirty rubber bands."

"The bag is so old too. Worn out," Hugh rumbled. "Judging by the rest of the house, it's not something Jason would keep."

"No, he'd have a fancy leather briefcase," Ellie agreed. "Or one of those hard silver ones they use in spy movies."

Her heart thumped. Her hands trembled. She had a bad feeling about this.

Reaching down, she zipped the gym bag back up and went to push the drawer closed, but one of the handles had fallen out and caught against the drawer slide. She pulled the drawer open again and flipped the bag's handle safely inside—and froze.

Both handles were wrapped in red duct tape.

Red. Duct. Tape.

She swung her backpack off her back and tore it open. Her bolt cutters were still there, waiting to be whacked against something—or someone. She pulled them out, putting the grips next to the bag's tape-wrapped handles. They matched.

Her lips curled into a snarl. Her vision narrowed. "Fergus," she spat.

She was going to kill him, right after she discovered why his bag had ended up full of cash and buried at the bottom of Jason's filing cabinet. She stuffed the bolt cutters back in her knapsack and zipped it up, took a picture of the bag of cash, then kicked the bottom drawer closed.

"Who's Fergus?" Hugh asked. "Where are we going?"

"We're going to ask an old friend a few questions," she said, stomping to the study door. She let Hugh slip out, then flicked the lock on the inside of the doorknob. She scanned the space to make sure it looked undisturbed, turned off the light, and closed the door. "Follow me. We're getting my dog and leaving."

The game had just changed. Ellie had known, on some level, that if Jason was willing to poison innocent sheep, he'd be willing to do worse things. The waterfront resort was his legacy, and he'd stop at nothing to get it built. Sticking to philanthropy just wasn't in Jason's blood. He'd always wanted his name on something bigger.

But that bag of cash told her that it wasn't just the island's rich elite who were vying for a piece of the luxury resort pie. There was more going on, and Ellie intended to find out what it was.

First, she'd get Louie back. Her dog wasn't going to spend one more minute in Jason's possession. Not after she realized that she hadn't known her ex-fiancé at all.

They were halfway to the back door when they heard the car pull up. Hugh's heavy hand landed on Ellie's shoulder, his eyes wide. He put a finger to his lips, glancing toward the front of the house. "Someone's pulling up."

"Crap." Ellie looked at the back door, her heart breaking. "If we go outside to get Louie, there's a chance he'll bark or alert that we're here."

"We have to hide."

Ellie's heart thumped. Everything was going wrong. How had she ended up here? She grabbed Hugh's arm and pulled him toward the nearest doorway. It was an opening with no door that led to the basement. They rushed down the stairs, scanning the room. The large carpeted space had a relatively low ceiling and a large media room. It was comfortably cool year round, and Ellie had loved snuggling down here to watch a movie.

She heard the front door open, then close. The alarm panel beeped, then beeped again. A grunt, and it beeped a third time. Uh-oh. She paused at the bottom of the stairs, listening. Hugh stood close by, his front brushing her back, his head angled toward the door at the top.

Footsteps echoed down the hallway above them, moving closer. Her heart stopped when they paused at the top of the basement steps.

Panic gripped Ellie's throat in a tight fist. This was bad. This was really, really bad. The basement might be comfortable, but now she cursed it for its lack of hiding spaces. "Over here," she mouthed, and she dragged Hugh to the basement powder room. She shoved him inside, following close behind and then closing the door in one quick movement. It gave an almighty squeak, the noise impossibly loud to her pounding ears.

She froze, eyes wide, listening. The footsteps above their heads paused, then approached. She heard them on the hardwood near the basement doorway, then muffled creaks on the carpeted steps down to the basement.

Ellie closed her eyes, biting her bottom lip, and prayed to every saint and deity she could think of. If Jason found her hiding in his bathroom with Hugh, her life would be over. She'd never find out why he had that cash, and she'd never get Louie back. Her public humiliation would never end. Palms sweating, she tried to regulate her breathing as panic and fear warred within her.

Seconds ticked by, and she heard no movement. Then the footsteps retreated up the stairs and returned to the hardwood above.

With an exhale, she leaned against the closed door and shut her eyes. "I forgot about the squeak," she whispered. "Jason said he'd fix that but never did."

When Ellie finished speaking, she opened her eyes—and realized just how small the bathroom really was. Hugh was directly in front of her, leaning against the vanity. A toilet took up the rest of the space. They barely had three inches of space between them. She shuffled to the side to stand in front of the toilet, her chest brushing his along the way. It gave her an extra couple of inches of space, just enough room to turn around and lean her hands against the wall.

Her heart pounded so hard and so fast it made her head spin. They were going to get caught. They were *so* going to get caught.

Baby's Second Mug Shot was about to get passed around every dinner table on Fernley.

Light entered the powder room through a window well that opened onto the backyard. She knew that it was near Louie's doghouse, but when a shadow fell across the window, she nearly screamed. The squeak that fell from her lips sounded far, far too loud in the small space.

Then Hugh was there, his body at her back. He wrapped one arm around her stomach, his other hand stroking her arm. "Shh," he said, his jaw touching her temple. "Quiet."

Normally, she'd hate having a guy shush her, but these were extenuating circumstances. His body was a warm wall at her back, his muscular arm banded tightly across her stomach. She found herself leaning into him, closing her eyes.

The last thing she should've been doing was accepting soothing strokes from this man, especially after what had happened on the doorstep. But he was there, and she didn't have much choice. She might as well take whatever comfort he could provide. As her heartbeat slowed, she let herself sink into Hugh's chest.

They listened to Jason's voice as he spoke to Louie. His words were muffled, but they could hear the dog woofing, his shadow darting over and back across the window well.

"He's just filling up his water bowl and feeding him," Ellie whispered. "He can't see us."

Hugh's hand ran down her arm from shoulder to elbow, then back up again. She found herself leaning into him, letting his movements calm her racing heartbeat. He smelled incredible, fresh and male and musky.

He moved his hand down to tangle with hers and wrapped both arms around her body. They seemed to fit together so perfectly. He lulled her into a calmer state of mind, holding her close to his warmth and his bulk. It felt . . . nice.

Until she felt the bulge in his pants.

Her heart stuttered. Her brain went offline for a full second and took its sweet time booting up again.

The man had a *boner*. What in the world was *wrong* with him? This was a life-or-death situation! They were about to get found out and arrested, and he was *turned on*?

Stiffening, Ellie rocked away from him as her eyes bulged. "Hugh. Are you—" She couldn't even say the words. She stared at the wall, wide eyed. Her heart was back to jackrabbiting in her chest.

He leaned away from her, disengaging his arms and angling his hips back. He spoke in a low voice. "That was an accident."

She scoffed, half turning to stare at him. "An *accident*? What are you, thirteen?"

His jaw clenched. His cheeks were flushed, and he stared at a spot on the wall above her head. "Can we just forget about it?"

"What, forget about the fact that you just got a boner while you bear-hugged me for no reason?"

"There was a reason," he hissed back, eyes dropping to meet hers. "You were panicking. I wanted to calm you down."

That made Ellie want to look away, and for some reason, she decided to look down at his crotch. His jeans were still bulging. For crying out loud. "You're sick," she whispered, turning back to stare at the wall. She ignored the way her heart pounded and how her inner thighs trembled slightly. "Did it turn you on that I was scared?"

"What? No! Ellie, listen, this has nothing to do with you."

"Ex*cuse* me?" Next thing he'd tell her the kiss had nothing to do with her either.

They fell silent as a shadow passed the window well again; then they heard the back door open and close. Hugh shifted, the cloth of his shirt making a soft whisper of sound. His voice was strained. "Your butt was rubbing up against me, and I had my arms around you, and . . . look, I—I didn't get hard thinking of *you*, specifically. It was a physiological reaction I couldn't control."

Well. What a freaking Casanova. "Is that supposed to make me feel better? Earlier, did you just fall over with your lips puckered and happen to make out with me?"

"What, you *want* me to get hard at the thought of you right now?"

Ellie spun around, intending to give him a piece of her mind. But then she was facing him, and all the words just evaporated from her lips. He had no right to be this gorgeous, all wound up and flushed and muscular. It wasn't normal. Regular people didn't look like that. She blinked, glared, and huffed.

"Let's just forget about it," Hugh said, the cords in his neck tensing. "Please."

Ellie was never going to forget about it. She felt hot all over, and she couldn't think straight. She needed to get out of this bathroom. "Fine."

"Good."

"Just—next time you manhandle me, try to keep your cock away from me."

He closed his eyes and put a hand on the countertop. "Ellie, don't say the word 'cock' right now. Please."

She reared back. "What's wrong with the word 'cock'? You know what, I don't want to know. All right? I'm sorry! Keep your erection away from me. Is that better?"

His eyes opened again and met hers, full of fire and menace. "You're not helping."

Ellie's heart fluttered. In a remarkable display of discipline, she resisted the urge to look at his crotch again. Instead, she lifted her chin and arched a brow. "What, 'erection'? Now I can't even use a medical term?" Her mouth just would not stop going, spewing out thoughts as soon as they popped into her head. "Oh my God, is this turning you on? Me just standing here saying 'cock' is enough to get you going? Wow. That whole kissing thing is making a lot more sense now. You're just a hormone-riddled savage."

"Ellie," he growled. "Stop it."

Heat flushed through her chest, down to the pit of her stomach, and all the way to her thighs.

Oh no. Was she actually *flattered*? She needed to get a grip on herself, because this day was quickly spiraling out of control. Now she actually *wanted* Hugh Hartford to find her attractive. She wanted him to have a big ol' boner because of her.

Adrenaline was to blame. It scrambled her brain cells, getting all her wires crossed and confused. That's what was going on. She didn't actually want this man to be interested in her, because she sure wasn't interested in men. How could she be, after what she'd endured with Jason? The kiss was an aberration, and this was . . . she didn't know. It was battlefield lust. Her fight-or-flight response had been activated, and now she was horny.

Or something.

She turned to face the toilet. At almost the same time, Hugh turned and leaned against the vanity, so they were side by side in the small space. That was better than face to face, at least. They listened to the footsteps over their heads. A toilet flushed somewhere in the house. More water rushed. Footsteps moved to the far side of the house, where the kitchen was.

Ellie began to sweat. Two bodies in this tiny room heated the place up more than was comfortable. She fanned herself, listening to the never-ending footsteps above.

Hugh must have been feeling the heat as well, because he took off his fleecy top to reveal a marled gray tee beneath. Ellie caught a glimpse of his stomach while he disrobed, which made her heart jump up and get stuck in her throat. Sweat beaded near her hairline.

"How long is he going to be here?" Hugh asked, his voice still barely above a whisper but no longer rough.

She shrugged. "I don't know. He used to work at the Brownlow Foundation all day long, but that was when he was screwing his head of fundraising. It's probably less exciting to be at the office now."

Hugh glanced at her, and she felt like he could read every emotion she tried to hide. She couldn't look at his face, and the close quarters made her feel faint. She didn't want to take her cardigan off, because she needed every barrier she could find between his body and hers, but dampness gathered between her shoulder blades and under her arms. She took off the cardigan. Hugh shifted slightly beside her as if he, too, wanted to put more space between their bare arms.

"Did you get that top at the outdoor store on Fifth Street?" Ellie whispered, pointing to his fleece. It had an I HEART FERNLEY logo on the breast, so she knew exactly where it had come from, but she needed to think about something other than the kiss, or the boner, or her ex-fiancé discovering them there.

"Yeah," Hugh replied. "Gets colder than I was expecting in the evenings."

Ellie nodded. "It does. Even in summer."

Now they were talking about the weather. It should have been a safe topic, but the fact that they'd reverted to small talk only made her more aware that she could feel the heat of his arm next to hers.

Hugh cleared his throat. "Any chance Jason'll come down here?"

Ellie shook her head. "He usually watched TV upstairs in the second living space. He said it was too dingy down here." Maybe that's why Ellie had liked the basement so much. It was her sanctuary. The place where she could come and be herself, shed the skin she wore whenever she was around Jason and his peers.

The thought clanged through her, and she realized their relationship had been doomed from the start. Had she ever felt at home in this house? Had she ever felt comfortable with Jason? The only place she could stand to be for any length of time was alone in the basement.

After another grueling few minutes that felt like hours, when they listened to more footsteps that faded back down the hallway, Hugh jerked his chin at Ellie. "You mind swapping places?"

Weird, but okay. "Sure." She gave him as much room as she could and went to lean against the closed door. She considered opening it, but then the footsteps came back down the hall again. Seriously, did Jason ever just sit down? Why did he seem to be walking over and back in front of the basement's doorway?

The sound of a zipper sliding brought her attention back to the room. Hugh had left his sweater on top of the sink, beside hers. Now, he stood above the toilet, legs spread, hands at his groin.

"Um. What are you doing?"

He glanced at her, then at the toilet bowl. "I have to pee."

"Not in here you don't. Not with me standing a foot away from you."

He dropped his arms to his side. "What do you expect me to do?"

"Hold it in!"

"Ellie. Don't be ridiculous."

"Excuse me? I never even peed in the same room as my ex-fiancé. I don't want your aerosolized pee particles getting all up in my nasal cavity! That's disgusting. You're disgusting."

"My aerosolized—" He stared at her, then shook his head. "Look, we don't know how long we're going to be stuck in here. You can step outside, but I have to pee."

"There's no door at the top of the stairs," she reminded him in a forceful whisper. "If I step out there, he'll hear the door squeak, and he'll come to investigate. Then he'll see me standing there. Either way, he'll probably hear you peeing. You can't do it."

"He'll hear me peeing through the bathroom door and up the stairs? I doubt it."

"It's a risk."

"Your constant whispering is a risk too, but that doesn't seem to stop you."

"You can't pee while I'm in here." This was a hill she would die on.

Hugh took a deep breath. "Ellie, I have to pee. It's nonnegotiable. You can either turn your back or step outside."

"Do you *want* Jason to find me? Because asking me to go out there is basically begging Jason to come investigate. The bathroom door squeaks. We know this. It almost got us caught when we first came down here."

Hugh's jaw tensed. He held her gaze for a moment, then turned back to the toilet. He reached for his zipper again.

"Okay!" Ellie hissed. "Fine! You can pee. But you have to sit down."

He let out a frustrated little huff of laughter and turned to stare at her. His expression was incredulous. "You want me to sit down? How is that any better?"

"Less splashing. I don't want to be in the blast zone. I've seen the aftereffects of a man letting loose on a toilet, and if I'm going to be in the same room as you when you do this, I just want to make sure I don't get your bodily fluids all over me." She narrowed her eyes. "And if you tell me that sentence just turned you on, I'm going to get the bolt cutters out and bash you on the head again."

Hugh looked like he wanted to argue. There was a long, tense moment; then his shoulders dropped. "Fine," he relented. "But you'll have to turn around unless you want to get a full-frontal view of me." His hands were already undoing the top button of his jeans, and Ellie caught a glimpse of the black underwear beneath.

She spun around and stared at the wall.

Seconds ticked by, one after the other. Nothing happened.

"Everything okay back there?" she asked, crossing her arms and shifting her weight from foot to foot. "For someone who so desperately had to pee, there doesn't seem to be much urine coming out of you."

"Just—give me a minute. I'm stressed out."

A few more moments passed, and Ellie heard a tinkle. Then there was the rustle of fabric, a zipper, and Hugh clearing his throat. "All right," he said. "I'm decent."

Ellie turned back around and gave him a tight smile. She hunted through her bag and came out with a little travel-size bottle of hand sanitizer. Hugh rubbed some on his hands, thanked her, and handed it back. Once it was safely in its designated pocket, Ellie reached over and put her finger on the toilet's flush lever.

Hugh caught her wrist and pulled it away. "What are you doing?"

She pulled her hand away from his. "What do you mean? I'm flushing the toilet."

"Ellie, Jason will hear the flush."

Hmm. That was a good point. If her brain was fully operational right now, she would have thought of that herself. Still, she set her jaw. "You expect me to stand here in the same room as a bowl of your pee for an indeterminate amount of time? It'll stink!"

He shut the lid on the toilet. "There. Happy?"

"That urine is going to stain the bowl if it sits there. It'll get all scummy and disgusting. You have to flush it."

"This isn't even your house! Why do you care?"

An excellent question, one that Ellie couldn't answer. She knew it was unreasonable. She knew it was ridiculous. But she couldn't bear the idea of standing in a room with someone else's pee just . . . sitting there. Plus, Hugh was taking up so much space, and she was finding it harder and harder to look at him. The whole boner situation had really thrown her, and she kept thinking about their kiss. She hadn't expected a man like him to be attracted to her, and she definitely hadn't expected to like it. In fact, liking it was the worst part of this whole debacle. It meant she was opening herself up to getting hurt again, when she should be focused on ruining Jason's life.

She stared at the closed lid of the toilet. She wouldn't flush it. Of course she wouldn't. She wasn't stupid. But she wanted to, mostly because it was the only thing in this whole disastrous nightmare that made any sense.

Hugh stood in front of the toilet, blocking her access, reading her mind. He pinched the bridge of his nose. "You drive me crazy," he mumbled.

"Well, that's what you get for coming along when you weren't invited." She knew she sounded petulant and unreasonable, which was pretty much in line with how she felt. She took a deep breath and tried to get her bearings. "We have to get out of here," she said. "I want to get Louie and go talk to Fergus about that bag of cash."

"Is there any way we can sneak out? A basement door? Can we make a run for it after the door squeaks?"

Ellie's eyes widened. She met Hugh's gaze. "The old cellar," she whispered. "We can get out through the crawl space."

CHAPTER 13

Hugh watched as Ellie set her backpack on the vanity and unzipped it. She pulled out a small bottle of water, a length of rope, and the bolt cutters, staring at them intently.

"The solution to the squeaky door is here," she whispered. "I know it is."

"What about your hand sanitizer? We could squirt that on the hinges and try to open the door really slowly."

She shook her head. "Slower is worse. And would hand sanitizer really help?"

Hugh shrugged. "It's kind of lube-y."

"'Lube-y'?" she repeated, flicking her gaze to meet his. Her cheeks flushed, and she glanced away again. "It's alcohol based. I don't know what kind of lube you usually use, but I hope it's not alcohol based."

He bit back a grin. "What else have you got in your bag of tricks?"

"Nothing." She clicked her tongue and put the water, rope, and bolt cutters back. Then she grabbed her cardigan and his sweater, folding them before slipping them in the backpack too. She stared at the fabric, scowling. "I knew I forgot something. I should have brought the WD-40. The only other things I have are the lockpicks, my phone, and . . ." She straightened, inhaling sharply, then unzipped a small pocket at the front of the bag. She pulled out a tube of lip balm that was so old the label was faded and scratched, lifting it like Indiana Jones grasping the Holy Grail. "And this."

If they hadn't been trespassing in another man's home, Hugh would have laughed triumphantly. As it was, the situation was stressful and confusing, and his body had already betrayed him more than once. Even watching her take her cardigan off had been nearly too much to bear. He gave Ellie a sharp nod, then watched her wind the bottom of the tube so a good amount of lip balm was sticking out. She started at the bottom hinge, rubbing furiously, trying to get the lip balm into every crevice before moving on to the middle hinge.

The top hinge was too high for Ellie to reach comfortably, so Hugh took over. He applied the balm liberally, hoping it would work. It had to work. If he got caught here, he worried that Jason would use it as leverage to force him to sign the deal. Otherwise, he'd be arrested. Two outcomes he'd rather avoid.

They used the entire tube of lip balm, scooping out chunks from the plastic bottom of the tube to rub into any spots that looked ungreased. Finally, the two of them stepped back and exchanged a long glance.

"Ready?" he asked.

Ellie nodded. "You open the door. If it squeaks, I'll go out and distract Jason while you make a run for it. The entrance to the furnace room is under the stairs, and the crawl space is in the back corner. You might have to break the lock on the trapdoor to get out, so you should take the backpack." She handed it over.

Hugh loosened the straps and slipped it on, then vowed, "You're not going anywhere without me, Ellie."

She gave him a fierce grin. "Don't be a hero, Hugh. Just get yourself out of here and pretend you don't know me." Then she nodded at the door, and he turned the handle. Inch by inch, the door opened, and cool air started to filter in. They both let out a sigh of relief at the change in temperature. Hugh's shirt was stuck to his back, and he could see damp patches on Ellie's tank top. Getting out of here would be a relief.

He took a deep breath, stealing a glance at Ellie. Her jaw was set, her shoulders back. It was impossible to be in Ellie's presence and not get caught in her tailwind. She was a force of nature. Hugh had lived his life on autopilot until Ellie had jerked him into her slipstream.

The door opened wide enough for Ellie to shimmy through, but Hugh needed more room. He met Ellie's gaze through the widening opening, then pulled the door the last three inches so he could exit and finally get out of here.

Squeeeaaaakkkkk!

The door let out a plaintive wail in the last inch, as loud as a gunshot to Hugh's ears. He paused, heart thundering, while Ellie's head whipped toward the stairs. They stood still as statues, Ellie in the open, Hugh in the powder room, waiting for Jason to descend the steps to the basement and catch them red handed.

But nothing happened. No footsteps sounded above them. Total silence pulsed in the air. Hugh let out a breath and eased through the opening, after taking the backpack off so he could make it through without opening the door any wider. Once he was out of the powder room, he nodded at Ellie and crept toward the stairs. They made it to the furnace room door, and with one last listen for any noise in the silent house, they went through the door.

Darkness enveloped them. Ellie reached back, sliding her hand down his arm until she reached his palm. She braided her fingers through his and tugged him closer. Little shivers danced over the surface of his skin everywhere she touched.

"Cell phone flashlight," she whispered, her breath coasting over his cheek.

Hugh dug his phone out of his pocket and flicked it on, and light illuminated the dank, dark space.

He shone his light around the room, with its low ceiling and shining silver ductwork. Cobwebs clung to every corner, along with old tools and boxes of various sizes. "Why didn't you hide us in here to begin with?"

Ellie pursed her lips. "I was panicking. I forgot about it," she said. "This place gives me the creeps. I never came in here when I lived in the house."

She forged ahead, circling around the furnace to the far side of the room. The ceiling was lower on this side, the darkness stygian beyond the light. Ellie crouched down and led him to the far corner of the room, finally stopping at an angled cellar door.

Hugh looked at the door and tried it with his fingertips. It didn't budge. An old, rusty lock was their next barrier.

Ellie huffed, then brightened. She hurried back toward the furnace, pausing to gag and flail her arms at a cobweb that attacked her face, then reached up to grab something off the wall near the entrance to the room. Keys jangled. She came back, beaming. "Jason kept misplacing the keys to the cellar until his mother installed a hook down here," she explained in a hurried whisper.

She pulled out an ancient-looking skeleton key. "This is one of the only things Jason didn't change when he renovated the place," she explained, grinning. Then she fit the key in the lock, and it slid open with a satisfying clunk.

"I'll go first," Hugh said after Ellie had darted back to replace the key on its hook. He pushed one side of the old cellar door up and paused, listening to the sounds of the forest outside. Then, moving quickly, he pushed it open far enough for him to lift himself out. Not letting the door drop, he held it open with one hand and helped Ellie out of the cellar with the other.

They were at the side of the house, with the gate to the backyard to their left. It was padlocked, so the only way out was toward the front. They'd have to pass the windows of the study and the formal living room to make it back out to the open forest.

Hugh closed the cellar door gently, heart thundering. A snuffling sound drew his attention toward the backyard, and Ellie let out a pained-sounding sigh.

She crouched near the fence, putting her hand against it. "I'm coming back, Louie," she whispered. Then she dug through her backpack and took out more treats, shoving them between the fence planks for her dog. While he was munching, she took off her shoe.

"What are you doing?" Hugh whispered. "We have to go."

"Louie loves socks." She tore her left sock off and stabbed her bare foot back into her shoe. "I don't want him to forget me."

"No one could forget you, Ellie. Especially not your dog."

She threw Hugh a quick glance, then looked away. "Still." She stood and shoved her sock through one of the gaps in the privacy lattice before sticking her face against it to peer through the cracks. She smiled when Louie pounced on her sock, tail wagging furiously. Through the gaps in the fence, the movement looked almost like stop-motion animation.

"We have to go," Hugh repeated softly.

She nodded, tearing herself away. They hurried along the side of the house, stopping when they reached the big picture windows that looked out from Jason's study. Hugh paused, glancing inside. Empty. They continued on and stopped at the front living room windows.

Jason was inside, sipping a mug of something, looking over some documents spread out over the big square coffee table. They looked like the blueprints of the resort, but at this distance, Hugh couldn't be sure. Ellie crouched beside him, her arm leaning against his.

She swore. "That rat *bastard*."

Hugh blinked.

She thrust her finger toward the window. "He's using a coaster!"

This woman would never make sense to him. He met her gaze. "You got something against coasters?"

"No, Hugh. I like coasters. But for the entirety of our relationship, Jason refused to use one. I always thought he was doing it as a weird power move over me, but when I tried to explain it to anyone else, it made me sound like I was completely insane." Her lips turned down, eyes narrowing. "But now I know. He only refused to use a coaster with me because he knew it bothered me. Sometimes, I'd put a coaster down under his drink and he'd take a sip, then put the drink directly beside the coaster. It drove me nuts."

Hugh hadn't known Ellie very long, but their acquaintance had been a trial by fire so far, and he knew that look on her face. She was stubborn and angry and hurt, and she wanted to do something impulsive. He eased away from the window and pulled her with him so they were out of view.

She scowled. "You think I'm crazy," she whispered. "I know you do. Everyone does."

He crouched in a squatting position with his back to the exterior wall of Brownlow's house, the backpack on the ground between his spread knees. He shook his head. "I don't think you're crazy."

She snorted, throwing him a sideways glance. Her gaze drifted toward the window again, and Hugh knew he had to stop her from drawing attention to herself.

"My dad had a secret second family," he heard himself say. The words just fell out of him—words that he hadn't been able to speak out loud even when his mother had dragged him to a child psychologist. He'd seen the nice older lady for months after his father had left them for his other family all those years ago. All he remembered about the sessions were the psychologist's funky red eyeglasses. "He left my mom and me for the other family after she found out."

Ellie startled, moving away from the window to meet his gaze.

"His new wife came from wealth, and my dad had always had a taste for the finer things. In the end, my mother and I just weren't enough." He gave her a brittle smile. "I know what it's like to be lied to over long periods of time. I've felt the whiplash of finding out the truth."

Cracks appeared in Ellie's expression, a hint of the woman behind the anger. Under an overcast sky, with the trees whispering around them, she stared at him with dark-blue eyes, and Hugh felt a connection with her he'd never experienced before. He held her gaze. "I believe you about the coasters. It's the little things that really screw you up. My dad used to call me his favorite son, and it was all a big joke because I was the only son—until I found out there was another one that he called his favorite too. Even though he told so many lies that were so much worse, that's the one I used to think about at night when I couldn't sleep."

Her shoulders dropped. She let out a long breath and glanced at the window again. "I feel like I'm drowning."

Hugh's chest tightened. He wanted to comfort her, but he knew that the longer they stayed there, the higher the chance that they'd be seen. "Come on," he said, then dropped to his hands and knees. "Let's get out of here."

They crawled along the window, taking a small break to catch their breath when they reached the front of the house. They leaned against the corner of the house, glancing at the driveway and at the front porch, where they'd shared their first kiss.

Hugh turned to check on Ellie where she leaned against the corner of the building. For the first time in what seemed like forever, her lips curled into a smile. She grinned at him, a mischievous sprite that had appeared in his life with the express purpose of messing up all his carefully laid plans. He grinned back, welcoming her chaos with open arms.

Then, without exchanging another word, they sprinted back to the car, got in, locked the doors, and burst out laughing.

CHAPTER 14

Ellie's body couldn't decide if it was exhausted or ecstatic, which made giddiness arc through her chest in odd little waves. Light-headedness made her blink over and over again as she caught her breath.

She hadn't found evidence of the sheep poisoning, but she had a lead—and a partner. When Hugh had appeared behind her on the doorstep, she'd wanted him to leave. But something had shifted between them.

She let her head fall against the headrest as Hugh turned the key in the ignition. The "Drive Tunes" playlist came on, with "What I Like About You" by the Romantics starting along with the car. The guitar chords danced out of the speakers, and Ellie couldn't help but lift her hands to do the four rapid claps that marked the start of the song. To her surprise, Hugh had the same urge; they clapped in sync to the song and each other, then exchanged a wide-eyed look.

Shock and delight flitted through Ellie, sprinkling her skin with goose bumps. When, a few seconds later, they both shouted the song's "Hey!" it was game over. Ellie cackled as Hugh grinned and put the car in gear. They bobbed their heads to the music, sang along, and let the tension of the past couple of hours drain away.

Ellie lowered her window and let the breeze mess up her hair, leaning into the cool, crisp sensation with closed eyes. She felt comfortable with this man in a way that was as captivating as it was unfamiliar. He sang along to bits and pieces of the lyrics, his voice deep and warm as it wound around her. She didn't want the moment to end. For a few precious minutes, she lived in a world where Jason Brownlow didn't exist, where she was carefree and content and safe.

Hugh didn't view her through the lens of her arrest. He saw *her*.

Ellie wanted to revel in that feeling, because it was exactly what she'd been missing for six months. She'd been disgraced, her reputation shot, her complaints falling on deaf ears.

Maybe, if she was able to figure out what Jason was up to and expose him, her reputation on the island would be fixed. Maybe more people would see her, respect her, understand her.

The way Hugh did.

But they drove on and reality intruded. She was still the laughingstock of the island, and she had no proof of anything. She couldn't count on that changing unless she succeeded in exacting her revenge.

Ellie had things to do. She couldn't let Jason bully her parents, and she needed to get Louie back as soon as possible. So once they'd driven halfway to Carlisle, Ellie directed Hugh to the central part of the island, where Fergus O'Hara lived.

"You don't have to come with me," she said when they'd turned off the main road and onto a narrower two-lane street that curved in and out of the trees. "The longer you hang out with me, the more people will notice. Your reputation will be shot. People will talk. You can just drop me back home, and I'll drive myself to Fergus's."

Hugh's hands kneaded the steering wheel. He threw her a quick glance. "You done?"

She turned her head to the window to hide her smile. This time, she didn't push him. The truth was, she wanted him to come along. She wasn't ready for their partnership to end.

And maybe, in a hidden corner of her mind, she entertained the idea that he might kiss her again. Maybe they'd do it somewhere more appropriate, where they'd have time to explore each other's tastes and bodies. Maybe, for the first time in a long time, she could enjoy intimacy with a man without feeling like it was part of a bigger transaction, the way it had always felt with Jason.

She straightened as the thought turned to realization. Her entire relationship with Jason—from the moment he'd bought her a drink at the Fernley Hotel three and a half years ago—had been transactional. He'd spoil and lavish her, and he'd expect sex and devotion. He'd use money and connections to advance her business, only to keep her by his side as an object to show off, parade around, and condescend to. Jason had moved Ellie into his house when her lease was up and money was tight, only for her to discover the home was a stage covered in invisible eggshells. She was expected to dance across it without breaking a single one. Day after day after day.

Thinking back on it now, Ellie realized it was an impossible task. From the moment she'd crossed the threshold, she was never going to succeed—and yet, she still blamed herself for her failure.

Their relationship always felt like a battle for one-upmanship, fraught with undercurrents that Ellie had struggled to understand.

Had he ever truly loved her? Was he capable of it? Was *she* capable of it?

Maybe she was cursed to repeat her mistakes. How could she trust another man to cherish her if she couldn't even trust herself to notice a house full of eggshells?

Hugh turned the music down. "You okay?"

She blinked, glancing at the man in the driver's seat. His dark hair was unruly, his body relaxed as he drove the car along the winding road. He had one hand on the steering wheel and the other on the window frame, utterly at ease. It was comforting to sit beside someone like him. She realized that even though his presence pushed against her skin like it had always done, she didn't really hate the sensation anymore.

"I'm fine. Just undergoing some deep, existential realizations over here."

His lips tipped up, but he didn't take his eyes off the road. "Any you want to share?"

"My relationship with Jason was a sham, and I think I'm doomed to be alone forever."

He snorted. "I used to think that too."

"What changed?"

He didn't answer, just gently shook his head and took the next turn Ellie pointed out. Then they'd arrived at their destination, and the time for conversation was over.

It was time to figure out what Jason was up to, how Fergus was involved, and how Ellie could use that to bring her ex-fiancé down.

Fergus O'Hara lived in a run-down bungalow clad in dark-brown siding. The window frames were painted a deep forest green that was peeling and flaking all over, and the overgrown lawn was littered with rusty detritus from engines and boat parts. It was a total dump. His mother would probably be ashamed, except in her eyes her son could do no wrong.

They parked on a patch of gravel littered with weeds, and Hugh cut the engine. Through the windshield, they watched the house.

"Is he home?"

"His car's there." Ellie pointed to the pickup truck next to the front door. It was silver and about ten years old, and it was relatively well maintained compared to the rest of the surroundings. Hitched to the pickup truck was an old boat on a trailer, its dull black motor tilted up to the cloudy sky.

"What's the plan?"

"The plan is to squeeze Fergus until he admits the cash is his and explains why it was at Jason's house. Then we can reassess."

"You think he'll talk?"

Ellie's brows lowered. "I'll make him talk."

They exited the car and marched to the front door. Ellie took the lead. She rang the doorbell, then banged her fist on the door, her blood starting to thrum.

When no one answered, she peeked through the window beside the door. Through the gauzy curtain, she could see an old rug and a tipped-over chair, but not much else.

"Let's try the back door," Hugh said, and he started walking around.

Ellie followed. When they reached the back porch, she saw a familiar-looking blackberry pie set out on top of the porch handrail. A bird pecked at it tentatively and flapped away. Even animals didn't want any of Mrs. O'Hara's pie.

Ellie snapped a picture for her grandmother and sent it along with the caption "Even the birds think cyanide would be an improvement," then followed Hugh to the sliding glass door at the back of the house. The interior of the house was a mess, with old beer cans and pizza boxes littered on the floors and tables, a thick layer of grime coating every visible surface. She curled her hands around the sides of her face to get a better look through the glass and spotted a pair of feet sticking out from the end of the couch. One was bare, and one was covered in a hole-ridden sock.

Bingo. Fergus was home.

She knocked on the sliding door before trying to tug it open, but it was locked. "Fergus!"

The feet wiggled, then moved. An eternity later, Fergus stumbled out of the living room and squinted at the back door. He was a tall, lanky, brown-haired man who had developed a small potbelly in the years since he and Ellie had been in high school together. His hair was permanently greasy, falling in loose curls that brushed his shoulders and did their best to hide his receding hairline. His beard was mostly scruff, crawling high up his cheeks and low down his neck. He had not aged well.

Fergus frowned slightly, then unlocked the door and slid it partially open. The smell that wafted out was . . . unpleasant. A mix of rotting food, body odor, and marijuana. "Ellie," he mumbled, scratching his stomach through his stained tee. "What are you doing here? What time is it?"

"We have a few questions for you," Ellie said, propping the sliding glass door open with her foot.

Fergus seemed to notice Hugh's hulking figure for the first time. His brow furrowed, brain obviously struggling to process so many stimuli. "Who's that?"

"That's Hugh," Ellie said, and she shoved the door open all the way.

"Hugh," Fergus repeated under his breath, then shook his head like he was trying to spark up his last remaining brain cells. He turned around and led them to the kitchen.

Ellie saw evidence of Mary's presence in the mop and bucket in the corner and the dirty plastic containers stacked in the sink. She probably brought her son food, then came by and did the dishes for him. Fergus obviously didn't clean anything himself.

He opened the fridge and glanced in, burped, and closed the door again before opening a pizza box on the counter and grabbing a slice. He leaned against the kitchen counter and munched on the cold pizza while he studied his two guests.

Ellie didn't want to touch anything, but she set her backpack on the small round table and unzipped it. When she pulled out her bolt cutters, Fergus threw his hands back, a piece of pepperoni flying off to tumble into the sink.

"Deal's done, Ellie," Fergus said. "You bought them fair and square. Buyer beware."

She zipped the backpack up again and set it on the ground, holding the bolt cutters by their tape-wrapped handles. She tested them out, opening and closing them a few times. "I'm not trying to get my money back," she said, and Fergus's shoulders relaxed.

Hugh rounded the table and ended up beside Fergus. He swept his hand toward one of the kitchen chairs, and Fergus stared at him for a moment before taking a seat. Hugh stood behind him, looking very imposing. Ellie was glad he'd come along.

In the middle of the table was a wooden box carved with an intricate pattern. Fergus pulled it closer, then opened the lid and removed a prerolled joint and a lighter.

"Before you do that," Ellie said, "answer a couple of questions for us, Fergus."

Hugh grabbed the items from the other man's hands and placed them in the box again, pushing it out of reach.

"Hey! You can't come to my house and tell me what I can and can't do."

Ellie slammed the bolt cutters on the table with a loud bang. "Why does this red duct tape match the handles of a duffel bag full of cash in Jason Brownlow's house?"

Fergus's eyes widened for a moment; then his face settled into a blank expression. "I have no idea what you're talking about."

"Bullshit."

"You guys are being pretty rude, you know that?" He made to get out of his chair, but Hugh's hand clamped onto his shoulder and pushed him down again. Fergus landed on the chair with a grunt.

"What's up with the cash, Fergus?"

"Cash? What cash?"

"Your poker face needs work."

"I don't know what you're talking about."

"A bag of yours containing a lot of money ended up in Jason Brownlow's possession. Why." Ellie bit off the last word, speaking through clenched teeth. She wasn't leaving until she had information.

Fergus leaned back, ignoring Hugh's hand on his shoulder. He crossed his arms. "Say there is a bag of cash," he said slowly; "how the hell do you know about it?"

Ellie picked up the bolt cutters again and shoved the table out of the way. "Answer my question, Fergus."

"No, no, no." He shook his head, his greasy curls springing up and down in outrage. "I want to know how you found out about a bag that belongs to Jason when you don't even live in his house anymore. Because everyone knows he kicked you out after you tried to trash his car."

Ellie had the urge to defend her actions, but she tamped it down. There were more important things at play right now than her humiliation. She opened the bolt cutters and put them against Fergus's ear. "Tell. Me. About. The cash."

Fergus's neck muscles were tense, and he gulped thickly. "No."

"I'll cut off your ear, Fergus, and these bolt cutters aren't sharp. It'll be messy."

Hugh cleared his throat and caught Ellie's gaze. He widened his eyes slightly, as if asking if she was serious.

She didn't know the answer to that. Did she want to hurt Fergus? Of course not. He'd likely never amount to much, but he still deserved to keep both of his earlobes. He'd provided most of their high school with recreational drugs and had never really moved on from that particular pursuit—as evidenced by the smell in this place and the contents of the box on the table—but he wasn't exactly Pablo Escobar. He could actually be kind of funny, if you caught him on one of his more lucid days. He was part of the island. He was Fernley.

But Jason was threatening her parents, and Ellie needed answers.

"I'll do it, Fergus. Answer me. Why did you give Jason a bag of cash?"

"I'm not a narc. I'll never tell you why. Never!"

"So you admit the bag of cash was yours?"

"What?" Fergus opened his eyes and stared at her. "Damn it, Ellie. I mean, no! No, it's not mine. I never said that. What cash? Stop tricking me! I won't talk! Ever!"

Hugh held Fergus to the chair and finally spoke. "If you tell us about the cash, we'll leave."

"Who is this guy, anyway? Why'd you bring him here, Ellie? I thought you were cool."

His earlobe was still in the jaws of the bolt cutters. She looked at the little dangling bit of flesh and wondered if she had it in her to snip through it. That was a bright line that she'd never even come close to crossing, but now she was here, with her toes up against it, moments away from taking a big step into a different kind of future.

A future full of severed ears and mysterious bags of money.

She needed to protect her parents. She needed to safeguard their land. She needed to ruin Jason Brownlow's life for what he had done to her and her family. She needed everyone to know she wasn't crazy and wasn't wrong.

Ellie dropped the bolt cutters, and Fergus let out a breath. He let out a dizzy little chuckle. "I knew you were joking, Ellie. Good one. That was funny. Wait—what are you doing?"

She pulled out her phone. "I'm calling your mother."

Fergus's eyes grew wide. "My mother? Why?"

"I'm going to tell her that in fifth grade, when you said you were working on a science fair project, you were really with me, hiding stink bombs in Mr. Moseley's car."

"She won't believe you," Fergus said, shaking his head frantically. "Don't do it. She'll only get mad at you. She hates you, Ellie."

Ellie narrowed her eyes. Hugh shifted his weight, his hands still holding Fergus down. She glanced at him, but all he did was stare back, leaving Ellie in the driver's seat.

She suspected Fergus was right. He could do no wrong in Mary's eyes, and any past transgression would only be a new mark against Ellie's character.

She pressed the call button and put it on speakerphone. It rang, oddly loud in the dirty kitchen. Fergus leaned back, the tension melting away from his muscles. He thought he'd won.

Ellie narrowed her eyes.

"Hello?" The voice coming through her phone's speaker was tinny and feminine.

"Hi, Mrs. O'Hara, it's Ellie Davis calling."

"Ellie," she said, not quite hostile but not quite pleased either. "What can I do for you? Is this about the wood? How's Lionel's nephew settling in?"

Hugh arched a brow, and Ellie bit back a smile. She racked her brain, trying to think of some way out of this. What could possibly make Fergus talk? He wasn't scared of physical threats—and Ellie was too chicken to act on them anyway—and he was completely confident in his mother's love.

Ellie had nothing. She had no leverage. She couldn't get Fergus to explain himself, and she couldn't go to the police and admit that she'd sneaked into Jason's house either.

Ellie stalled. "Hugh's great. He told me it was a pleasure to meet you."

Hugh's lips tilted, amusement dancing in his eyes. Fergus was silent, arms crossed, looking completely at ease.

"Actually, Hugh was wondering about your blackberry pie recipe," Ellie rattled on, furiously trying to come up with something to use against Fergus. "He loved it and said he wanted to try baking it himself."

"Well!" Mary exclaimed. "Isn't that wonderful? You know, I don't give out my recipe, but if he wanted to come watch while I make the pie, I'm sure I could make an exception . . ."

Hugh's eyes widened, and he pinched his lips, clearly conveying that he was *not* happy with that idea. Ellie bit back a smile, rolling her lips inwardly as she tried to compose herself. She shifted the phone to her other hand, turning around so she wouldn't see Hugh's face. If he kept looking at her like that, she'd burst out laughing.

"That's such a lovely suggestion, Mrs. O'Hara," she said, and Hugh made a strange, strangled grunt behind her. "I'll let him know . . ."

Her phone buzzed. Grandma had received the photo of Mrs. O'Hara's pie and responded with seventeen laughing emojis.

Her gaze had drifted out through the sliding glass doors, to the pie sitting on the handrail of Fergus's porch. She whipped back around, staring at Fergus as triumph blasted through her. He jerked back, frowning at her.

"Actually, Mrs. O'Hara, that isn't the only reason I called." A little wicked smile curled Ellie's lips. The first hints of fear entered Fergus's expression. She could almost hear his brain huffing and puffing with effort, trying to figure out what she was up to.

"Oh?"

Her smile widened. "I happened to stop by Fergus's today, and I was sad to see one of your pies—"

"OKAY! OKAY! I'LL TALK! Mom, I love your pie! It was delicious! I ate it all! It's always delicious! The best, Mom!"

"Fergus, honey, is that you?"

"Oh, I have to go, Mrs. O'Hara. Bye-bye!" Ellie hung up and pointed at Fergus. "Talk, or your mom finds out you've been feeding her award-winning pie to the birds, asshole."

"Her pie is disgusting!"

"Talk."

"The birds don't even eat it!"

"Talk."

Fergus groaned, slumping back on his chair. "Ellie, you don't want to know about the cash. You really, really don't want to know."

She pulled up a chair and sat down across from him, grabbing the bolt cutters from where she'd left them on the table to lay them across her lap. She didn't know why; it just felt more comfortable that way. She stroked them lovingly. Useless things.

Fergus leaned his elbows on his knees and dropped his head in his hands. "Ellie, you don't know what you're asking."

Ellie stayed silent, watching him. Hugh backed up slightly and leaned against the kitchen counter, giving Fergus a bit more breathing room. She exchanged a quick glance with Hugh and saw the tug of his lips, the light in his eyes. She loved that look. She felt proud, in control, excited.

A deep, pained breath slid through Fergus's lips, and he finally met Ellie's gaze. "I've been dabbling in the import-export business," he admitted. "The Canadians have been buying some product from me."

"'Product.'"

"You know," Fergus said, tilting his head from side to side. "Mary Jane."

Ellie grew still. "You've been trafficking *drugs*, Fergus? Are you kidding me?"

"It was supposed to be just one time," he cried, throwing out his arms. He dropped his shoulders. "But then . . . the money's too good, Ellie. I can't stop. There's just nothing else I'm good at."

"I thought weed was legal in Canada," Hugh said.

"There's still a market for it," Fergus answered with a shrug.

The weight of the revelation pressed down on Ellie. Suddenly, she was worried for Fergus. He wasn't a friend, but she didn't want him to throw his life away. "You're going to spend the rest of your life in jail if you get caught."

"Who's going to catch me?" He shrugged, scoffing. "I just drive the *Sea Stallion* over to a little uninhabited island across the border, make the drop, and it's all over. Easy." The vessel in question was the little metal canoe with a two-stroke motor that was barely watertight currently sitting hitched to his pickup truck in the front yard.

Ellie shook her head. "So what's this got to do with Jason?"

"Well, you know, there's only so much money you can stuff under a mattress."

Ellie didn't know what to think. She was too shocked to respond. Maybe Fergus was a baby Escobar, after all.

"Brownlow's been washing your money," Hugh said from behind Fergus. "Let me guess: he's using the charity."

Fergus met Ellie's gaze and pointed a thumb over his shoulder. "What he said."

"Money laundering," Ellie breathed. This had just ballooned way beyond her expectations. She thought this was about a few dead sheep, a luxury resort, and a little patch of waterfront land—but there was more to the story. Jason was tangling with some very, *very* illegal activities. Suspicion snaked through her, and she had to ask: "Does this have anything to do with the resort?"

Fergus snorted. "The whole point of the resort is to expand this operation. Once construction starts, I'll be able to offload a lot more product."

"Where are you even getting—" Ellie bit off the end of her question. "Actually, I don't want to know."

"That's what I tried to tell you," Fergus said with a shrug.

"Where does Jason fit into this? How does he get the money?"

"We meet after I do a drop, and I give him the money."

"When's the next meet?"

Fergus looked uncomfortable. "I don't know."

"Lie."

"Come on, Ellie. I can't tell you that."

"Fergus," she warned. "You've told us this much. Why stop now?"

He dropped his head in his hands. "This was a mistake."

"When's the next meet?" she repeated.

"The day after tomorrow," he mumbled. "We usually meet by the dumpsters behind the grocery store to do the exchange." He straightened up and leaned back, shaking his head. "I'm sorry, Ellie."

"Why are you apologizing to me?"

"He wasn't good to you," Fergus said quietly. "And now I'm in business with him, and . . ." He sighed. "I'm just sorry, okay?"

"You should stop," Ellie answered quietly. "You should stop this, Fergus. It's madness. You're going to get yourself in real trouble."

He nodded. "I know." A crooked smile. "So should you. Just forget about everything and leave, Ellie."

"I can't." It came out like a croak.

Fergus spread his hands. "Neither can I."

With no other questions to ask and too many thoughts swirling in her mind, Ellie stood to leave. She stuffed her bolt cutters in her bag and put one strap over her shoulder, heading for the front door. Fergus and Hugh followed. Once they were outside, with Fergus standing in the doorway, Ellie turned to meet his gaze.

"If you're making so much money, why'd you charge me three hundred bucks for these crappy old bolt cutters?"

Fergus shrugged. "Gotta keep up appearances somehow."

She glanced at his run-down house, his old car, his shoddy boat. She wondered what the point was for Fergus, because he sure didn't seem to be using any of his ill-gotten earnings.

Feet crunching on gravel, she followed Hugh to the car and let him open the door for her. She slid inside and clicked her seat belt, watching the big man circle around the front of the car to get behind the wheel.

Exhaustion crashed into her. She sank into the seat as despair weighed down her limbs. Money laundering was the last thing she'd expected to find today. She thought Jason wanted to build the resort as his legacy; she didn't think he was involved in this kind of criminal activity.

It made her feel so stupid for having dated him for so long. How had she not seen what kind of man he was? Up until she walked in on him with another woman, Ellie'd had no idea he was so despicable. Not only was she embarrassed about her arrest and mug shot, but she now felt even more humiliated for falling for Jason's charm in the first place.

She had to ask herself: Was she *stupid*? Was she a monumental idiot, the likes of which had never been seen? Did she deserve the derision of everyone on the island?

And, to top it all off, Ellie was scared. If Jason was happy to get involved with international drug trafficking—even if the main operator was only Fergus O'Hara—what else would he be willing to do? Were she and her family in real danger?

It was all too much for her to bear. All she wanted was to get her dog back and for her parents and grandma to be safe. Now things were spiraling out of control, and it might be too late to turn back.

Before he started the engine, Hugh turned to look at her. "How are you doing?"

"Peachy," she deadpanned.

It was a surprise when he reached over and tucked a strand of hair behind her ear. His touch was soft, his finger warm. "You want to grab some dinner?"

The offer was tempting, but the tiredness in Ellie's bones made her shake her head. "I'd like to go home now, please."

Was that disappointment she saw in his gaze? It was hard to tell.

A few raindrops started to splatter on the windshield. Hugh started the car, flicked on the wipers, and took her back to her parents' house.

CHAPTER 15

The day after their confrontation with Fergus, Hugh finished his breakfast at the Sunrise Diner and leaned back against the booth. The seat creaked as he shifted his weight, the table wobbling slightly as he set his mug back down after taking a sip.

He liked it here.

It had hit him that morning, when he'd walked out of the hotel and taken a deep breath of sea-scented air. This was a place that felt like home, even when he didn't know every bend in the road or every hidden inlet on the island's craggy coast the way Ellie did. The dense forests budding with new leaves, the first flowers blooming, and the cool dampness of the air made him feel refreshed and at peace in a way he'd never experienced before.

It was also the location of the Fernley Luxury Resort and Spa, which was apparently a complex money-laundering operation that happened to have his name all over it. He couldn't stay here. He couldn't be on the island when he refused to green-light the use of his land. If Jason Brownlow was involved in some seriously illegal activities, Hugh didn't want to be anywhere near here when he torpedoed the entire project.

Jason needed Hugh for the project to go ahead. Hugh had the only access road onto the proposed construction site. When Hugh told Jason he wasn't signing the contract, Jason would be very, very angry.

If Hugh was smart, he'd leave on the next ferry and never look back. But leaving meant he'd never see Ellie again. It meant she'd be on her own to contend with whatever wrath Jason meted out. And knowing Ellie, she wouldn't run away and keep herself safe; she'd take the brunt of any aggression on herself to protect the people she loved.

Hugh couldn't let her face the fallout alone. He didn't *want* to leave her here alone. He wanted to protect her while she protected her family. He wanted to be the one she could turn to, the one she could lean on.

The strength of that feeling surprised him. He'd known the woman a little less than three days—but what eventful days they'd been. Between her initial attack with the bolt cutters and their escape from Brownlow's house, they'd forged a connection that belied the short amount of time they'd known each other.

Coming to Fernley had forced Hugh to take a good look at himself. He'd grown up despising his father for abandoning him, for starting a family with a younger, wealthier woman without even having the decency to break up with his mother first. He'd convinced himself he only wanted enough money to live a comfortable life, because he wasn't like his father. *He* wouldn't abandon his commitments for a few empty luxuries. He wouldn't ignore his firstborn for years because he'd decided to start over with his new wife and her overflowing bank account.

At least that's what Hugh had told himself until money had landed in his lap, and he'd actually considered signing the deal and getting out of here without doing any due diligence.

What if he hadn't met Ellie that evening at Lionel's? What if Spencer had chosen another night to spread the milkweed over the Davises' grazing pastures?

Hugh would have signed the contract and sold his soul to a devil in a down vest.

Staying here to help Ellie was Hugh proving to himself that he was nothing like his father. He'd refuse to participate in the resort. He'd turn down millions of dollars because he had integrity, and he was able to put other people's needs above his own.

Now he had to figure out how to do it in a way that wouldn't put him, Ellie, or her family in danger.

Sighing, Hugh took another sip of coffee and pulled out his phone. He dialed and put the device to his ear.

"Hi, Hugh," his mother, Faye, said after two rings. Her voice sounded clear, if a bit tired. "How are you doing?"

His shoulders relaxed. "I'm okay, Mom." They slipped into a familiar conversation, their weekly chat about everything and nothing that had gone on. His mother still lived in Arizona, in a small two-bedroom house that she'd scrimped and saved to buy after their life had spiraled.

She'd made a good life for Hugh despite what his father had done. She was steady and had a core of steel that never broke. She would adore Ellie.

Finally, his mother asked, "Have you figured out what you're going to do about the land?"

Hugh sighed. "There's some shady stuff going on. I'm not going to go through with the resort, but I have to figure out how to get out of the deal."

His mother hummed. "People'll be upset if you back out?"

"Very."

"That's just like your father, to dump that on you."

"You think that's why he left it to me? To make my life difficult?"

She was quiet for a moment, then clicked her tongue. "No, I don't think that. Your father was thoughtless, but he was very rarely malicious."

"How can you say that after what he did? He lied to you for years, Mom. He left us for his do-over family."

There was a short pause, and Hugh heard his mother sigh. Despite the trauma that they'd endured together, they had never talked about his father's betrayal. Not since Hugh had gone to a few therapy appointments as a child. The boiling mass of anger and bitterness that had grown in his heart was a secret he kept to himself. Maybe keeping it hidden was a way to protect his mother, to shield her from more hurt.

"He made a thousand small decisions that led to a big betrayal," Faye replied in a voice that sounded more tired than sad. "I don't think he ever really thought of the consequences until it was too late. Thoughtless, not malicious. He wasn't smart enough to be Machiavellian."

"But he just moved on and forgot about us." An old ache pulsed in his chest. This is why he hated talking about what his father had done. This is why he kept his own feelings locked up.

"Oh, Hugh," Faye said softly, "if he'd forgotten about you, he wouldn't have left you the land. He wouldn't have tried to reach out to you before he died."

Hugh jerked. "You knew about that?"

Faye let out a soft chuckle, half-rueful, half-bitter. "He sent me an email three or four years ago and tried to get me to talk to you on his behalf. I told him that wasn't my problem to fix."

"I hated him for so long," Hugh admitted quietly. "And now he's dead, and . . ."

"And you'll never get any answers."

A heavy sigh slipped through his lips. "Yeah."

"My sweet boy. It's okay to grieve someone even when you're angry with them. Just because you're sad they're gone doesn't mean your anger isn't valid."

Hugh stared at the opening in the wall in front of him, where he could see the diner's chefs moving around the kitchen. "Maybe I should have taken his calls. Maybe I'd know if he was involved in this mess with the resort, or I'd be more prepared . . ."

"You did what you could, when you could," Faye corrected gently. "Beating yourself up about it now serves no purpose."

Hugh rubbed his forehead, not wanting to think of his father as anything other than a deadbeat. Alex had chosen to play happy house with his new wife and children, chosen to start his new life before moving on from his old one. Once his secrets had been discovered, Alex had *left*, and he hadn't looked back. A few phone calls when Hugh was in his thirties didn't fix a lifetime of absence. "I wish I was as good a person as you are, Mom, because I just can't bring myself to forgive him."

That made her laugh. "I was furious for years, honey. But all my anger ever did was hurt me, hold me back."

"I sense you're trying to tell me something here."

When she spoke, Hugh could hear his mother's smile. "You'll figure it out. You're much cleverer than your father or I ever were. The answers are probably on that island, on the land he left behind for you. Once you figure out what you want to do, you'll be able to forgive your father and heal."

"Yeah."

"You don't sound convinced."

"That's because I'm not."

A soft chuckle. "Keep digging," Faye advised.

They hung up not long after, but those two words rang in Hugh's head, and he understood his mother's wisdom. He had to keep digging, keep searching for answers.

His father had tried to reconcile with Hugh in the years before he died. Hugh had pushed him away, and Alex had responded by willing him this land. It had felt like nothing more than a blatant attempt at emotional bribery.

Worse, though, was the feeling that Hugh was *still* getting the scraps of his father's love. Once, falling down an angst-ridden rabbit hole, Hugh had found his half siblings on social media accounts. He'd seen the mansions, the luxurious European vacations, the expensive cars. He'd seen his father, smiling, in his element, with his arm around his true favorite son against the backdrop of the white walls and azure water in Santorini.

Would Alex still have let Hugh inherit this property once the resort was built and the money was rolling in? He'd told Hugh about the inheritance when the acreage was just a forested, windblown property on a speck of an island off the coast of Washington State. If the heart attack hadn't taken him, would Alex have left the inheritance as it was, even if Hugh had continued to push him away?

Hugh doubted it.

And then there was the question of the criminal activity. Did his father know? Was he involved?

If his father had been party to the criminal schemes, it meant Alex had left the land to Hugh to protect his other family. It was one last potshot in Hugh's direction, a clear sign of how little his father had cared. *Here,* the land proclaimed. *Deal with this one last mess before you can move on.*

Or worse, maybe it was a message that Alex thought Hugh wouldn't care about the immoral nature of the deal. Maybe his father thought Hugh was just like him. Money was more important than morality.

But if his father *hadn't* known about the drug trafficking and money laundering . . . well, that was murkier. Was it a true attempt at reconciliation, and would it have still been Hugh's once it was worth a fortune?

As Hugh sat there, feeling warm sunlight against his shoulders through the windows at his back, he didn't know which option he wanted to come true. Hating his father was easier than forgiving him.

After leaving cash on the table and a bit of cold coffee at the bottom of his mug, Hugh exited the diner and headed down the slope to walk along the coast. He didn't know what to do, what to think.

"Hugh!"

Turning at the sound of his name, Hugh saw Jason jogging toward him with Ellie's dog at his side. Louie came bounding up to Hugh, demanding rubs, tail wagging furiously. Louie ducked his head under Hugh's hand and wiggled his body nearer.

"He likes you," Jason noted. "Usually he's a lot more hesitant with new people."

Hugh scratched Louie's head, remembering the look in Ellie's eyes when she'd hugged her dog the day before. He couldn't leave this island while Jason had Louie. He couldn't walk away from her or this mess. He straightened. "Cute dog." The words came out slightly strangled, so he cleared his throat to hide his discomfort. He hated lying, and standing here pretending to be cordial with Jason made him want to scream.

"Yeah," Jason said, smiling broadly. "Hey, listen, you're planning on coming to the Brownlow Foundation Gala on Saturday, right? All the other investors all really looking forward to meeting you. We'd love for you to stop by."

"Oh," Hugh answered noncommittally.

"Alex had been talking about coming out and meeting the team, but it unfortunately never happened. We'd really like to bring you into the fold. Saturday's event is the perfect chance to meet everyone."

"My dad never came out here?" Hugh asked. If that was true, it pointed toward Alex not knowing about the shady side of the project.

"We only met once, a little over a year ago," Jason said. "My lawyers had contacted him about the land, and he wanted to meet me in person." He smiled again and spread his arms. "The rest is history."

Hugh grunted. "Right."

"He was a good man," Jason said, and it sounded like he meant it. His smile widened. "So I'll see you Saturday?"

"Yeah," Hugh answered, not really meaning it. Saturday was three days away; he had time to come up with an excuse.

A woman had been walking down the sidewalk behind Jason carrying two coffees, and she came to a stop beside the other man. She smiled at Hugh, then tilted her head up at Jason in a quiet demand for a kiss. Jason leaned over and kissed her on the lips before taking his coffee.

"Hugh, this is Jade. Jade is our fundraising manager at the Brownlow Foundation. She's a genius. Aren't you, baby?"

So this was the woman Ellie had walked in on at her engagement party. The petite blonde woman smiled at Hugh, extending a hand, palm down. Not quite sure what to do with that, Hugh grasped her fingers and awkwardly shook them.

Jason hooked an arm around Jade's shoulders and tugged her close. "Hugh met Ellie," he said, a conspiratorial smile tugging at his lips. "I told him to stay away."

"She's insane," Jade said, shaking her head. "Certifiable. It's a little scary, actually. She came at me with a baseball bat after Jason broke up with her. That's why she got arrested."

The lie rankled. Hugh wondered how much of this Ellie had endured since her failed engagement party. He was a stranger to Jade, and she felt comfortable saying such nasty things about another woman. If they could say these things to him, what were they saying behind closed doors? What were they saying to friends and acquaintances?

No wonder Ellie had snapped.

It annoyed him that these two reveled in saying awful things about a woman who wasn't here to defend herself. It especially annoyed him because Ellie wasn't crazy or unreasonable. She was just . . . impulsive. Intense.

"Welp," Hugh answered, wanting to escape. "I'll leave you to it. I'll see you around."

He turned on his heels and walked back to the hotel, abandoning his idea of a coastal walk. There were two things he needed to do before he could leave the island and refuse to sign on to the project. First, he had to figure out if his father had been involved in the laundering. He'd comb through all the correspondence that he'd acquired between his father and Jason about the project. He wanted to go through it once more with fresh eyes. The clock was ticking; he'd have to tell Jason to kick rocks sooner or later, and he had a feeling he wouldn't be very welcome on the island after that. If he wanted answers about his father, he needed to get them as soon as possible.

And second, Hugh needed to talk to Ellie. After a conversation like the one he'd just had, all he could think about was the injustice of Jade's and Jason's accusations. Whatever she planned, he wanted to be involved. The only problem was that he still didn't have her phone number, and he wasn't exactly sure what he'd say to her once he did. The urge to help her was so strong that it hardly made sense.

And he had to tell her he owned the land next to her parents. He had to tell her he was part of the resort project.

But the thought of the land was so closely intertwined with the thought of his father, and Hugh hated the thought of Ellie lumping him in with Alex. Admitting the truth about the inheritance would be as good as saying his integrity was for sale.

So he'd start with the first item. He'd go through emails and documents, looking for clues of his father's guilt. Then he'd talk to Lionel about Ellie or see if he could find an excuse to drop by her parents' house.

But when he got to the Fernley Hotel, Ellie was sitting in the lobby. She stood as he walked through the sliding glass doors. The sun shone through the window to gild her hair and skin, glinting on the dangly earrings she wore again today. Her hair was down, and her eyes were solemn.

Hugh wanted to wrap her in his arms and kiss her until she laughed, and suddenly his feelings made sense. He wanted to help Ellie because he cared about her. Because she was magnetic, and funny, and considerate. He wanted to be one of the people for whom she'd go to war—as long as he'd get the privilege of jumping in front of bullets for her when she did.

He stumbled, hit by the force of his desires. Recovering quickly, Hugh came to a stop in front of her and said, "Hello, Ellie."

CHAPTER 16

Ellie had intended to wash her hands of Hugh Hartford. She'd gone home the night before and decided that although Hugh was a great accomplice, he was an even greater liability. He knew too much.

Worse than that, though, was the fact that Ellie had trusted him with all that knowledge. Trust was a good way of getting burned. Trust got you in trouble. She'd twisted and turned all night and decided that the only option was to cut Hugh out of this whole mess and protect herself.

Then she'd woken up to Etta James playing on the record player and her parents slow dancing in the living room, and Ellie's heart cracked in a thousand places. She cared so much about her parents and her grandmother, about Wynn and Spencer and Lionel—every one of the patchwork of people that made up this island—and a wave of anxiety nearly knocked her down. She needed *help*. The meeting with Fergus had thrown her, and the only other person who knew the whole truth was Hugh.

So here she was, standing in front of the man, looking up into his milk chocolate eyes, feeling that little knot in the pit of her stomach slowly loosen. Even the revulsion she felt at being here, in this hotel, just a few feet from *that* conference room, seemed to fade a little bit when he approached.

"Hi, Hugh," she replied, then tilted her head to the check-in desk. "They told me you were out, and I don't have your number, so I figured I'd wait."

He nodded. "What's up?"

"Can we go for a drive?"

He followed her to her car, and they set off toward the national park that hugged a few miles of the northeastern coast of the island. To get there, she had to pass Lionel's and Jason's driveways. When they passed the big mansion they'd broken into, she saw the same black SUV as yesterday parked on a side street. Slowing down to catch a glimpse of the driver, she saw the shape of a man, but nothing more.

Were these people involved with the charity, with the money laundering? Did Jason have dangerous associates? How deep did this thing go?

Heart thumping, Ellie kept driving. She'd hardly slept, and now she was seeing shady people at every turn. The SUV probably belonged to tourists or a new resident. This area was dotted with lots of properties, many of them uninhabited during the winter months. It could be a short-term rental. It could be someone's family member. Ellie needed to get a grip. She wanted peace and trees, not a reminder of the mess she'd stumbled upon. Quiet solitude would help her put into words what she planned to do.

Hugh took up a lot of room in the car. He'd pushed his seat all the way back, his knees spread in the space available. One arm leaned on the center console, while the other was propped on the window, his long fingers tapping to the beat of the classic rock radio station playing on the car's old sound system. His presence made it hard to breathe, so when they arrived at the national park, Ellie was glad to get out and gulp down a deep breath of air.

"There's a nice spot just ten minutes away," Ellie explained. "You don't mind walking, do you?"

Hugh shook his head and gestured for her to lead the way. The path through the trees wasn't wide enough for them to walk side by side, but she didn't mind Hugh's presence at her back. The forest was quiet and calm, sunlight poking through the clouds intermittently as they walked.

"I wanted to know your thoughts about yesterday," she finally said, thankful that she didn't have to look at his face. "About what we found out at Fergus's."

"I was surprised he admitted anything," Hugh said, his voice deep and velvety behind her.

"So you believe him?"

Hugh hummed, and Ellie glanced over her shoulder briefly. Dappled light danced over his shoulders as he shrugged. "Yes," he finally said. "We both saw the cash."

Ellie nodded, taking the left fork in the path that split off into a network of mountain biking trails and narrow animal tracks. They passed old madrone trees, with their stunning orange bark peeling in papery strips, and ended up on a rocky beach lined with driftwood.

Taking a seat on an ocean-bleached log, Ellie stared at the waves gently lapping the shore and tried to order her thoughts. She needed to word this conversation carefully.

Hugh watched her, then picked up a flat rock and skipped it over the calm water. The island was full of these secret spots, inlets and corners that made you feel like you were alone in the world with nothing but trees and moss and rocks and water to keep you company.

"What are you going to do?" Hugh inspected the shore for another flat stone. He found a satisfactory one, brushed off the gravelly sand clinging to it, and launched it at the water. It skipped six times before sinking. He turned to look at Ellie. "You still want to ruin Jason's life?"

Jaw set, she nodded. "More than anything. But I'm not stupid; I realize I'm in over my head."

"So what's the plan?" At her raised eyebrows, Hugh said, "I can tell you have a plan, Ellie. It's written all over your face."

It surprised her how easily he read her. She met his gaze and dipped her chin. "I have to go to the police with this. It's too big for me to take Jason down on my own; I don't know what other kind of illegal stuff he's into. I was hoping you'd come with me and make a statement too." No matter what she thought of Sheriff Jackson, she couldn't believe that he'd let something like this happen on Fernley. If the sheriff knew what Jason was doing, he'd stop it. Ellie had to believe that. Drugs, money laundering—it was too big to think the cops wouldn't help.

The hard part would be getting them to believe her.

She held her breath, unsure of how Hugh would respond. In those brief moments that hung in the air after the end of her sentence, she realized she wanted his support. She wanted to know Hugh was on her side. She wanted him to care.

He let out a breath. "I'm happy to hear you say that, Ellie. I think it's a good idea."

Hope blossomed in her chest. "So you'll come with me?"

A sharp nod. "Of course."

Then her phone rang. She dug it out of her cross-body bag and swiped when she saw Wynn's name on the screen. "Hello?"

"Ellie," Wynn panted. "Ellie, you have to come to your office. Someone just smashed the window and trashed it. Your dad took off to chase them down."

Ellie was out of breath by the time she made it to the car, Hugh panting equally hard behind her. They had sprinted the whole way back. Jumping into her hatchback, she waited for Hugh to click his belt and tore out of the parking lot in a spray of dust and gravel. The Corolla's little engine struggled up the hill leading to the main road, obviously unhappy with Ellie's aggressive driving. Ellie's knuckles were white as she gripped the steering wheel, taking turns far faster than she should.

Hugh was silent and stoic despite his death grip on the handle above the door.

They careened into Carlisle at top speed, turning onto a side street near the top of the town's big hill. It was the first time Ellie had driven down this street since the day she'd gotten out of jail after her arrest. She'd come here to grab her laptop and lock up, then avoided the building entirely. Ellie slammed on the brakes when she saw Wynn and Claude on the sidewalk in front of her old business's office.

Her heart wilted. She gripped the steering wheel, blinking rapidly, not processing what her eyes were telling her. Her breath started coming faster, her heart pounding uncomfortably hard against her rib cage. Panic sank its claws into her chest.

Then a warm hand slid onto her thigh, and she turned to see Hugh's eyes studying her. "You okay?" he asked, voice low.

She looked at the shattered front window and the door hanging on only one hinge. Through the starburst of broken glass, she spied carnage inside.

"I don't know," she answered honestly. His fingers squeezed her thigh.

They stepped out of the car and joined Wynn in front of the building. Claude came nearer and put a hand on Ellie's shoulder, tugging her into his chest. "We'll clean it up, Ellie-Belly." He hugged her tight, then let her pull away to look at the remains of the business that had once been her biggest source of pride.

Her files had been upended and scattered over the floor. Banners and reusable party decorations were destroyed. The door to the bathroom was open, and the toilet was overflowing with wads and wads of toilet paper. The walls had been spray-painted with insults and swear words, calling her a psycho, a crazy bitch.

Ellie took it all in without saying a word.

"I was driving by," Wynn said. "I stopped at the corner when I saw someone walk out of the building. Looked like a guy, but they were wearing a hoodie and I didn't recognize them. They tore the sign down and used it to smash the window, then took off."

"Bumped right into me." Claude took up the narrative, squeezing Ellie's shoulder. "I was just around the corner, and I heard Wynn shouting and honking."

Ellie frowned. "What were you doing here?"

Her father rolled his lips in and tilted his head from side to side. "Sometimes I come check on the building, Ellie. I know it's been hard on you, so every couple of days I just come down to make sure everything's okay. That way, when you decide to come back, there won't be any nasty surprises."

She looked at the big ol' nasty surprise in front of her, feeling raw.

"I'm sorry, Ellie." Wynn looked like she was about to cry.

Ellie shook her head at the cast Wynn kicked up. "Don't be. I'm glad you didn't chase anyone. You could've gotten hurt." She looked at the ankle again. "More hurt, I mean."

"I would've chased them if it wasn't for this stupid boot and the one-way street. I went around the block, but I lost them."

Ellie followed Wynn's hand gesture to the far end of the street, and—

"Hey!" She took off at a sprint toward the black SUV pulling away from the corner. "Hey! Stop!"

Her arms pumped as she sprinted, screaming like the crazy psycho everyone thought she was, but the car turned onto the nearest road and took off in a squeal of tires. Ellie slowed to a stop, anger and fear and worry warring within her. She watched the car disappear around a bend and dropped her shoulders. Her chest heaved, her lungs burned, and she let out a yell that held all her pent-up anger.

Who *was* that?

They were gone now, anyway. She had no choice but to turn back toward the decimated office that had once been her second home.

Hugh had taken off when Ellie had. Now he stood before her, searching her face. "What's wrong? Who was that?"

Ellie dropped her gaze. "I've been seeing that car . . . I don't know, Hugh. It could be no one. I don't know what's going on. I'm losing my mind."

They walked back, and Ellie shook her head when Wynn and Claude tried to ask her why she'd sprinted after the car. "I've been . . . seeing that car around." She cringed at how ridiculous it sounded. "I don't know. It's probably nothing."

"You think they did this?" Claude looked at her office, frowning. "But . . . why?"

"Jason—" Ellie stopped herself. Only Hugh knew about the money laundering. They didn't even know she'd been inside Jason's house. She wanted to tell her father and Wynn, but she was afraid of putting them in danger. Everything was happening too fast.

"You think this has something to do with the sheep?" Claude swung around to meet her gaze. "You think Jason did this? Ellie . . . we don't even know that he was behind our sheep getting sick. Not for sure."

"You don't believe Spencer?"

Claude sighed, rubbing his forehead. "Of course I believe Spencer. It's just . . . it's just too much. I don't know what to think. It's a big jump to think Jason would go from that to this." He pointed at the vandalism before them.

Was it, though? Ellie said nothing.

Hugh walked to the entrance of her building and propped the crooked door against the wall so it stayed open and upright. His shoes crunched on broken glass as he stepped inside, glancing back once to meet Ellie's gaze. His expression was unreadable.

Ellie was empty inside. She felt nothing. Her heartbeat had returned to normal, and she was no longer breathing heavily, but seeing that car had torn away the last scrap of reason from her mind. Everything was spiraling out of her control.

She was completely lost as she stared at the devastation around her. She'd already destroyed her business months ago, so this was just an extra kick in the ribs. After Ellie's disastrous engagement party, work had dried up between one day and the next. Every single booking she'd had got canceled, and suddenly she had no livelihood and an arrest on her record.

The bump in status she'd enjoyed as Jason Brownlow's fiancée had ended, and she'd crashed right back down to her proper place in Fernley society: at the bottom. Without Jason beside her, no one wanted to hire her to plan their events on the island. Her phone calls went unanswered, unless a client was asking for a refund.

It had made her feel like a fraud. An unworthy, idiotic fraud who hadn't understood that her success had been handed to her with a long list of conditions, which included remaining attached to the Brownlow name.

So, really, her business had failed six months ago. The physical destruction of her office didn't really make a difference. But it *hurt*.

"I'm calling the cops," her dad said.

Ellie nodded absently, following Hugh inside.

"This was your place?" he asked, taking in the mess, the insults, the vindictiveness of it all. This attack felt personal. It wasn't just some dumb kid letting off steam; this was a message.

Ellie met his gaze. "I was an event planner. I started working from home, but eventually I needed more space. This was my sanctuary."

"I figured." Hugh toed the corner of a sign that read ELLIE'S EVENTS. It had landed against her desk when the vandal had thrown it through the window, broken glass littered around it. The sign was badly chipped and had a big dent down the middle.

Ellie's eyes prickled. "Wynn designed that sign. She's a really good graphic designer," she said, like it even mattered. None of this mattered. Her business was already dead. She'd lost all her clients when she got arrested, been blacklisted by almost everyone on the island. And those who still supported her didn't have the money to hire event planners or the guts to go against a Brownlow.

But this attack—it hurt. It hurt a whole lot more than Ellie could handle.

Hugh's arms came around her, and she was engulfed in the warmth and safety of him. She wet his shirt with her tears and hoped he didn't notice, clinging to his back with stiff fingers.

"The police will find whoever did this," Hugh murmured. "Okay? We'll clean it up, and everything will be okay."

"I don't believe you, but thanks for saying it anyway." She sniffled, wiping her eyes with the heels of her hands before pulling away from him.

A broad hand slid over her jaw. Hugh swept his thumb across her cheek and let out a long sigh. His touch felt so nice it was almost painful. She wanted so badly to believe that he was as good as he seemed. He'd appeared in her life out of nowhere, and now he was the one person she felt she could lean on, the only one she could confide in.

It scared her how quickly her feelings had mushroomed. She barely even knew him.

But he touched her cheek and pulled her in for another hug, tucking her head under his chin and stroking her back in slow, smooth movements. They fit together.

The single whoop of a police siren pulled her out of her Hugh-induced daze. She turned to see a cruiser pull up outside the building, its lights flashing red and blue. Both front doors opened, and Sheriff Bill Jackson stepped out of the passenger seat, while his partner, Deputy Dave Hunt, got out from behind the wheel. They surveyed the damage from behind their aviator sunglasses, nodding to Claude as they strutted inside.

Bill Jackson was a slim man with broad shoulders and a uniform that might be a size too small. He carried himself with absolute confidence, with half-inch-long dark hair standing stick straight on his head and a thick mustache quivering above his upper lip. He policed Fernley like it was a hotbed of criminal activity instead of an island where most of his callouts related to troublemaking teens and stray sheep.

Although, judging by the discoveries Ellie had made lately, she wasn't so sure that assessment was true anymore. Fernley had a well-concealed underbelly.

Deputy Hunt was tall and wide, with rosy cheeks and a bulbous nose. He worshipped Bill Jackson, which was just the way Jackson liked it.

Sheriff Jackson hooked his thumbs into his utility belt and let out a whistle. "Quite the mess."

Ellie squared her shoulders and nodded. "Wynn and my dad saw the guy who did it. They called me."

"Did they, now." Jackson arched a brow over his aviators. He pulled the glasses off and gave Ellie a narrow-eyed look. "They didn't call us right away, then?"

"We called you as soon as Ellie got here," Claude answered from the sidewalk, looking in through the broken window.

Deputy Hunt kicked a piece of glass and popped the gum he was chewing. "Strange that you didn't call us first."

Ellie tamped down her frustration. "Shouldn't you take their statement or something?" She thrust her arm at Wynn and Claude. "I saw a car too. I've seen a car around for the past couple of days. A black SUV. I think it's them."

"'Them,'" Hunt repeated. He glanced at the sheriff, who gave him a subtle nod of approval.

"Yeah," Ellie said, panic nipping at her heels. "Well? Don't you want descriptions, statements?"

Jackson looked at his partner and pointed his thumb in Ellie's direction. "Tellin' us how to do our jobs."

"Where were you when this was going on, Davis?" Deputy Hunt asked, still wearing his shades despite the low light inside the office.

Ellie blinked. "I was in the national park."

"Interesting." Jackson crossed his arms.

Ellie wanted to scream. She didn't have time for small-town-cop peacocking. She didn't have time to stroke Sheriff Jackson's ego. She just wanted to be taken seriously. She wanted *one thing* to go right.

Deputy Hunt looked at his partner, then asked, "How long were you at the park?"

She shrugged, frustration increasing. "An hour or so? Aren't you going to ask Wynn about the guy who did this?"

"I can tell you what he was wearing," Wynn supplied.

Jackson's mustache quivered. "I'm asking the questions here. Why did you go to the park?"

Ellie's chest burned. Memories flooded her from the last time Jackson had interviewed her. She'd been angry and scared and hurt, and he'd treated her like a murderer. They hadn't even given her any medical attention before launching into an interrogation. Her humiliation had been so complete, so all encompassing. It had swallowed her whole. The world crowded in on her, broken glass and trashed belongings swimming in her peripheral vision.

Even now, when she was clearly the victim, she was being treated with suspicion.

Hugh spoke in a low, rumbling voice. "I was with Ellie for the past couple of hours. Whatever you're suggesting, it's off base."

Ellie swiveled her head to stare at him, shocked to see a muscle feathering in his cheek. Hugh was very, very angry.

A petal unfurled in her chest, soft and slow, at the sight of this great big man coming to her defense.

Both cops turned to look at him. Hunt popped his gum. Jackson shifted his hands to his hips, just above his gun. She could almost see the green-and-blue feathers poking out from behind the sheriff's shoulders, quivering gently. In a moment, the peacock's train would fan out behind him and start rattling menacingly.

"Can we focus on the break-in?" Ellie said, head beginning to pound.

"You got cameras?" Jackson asked, eyes still on Hugh.

Ellie shook her head. "No."

Jackson swung his gaze to her. He shrugged, then turned to Wynn. He took a quick description of the perpetrator, jotting down a few words, then whistled for Deputy Hunt to follow him to the car, and they were gone.

Hugh watched them, vibrating with rage. "That's it? That's what the cops are doing about this?" He spun around to look at the carnage, finally meeting Ellie's gaze.

And she knew—she knew her earlier plan would never work. She couldn't go to the Fernley police with the information she'd gathered. Not after this.

If they didn't help her in the face of this much vandalism, they'd never help her. She could phone a tip to the FBI—but then what? They'd investigate, they might discover something, but how long would it take? Months? Years?

The Fernley Luxury Resort and Spa would be built by then. Her parents would lose their land; the pressure Jason was putting on them would only increase. The island would become a cesspit of crime, and the entire community would be at risk.

And what if the authorities *didn't* investigate? What if Ellie sat on her hands for all those months and years, watched her parents crumble to the pressure and lose their land . . . and nothing came of it?

If Ellie was going to stop Jason Brownlow from building his resort, she'd have to do it herself.

"Let's clean this up, Ellie-Belly," Claude said, his face grim. Ellie nodded and got to work.

Wynn sat and kept them company, straightening paperwork and doing tasks she could at the desk, while Ellie and Hugh started taking care of the glass.

Claude left for a while and returned with Helen and a bunch of cleaning and construction supplies, and they all got to work fixing the place up. Her family, picking up the pieces once more. She didn't deserve them.

Ellie stared at the spray paint on the walls. Hugh walked up beside her and read the words that had been branded there.

"I lost all my clients after the arrest," she told him, half to fill the silence and half because this felt like the true end of her business, and she needed to say it out loud. It felt almost like mourning to see all her hard work destroyed so brutally, grief of a kind she'd never experienced before. "The business was already dead, but this still hurts. This building was an early inheritance from my grandma. She told me she wanted to be able to watch me succeed while she was still alive." She gave him a sad smile. "Didn't exactly work out."

"It's not over." Hugh's hand brushed her lower back.

"Look around, Hugh." She shook her head. "The only thing I can do now is ruin Jason's life. Revenge is all that's left. There's nothing else for me here."

A drill whirred as Ellie's father put a piece of plywood over one half of the window opening. He'd knocked out all the broken glass, so all that was left was a gaping hole. Hugh moved outside to help him, and Ellie exchanged a glance with Wynn. Her best friend just gave her a sympathetic smile. Ellie walked over to the desk to ask for a hug—and froze.

She reached for a scrap of fabric on the corner of the desk. It was an ankle sock just like the one she'd dropped over the fence to give to Louie. In fact, it was the exact ankle sock she'd dropped over the fence to give to Louie. Her heart pounded. Her vision narrowed. From a distance, she heard Wynn call her name, but all she could do was stare at the sock.

In some corner of her mind, she'd known Jason was behind the vandalism here. But as she rubbed her fingers over the fabric, Ellie realized she still hadn't quite believed it.

Now she knew. Jason had done this as a warning—or a threat.

A scuff on the floor drew her attention to the entry, where Hugh stared at the sock with murder in his eyes. He lifted his gaze to hers. Fear was a writhing snake in her gut, but Hugh's face was calm, determined. She slipped the sock into her pocket and touched Wynn's shoulder.

"I'm okay," she said and then hugged her friend.

Later, after Claude and Helen had gone home and Wynn had been called away, Ellie swept up the last of the mess on her office floor and glanced at Hugh. "I have to tell my family what's going on before I do anything else. This involves them now. I have to tell them about what we found."

"I'm in," Hugh said quietly. "Whatever it is, I'm there, Ellie."

After he said that, Ellie couldn't speak for a while.

STEP THREE: STRATEGIC OFFENSIVE MANEUVERS

CHAPTER 17

Ellie and Hugh arrived at her parents' house a short while later. She was glad that he was beside her, grateful to have someone who knew everything that was going on. It felt less daunting to have someone by her side when she spoke to her family about what they'd discovered over the past couple of days.

As they stopped in front of her parents' house, Ellie glanced at Hugh and wondered if she could truly trust him. They barely knew each other, but they'd already been through so much. The way he'd comforted her in her office couldn't have been false . . . could it? It scared her to rely on someone so quickly. Opening up to Jason had ended in disaster.

The front door opened when Ellie parked, her grandmother standing in the doorway. Mabel looked worried, but her eyes brightened when she saw Hugh, and she waved vigorously like he was a long-lost friend. "Come in!" Mabel called out. "Come in, come in! Helen, Ellie brought the boy with her!"

Ellie's face turned hot. She stole a glance at Hugh to see his reaction and was relieved to see he looked amused rather than horrified. Her family was loony, but they were hers, and they were lovely. She gave Mabel a kiss on her soft, wrinkled cheek and slipped inside.

"Hugh!" Claude boomed, striding forward to shake hands with violent pumping actions. "Didn't know you'd be coming by after the cleanup. It was nice of you to help, by the way, very nice of you. I'm sure Ellie appreciated it. Can I get you anything? What are you in the mood to listen to? No, don't sit there. Here, this side of the couch. The sound is best when you sit right here in front of the speakers. Comfortable? Good. Okay, Ellie, what should I put on?"

"I don't know, Dad. I'm not sure we need a soundtrack for this conversation."

"Nonsense."

"Hi, Ellie-Belly," Helen called out from the kitchen. "I'm just putting out some snacks. Does Hugh have any dietary restrictions?"

It was strange having a man in her parents' house again. Jason had always looked down on her family. He'd always been snide and slightly conceited, and Ellie, being immature and naive, had accepted his judgment. She'd stopped bringing him around here, stopped having so many family dinners, even though she'd missed them dearly. She'd made herself small to fit into the box her ex had created.

But Ellie wasn't that person anymore. She'd been dragged through the muck and had her reputation destroyed—and her family still loved her despite it all.

As her family rushed around Hugh like he was visiting royalty, Ellie realized she'd been embarrassed of them before. She'd wanted to hide them away, to put some distance between their reputation and hers. She'd wanted so badly to be accepted by Jason and his peers that she'd looked down on her own family. Suddenly, she was ashamed of herself for it.

Her parents had been vocal protesters in the Fernley counterculture in the seventies and eighties. They'd fought for environmental protection on the island, had set fire to the mayor's house, had marched in the streets and sung "Kumbaya" and made their presence known. They'd been *loud*. Especially her mother.

What was there to be ashamed of? Ellie should've been *proud*. Her family fought for what they believed in. They didn't back down. Just like Ellie.

Where the hell did she think she'd gotten it from?

She'd spent so long trying to deny her family's past that she hadn't realized they were right all along.

But they were also *very* excited by Hugh's presence. Her grandmother was flapping around, barking out orders to her mother in the kitchen. Her dad was pondering his music collection like the future of the country rested on his choice.

Slightly nervous to see Hugh's reaction to their antics, she met his gaze. If he judged her family harshly, it would break her heart. No matter what he'd said before, no matter how much support he'd promised, if he rejected her family's advances, she'd never forgive him.

He leaned back on the couch and slung an arm over the back of it, looking slightly oversize for the small sofa—and he grinned. "I'll eat anything."

Relief was a cool breeze blowing over Ellie's skin. "He'll eat anything!" she called out to her mother.

"Great!" Helen came breezing in with a tray of bread, crackers, spreads, fruit, cheese, and nuts. The tray was an antique that had belonged to Claude's mother, a wooden board with a floral inlay. Helen set the whole thing down and beamed at Hugh. "Eat, eat!"

Mabel dragged a chair over to sit next to Hugh, crossing her legs and leaning over to stare at him. "Not a bad-looking man you've got here, Ellie. Certainly an upgrade from the previous model."

That was a comment Ellie wasn't going to acknowledge. She took a seat next to Hugh and grabbed a grape as her father put on an old album by B. B. King. Ah, so her father was more stressed than he was letting on. The blues was Claude's comfort music.

"How are you holding up, Ellie?" Helen asked.

Ellie shrugged. "Fine, considering."

"She'd be a lot better if the police on this island were worth a damn," Mabel grumbled. "Isn't that right, Hugh?"

"Yes, ma'am."

Mabel grunted and patted Hugh's arm, satisfied.

"I have something to tell you," Ellie said, reaching for another grape, "but you have to promise not to get mad."

Her parents exchanged a glance, and it was her father who spoke. "We'll do our best, Ellie."

"Hugh and I went to Jason's house yesterday. We found a duffel bag full of cash."

Helen stiffened on the couch beside Ellie. Mabel made a squeaking noise, and Claude's gaze sharpened.

"It was Fergus O'Hara's," Ellie continued, "and he admitted to us that he's been laundering money through the Brownlow Foundation. The new resort is going to be used to expand their operations."

Outraged noises exploded out of everyone in the room. Ellie froze in her seat until Hugh's hand appeared on her upper back like he'd been able to sense her discomfort. His thumb carved a slow track between her shoulder blades, soothing away her anxiety.

"How did you get Fergus to admit to that?" Claude asked.

"She got him to rub his last two brain cells together," Mable cut in, snorting.

Ellie huffed and spread her hands. "Is that important? I think he was telling the truth."

Her mother leaned back on the couch and stared at the ceiling. "We have to tell the police."

"I *can't*," Ellie answered. "Dad, you saw how Sheriff Jackson spoke to me, right? What would I do, tell him I broke into Jason's house? Ask him to launch a forensic financial investigation on Jason's charity? They're going to think what everyone thinks—that I'm just some crazy ex-girlfriend out for revenge."

"We'll phone in a tip to the authorities," Helen suggested.

Claude looked lost. "What authorities?"

"The FBI?" Helen suggested, shrugging. "The . . . the government?"

Ellie shook her head. "How long's that going to take to pan out? If ever? By the time they investigate, he'll have half the island flattened and turned into his own personal amusement park for rich people."

Hugh made a noise, and everyone turned to look at him. He looked slightly startled at the attention and said, "So, um, about the resort . . ."

"Everyone involved in that thing is a criminal, as far as I'm concerned," Ellie said when he didn't finish his sentence. She gritted her teeth. "Who would actually agree to a project like that? Only money-hungry leeches, that's who. Don't you think?"

The movement of Hugh's thumb stopped between her shoulder blades. He pulled his hand away, placing it on the back of the sofa behind her. When Hugh looked at her, his eyes were full of worry and hurt and something like grief. "Yeah," he finally answered, dropping his gaze to the floor. "I agree completely."

"This isn't just about the sheep anymore," Ellie said. "This is about the whole island." She pulled out the sock. "When Hugh and I went to Jason's place, I left a sock for Louie."

"You encourage that dog to steal socks, Ellie," her mother grumbled, clicking her tongue.

"I found it on my desk this afternoon."

All eyes landed on the sock.

Claude blew out a breath. "You're saying Jason did that. He wrecked your office."

Ellie nodded. "And I can't use this to prove it to the cops, because I'll be admitting to breaking into his house." She took a deep breath. "Jason is willing to kill your sheep, wreck my office, use his charity to launder money, and get involved with drug trafficking. He roped in Spencer and Fergus—"

"Fergus might have instigated the drug thing," Helen cut in.

"You think he'd come up with a plan like that all on his own?" Mabel snorted. "Not likely."

"Where will it end?" Ellie said. "I have to stop him. Or at least I have to expose him. Everyone on Fernley should *know* about this. The residents of this island have a right to learn the truth."

This wasn't about her dog, or her parents' sheep, or her parents' land, or even the resort development. This was about the island as a whole.

"They've known the truth about what Jason did to you this whole time," Claude cut in angrily, surprising Ellie with his vehemence. "Did that change anything? Did that make people turn their backs on him, after how he treated you?"

When Hugh's hand slid back onto Ellie's shoulder and squeezed the place where her neck met her shoulder, the tension in her body eased. She no longer felt alone—hadn't felt alone since Hugh showed up in her life.

"Maybe the community needs something bigger than him cheating on me to come to terms with Jason's true character. They need to be smacked in the face with his rottenness."

"I really think we should just call the authorities," Helen insisted. She was looking at her phone. "The FBI have a tip line. We can call right now!"

Of all the people in the world to be pushing them *not* to take things into their own hands, it had to be Ellie's mother, the woman who had raged and rampaged on the island for all her youth.

"There's no *time*, Mom," Ellie said. "I need to stop him *now*. Before construction starts. Before he pushes you out of your home. And what are you going to say? 'My daughter's ex-fiancé threatened her with her own sock'? That'll go over well."

Helen huffed, staring at her phone. Her lips were pinched.

Ellie straightened as an idea sparked. "The gala." She jumped off the couch and hurried to the kitchen, then pulled the flyer off the corkboard. It was just as sleek and pretentious as the last time she'd looked at it, but this time, her lips curled into a smile.

Walking back to the living room, she held up the brochure. "This isn't just a charity event; it's the time when Jason is going to pitch his resort to all the richest people on the island. He's been planning it for a year. I helped him come up with the idea. He has people flying in from all over to attend this thing."

Mabel leaned forward, blue eyes sparkling. "You want to expose him in front of all his potential investors."

"What better time to blow up the project before it gets off the ground?" Ellie let out a breathless chuckle and shook the glossy piece of paper. "This is it. This event is where it all ends."

Hugh's throat was so tight he could hardly swallow past the constriction. The words were on the tip of his tongue; all he had to do was admit that he owned the land next door and tell them that he had no intention of signing the deal his father had negotiated with Jason. The resort was dead in the water already.

But that would be admitting he was nothing more than a money-hungry leech. He'd have to look Ellie in the eyes and tell her what had brought him to this island—and it wasn't a desire to reconnect with his grumpy old boat mechanic of an uncle. He'd have to defend himself and explain that he was nothing like his father, even if his father had seen fit to will him that land and, by extension, the resort deal.

The problem was, Hugh didn't know if he'd be telling the truth. He *had* wanted the money from the resort deal. When he'd disembarked from the ferry a few days ago, he'd already spent that money in his mind, on his mother's mortgage and his own music studio.

He'd known Ellie for four days. Less than a hundred hours. Hugh had spent more time poring over the wills and deeds and legal documents pertaining to his inheritance than the entirety of his relationship with Ellie, but it was enough. He already knew he had to kill the deal with Jason as soon as possible, if only to prove to her—to himself—that his integrity wasn't for sale.

But would she believe that once she knew what he'd inherited?

Whether or not his father knew about the criminal activities planned for the resort no longer mattered. His father was dead—what did it change whether he was a big piece of shit or a little piece of shit? Either way, he'd abandoned Hugh and his mother. Alex had deserted them for his do-over family, and Hugh had been left out in the cold, belated attempts at reconciliation or no.

It was over. He was never getting those years back. He had to let himself heal from that pain, whether or not his father was guilty of more crimes. Maybe his father had willed him the land as a bribe to try to wriggle his way into Hugh's life. Did it matter? It hadn't worked.

One thing he knew for sure was that he couldn't keep lying to Ellie. It was a lie by omission, and he barely knew the woman, but it was time he came clean.

Sitting in her parents' cozy living room, surrounded by the palpable love that existed between each member of Ellie's family, Hugh felt a sense of peace he'd never experienced before. This was a family who had each other's backs. They accepted each other, flaws and all, and were ready to go to war for Ellie. He wanted to be part of it. Everything he'd learned about Ellie drew him closer to her, made him want more.

As he listened to Ellie's mad genius while she laid out her plan for the Brownlow Foundation Gala, Hugh's heart expanded in his chest. He'd give her the death of the resort as a present. He'd go to Jason and tell him he wasn't signing any contract, and this whole mess would be over. Then, when he told her about the land and the resort deal, it wouldn't feel like he was lying when he said he didn't care about the money.

After Ellie had laid out the broad strokes of her plan, she offered to drive him back to town. They walked outside, and Hugh veered off to look at one of the small pastures where sheep grazed. He leaned against the fence and watched the animals, who watched him back.

Ellie came to stand beside him. "My parents started with just one sheep about seven years ago, after they'd retired from their jobs. My dad was a high school science teacher, and my mom was the school nurse. They've been much happier since they started doing this, but this whole mess is stressing them out. They won't show it, but I can tell. My dad walks the pastures every day to make sure they're clear. He jumps when he hears noises outside. My mom looks like she hasn't slept right in six weeks."

A sheep let out a baa, as if it were agreeing with Ellie's words.

Hugh slid his hand over so it covered Ellie's on top of the fence. It surprised him how easy it was for him to touch her, how right it felt to be beside her. He'd never felt so comfortable with another person before. He'd spent his life suspicious of others, waiting for them to turn around and betray him. It wasn't like that with Ellie. She'd unlocked some secret compartment of his heart and shown him everything he was missing.

And he'd only known her four *days*. How much better could life be with her after four weeks? Four years? Four decades?

He squeezed her hand. "It'll be over soon."

She was quiet for a beat, then turned her head to glance at him. Dusk settled over the hollows of her face as she searched Hugh's eyes. "You really believe that?"

Hugh nodded. "I'm sure of it."

"You probably shouldn't help me, you know," she said, turning her palm around so it was against his. She curled her fingers around to grip his hand and turned back toward the sheep. "I know I'm reckless, and I'm happy to ruin my own life, but you have so much more to lose than I do. You should just leave this island and never look back."

Yes, he probably should do that. But he wasn't going to. "That's not an option anymore," he told her.

In the falling dark, he thought he saw the corner of her lips curl into a tiny smile.

Ellie drove him back to the hotel and parked near the lobby door. Hugh met her gaze and had the impression he'd just stepped into a new phase of his life. He slid a hand over her cheek and pulled her in for a kiss, unable to resist the temptation.

This woman was under his skin. She was fire and lightning given human form, and he was hooked on her. Being with Ellie made Hugh feel alive. It made him think there was more to life than just music and a bleak future. She made him think about the future, point blank. He kissed her softly, trying to convey the strength of his feelings, then pulled away to press his forehead against hers. It made no sense to be this infatuated this quickly. It threw him, confused him, rocked him to his core.

"I'll see you tomorrow," he said.

She nodded. "Yeah."

They finally exchanged phone numbers, and then Hugh got out of the car and watched her drive away. He waited until she was out of sight before heading to his rental vehicle, then got on the road toward Jason Brownlow's house.

He'd waited four days too long. It was time to torch the contract his father had written.

CHAPTER 18

The porch light shone down in a cone of buttery yellow, illuminating the welcome mat where Hugh had first kissed Ellie. He still felt the whisper of her lips on his from their earlier kiss, the gentle touch of her fingertips against the side of his neck.

He was doing the right thing. It was impulsive to blow up this partnership after four days, especially after three months of research and due diligence, but Hugh couldn't go on any longer without taking action. He wouldn't participate in criminal activities, and even if that hadn't been a factor, he wouldn't partner with someone who bullied Ellie and her family.

After parking the car, Hugh took a deep breath and headed for the front door. It only took a few moments for it to open after he'd rung the doorbell.

Jade stood in the opening, smiling in surprise. "Hugh! How lovely to see you. Is Jason expecting you?"

"Uh—no. Sorry." Hugh resisted the urge to rub the back of his neck. He tried to keep his muscles relaxed, to avoid betraying the tension writhing in his gut.

"Come on in," she said, opening the door wider. "Can I get you a drink? Coffee? Tea? Beer? Water?"

"Water is great, thanks." Hugh wondered if Ellie knew that Jason had already moved his affair partner into his house. The woman led him to the front living room, where he'd spied on Jason through the window the day before. Had it only been a day? It felt like an eon.

Jade gestured to a chair and disappeared down the hallway, calling out for Jason. A few moments later, Jason appeared. "Hugh," he boomed, smiling. "How can I help you?"

They shook hands, and Hugh said, "I was hoping to talk to you about the resort project."

"Oh?" He sat down in front of the large coffee table, leaning back to spread his arms across the tops of the cushions. Hugh sat in the armchair to his left, girding himself for the conversation that would follow.

"Here we go!" Jade singsonged as she entered with ice water. She set the glasses down, then fetched coasters from the side table to slip them under both glasses. "Can I get you boys anything else?"

Jason took a sip of water and smiled at his girlfriend. "No thanks, honey. That's all." His tone was mildly dismissive, and when he set his glass down, it was slightly to the left of the coaster, directly on the wood table.

Hugh looked at the condensation-covered glass, slowly dripping water onto the nice timber table, and remembered what Ellie had said about coasters in her own relationship. He lifted his gaze and saw Jade staring at the glass on the table, her smile slightly frozen on her face. Then she recovered and said, "Okey dokey! Holler if you need anything!" and swept out of the room.

It was odd that such a small thing could feel like such a big revelation to Hugh. He'd seen the man use a coaster when he was on his own, but he purposefully avoided doing so when it had been put there by someone else. It was a tiny, infinitesimal power play that probably would have gone unnoticed had Ellie not mentioned it.

His resolve strengthened. He met the other man's gaze and decided to be as direct as possible: "I've decided not to go ahead with the project."

Jason blinked. "I'm sorry—what?"

"I've reviewed everything, and I've decided I don't want to be involved in the resort project. I understand that this isn't what you wanted to hear, and I apologize for disappointing you." He hated apologizing to this man, but he made his voice as neutral and intractable as possible. He wanted it to be clear that although he was being polite, he would not change his mind.

Jason laughed. "Hugh! Don't be ridiculous. You're leaving millions of dollars on the table. Your land is too steep for farming and too wooded for grazing. It's worthless without the resort."

"Regardless, I've made my decision."

"Why?"

Hugh wanted to be careful. He wasn't afraid of Jason, but he had no idea what the other man was capable of. He spread his arms. "I reviewed the documents and decided the risks are too high for me."

"Risks? What risks? We're building a money-printing machine, Hugh."

Oh, Hugh knew that. He held the other man's gaze. "I understand your disappointment, which is why I wanted to tell you in person."

Jason's face darkened. He leaned his elbows on his knees and looked Hugh in the eyes, his gaze flinty. The jovial mask had been ripped away, revealing the expression of a man Hugh had never met. "You're making a mistake, Hartford. You'll regret this." The words were spoken in a low voice, the menace in them clear.

"Maybe," he replied. "But I don't think so."

"Is this because of Ellie Davis? I know you've been hanging around with her." He leaned back, straightening the collar of his shirt. "People talk on this island, you know. Not much happens that I don't find out about eventually."

Hugh paused. Jason was bluffing, surely. "This has nothing to do with anyone but me," he said.

"Have you fucked her yet?"

"Excuse me?" Hugh growled before he could stop himself.

Jason spread his palms, a good old boy grin spreading over his lips. "I get it, man. She was good for a while."

Hugh stayed silent and regulated his breathing. If he spoke, he was afraid of what would come out.

"Look, I've been there." Jason sounded understanding, which made Hugh want to wrap his hands around the other man's neck and squeeze. Jason looked like he could tell what Hugh was thinking, and he smiled a lizard smile. "It happens. The crazy ones do that to a man. But no pussy is good enough to turn your back on millions of dollars. You know that. We both do. Take a couple of nights, come to the gala, and we'll talk."

"We don't need to talk. I'm out." It was an effort to keep his voice steady, but he just about managed. "I know this is a disappointment for you. Maybe your next project will work out."

Jason threw his head back and laughed. "You think this is the end? It's the end for you—not for me." Jason's lips were still curved as he took in Hugh's confusion. "The resort project *will* go ahead. If I have to dredge up the entire coast of Fernley, I'll do it. I have the land. I have the money. I have the support. Then your property value will plummet, because who wants to live right next to a busy hotel? If you refuse to sign the deal your father negotiated, you're not just losing out on the cash cow that this resort will be. You're destroying any chance at making anything of yourself."

Hugh stood. "So be it."

"Your father would be disappointed in you."

Once upon a time, that comment might have hurt Hugh. It would have cut to the core of what had always bothered him about his father's abandonment: that he wasn't enough, he'd never be enough. But today, the words bounced off him and clattered to the floor.

For once in his life, he knew he was making the right decision— and he was doing it for someone else.

Calm draped over him like a comforting blanket. Nothing this man could say would bother him. "Go fuck yourself, Jason."

Jason laughed, and it was an ugly sound. "Get out of my house. Oh, and tell Ellie I said hi."

The door loomed in front of Hugh, its handle cool under his fingertips when he turned around and asked, "Ellie's office—was that you?"

Jason's blond eyebrow arched. He looked bored. "Would it matter if it was?"

"Yes."

A snort. A shrug. "Maybe it's a good thing this deal fell through. I don't think we would have worked well together."

Hugh walked out the door and heard it slam behind him. A distant bark echoed in the silent forest, and Hugh knew this wasn't over. Louie was still here. Jason was still building the resort. Ellie was still in Jason's sights.

After that conversation, Hugh knew exactly where he stood. He'd help Ellie get her dog—and he'd help her get even.

CHAPTER 19

Ellie met Hugh at the ferry terminal the next morning. She'd already parked and bought a couple of coffees, so she was sitting on a bench watching when he walked down the hill. His strides ate up the distance between them, movements full of relaxed grace. The morning sunshine gleamed on his dark hair. He wore jeans and a dark tee that clung lovingly to his shoulders and arms. His eyes were pale in the light that bounced off the water behind Ellie, his lips curving into a conspiratorial smile. He was truly a beautiful man.

"Ready?" he asked when he came to a stop in front of her.

Ellie presented him with the coffee she'd purchased for him. "Ready."

Today was the first step in her plan to take Jason down, once and for all. She'd gather all the evidence she could today and tomorrow, get Louie back on Saturday morning, then ruin Jason's life on Saturday evening, once her dog was safe at home. Once she had Louie back, there'd be nothing to stop her.

Her scheme was risky. It had a high chance of failure, and she was going up against the most powerful family on the island. But as far as Ellie was concerned, it was high time someone stood up to the Brownlows. She needed to cut out the rot so the island could heal.

The morning ferry had already departed, so the terminal would be relatively deserted until the afternoon. She led him past the handful of shops and stalls inside the terminal to a door marked *Staff Only*. Knocking loudly, she waited, but no one answered. "Maybe he's on the ramp," she said, and she led Hugh back outside and down toward the water.

The ferry terminal had a few long lanes where people parked their cars as they waited to drive onto the ferry, all currently empty of vehicles. They found Spencer by one of the barricades, fiddling with a lock. The blond man looked up when they approached and smiled broadly. "Ellie!"

"Hiya, Spence," she answered with a grin. "You remember Hugh? He's the one who tackled you to the ground and tied your hands together like he was competing in a rodeo."

Hugh glowered at her, which made her laugh. He turned to the other man and extended a hand. "Sorry about that, Spencer. I thought you were dangerous. Truce?"

Spencer just smiled and shook Hugh's hand. "Of course. Maybe you could help me with this as repayment. I just need you to hold the gate up a few inches so I can fix the latch."

Hugh positioned himself and lifted the steel gate, his biceps straining against the fabric of his tee. His forearm muscles were corded, flexing with effort as he held the heavy metal gate in place. Even his leg muscles fought against the confines of his jeans. It was obscene. Ellie had to look away.

Hugh looked down at the waves crashing against the pier's pillars. "Pretty important gate, huh? Wouldn't want people falling down there when a ferry's nearby."

Spencer's face had gone red from exertion as he struggled with the half-rusted latch. "Oh no," he replied absentmindedly. "They'd probably die in the ferry's propellers, and then we'd have a real mess on our hands." He grunted, bending the latch in place to secure it. "There. Thanks, Hugh." He beamed at the other man and wiped his hands on a rag. "Now, what can I do for you?"

"Well," Ellie started. "I need a favor."

"Anything," Spencer replied. "After what I did to your parents' sheep, I'll do anything I can to fix it."

A while later, Ellie and Hugh left the ferry terminal side by side and headed up the hill to where Ellie had parked her car. Spring had officially arrived in Carlisle, seemingly overnight. Flower baskets hung from every lamppost, their colorful blooms fluttering in the breeze. More flowers were bursting from decorative planters that lined the sidewalks at even intervals. The town was ready to accept its influx of tourists with open arms.

The scent of seaweed overlaid with floral perfume wrapped itself around Ellie, reminding her of all the things she loved about this island, about her home. After a dreary, drizzly winter, Fernley was the most wonderful place to spend the summer. There was the pie-baking contest and the jazz festival and the art exhibitions. Live music spilled from every venue multiple nights per week, and in the town square, a gigantic open-air cinema played movies every Friday and Saturday evening. The entire island came to life, and Ellie could feel the first stirrings of that beautiful season.

The truth was, Ellie didn't want to leave. She'd only felt like she had to—she'd had no other choice. But now . . . "I'm still trying to figure out why you're helping me with all this." Ellie stole a glance at the man beside her, tracing the line of his jaw with her gaze.

"Maybe I'm an adrenaline junkie."

She snorted. "Right."

"Maybe getting hit in the head with a pair of bolt cutters permanently damaged something in my brain."

She laughed harder. "That sounds more likely. It would explain a lot, actually."

He grinned, then glanced farther up the street and pointed to a shop with a pale-blue sign out front. "You want ice cream?"

Ellie followed his gaze and let out a squeak. "Scoopz is open! *Ohmigod.* Yes, I want ice cream!" She grabbed Hugh's arm and dragged him up the hill. "This place only opens for the summer months. It's the best. Rhonda makes all the ice cream herself, and she has specialty flavors all the time. She's a genius."

They entered the tiny ice cream shop just as a red-haired woman slipped a massive tub of ice cream into the slot open for it in the display freezer. Rhonda was a short, curvy woman of about fifty. She had four children, and her ice cream shop had been legendary since she'd opened it two and a half decades ago. People came to the island specifically for a cone. She beamed at the two of them. "Ellie! You're my first customer of the year. That's good luck, you know."

"I'm going to need it," Ellie said with a grin. "Rhonda, meet Hugh. Hugh, this is Rhonda Roberts. Everyone agrees that she should have won the Fernley Com-Pie-Tition by a landslide. And you've tried Mary O'Hara's pie, so you know I'm telling the truth."

"She fed you that monstrosity," Rhonda commiserated, shaking her head. "I'm so, so sorry."

Hugh grinned, and Ellie nearly dropped her panties on instinct. Maybe she should knock herself in the head with a pair of bolt cutters to see if it would help. Hugh nodded to Rhonda. "It was pretty terrible."

"Well, losing wasn't all bad," Rhonda answered, grabbing wooden sample spoons from a bowl and then loading them up with ice cream from one of the tubs. "I got so frustrated after the ceremony that I dumped the whole pie into a tub of ice cream and mixed it up. This was the result."

They tasted her apple pie ice cream, and Ellie nearly had an orgasm right there in the store. (She really should not have been thinking about orgasms with Hugh standing right there, but Rhonda's ice cream was that good.) Vanilla ice cream dotted with black specks from actual vanilla beans, delicious pie crust, and delicately spiced filling all came together to create something magical. They both got double-scoop cones of her new creation.

When Rhonda handed Ellie her cone over the counter, she gave Ellie a wink. "I like him," she said quietly, tilting her head toward Hugh. "I always knew you could do better than Jason."

Ellie blinked. Just like Gemma, Rhonda was telling her she was on her side. Maybe the whole island wasn't against her. Maybe they never had been.

Ellie and Hugh stepped out onto the sidewalk and headed back down the hill toward the boardwalk near the water. They ate their ice cream and enjoyed the sun warming their skin, walking slowly as the sights and sounds of Carlisle kept them company. They wandered down to a tiny crescent beach lined with washed-up logs and sun-dried seaweed, taking a seat on one of the pieces of driftwood. A seagull stared at them curiously for a moment—very intent on their cones of ice cream—then flapped away.

"What do you think of Fernley?" Ellie finally asked, licking a drip of ice cream before it reached her hand.

Hugh watched the movement of her tongue for a moment. Then he blinked and looked away in an awkward, jerky movement and replied, "I like it. It sounds crazy, but it feels like home. And I've been here less than a week."

Ellie's chest fluttered at his words. Even though she'd wanted to leave the island, this was where she'd grown up. She knew every inch of this place, from the ruggedly beautiful coastline and forests to the cozy corners of Rhonda's ice cream shop. She didn't want to leave unless she had to. It felt good to know that Hugh could sense the magic of this place, that he appreciated it.

"After my dad left, I never really felt like I had a home," Hugh continued, eyes on the horizon. "My mom and I were a team, but . . . I don't know. It's different when you're struggling to survive versus actually being content somewhere."

Ellie chewed on a piece of pie crust from her ice cream. "Are you close with your mom?"

He nodded. "It was just the two of us against the world. She dated a guy for a little while when I was about fifteen, but it didn't work out. Then she said she was just going to work on herself for a while. After I moved out, she dated now and then, but nothing ever stuck."

The log was smooth and polished beneath Ellie's palm as she ran her hand over it, mulling over Hugh's words. Her ice cream tasted sweet, with the occasional splash of tartness when she bit into a spiced apple. "You ever talk to your dad?"

Hugh glanced over and shook his head. "The past three years, he'd call every few months. I answered a few times, but the conversations always left me feeling worse. But now he's dead, and I can't help but feel . . ."

"Like you missed your chance?"

He nodded. "Yeah. He wasn't a good guy." Swallowing, Hugh let his gaze drift to the horizon. The Olympic Mountains were just visible in the distance, a hazy, jagged line above the glittering sea. "He married my mom thinking she'd inherit lots of money from my grandparents. But my grandparents didn't have any real wealth; they just had a nice house they'd bought a long time ago, and they were careful with their money. Grandpa told me that when I was sixteen or seventeen, about my dad thinking there was money where there was none. He was angry at my dad. We all were. After my dad found out there was no inheritance, it only took him a few months to start up with another woman, but we only found out about it three years later, when he had a baby and another on the way. Took me years to piece this all together from bits and pieces people told me, and still I feel like I don't know the whole story. Maybe I should have taken his calls and asked him for the truth. Asked if money really was what he'd chosen over us."

"I'm so sorry," Ellie offered when the silence stretched. "Money is weird, isn't it? I'm . . . honestly ashamed to admit this, but I think part of the reason I stayed with Jason so long was because of his money and his status." She grimaced. "It doesn't feel good to say that out loud."

Hugh's knee nudged hers. They paid attention to their ice cream cones, not looking at each other. After a long pause, Hugh admitted, "My dad wrote me into his will. He used his new wife's connections and capital to do some property investing, and I guess he was pretty successful. Getting the inheritance felt like a bribe from him from beyond the grave. For what it's worth, I'm ashamed of myself for taking it."

A weight she'd never noticed lifted off Ellie's shoulders. She glanced at Hugh, noticing the way the sun shone on his dark hair, the way his jaw moved as he enjoyed his ice cream.

He didn't think she was contemptible for staying with Jason. He understood it, could relate to it. With a light spring breeze ruffling her hair and the warm rays shining on her face, Ellie was afraid she was falling for him.

Hugh took a deep breath and squared his shoulders. His throat worked as he swallowed, and he glanced over at Ellie with a look in his eyes she didn't understand. It seemed like he wanted to say something and was trying to find the right words.

If they kept talking about money and shame and their pasts, would Hugh's opinion of her change? Ellie was only just coming to grips with all the ways she'd been wrong—and all the ways Jason had manipulated her. She wasn't sure she wanted to probe any deeper. What if Hugh didn't understand her, after all?

Needing to change the subject, she swallowed past the constriction in her throat and tried to think of something to say. "What about you?" she finally asked.

He turned to look at her. "Me?"

"You ever meet someone who stuck, or did you take after your mom?"

He held her gaze for a long moment. "I used to think that person didn't exist. My relationships never lasted long."

Used to. His words rang in Ellie's head, and she wondered if they meant what she thought they meant. Was he saying that things were different now? Maybe different . . . because of her? Her heart skipped as she fought to keep her voice level. "Well, I'm not exactly an authority on healthy relationships."

Hugh shifted, his knee brushing hers again. He bit into his ice cream cone and chewed thoughtfully. "You know that getting revenge on Jason probably won't help, right? You're still going to feel like garbage."

"I don't know. I think seeing him get his comeuppance might be worth it. He's an ugly crier." She popped the last bit of her cone into her mouth and crunched down on it.

Hugh grinned, and Ellie's stomach fisted. He was gorgeous, with gleaming dark hair and those pale-brown eyes. She wanted to run her fingers over his jaw, feel his stubble beneath her fingertips. She wanted to kiss him again and feel that breathless, dizzying sensation that she'd only ever experienced in his arms.

She was sick with it—the wanting. Her life had been upended six months ago, and now she was tumbling all over again. Hadn't she learned her lesson with Jason? Shouldn't she focus on her plan instead of lusting over this new man? It was dangerous. Foolish. Reckless.

But she still wanted him.

As she wiped her sticky hands on a napkin, Ellie tried to swallow past the lump in her throat. She felt flushed and uncomfortable, her heart thumping. It was probably the thought of the gala. Yeah—that was it. She was just nervous about finally facing Jason.

Hugh finished his ice cream cone and crumpled his own napkin in his fist. "So, what's next?"

Ellie's gaze snagged on his forearms and the way they corded and flexed. She blinked to gather the last remnants of her wits so she could make her brain make her mouth make words. It was hard. "Now, we case the spot for tonight's surveillance operation."

CHAPTER 20

Ellie had started to enjoy being in the car with Hugh. They'd taken his vehicle, since she thought it was less recognizable than her red hatchback, and as soon as he'd gotten behind the wheel, Ellie felt a hard bead of tension soften within her. The "Drive Tunes" playlist belted out "You Sexy Thing" by Hot Chocolate, and they both bobbed their heads to the beat. She directed him to the far side of Carlisle, where the grocery store lived in the middle of a large parking lot at the end of a strip mall. There had been a lot of uproar when a major chain had established itself here, because there were fears that the small greengrocer and butcher would go out of business.

The big store had affected many small businesses, but most of them had survived. This island was full of survivors.

It was comforting for Ellie to know that. It made her feel like she belonged here, despite what some of the residents thought of her. And what if there were more Rhondas and Gemmas and Traceys? What if she'd been wrong about her reputation—or looking for validation from all the wrong people?

They circled the grocery store and spotted the dumpsters.

Hugh slowed and slid into a parking spot, leaning his forearms on the wheel. "It's going to be tough to get a clear line of sight from anywhere if they go behind the dumpsters."

"That's why I brought this," Ellie said, pulling out the trail camera she'd used to catch Spencer in the act of spreading milkweed over her parents' pasture. She grinned at Hugh's raised eyebrow. "It has no audio, but it'll get us some visuals."

"Is this legal?"

Ellie stared at him. "What's that saying about shutting the barn doors after the horses have bolted?"

He laughed. "Point taken."

The second piece of the puzzle was soon in place. Ellie adjusted the camera and checked the view on her phone, nodding to Hugh when she was done. "That's it," she said. "Let's go to the office."

They headed to the event management office, which was now boarded up and mostly cleaned. Ellie directed Hugh to park behind the building in one of the three available spaces, then unlocked the door and led him inside. It still made her heart squeeze to enter the dark space, her gaze catching on the words spray-painted on the walls. She turned her back on the insults.

Hugh stood near the back door. "Are you sure about this, Ellie?"

A shaft of light from a high window on the back wall fell across Hugh's face, and she could see he was worried—and it looked sincere. Her stomach fisted. She licked her lips and exhaled heavily. "Hugh, if you don't want to be involved, I won't hold it against you. But I have to do this."

He walked toward her, his steps echoing on the bare floorboards. He stopped when he was only inches away, then lifted a hand to tuck her hair behind her ear. "I understand. I like you too much to back out now, anyway."

Lips curling, she had to stare at his chin to pull herself together. It was so rare that people outside Ellie's inner circle actually understood her. She was the type of person people warmed to over time. That's why it had shocked her so much when Jason had shown interest in her to begin with. On Valentine's Day, when they'd been dating for about two years, Jason had called her an "acquired taste." For some insane reason, Ellie had taken it as a compliment.

Was it any wonder she didn't quite trust Hugh's attention? It terrified and flattered her in equal parts. She wanted so badly for him to like her for who she was, without the shadow of her family's past, without the shame of her mug shot and its aftermath.

"We should get to work," she croaked, and she pulled away from him. After digging a tripod out of the closet—one she'd used for her social media posts when her business had been booming—she set it up and placed a chair in front of it. Hugh flicked the lights on. Ellie placed her cell phone on the tripod, checked the frame, and adjusted the chair.

It took an hour to record. She'd put together a script the night before, but it took a few takes to get it all down. Once the chair and tripod were put away, Ellie reviewed the footage and gave a quick nod. "Got it."

Hugh was solemn as he dipped his chin in response. He drove her to her vehicle, still by the ferry terminal, and they promised to meet that night for their stakeout. Ellie drove back to her parents' place, fired up her laptop, and got to work editing.

Hugh was on edge for the six hours that followed. He forced himself to eat, then paced his hotel room until the carpet threatened to wear out. He went down to the lobby bar to have a drink and nearly had a heart attack when Jason Brownlow walked through the doors.

Jason slowed, eyes darkening when they met Hugh's. "Change your mind yet?" he asked.

"Nope."

Jason snorted and kept walking, and Hugh overheard him asking the employee at the front desk about the ballroom setup for his event. He then walked off down a hallway with the worker and moved out of sight.

The day after next, Hugh would be exposing that asshole for the criminal he was, and Hugh was glad.

When it was finally time to go, Hugh met Ellie at the back of the hotel. She was in the driver's seat of her car, her fingers drumming on the steering wheel, her jaw clenched. As he sat beside her, Hugh immediately felt better.

"Ready?" Ellie asked.

"Let's do it."

They drove past the strip mall with the grocery store and parked down one of the many gravel roads that crisscrossed the island. Ellie checked her backpack and nodded to him, and the two of them crept through the forest and reached the edge of the parking lot. She wore dark jeans and a black hoodie, and she walked with quiet, light steps as she circled to the bushes they'd scoped out earlier.

They hunkered down to wait. As he scanned the open pavement, Hugh's heartbeat kicked. There was a very, very high likelihood that this was a mistake, but he was used to feeling that way. Almost everything he'd done since he'd arrived on Fernley was probably a mistake—it just didn't feel that way when he was with Ellie.

"So, um, I've been meaning to ask," Ellie said quietly. "Are you busy tomorrow night?"

He arched a brow and glanced over at her. "Why? I thought you said tomorrow night was the calm before the storm. We're supposed to lie low. Has that changed?"

Ellie bunched her lips to the side and threw him a quick glance. "Tomorrow night is ODNT."

"ODNT?"

"Old Dog New Trick," she said. "My dad's band."

"Your dad's in a band?"

She smiled, and Hugh couldn't quite stop his own lips from curling in response. "He started playing the saxophone about ten years ago. He and a few of his friends put the band together and play a gig a month or so. More in the summer. They're pretty good, if you're into a bunch of sixty-year-olds playing classic rock covers." She let out a little huff. "My mom asked me to invite you."

Hugh was flattered in a way that was completely out of proportion with the invitation Ellie had extended. His chest warmed, his cheeks threatened to crease . . . but that was silly. He fought to keep his expression neutral, to not show her this embarrassing, needy part of himself. Hadn't he craved being part of a community? Hadn't he always wanted a big family? Ellie's family had welcomed him with no hesitation. He'd belonged to their clan from the moment he mentioned he liked music—and who doesn't like music? They—along with Ellie—had made him feel like he had a place in the world.

He hadn't had a place in the world since he was a preteen, when he thought his parents had a loving and healthy marriage. A simple invitation to see Claude's band knocked him so hard that he almost fell back onto the moss and leaves behind him.

Hugh nodded, returning his gaze to the parking lot. His throat was tight, so all he managed to say was, "Cool."

"You know what, forget it." Ellie shook her head. "I know it's lame. Listen to me, 'My mom asked me to invite you to watch my dad play the saxophone.'" She let out a self-deprecating laugh. "I'll just tell them you're busy."

"No," Hugh cut in. "I want to come. What time?"

Her eyes shone as she turned to look at him, hope a beacon in them. This was a side of Ellie that she usually tried to hide; the vulnerability in her gaze was something Hugh had only seen a few glimpses of since he'd met her. Maybe he was wrong to hide his own vulnerability. Wrong to hide how much it meant to him to be invited.

Maybe Ellie felt the same way he did.

"Their set starts at eight," she said, voice raspy.

"At the hotel? I saw a poster about live music on Fridays."

Ellie laughed, and she was back to herself again, unflappable and irreverent. "No. They wouldn't let riffraff like us invade their swanky hotel bar. It's at Mickey's. I'll send you the address."

Hugh wanted to kiss her again. Under the shadows of the trees and bushes, the angles of her face were striking. Her eyes were inky pools that drew him in. He would follow this woman to the bowels of hell just to see her smile again.

He suspected that was exactly what they were in the process of doing.

Then a car drove into the big lot and parked near the back corner.

"Showtime," Ellie whispered.

Later, when they parted, Hugh promised to meet her at Mickey's just before eight o'clock. Ellie's grin ripped a slash across his chest, exposing his beating heart for all to see.

CHAPTER 21

Mickey's Bar was near the ferry terminal, down a side street that looked pretty foreboding in the dark, except for the lively music that fell out of the door every time it opened and the fairy lights strung up around the patch of pavement out front. The building was painted black, with gold lettering on the sign above the door proclaiming it MICKEY'S BAR in a graceful arch.

The interior was dark, just this side of dingy. A bar of reclaimed wood ran the length of the building, its edge a brass curve. On Friday nights, the space inside was mostly standing room, with a few barrels and high-top tables dotted around where people could gather. It was loud, it smelled like alcohol and sweat, and the beer was terrible. Ellie loved it.

Ellie had spent many an evening in this place in her youth, but she'd really come to love the evenings that ODNT played. They were *good*. On nights her father played with his band, the bar would be packed from wall to wall with all the hippies and radicals who usually didn't stir from their properties. There was something about the music—its honesty, its rawness—that connected with people.

And her father was pretty darn good on the saxophone.

Ellie sipped her terrible beer and tried to get the nervous jitters out of her limbs. She'd worked hard to put together her revenge. She could almost taste the blowback she'd get after everything about Jason was exposed, but what other option did she have? The police didn't take her seriously. If she did nothing, Jason could bully her parents and every resident of this island until he owned—or destroyed—the whole thing.

She'd spent the day working at her computer and pretending that everything was normal—Hugh had told her he'd do the same—but nervousness had plagued her from the moment she'd opened her eyes. Without Hugh there to distract her, Ellie realized she might be in over her head. But how could she turn back now?

Tomorrow, while Jason was busy getting ready for the event, she'd take her dog back, and then he'd have nothing over her.

Tonight, however, she could sit on one of the wobbly barstools and listen to her father's band. She could stomp her feet on the floorboards and let her mother drag her over to the tiny dance floor. She could enjoy one last night before she took a bazooka to her life and pulled the trigger—again.

"What time is Hugh getting here?" Wynn asked, squeezing a lime into her vodka-cranberry. Wynn preferred fancy cocktails, but booze plus mixer was about as elevated as it got in this place, so she made do. Her booted foot was swinging back and forth as she bobbed her head to the music playing over the speakers.

Ellie stole a glance at the front door. "I'm not sure. I told him the set started at eight."

"He'll be here," Wynn said with absolute confidence. "Hugh's trustworthy."

Despite the voice in her head telling her that she didn't even know the man, Ellie agreed with Wynn's assessment—until her father's band took the stage and there was still no Hugh in sight. She tried not to let the disappointment she felt show on her face, and she reminded herself that it was still early.

Her father met her gaze from his corner of the small stage, winking. He wore a flat blue tweed cap, a white button-down paired with a vest that matched his cap, and jeans. His feet were clad in ginormous white sneakers. He looked like a total dad, and Ellie loved him for it.

The lead singer / guitarist was a man named Sandler, whose head was covered in a thick coating of inch-long silver hair, everywhere except his ears and the space between his upper cheeks and the top of his fore-head. He was Tracey's husband and co-owned the Sunrise Diner with her. The bald pate of their bassist, Ned, shone brightly under the stage lights, reflecting almost as much as his round glasses. The drummer was a new (and young) addition—Spencer Wisneski. Spence grinned under the lights and counted them in as he hit his drumsticks together.

Van Morrison's "Moondance" started, and the crowd erupted. Ellie's lips curled into a smile as Sandler's voice filled the space. Tracey danced her way over to Ellie and bumped Ellie's hip with her own. She smiled at Wynn and said, "I'd ask you to dance, but I think you're out of commission this week."

Wynn grimaced at her crutches, propped against the bar beside her. "Unfortunately."

"Come on, Ellie," Tracey said as she dragged her out of her chair. With no choice but to follow the older woman, Ellie laughed and let herself be led to the dance floor.

So what if Hugh didn't show? She didn't even know the man. He was helping her out temporarily, and then they'd part ways. No one ever stuck around with Ellie—especially not with her reputation. It was probably only a matter of time before Hugh came to his senses and lost interest. It was a good thing that he wasn't here. She was getting far too attached, anyway.

She danced with Tracey through three songs and was sweaty and laughing by the time she stumbled back to Wynn at the bar—except in her friend's place was a large, dark-haired, very amused man.

"Nice moves," Hugh said in greeting, his lips curling.

Ellie blushed. "You're late. You missed some of ODNT's greatest hits."

"I made a pit stop," Hugh answered, and he pulled up his jeans to show off his ankles. For a moment, Ellie didn't understand. One foot was wearing a sock, and the other one wasn't. Then Hugh said, "I figured I wanted to get on Louie's good side sooner rather than later."

Ellie's eyes widened. "You . . ."

"Sneaked through the forest and gave your dog my sock. Yep." Hugh's cheeks flushed slightly, and he shook his head, like he couldn't believe it himself.

She couldn't stop herself from throwing her arms around Hugh's neck as he wrapped his around her waist. His body was a warm, solid wall that felt like heaven pressed against hers. She pulled away, heart soaring, and shook her head. His hands were still on her waist, their warmth soaking into her skin, scrambling her brain.

"Did you really go visit my dog to give him one of your socks? *Really?*"

"Thought I got caught. The lights came on, and I had to hit the ground—but then I realized they were motion activated by the dog in the backyard." He pointed to a green stain on his knee, grinning.

Ellie snort-giggled and pushed a strand of hair off his forehead. "You're crazy."

"I'm in good company then, huh."

Ellie tried to look stern and offended. She really did. But her face broke into a wide grin without her permission. "Careful, tough guy. I got bolt cutters, and I'm not afraid to use them."

"Bring it on, babe."

Ellie's heart turned over. She couldn't think of anything to say, so she just grinned at him like a lovesick loon.

Warm brown eyes circled her face, a soft smile still toying at the edges of Hugh's lips. She loved the way he looked at her. She'd never felt so beautiful as when he stared at her like he wanted to memorize her. His hands squeezed her waist. "Get you a drink?"

"Sure."

She slipped onto the stool beside him and ordered another beer. She turned to watch her father play a killer sax solo, trying not to get distracted by the way Hugh's leg pressed against hers.

He touched her elbow. "You're right," he said in her ear, his breath warm on her skin. "ODNT is good."

"They just started writing their own stuff," Ellie bragged. "They'll play a few originals as the night goes on."

Hugh smiled. They were in a cocoon, a temporary reprieve from the revenge plot she'd concocted. While her father played his sax and the bar's patrons bobbed to the music, nothing outside these walls existed. Ellie found herself relaxing and leaning into him, so there was always some part of her body touching some part of his. When she leaned forward to take a sip of her beer, his hand would touch her lower back. When they both turned to look at the tiny stage and multitude of dancers, his side would press hers. When he turned to speak to her, his knee would notch between hers, his heel hooked around the bar stool's crossbar.

"I'm a little jealous," he said between songs, "Your dad is way cooler than my dad."

Ellie laughed, pleased and slightly woozy. Hugh's hand slid onto her knee, his thumb making small circles on the inside of her thigh. She couldn't think straight when he touched her like that, but she managed to say, "He's the best. And look at my mom."

Hugh followed the direction of her gesture, and they both smiled as Helen danced in front of Claude as they started their next song, obviously his number one fan. Mabel sat behind her with Greta and Harry, eyes half-closed, head bobbing to the music. Wynn had apparently relocated beside the old dragons, and she gave Ellie a little wiggle of her eyebrows and a wave.

"You're lucky," Hugh said. "I never had parents who loved each other like that."

"Even when they were together?"

Hugh shook his head. "I only have a few memories, but none of them looked anything like this."

"I'm sorry." Ellie touched his hand. His fingers squeezed her leg, that maddening thumb stroking over the inner part of her knee.

"I think a part of me believed that kind of love didn't exist." Hugh glanced at Ellie's parents, smiling softly. "You can feel it from a distance, can't you? How much they love each other."

Ellie huffed and took a sip of her drink. "Yes. You know, I felt like such an idiot for thinking I'd found what my parents have in Jason. Maybe that's why I fell for him; I wanted so badly for him to be the one."

Hugh nodded, his gaze telling her that he understood her completely. She'd never felt this way with a man. It had never been so easy to speak her heart.

That was trust, wasn't it? Not being afraid to speak what was true.

He'd met her when she was almost at her worst, when she'd endured humiliation and derision, when she wanted to fight until her knuckles were bloody and the rest of her dignity had been burned away. And yet, he kept coming back. He kept telling her again and again that he was on her side.

That kind of support and acceptance was a first for Ellie. From the time she was in school, Ellie was always the troublemaker, the distracting one, the embarrassing one. But with Hugh, she could just be herself.

When the band started a new song, Hugh put down his half-finished drink. "You want to dance?"

A smile tugged at Ellie's lips. "Yeah," she said. "I do."

ODNT did an amazing cover of Whitney Houston's "How Will I Know." They rock-ified it and sang it in a lower key to highlight Sandler's deep baritone, and it always got everyone out on the dance floor. In the middle of all that movement and chaos, Hugh wrapped his arms around Ellie and made her feel like she'd found someone who truly saw her.

They spun and swayed between other couples and dancers, and Ellie couldn't wipe the smile off her face, no matter how hard she tried. When the band transitioned to the next tune, Hugh pulled her close and said, "Let's go get your dog back."

She stared at him, wide eyed. "Right now?"

He grinned. "Yeah. I scoped it out when I was there. I think we can do it, and I hate the idea of you or Louie waiting any longer than you need to."

Ellie's heart stopped. Dancers spun around them. Music swelled. Ellie stared into Hugh's warm brown eyes, and from one moment to the next, she tumbled head over heels in love with him.

CHAPTER 22

They took Hugh's rental car after a brief debate, for the same reason they'd taken his car to the supermarket parking lot. It was less recognizable. He'd watched Ellie grab her backpack from her own vehicle because "You never know when you might need supplies," and then she climbed in beside him.

He parked in front of Lionel's house, strode to the front door, and knocked, Ellie at his heels. When Lionel opened, the old man frowned at the two of them.

"Hey, Lionel," Hugh said. "Mind if I borrow some tools?"

His uncle's eyes narrowed. "What for?"

"Um," Hugh said. "A project?"

Lionel's gaze shifted to Ellie. He pursed his lips. Then he reached into his pocket and pulled out a set of keys, tossing them at Hugh's chest. "Don't break anything. Don't get arrested. I'm not bailing you out if you do."

The door slammed, and Hugh and Ellie were alone.

Ellie grinned. "And he didn't even charge you for the tools. He must really like you."

"Come on," Hugh answered. His heart beat unsteadily as they circled the house and headed for the workshop by the water. He'd been here once before, when he'd grabbed the crowbar for the front window.

This time, as they navigated the path through the trees and ferns, the moon lit their way, and the rain was nowhere to be seen.

He unlocked the workshop, flicked the lights, and headed for the pegboard on the left wall. He grabbed a hacksaw, while Ellie admired the long-handled bolt cutters hanging on the far end of the wall.

"These are way nicer than mine," she complained. "And I bet they didn't cost Lionel three hundred bucks."

"He probably also didn't buy them from a drug trafficker," Hugh noted.

Ellie laughed and grabbed the tool from the wall. "You don't know that."

Hugh grinned, and they headed back to the car. From there, it was a short five-minute drive to the same spot on the opposite side of Brownlow's property. Hugh parked exactly where he had before, near the picnic tables by the Fernley Coastal Trail.

They grabbed their new tools from the trunk of his car, leaving Ellie's backpack behind. Side by side, Hugh and Ellie stared at the shadowy forest, and Ellie glanced up at him. "I can't help but feel like I'm a bad influence on you."

He stared back at her, loving the way her blue eyes appeared black in the darkness. "Maybe I like bad influences."

The walk through the forest was full of nighttime noises, like the hoot of an owl and the rustling of tree branches. Hugh didn't speak as his pulse kicked. When they spotted the tall timber fence that enclosed Jason's backyard, they slowed and listened.

Only the sounds of the forest reached their ears. They moved closer.

Ellie eased around a tree. "There's a light on upstairs," she whispered. "You still want to go through with this? We could wait until tomorrow, when he's busy with the event."

If they waited, they risked Jason taking the dog with him to the hotel. A thousand things could happen between right now and tomorrow. Hugh had seen the darkness in Jason's eyes in the hotel lobby yesterday, and he'd twisted and turned last night thinking about this situation.

Ellie was strong, but he knew it would break her to lose her dog for good. He wanted to do this for her. He wanted to show her that he was on her side. Hopefully, once he told her about the property, she'd understand. She'd know that Hugh cared about her.

"We're here," he said. "Let's do it. Get Louie, keep him safe tomorrow, and execute the plan. Then Jason will be exposed, and no one will question you getting Louie back. This is *your* dog."

A fierce grin was the only response he got. Ellie brandished Lionel's spiffy bolt cutters and headed for the back gate. She paused when she got there, staring at the tool, then handed it to Hugh. "You do the honors," she said.

Hugh nodded, wrapping his hands around the grips. The blades were sharp, and they cut through the steel chain like it was butter. Ellie caught the two ends of the chain before they could rattle too much against the timber fence, then slowly unhitched the metal links from the gate so they could open it.

It swung open with a slight squeak.

"Not this again," Ellie grumbled. She stopped, sticking her head through the opening. Hugh poked his head above hers.

On the far side of the yard, Louie's head appeared in the doghouse opening. He came up slowly onto all fours, sniffing, then shifted forward. A chain linked his collar to a steel peg in the concrete, glinting in the moonlight as the dog moved as close as he could before the chain grew taut. Louie whined softly, then barked once.

"He tied Louie up," Ellie breathed.

As Ellie crouched beside Hugh, he watched her body go still. He followed her gaze to the upper windows where the light spilled out—and, before Hugh could say anything, she took off.

Ellie ran across the open yard, skidding to a halt near Louie's doghouse. Behind her, motion-activated lights blazed bright in the backyard. She heard Hugh hiss behind her, and a moment later, he ran past her to stick himself on the wall just around the corner. Ellie felt around Louie's collar. "Come on, boy. Come on."

Louie's tail wagged like crazy. He lifted his paws up onto her thighs, and she tried to hiss at him to sit, but Louie was too excited. He licked at her hands, his head twisting as he tried to lavish Ellie with affection.

"I'm trying to untie you," she whispered, hands trembling.

Then the back door slid open. Hugh reached over and yanked her toward him, spinning around so she was pinned against the wall.

"Louie?" Jason's voice called. "What's up? I heard you bark." The deck creaked as he stepped out. He huffed, then grumbled, "These stupid sensitive lights."

Ellie mouthed "Away" to her dog, pairing the word with a sharp hand gesture.

Louie stared at her, tilting his head. The deck creaked some more. Jason was getting closer.

"Go," she mouthed, shooing him away frantically.

Louie's tail wagged so hard his butt lifted off the ground. Jason's steps were getting closer, the stairs creaking as he descended them. Soon, he'd be walking along the concrete path toward the doghouse. He'd find Hugh and Ellie plastered against the side of his house, and the jig would be up. Not only would they not get Louie back, but they wouldn't be able to go through with their plan for the gala.

Ellie began to panic. Had this been a mistake? Should they have waited until tomorrow?

Then Louie stood and walked away, calm as anything. "Why'd you bark?" Jason asked. "Stupid dog. Did the lights scare you?"

Hugh's hand drifted to her waist, and Ellie looked up to see him shake his head. That's when she realized her muscles had all bunched at once, like she was about to pounce around the corner and attack Jason for insulting her dog.

The chain securing Louie to his doghouse rattled softly, and Jason let out a soft grunt. "I think you've outlived your usefulness, dog. That stupid bitch doesn't even want you back. So just be quiet and enjoy your last night out here. I don't need to keep you to keep her quiet anymore. She's learned her lesson."

Ellie's vision went red. Louie's last night? Outlived his usefulness?

The only thing that stopped her was Hugh's hold on her waist and the press of his thighs against hers. They listened to Jason's retreating footsteps, the creak of the deck, and the glass door sliding closed as Jason entered the house.

The motion-activated lights turned off.

"Wait," Hugh said softly when Ellie would have moved.

Ellie trembled. Her whole body had gone cold while Jason was outside and was now flooding with warmth. She heard the rattle of Louie's chain, and her heart kicked, but she forced herself to inhale softly and exhale slowly. She focused on the feel of Hugh's hands on her waist, his breath coasting over her cheek.

The door slid open again. There was a grunt and a rattle, and then the door closed again. Ellie heard it latch.

"Okay," Hugh finally whispered, after what felt like a whole year. "Let me go check if the coast is clear." He eased away from Ellie, and she watched him walk on quiet feet until he could poke his head around the corner of the house. Louie came closer to investigate, holding Hugh's sock between his jaws.

While Ellie leaned against the wall and watched, Hugh crouched, feeling at Louie's collar for the carabiner that clasped it to the chain. Ellie crept closer and watched him detach the chain and place it gently on the ground. Then he put his arms around her dog while Louie wiggled closer, obviously in doggy heaven as he tried to lick every bit of Hugh's neck and face that came near.

"Good boy," Hugh whispered. He picked Louie up and met Ellie's gaze. "Make a run for it and hold the gate open. I'll be right behind you."

Ellie nodded, easing past him. She glanced at the house. All its windows were dark except for the upper bedroom one. A shadow passed near the window behind the gauzy curtain, and she thought it looked like Jason. The motion-activated light fixture was hanging crookedly, wires dangling from its base. Jason must have disconnected it.

It was now or never. With one last look at Hugh and Louie, Ellie ran for the gate. The backyard seemed to stretch on and on and on, lengthening as she tried to speed up. Finally, she reached the gate and opened it, only to turn and see Hugh barreling past her while he carried her dog.

She shut the gate and hung the chain loosely closed so it wouldn't swing open again, then turned in time to see Hugh setting Louie down on the forest floor.

Louie bounded toward her, tongue lolling, ears up, tail whipping back and forth so fast it was a blur.

He was free. *He was free.* They'd gotten her dog away from Jason, finally, *finally!*

"Let's go," Hugh said, holding the tools they'd used to break in. He jerked his head toward the car. "We need to get out of here before they see that Louie's gone."

"Come on, Louie," she said, and she took off. Ellie sprinted between the trees, breathless laughter falling from her lips. Hugh moved like a shadow behind her, Louie bounding over the moss and ferns by her side. Her heart soared. She'd never felt so light. She flew across the landscape, dodging branches and jumping over roots that jutted up from the ground.

Through the foliage, Ellie saw the car's lights flash as Hugh pressed the fob to unlock the doors. Ellie crashed into the back door and opened it up, following Louie inside. Hugh jumped behind the wheel.

They slammed the doors in unison. Hugh dropped the tools on the passenger seat; then they were off.

Ellie clipped her seat belt as Louie flopped on the seats beside her. She laughed as her hyperactive dog sat up again, stuck his muzzle into her neck, and licked. Joy was fire in her veins. She scrubbed Louie's fur and buried her face in his neck, crying tears of joy and relief.

She had her dog back. He was safe. He was unhurt. Oh, Ellie hadn't been this happy in *months*.

Ellie caught her breath as Hugh tore across the island. She didn't have to give him directions; he already knew the way back to Ellie's parents' place. By the time Ellie had gathered herself together, they were almost there. She straightened up as Louie collapsed onto her lap, his eyes closing as she scratched behind his ears. His tail swept over the leather seats in a soft whisper of noise that soothed Ellie down to her marrow.

She met Hugh's gaze in the rearview mirror and smiled. "Thank you," she whispered, throat tight.

His eyes crinkled, and he returned his gaze to the road.

When they pulled up outside the house, Ellie wasn't ready to say goodbye to the man who had given her this precious gift. Without Hugh, Ellie would have waited until tomorrow, and who knows what Jason would have done by then? Even if she'd gone there tonight, without Hugh, she would've been caught. She'd needed his steadying presence, his calming touch.

"Come inside for a drink?" She tried to keep the hope out of her voice, but her relief must have been obvious when Hugh agreed.

Louie jumped out of the car after her and took off toward the pasture, running down to the end of the field, under the fence, and around the outraged sheep. They bleated their displeasure as Louie herded them. He ran back, tongue lolling. He sprinted down along the fence again and zoomed around the two of them, finally coming to a stop near the front door. Then he flopped on his side and immediately got up again. He ran over to Ellie and tangled her legs as she walked up the path to the front door.

"We're happy you're back too, buddy," Ellie said, laughing. Hugh knelt on the welcome mat and slid his hands over Louie's back in long, slow motions. Louie huffed, leaning his head on Hugh's shoulder. Hugh grinned, whispering sweet words to her dog. It made her heart grow in her chest.

When Louie flopped onto his side and presented his belly for rubs, Ellie knew her dog had just professed his undying devotion.

Her hands trembled as she tried to get the door unlocked. It had taken nearly a week to get her dog back since the first day she'd attempted it with Wynn, but it had felt like a lifetime. How had she waited so many months to ask for Louie to be returned through proper channels? Why had she trusted the sheriff to do the right thing? She should have known the only way to get Louie would be to take him back.

The three of them entered the dark house, and Louie rushed to his favorite spot on the rug by the hearth in the corner of the living room, rested his head on his front paws, and closed his eyes.

The touch of Hugh's hand on her lower back drew her attention away from her dog. Hugh stood close to her, so close she had to tilt her head up to meet his gaze. He slid a hand over her neck, thumb stroking her jaw.

"Hi," Ellie whispered, intelligence abandoning her when she needed it most. She couldn't help it. The man was too dang gorgeous for his own good. He'd just given her her dog back and proved to her that she could rely on him. He'd arrived in her life and lifted a veil from her eyes, shown her a future she hadn't dared believe in. He'd taken a hammer to the hard shell around her heart and shattered it into a million pieces.

She was besotted. She was silly. She was in love or lust, or maybe she was just lost. She wanted him desperately.

"Thank you," she breathed. "You saved my dog."

His fingers pressed gently into her nape as he pulled her closer. "You saved your own dog, Ellie. I was just along for the ride."

"Did you enjoy the ride, at least?"

His lips curled, head angling down toward her. "More than anything."

When Hugh's lips crushed hers, they stole every bit of breath from her lungs. She melted into his embrace, lost herself in his kiss. She was high on adrenaline—or maybe that was just the effect Hugh had on her. Hadn't he spun her like a top from the moment he'd pinned her to the muddy ground outside Lionel's house?

Groaning as he deepened the kiss, Hugh shifted the hand on her back so his arm was banded behind her. She loved when he did that, when he wrapped his body around hers like he wanted to feel every inch of her against his front. She wanted the same thing.

Ellie's fingers slid over Hugh's shoulders and curled around his neck, pulling him closer as her heart beat a riot inside her chest. Hugh responded in kind, sliding his hand down so it cupped her curves. They were entwined, inseparable. Ellie felt the world tilt on its axis, so she clung to Hugh with all her strength.

"Where's your bed?" His lips roamed down her jaw, her neck.

Ellie tilted her head back, drugged by the sensation of this man giving her all his attention, his affection. "Down the hall," she panted. "Second door on the right."

A yelp escaped her lips as Hugh lifted her over his shoulder. She dangled over his back, spying Louie's curious lift of the head from the corner of her eye. "I'm okay, buddy," she called out. "You stay there."

Louie stood at once and watched them until Hugh turned around and said, "I'll bring her back in a little bit."

Her dog lay down again, and Ellie laughed. "If he ends up listening to you more than me, I'll never forgive you."

Hugh's chuckle was warm as it vibrated through her stomach and thighs. He turned to the hallway and carried her down through the correct door. He paused just inside, set her down, and closed the door behind them. When he faced Ellie again, his eyes were dark as pitch and full of promises.

"I want you, Ellie," he rasped.

Simple words, spoken with such openness. Ellie felt stripped bare, free of the humiliation and shame that had slicked over her skin like oil for the past six months. It was a heady feeling, being *seen* like that. Being appreciated. It terrified her a little bit, but not as much as it thrilled her. She dropped her arms to her side and spread her palms, saying the only thing that came to mind: "You have me."

They came together in a storm of lips and limbs and lust. Hugh tugged her jacket off with impatient motions, his lips on hers. Then he was tugging her top off over her head and groaning at the sight of her bra, her bare skin. Ellie's stomach tightened. She loved the noises he made. She loved that her body was the cause of them.

Impatience nipped at Ellie, so she clawed at his tee until he helped her remove it. Then her hands roamed as they pleased over the broad expanse of his chest, feeling the coarse, curly hair that grew there, tracing the flat discs of his nipples. Hugh let out a heavy breath and tugged her closer by her belt loop. She crashed into him, liking the way his hand clamped on her hip.

"You've changed my life, Ellie," he said, sliding his other palm over her cheek. "It feels like I was stumbling around in the dark, and you turned on all the lights."

Her heart flipped and flopped in her chest, and all Ellie could do was cling to his shoulders for a moment. "You barely even know me," she whispered, hopelessly wanting to deny this connection between them, to hold on to some sort of safety as she tumbled headlong toward him.

A shake of his head. "I know you," he promised. "I've never known anyone better."

When he kissed her this time, he held her face and systematically destroyed any scrap of defense she might have erected against him. His skin was warm and smooth, pulled taut over the brawn of his muscles. He was heaven beneath Ellie's palms.

The bed was soft when she fell on top of her comforter, pillows scattered around her head. This time, Hugh's weight on top of her felt perfect. His hips notched between her spread knees as she ran her hands down his broad back, exhaling heavily.

Head spinning, she watched as Hugh propped himself up on his elbows and slipped the strap of her bra off her shoulder. He tugged the cup down, groaning at the sight of her bare breast, then brought his lips to her pebbled nipple. The rasp of his tongue against her sensitive flesh made her writhe and twist beneath him, wanting more friction, more pressure, just *more*.

Hugh laved her breast while he cupped it in one hand, then used the fingers of his other hand to trace the middle seam of her jeans. He was warm and pleasantly heavy, and his touches detonated a thousand tiny explosions below her navel. Ellie sank into the feeling, her knees falling open.

A tug—and her jeans were unbuttoned. Hugh slid his hand beneath the waistband and cupped her there, stroking softly against the outside of her underwear. It maddened her. When she tried to buck against his hand for just a bit more friction, Hugh chuckled and nipped at her jaw. "Don't be so impatient, Ellie," he rasped, his voice thick with need. Her own voice was lost somewhere she'd never find it, so she gave up and kissed him instead.

Her head spun. Her body sang. His fingers stroked and teased, pushing her panties aside and stoking the fire inside her until she could barely think straight. She didn't want to think straight. She just wanted to feel.

Impatient, Ellie shoved at her jeans and underwear, shucking them off. Now was not the time for modesty, for overthinking. Hugh let out a shuddering breath and shifted his body down along hers until his arms were wrapped around her legs. When his mouth touched her core, Ellie couldn't stop the moan that slipped through her parted lips.

His fingers tightened on her thighs as if the sound of her pleasure unraveled his control. "You taste like heaven, Ellie," he said. "Better than I imagined."

"You imagined?" Ellie panted, her hands twisting in the sheets.

A dark chuckle. "Yes, babe. I did."

Maybe it was vanity to be pleased by those words, but they still turned her on. Then Hugh's hand joined his mouth in its quest to bring Ellie to the brink of madness, and Ellie lost the rest of her faculties. Her vision went white, and pleasure tore through her body like a bolt of lightning. It almost hurt it felt so good.

When she returned to herself, Hugh was kissing the inside of her thigh, his eyes watching her with focused intentness.

"You're beautiful when you come," he said in a low rumble. "Makes me want to do it again."

"Hhnngf," Ellie replied.

He sat back on his heels, hands still on her thighs. There was an almighty bulge in his pants that drew Ellie's gaze, especially when those magic hands of his started unfastening the fly of his jeans. He stood to drop his pants and underwear to the ground, then stood naked before her.

He was truly a beautifully formed man. He almost didn't look real. And he was very, very hard. His cock, Ellie noted, was in proportion to the rest of him, which is to say, quite large. Ellie made her arms work long enough to take off her bra and toss it aside.

Hugh paused for a moment, watching her. She liked the way it felt to be the focus of his attention. She liked the hungry expression on his face, the way his lips parted ever so slightly at the sight of her naked body.

Shame had wrapped itself so tightly around her over the past months—the past years—that to have a man as attractive as Hugh look at her like that . . . well, it was more than flattering. There wasn't really a word for how good it felt. No other man had looked at her body like it was everything he wanted. No other man had accepted all her schemes and plans and asked to join in. No other man had told her he knew her better than anyone.

And for tonight—maybe only tonight, because who knew what fresh humiliation tomorrow would bring—Hugh was all hers.

She spread her arms in silent invitation.

Hugh let out a shaking breath and leaned over to dig through his jeans pockets. He pulled out a foil condom wrapper, and it took him two tries to rip it open. His hands were shaking.

Ellie wasn't doing much better. She watched him roll the condom on as she sipped in little breaths into her constricted lungs, her heart taking up so much space in her chest that she doubted she could take a full breath even if she tried.

He climbed onto the bed and used his hands to spread her knees apart again, sliding his palms up her thighs, over her hips, and all the way up her sides. His touch sent little darts of pleasure racing across her stomach. When he cupped her breasts and gently pinched her nipples, liquid heat puddled between her thighs.

"Hugh," she whispered. "I want you."

His erection nudged at her entrance as he draped his body over hers. Framing her face with his hands, Hugh replied, "You have me."

The deliberate slowness with which he entered her only made it feel more intense. Ellie gasped, clinging to him, fingernails sinking into the hard muscle of his shoulders.

He stopped, kissed her, then rocked his hips in slow movements designed, she thought, to drive her insane. Rational thought was a thing of the past. Nothing existed but Hugh's weight pressing her into the bed and the delicious intrusion of his cock between her legs.

She rocked to meet him, nipping at his lip, gripping his hair a little bit harder than strictly necessary—not that she could have stopped herself. Her movements became more frantic, and her nails dug a little bit deeper into his skin. Hugh responded in kind, hooking one of her legs over his elbow while he punched his hips forward again and again in hard, jagged motions. They both moaned.

"Hands and knees," Hugh ordered between harsh breaths, and the timbre of his voice made more heat twist in Ellie's core.

Ellie complied. What choice did she have? Sex had never felt like this before. She wasn't even sure this strictly qualified as sex. It had to be something more. She was delirious with it, drunk on it. On him. Tomorrow didn't matter—not right now. The gala, the resort, her ex—they were all nightmares from another life. They didn't exist in this reality.

"Hands on the headboard, babe," Hugh said, his own palms sliding over her hips. "I want you to hold on for this."

What followed stripped the last remnants of sanity from Ellie's mind. She fell into the ocean of pleasure Hugh delivered, sank, and drowned. When he pulled her body up to press her back to his chest, one hand banded across her chest to grip her breast, his other hand diving between her legs to tease that beautiful bundle of nerves, Ellie flew apart.

She cried Hugh's name as he urged her on, his arms wrapped tight around her like he couldn't bear for an inch of his skin to not be in contact with hers. His teeth scraped over her shoulder as Ellie's body arched, her pleasure absolute.

He joined her there a moment later, his body stiffening, his movements becoming jerkier. He breathed her name, his lips against her sweat-damp skin, and Ellie felt dizzy and raw and elated. She collapsed. Hugh grunted as he got off the bed, disposed of the condom, then came back to bed and wrapped her in his arms.

Resting her head on his chest felt almost as good as the orgasms had. She knew she should get up and go to the bathroom to clean up and get ready for bed, but her limbs were so heavy. She fell asleep.

Sometime later, probably only twenty minutes or so, she heard a scratch at the door, and she dragged herself away from the man snoring in her bed to let her dog into the room. Louie took one glance at the bed, then curled into a ball on his bed next to the door. Ellie listened to the silence of the house, ducked over to the bathroom, then came back and closed her bedroom door just enough that Louie could push it open if he wanted to roam during the night. Finally, she went back to bed.

As soon as she lay down beside him, Hugh curled an arm around her waist, and everything was all right in Ellie's world.

At least, it was all right for now. Tomorrow, as always, was another story.

CHAPTER 23

Hugh woke up slowly, blissfully, with his arm wrapped around a sound-asleep Ellie. She snored softly, her hair a curtain on the pillow below his chin. In that lovely space between true sleep and true wakefulness, Hugh lingered, loving the feel of her body against his.

They'd sealed something last night. He knew it even without being fully awake. His heart had settled into a different rhythm, a better rhythm. He was . . . happy.

From a distance, a woman's voice sounded. "Oh! Louie! What are you—Claude, did you know Ellie picked Louie up last night?"

"Is that why she left early?"

"Must be." The voice was closer now. "Ellie-Belly! We're making eggs for breakfast. Do you want—"

A shriek rent the air.

Hugh bolted awake, jostling Ellie, who tumbled off the bed and fell to the ground, dragging the sheets and blankets with her. Air kissed Hugh's groin, which alerted him to the fact that he was completely naked. He slapped his hands over his exposed privates.

"Oh, gosh! Oh, I'm sorry! Oh!" Ellie's mother stammered, holding the door open, eyes wide as she shifted her gaze from a naked Hugh to a naked-and-bedsheet-tangled Ellie.

Ellie rolled around on the floor for a second, trying to kick the blankets off while getting hopelessly more tangled. "Mom! Get out!"

"Right." Helen closed the door, then, a second later, cracked it open again. "I'm sorry. I didn't know you had company."

"Mom."

"Okay, okay. I'm getting out!" The door closed. A few seconds passed while Ellie lifted the blankets so they covered her face. Hugh clutched his cock, heart hammering from the adrenaline now pumping through his veins. When Helen spoke again, she did so through the closed door. "Is Hugh staying for breakfast? How does he like his eggs?"

Ellie lay mummified on the floor, unmoving.

Hugh cleared his throat. "Whatever's more convenient for you, Mrs. Davis."

"It's Helen, honey," she said. "How about scrambled? We'll make a big batch."

"Sure." It was strange to talk to someone while Hugh cupped his own balls, but then again, almost everything on this island had been strange so far.

"Okay, then." Helen paused, and a collar jingled. "Your dog needs a bath, Ellie." Then her footsteps receded down the hall.

Ellie flopped her arms down to her sides, taking the sheet with her. Her face was very red. She glanced at Hugh. Hugh glanced at her.

"Morning," he said. He took his hands off his groin, which immediately drew Ellie's attention, which made Hugh's penis want to show off what it could do. "Sorry," he said and then cupped it again.

Ellie snorted and shifted her gaze to the ceiling. She slapped her hands over her face and half groaned, half laughed. "We should probably get dressed and get out there. They'll come knocking if we take too long."

Hugh had a thought that he didn't like. "Is this a . . . regular occurrence?"

Ellie gave him a flat look. "No, Hugh. This isn't a regular occurrence. It will please your ego to know you're the first man who has slept in that bed in a very long time."

It did please Hugh's ego to know that, but he chose not to voice it out loud.

She looked at him then, and his heart swelled so much it crowded out his lungs. He couldn't go on without telling her about the land. He couldn't keep it from her. Ellie was everything he wanted in a woman; keeping a secret like that from her felt wrong on every level.

At first, he hadn't told Ellie because he didn't know or trust her. Later, he was ashamed that he owned the land at all. It had felt like too big a topic to broach, because Hugh would have to explain his messed-up family history and somehow prove that he wasn't a money-hungry leech like his father after all.

Now it was different. She knew about his father. She even knew about the inheritance, although she didn't know exactly what it was he'd inherited. For once, Hugh felt like he could tell her the land next door belonged to him, and that he'd refused to take part in the resort development. It wouldn't feel like a lie to say he was nothing like his father.

Today, he'd be emailing his lawyer's office to inform them that he'd refused the deal. He'd put it all in writing. His plan had been to wait until that was officially done—his involvement in the Fernley Luxury Resort and Spa completely ended—before broaching the topic with Ellie, but after last night . . . he couldn't wait any longer. "Ellie, I want to talk about something."

She squinted at him, holding the sheets to her chest. "Right now?"

Remembering that he was naked, Hugh tilted his head. "Well . . ."

"After breakfast," she said as she sat up. "I just know that my mom is probably telling my grandma about you, and Grandma will have no shame in coming here to pester us." The blankets were still wrapped around Ellie's body, so she clambered to her feet and pushed them down into a wrinkly cylinder, which she stepped out of. Hugh watched, because she was naked and beautiful and he felt stunned stupid at the sight of her.

She grabbed a towel and wrapped it around herself, and Hugh regained the ability to think.

"I'll grab you a towel for a shower," Ellie said. "You mind if I go first?"

"Go ahead," he said.

A short while later, when they'd both washed and made themselves decent, Ellie led Hugh to the kitchen. The timber table was laden with a breakfast feast and all the hardware required to consume it: artisan-style bread, butter, bacon, eggs, fruit, coffee with all its fixings, juice, plates, mugs, utensils—the works.

"Ellie! Try the bread," her father commanded. "I finally found a cast-iron dutch oven at the thrift store this week, and I played around with the oven temperature this morning. I think the crust turned out better, but your mom thinks it's too much."

"Nearly ripped my teeth out," Helen grumbled good naturedly into her cup of coffee. "And Ellie, your car's making a weird clunking noise." Helen watched her daughter slice a thick piece of bread. "You want me to call the mechanic to come have a look at it?"

"No, I'll handle it." Ellie took her slice of bread, slathered it liberally with butter, and handed it over to Hugh. "It's been making that noise for a while. Thanks for driving it back last night."

"Well, you were obviously busy."

Ellie's face went red all over. Hugh hid his grin and watched her butter a second piece of bread. She bit into it and chewed, tilting her head from side to side. "Pretty good, Dad. Hugh?"

Hugh nodded. "Really good."

Helen threw her hands up. "Ugh. I can never win around here."

"There he is!" Mabel said, hobbling into the kitchen. She wore a paisley dressing gown with her hair in rollers. She patted Hugh's arm on her way to the coffee machine. "Helen woke up the whole house with her screaming."

"I forgot about the car parked outside," Helen answered. "It just surprised me, is all. Ellie hasn't had overnight visitors since high school."

"You knew about that?" Ellie said, her mouth full of bread. "Quentin used to sneak out through the window before anyone was awake."

Helen just rolled her eyes.

They sat down as a family and ate breakfast together, like Hugh's presence was not only normal but also welcomed. He liked it—a lot. He was halfway through his scrambled eggs when Claude's heavy hand landed on his shoulder.

"Now," Claude said. "Hugh, I have a question for you."

Hugh swallowed his bite and straightened, throwing a glance Ellie's way. She gave her dad a questioning look but didn't interrupt. Hugh turned to look at Claude where the man loomed over his shoulder and nodded. "Yes?"

Claude met his gaze with eyes the same color as Ellie's. His hand was an iron clamp on Hugh's shoulder, his face solemn.

Here it comes, Hugh thought. He was about to get the hurt-my-daughter-and-die speech from an overprotective father. The funny thing was, Hugh almost welcomed it. He wanted the chance to prove to this family that he was worthy of their affection. He wanted to be a *part* of it. He wondered if they'd be as welcoming to his mother, if they'd make her feel like she was part of the tapestry of the island the same way they did him.

And he wanted to stand up for Ellie. She'd been beaten down so much it made Hugh's chest ache. All her bravado, her crazy plots, they just hid the vulnerable heart of her. Hugh wanted to be the one to protect it.

Claude squeezed his shoulder harder, gray brows lowering over his eyes. Then he said, "If you had to choose one album that's perfect from start to finish, what would it be?"

Hugh blinked. "Um. *Rumours* by Fleetwood Mac?"

Claude let out a whoop and smacked Hugh's back so hard he nearly got a face full of scrambled eggs. Then Claude gripped both of Hugh's upper arms and shook him violently. "I knew I liked this kid! Didn't I tell you, Helen?"

"You did," Helen confirmed.

"We have to put it on now. I'll be right back."

Ellie tried to hide her smile behind her coffee cup, but Hugh saw it—and grinned back.

While Claude went to put the record on, Mabel turned to her granddaughter. "Now, Ellie. We need to talk about tonight."

Ellie set her cup down. "What about tonight, Grandma?"

Mabel narrowed her eyes. "You're not doing it alone." She put up a hand. "No. I don't want to hear it. Your parents and I talked, and even your sister agrees with us. We can't let you go to that fancy event without support."

"You called Daphne?" Ellie complained.

"You're going to let us help," Mabel declared. "And that's final."

Helen stood and unpinned the invitation to the Brownlow Foundation Gala from the kitchen corkboard. "Your father and I will attend," she said in a tone that invited no argument. "We'll help you get inside."

Ellie sighed and rubbed her forehead. She grabbed another piece of bread and tore off a chunk of crust, tossed it in her mouth, chewed, and swallowed. Then she said. "Fine. I'll tell you what I have planned. But if you're going to do this, we have to do it my way. The plan isn't up for discussion. Understood?"

"The plan isn't up for discussion," Mabel repeated. "Got it."

"Ellie's the boss," Helen confirmed, grabbing the pot of coffee to fill up her mug again. "We're just your minions, Ellie-Belly."

"Very large minions," Mabel amended, eyes on Hugh.

Ellie just groaned, shook her head, and let out one last huff. "This is a terrible idea."

Unfortunately, Hugh completely agreed.

CHAPTER 24

As plans went, Ellie's was pretty bad. It was rudimentary, had a high chance of failure, and relied on rational reactions from irrational people. The evidence she'd gathered was shaky at best, but her own reputation was so shot she knew even the most bulletproof, irrefutable evidence would be cast into doubt just because she was the one presenting it.

She knew all this; she didn't need her family to remind her of it. They did, though, for two long hours. But where she'd inherited her mother's troublemaking spirit, it was matched with her father's mulishness. Her mind was made up. It wasn't going to change.

Hugh had left after breakfast, before the worst of the objections had started. His departure had left a big hole in Ellie's mood, which she didn't feel like acknowledging, especially when her mother had thrown a saddle over her highest horse, swung a leg over as she mounted, and started lecturing Ellie about being responsible.

Mabel was the first to give in. She threw up her hands, sighed, and said, "Oh, darn it all to heck. I'm getting dressed." Then she came back moments later wearing army fatigues, slapping bulky old night vision goggles on the table that she "got from a lover who was in 'Nam." Ellie didn't know what to say to that.

They argued some more.

Helen rubbed her temples. Claude pulled his hair out. Daphne was on speakerphone, trying to persuade Ellie to come stay with her in Seattle to cool off. Ellie was being impulsive, Daphne told her, and she just needed to take a breather.

Ellie had thought this through from beginning to end, from every angle, through to every possible outcome. Her plan was stupid, not impulsive.

What choice did she have? Jason had declared war on her parents, and no one would defend them except for her. Her parents could remain in their happy little bubble, tending sheep and growing vegetables, but eventually, the pressure would become too much. Sheep would die. Developers would exert more and more pressure on them to sell their land. Jason would win. Again.

Ellie was still mad. Furious. The anger that had slid over her skin when she'd discovered Spencer and the milkweed had grown roots and vines that crawled over her skin like a living wall. She was encased in it. Consumed by it.

It was *wrong* for a drug-trafficking, money-laundering adulterer to stomp all over the people of this island. It boiled Ellie's blood that he'd gotten away with keeping her dog for so long. The things Jason had said last night rang in her mind, stoking the flames of her rage. He'd kept Louie because he knew it bothered Ellie, because he thought it would keep her quiet and meek. He was *torturing* her. On purpose.

And yes, it bothered her that he'd cheated on her and humiliated her. Her business had been vandalized, and the police hadn't even blinked an eye. To them, she deserved it. That bothered her. She was a woman shunned, a leprous boil that should be excised from polite society. It was unfair. She was sick of it. Layers and layers of hurt and anger compounded on each other until Ellie saw no choice but to fight back.

Over the past week, the only thing that had made her forget her anger was Hugh's presence—and wasn't that a frightening thought? For a man to glide into her life and upend it in a single week was too much to bear. She felt torn in two; half of her wanted to luxuriate in the feeling of Hugh's laughter, his compliments, his lovemaking. The other half wanted to crawl under her shell and protect herself from the drop of the other shoe that would soon land on her head and squash her like a bug.

Last night—last night had broken something in Ellie's mind. It was sex, but it was more than sex. She'd drowned in more-than-sex without thinking of the consequences. She'd inhaled the scent of Hugh's skin and felt her atoms rearrange to make space for this man in her life. She'd *felt* something, some completeness that had always eluded her. She'd seen the mirage of a future that included more than jail and humiliation and revenge. A future she'd been happy to dismiss as childish fantasy, one that ended with sunsets and skipping.

He'd kissed her before he got in his car. He'd taken his time with it too, even though they both knew they had an audience of curtain-twitchers looking on. His hands had been warm as they held her jaw, his eyes liquid when he finally pulled away and met her gaze.

Ellie wanted so badly for it to be true, for that look in his eyes to be genuine. She wanted to be as special as he made her feel. But she'd been hurt before, and she was scared and angry.

Ellie had said, "What did you want to talk about earlier?" and Hugh had touched her cheeks like she was precious.

"You have a lot to deal with in there," he said, tilting his head toward her parents' house, "and I have some important emails to send."

"Ooh, important emails. Didn't know I was in the presence of such a big shot."

He'd grinned and kissed the tip of her nose, making her chest buzz. "Well, now you do. Don't worry about it. Tomorrow, when everything's over, we can talk. Okay?"

She'd choked out an "Okay" and watched him drive away.

Now that Hugh was gone, she wasn't quite so blinded by his presence. Now she was afraid.

And when Ellie was afraid, she got angry. Well—angrier.

Finally, after her family had broken off to sulk in their own corners of the property, Ellie brought Louie outside and filled the big old iron tub that lived near the shed. She ran the water and coaxed Louie into the bath, using dog shampoo to wash the stink of Brownlow out of Louie's fur.

She was mad that Jason had left Louie outside all this time. It had felt like a taunt, a jab, an arrow fired from a distance to remind her that he held all the munitions. And the blow had landed—for six long months, she'd felt that pain.

But she had Louie now. He couldn't hurt her dog. He couldn't hurt *her*.

Yes, her plan was bad. Yes, she'd probably fail.

What did she have to lose?

A couple of hours later, Ellie wrapped her anger around her like armor and drove to Carlisle. The Fernley Hotel was a beautiful building. Its ceilings were decorated with medallions and cornices. There were chandeliers in almost every room on the ground floor, from the lobby to the bar to the big ballroom. The carpets were plush, the walls covered in tasteful yet slightly generic art.

It made Ellie want to throw up. The last time she'd been here, when she'd met Hugh in the lobby, she'd had to hold her breath while she walked from the rotating glass doors to the lobby desk. She'd sat in a lobby chair and gritted her teeth as memories crowded her mind.

Now she sneaked in through the side door that Hugh held open and crept along a service corridor to a room adjoining the ballroom. She'd planned enough events to know the layout of the most upscale venue on the island, so she knew exactly which door to open. They entered a small room that held stacked chairs and folding tables. Ellie took a deep breath, staring at the door that led to the ballroom.

Staff could be heard through the door, setting up the multitude of round tables that would seat the gala's guests. Chairs dragged over the floor, people yelled out instructions, and silverware clinked as tables were set. Ellie turned her back on the door and tried to settle her nerves.

"Okay," she said. "This is where we do it."

They got to work. Ellie tried to ignore the comfort of Hugh's presence. She needed to be sharp. She was about to do something really stupid.

But when Hugh caught her hand and pulled her in for a kiss, she was too weak to resist. Hope was like poison in her veins, seeping into every corner of her heart. Maybe this was real. Maybe it could work. He combed her hair back from her face and kissed her forehead, and Ellie felt like crying.

She pulled herself together, though, and got back to work.

Finally, when night had fallen and the first guests began to arrive, Ellie was ready to exact her revenge. She was ready to ruin Jason Brownlow's life, once and for all.

CHAPTER 25

Hugh's job was to be the eyes and ears in the lobby, on the lookout for anything that seemed amiss. He sipped a glass of sparkling water at the lobby bar, trying not to look like he was staring at every guest arriving through the hotel's front doors.

It had started raining in the late afternoon, so bellhops and valets scurried around, helping people with jackets and umbrellas, while the guests peeled off their outer layers and revealed tuxedos and gowns. Delicate classical music floated through the lobby, and the sound of conversation swelled as more people arrived.

Hugh could have been one of them. If he'd made different decisions this week, he could have been heading down to the ballroom, his eyes shut against the truth.

He'd officially cut ties with the project today, informing his lawyer and Brownlow's team that he was pulling out of the project. It was done. So why did he feel this crushing sense of impending doom?

Brownlow smiled at every new arrival, his laughter grating against Hugh's skin. He shook hands with every guest, charm oozing off him like blood from a wound. After a while, Jason disappeared down the hallway and into the ballroom. Hugh texted Ellie to let her know Brownlow was heading her way. He got a thumbs-up back.

Ellie's parents arrived then, stepping out of their jackets to reveal clothing that didn't quite fit in with the glittering gowns and jewels dripping from the other guests. Helen wore a black wrap dress that hit her just below the knee, a thin gold chain circling her neck. Claude was in khakis and a white button-down. They looked apprehensive. Hugh wanted to tell them to go home, but they had a role to play tonight too.

He sipped his soda water—and waited. His next task wouldn't be for a while, until after the initial commotion had occurred.

The agony was in waiting. Ellie knew it would be bad, but she hadn't realized it would be *this* bad. A second text from Hugh told her her parents were headed to the ballroom. It took an eternity for all the guests to be seated, for the classical music to die down, and for the sound of a man's voice to start droning through the speakers, his words interspersed with polite applause.

Ellie took deep breaths.

She could imagine Jason, standing in front of a podium, light shining on his golden hair, looking completely at ease, completely confident.

Not for long.

Her lips curled into a snarl.

She texted her grandmother, who was in position. Mabel had what Ellie hoped was the safest job—getaway driver. She'd grumbled but finally accepted her mandate and promised to stay in the car no matter what. Ellie thought there was a fifty-fifty chance of Mabel actually listening to her orders. She'd brought the night vision goggles, though, so maybe the chances were more like seventy-thirty in favor of Mabel going rogue.

An unsteady, thumping heartbeat made it difficult for Ellie to keep calm. She paced the small storage room, willing her pulse to slow. Timing was everything. She had to wait for the exact right moment to go out there and hijack the screen so she could expose Jason's crimes.

Time crawled. Sand dripped through the hourglass one grain at a time. Ellie felt itchy and warm. Way too warm. Sweat ran down her spine and dampened her shirt.

Finally, her phone buzzed. Her dad was giving her the signal. Time to go.

She exhaled and slipped out of the storage room and behind a curtain she'd arranged earlier to block her movements. She dropped down, spying the little table that held a laptop and a network of cables and electronics. It was unoccupied, just like her father had indicated.

It was a short distance to the table, and she made it without being seen. She grabbed the laptop from the top of the table, pulled out the cables that were connected to it, and plugged in her own. It took too long for it to load. Way, way too long.

But she'd worked with the Fernley Hotel's projector before, so she knew exactly how to connect everything. With trembling hands, she stuffed the laptop under the tablecloth draped over the electronics table to hopefully buy herself a few more seconds—and pressed the key to connect to the projector.

Spencer's face appeared on the screen, sitting in his office with the harbor as the backdrop. He looked guileless. Innocent. Heartbroken. Ellie pressed play, then jumped behind the curtain where she'd originally entered the ballroom.

She heard Spencer's voice, loud and clear. "Jason Brownlow lied to me. He made me poison Claude and Helen's sheep, but he told me it was good for them. I was supposed to keep it a secret."

The room went silent. Ellie reached the doorway, still concealed by the curtain, but she couldn't go through to safety. Not yet. She had to stay—had to time this next phase of the plan properly. She crouched.

The next shot was Jason and Fergus exchanging a bag of cash—and a cut to the picture of the duffel bag in the filing cabinet. Murmurs went through the room.

Jason sliced through the crowd, his face like thunder, just as her own face popped up on the screen.

"Jason is using the Brownlow Foundation to launder dirty drug money through this island. He's defrauding us all, and he's trying to intimidate my parents into selling their land so he can launder even more of it."

The murmurs intensified.

Jason looked seconds away from murder. "Shut it off," he barked, and a poor sod rushed toward the laptop and clicked frantically before finally realizing all the cables to his laptop were disconnected. He looked utterly panicked.

Jason was close now, his long steps eating the ground between them. He'd come around the last table and be able to see Ellie soon. So soon. Just a few more steps—

Jason saw her.

He changed his trajectory, charging toward Ellie. She made a strategic retreat to the storage room off the ballroom just as the video and audio feed cut out. The poor AV guy had pulled the plug on the projector and microphones, and an awful squeal went through the room. Guests shouted.

They'd had mere seconds to get the accusations out into the public. Ellie hoped it would be enough—and knew it wasn't. No one would believe her. Not from a photo of a bag of cash and the word of a harbor worker.

Ellie ducked into the room as her heart pounded. She could almost feel his footsteps coming closer, as if the soles of Jason's feet were stomping on her chest. *Bang, bang, bang.* Her bones ground under the pressure. She turned in the storage room to face the ballroom door.

A second later, it flew open. Jason stood silhouetted in the doorway, fists clenched, eyes slitted. "You *bitch*," he hissed. He slammed the door behind him and turned the lock.

Another squeal in the main room, with cries of outrage from the crowd. Ellie hoped that noise was what she thought it was, but fear clouded her mind.

Her ex-fiancé was steps away from her, and she hadn't prepared herself for the impact of his presence. She'd hardly seen him since her arrest, other than a few passing interactions when she'd tried to get the sheriff to get her dog back.

Now he was here, tall and blond and terrifying. The snarl on his lips betrayed the rot beneath the surface. He was an evil, horrible man.

Jason stepped forward, and Ellie fought the urge to shrink back. The light in the storage room was fluorescent, buzzing above their heads. One of the lights flickered, causing shadows to dance under Jason's eyes. He looked like a demon come to life.

"Do you think this is going to stop me?" Jason said, voice oddly calm. "Do you think spreading your legs for Hugh Hartford will stop me?"

Hugh? What did Hugh have to do with this?

Didn't matter. *Stick to the plan.* "You've been using the people of this island," Ellie said, trying to keep her voice from trembling. "You've been using your charity to lie to all of us. I know you've been laundering money through the Brownlow Foundation, Jason. I have proof."

Fear clogged her throat as Jason took a step forward. She'd loved this man. Maybe not an everlasting love, maybe it was nothing more than infatuation, but she'd believed that he was good. Now, all she could see was a heartless monster who hurt innocent animals, who used everyone around him for his own personal gain.

Jason took another step forward and laughed. "Ellie, honey, give up. You're never going to win."

Anger boiled through her, burning away the fresh fear that had held her body frozen. She dug her fingernails into her palms. "I know about the drug trafficking. I know you're planning on using the resort to expand your operations."

Jason arched a brow. "Oh, sweetheart. It's cute that you think you can do something about it."

The pet names were really getting on Ellie's nerves. How dare he speak to her in that condescending way? He'd never respected her. Never treated her as an equal. "You killed my parents' sheep."

"Spencer Wisneski did that."

"You ordered him to!"

"He volunteered." A cruel smile. "It's not my fault the man can't look up what milkweed does to a sheep."

Distantly, she heard a swell of noise from the ballroom.

The edges of her vision turned red. She'd been *engaged* to this monster. This piece of dirt. "You're an awful person."

He spread his hands. "You're the one with the criminal record, Ellie. Who's going to believe any of this shit?"

"Everyone on this island will believe me, because it's true." They had to. This *had* to work.

Jason let out another cruel laugh and took a step closer. "I mean, money laundering? Really?" He scoffed. "Please. How about your little excursion breaking into my house? You think the police will believe me when I tell them that my alarm was disabled and I found one of your socks in my dog's house?" A tiny, triumphant smirk. "Because I do."

"*My.* Dog."

He laughed, an ugly, rasping, cackling sound. "Maybe I'll make a complaint to Bill Jackson about someone breaking into my backyard and stealing my dog. Then again, I'd been planning on putting him down today, so maybe I'll let you keep him."

Oh no. If he'd executed her dog, Ellie would've killed Jason, and she wouldn't have even been sorry.

"And I know it was you who wrecked my office," Ellie snarled.

The door to the ballroom rattled behind him, and Ellie gave it a panicked glance. Not yet. *Not yet.* The lock held, though, and whoever was there stopped trying.

Lips curled, Jason took a step forward. The storage room suddenly felt very, very small. "Yes, that was me. Did you know I only had to pay that kid fifty bucks to do it? I would have paid fifty thousand. It was worth it to put you in your place, because you obviously didn't get the message the first time you tried to stick your nose where it doesn't belong. I thought a night in jail would set you straight, and for six months, I guess it did. But you never learned your lesson, did you, Ellie? You went back to that dump your parents own and decided you needed to come back and annoy me some more. I felt like being a bit more direct this time. This is what happens when you get in my way, Ellie. You lose *everything.*"

He stepped forward again, his hand flying out to grab Ellie's neck. He slammed her against the wall—and the door beside them flew open. Hugh stalked in from the hallway door, panting like he'd run here, and ripped Jason's arm away from Ellie. He put himself between Ellie and Jason. "Do *not* touch her."

Ellie put her hand to her neck, trying to catch her breath.

"Oh, the white knight to the rescue!" Jason laughed. "How cute. Have you picked the baby names yet?"

"How long have you been using your charity to wash money, Jason?" Ellie asked, voice rough, throat aching. "Brag about it. I know you want to. You're probably dying to let me know just how clever you are."

Another scoff. "I'm not an idiot. Not like your knight here, who decided to turn his back on the business deal of the century. How did you convince him to do that?"

Hugh went very, very still in front of her.

Ellie frowned. "What?"

Jason looked at her. At Hugh. Back at her again. A slow, dark laugh fell from his lips, the sound burning against Ellie's skin like acid. "You didn't know," Jason said quietly, gleefully. "He didn't tell you."

"Tell me what?"

"Ellie, don't listen to him," Hugh said. "I can explain."

"Tell me what?"

"Hugh owns the land next door to your parents' place. His father negotiated a deal with me, buttoned it up, then went ahead and croaked right before he signed on the dotted line. Then Hugh, the genius, reneged on it. Turned down more money than you can imagine. All he had to do was sign the papers, and he refused. I think it was your magic pussy that convinced him, actually, so at least you have that going for you." A wicked, cruel smile. "He'll tire of it, though. I sure did."

Words passed through Ellie's ears, her neurons fired, and her brain tried to make sense of the inputs. She stood there, blinking, unable to process. The earth tilted beneath her feet, and she felt like tumbling to the side. It took all her energy just to stay upright, just to understand what was being said.

Hugh . . . owned the land next door? Hugh had been about to do business with *Jason Brownlow*? *That's* why he was on the island? That was the inheritance he'd hinted at?

"Since when?" she screeched—or maybe it came out as a whisper. She couldn't tell. The ringing in her ears was too loud.

Hugh turned, reached a hand toward her. She flinched. His eyes were tortured. He shook his head. "I wanted to tell you, but I knew you'd be mad. I wanted to help you."

The steel jaws of an old trap sprang shut around her ankle. With eyes wide open, Ellie had walked right into it. She'd trusted Hugh with her secrets, her plans, her heart. She'd *trusted* him, and he'd lied to her.

Just like Jason.

Except this time was worse, because Ellie should have known better. She was supposed to have learned her lesson, and somehow she'd let this man worm his way into her heart over the course of a few measly days.

She was a fool. A pathetic, groveling, needy fool who couldn't read a man's intentions to save her miserable life.

"You . . ." The betrayal was a dagger through her back. It slid right under her ribs and pierced her heart. She felt the blood welling in her chest cavity, felt herself dying where she stood. "You came to Fernley because you were doing business with Jason? And you didn't *tell me?*"

Jason laughed. "Oh, this is fantastic. This is better than when you walked in on me and Jade, Ellie. You should see your face."

And that's when Ellie realized a lot of people could see her face. Because this was her plan. Her stupid, rudimentary, probably-going-to-fail plan had gone exactly how it was supposed to. She knew that her original video would be cut off as soon as it started playing.

But the damage would be done—because Jason would be angry. And when Jason was angry, he got vindictive.

The whole point of the original video was to get Jason right here, with her, saying everything he'd just said. She'd known he would follow her when he spotted her. Ellie had been counting on it.

Which was why right at that moment, in the main ballroom, streaming live from the phone she'd set up on a tripod on top of a stack of chairs in the corner, her face was on the big screen. The entire ballroom full of people had witnessed her discovering that Hugh had lied to her.

That's what Hugh had been doing. That had been his second job. When the first video got cut off, Claude and Helen distracted the AV guy, and Hugh connected the live stream to the projector. And, because Ellie didn't do things halfway, it was also streaming live on social media, so everyone on the island could tune in to the next episode of the *Ellie Davis Embarrassment Show.*

Her humiliation was on display for all to see. Again.

"Ellie, I was never going to sign the deal with him. From the moment I met you. I promise."

She stared at Hugh and saw a stranger. She'd trusted him. She'd *trusted* him.

The pain in her chest was unlike anything she'd felt before. It made her fingertips tingle. She felt like she was floating. Or sinking. Or dying.

He'd lied to her. Over and over again. He'd held her in his arms, and it had been a lie. All of it. Every moment—even the night before.

Hugh was no different from the man gleefully cackling behind him. Hugh didn't respect her or see her or know her. Like Jason, he'd led her along by her nose because—why? Jason had done it because he was a terrible person driven by greed who wanted to use her for personal gain and was all too happy to toss her aside when it became clear he wouldn't get what he wanted.

Was Hugh the same? He'd come to the island to secure his inheritance—to make sure he got the money he pretended he didn't want—and had let Ellie make a fool of herself. He'd indulged all her stupid criminal schemes and then had gone home and laughed at all her bumbling.

Well, he had company now, didn't he? Jason was wiping tears from his eyes, and the rest of the island would be laughing along with him as they watched. The humiliation was so potent It made her dizzy.

"I'm almost glad our deal fell through," Jason said, his voice sounding like it came from underwater. "This is better than I could have imagined." He laughed again, and Ellie felt utterly empty. Stripped raw. "I dated her for three years, even promised to marry her just so I could persuade her parents to sell me their waterfront land, which was a waste of time . . . but it was worth it. For this, right here, it was all worth it."

Hugh's fist connected with Jason's jaw in a crack of sound that made Ellie flinch, but that must've been a purely physiological reaction. Her brain had sent a message to her muscles to jump, and so she had. Inside, she was getting colder by the second, emptier. The pain that had rocked her chest was fading, until she couldn't feel anything. She touched her face to make sure it was still there.

Jason staggered back, and Hugh lunged forward again.

Ellie supposed he was defending her, somehow. But every blow Hugh landed felt like it was aimed at her. She couldn't think about anything, because the shame and humiliation were too overwhelming. Too familiar.

It had happened *again*. She'd trusted a man, fallen in love with him—in a *week*, no less—and it had been based on nothing but lies. When Jason had betrayed her, she'd wanted to rampage. She'd been so hurt, so angry, so *hot*. All her emotions had burned.

Now, she wanted to fade away until she forgot her own name. Her skin was a thin layer of ice over cold, cold flesh beneath.

When the side door opened again, she was in a daze. It took her a few blinks to focus on her grandmother. A black-and-white bullet rushed in beside Mabel, crashed into Ellie's legs, and nearly laid her flat on the floor before she caught herself on a stack of chairs.

Jason let out a yell. She saw him flip Hugh onto his back, his fist raised high, ready to come down on the other man's face.

Louie lunged. Her dog clamped down on Jason's forearm just as Jason brought it down toward Hugh's face. The dog deflected the punch enough that it glanced across Hugh's cheek as he dodged, giving him time to roll over and regain his feet.

Jason screamed, and blood welled from Louie's bite. The dog held on. Ellie must have cried out, because her dog let go and came to her. Jason staggered to his feet and faced her, fury painting red streaks across his cheeks. Hugh sidestepped between them, cutting her line of sight.

The world was blinking lights and odd noises. None of it made sense, except for the hand Ellie curled around Louie's collar.

"Ellie, honey," Mabel said from the doorway. "We have to go, *now*." She was still wearing the camouflage pants, but she'd put on a wooly sweater and a rain jacket on top. The night vision goggles were hanging around her neck. She looked odd.

Ellie wanted to tell her so, but what came out was a jumble of words. Finally, she managed to say, "You're not supposed to leave the car."

"We have to go," Mabel repeated more softly. "Come here, Ellie-Belly." She beckoned with a wrinkled hand, her eyes swimming with concern.

The men were on the floor again, wrestling, their faces red, anger pouring off them in thick, noxious waves. Ellie would've laughed about how ridiculous they looked if she remembered how. She stepped around a tumbled chair and followed her grandmother, Louie's warm body at her side. Her fingers gripped his collar like it was the only real thing in the world.

"Through here," Mabel said hurriedly, hobbling to a fire exit. "There you go, baby girl, good. A few more steps now."

Ellie's arm ached where Mabel gripped it, but it felt oddly detached from the rest of her. The ache was more of a memory, an echo of what she thought her arm should feel. It wasn't actually real. The collar was real. Smooth leather, warm fur beneath her knuckles. She clung to that feeling and forgot the pain everywhere else.

An alarm went off, and Ellie wondered absently if it was because they'd opened the fire door. She guessed it probably was.

Rain came down in heavy sheets, blurring the already-hazy edges of Ellie's vision. She stumbled on a step and caught herself on a handrail. Her grandmother's face was drawn, so concerned she looked ill.

"Come on, Ellie, darling," Harry said, hobbling up from the bottom of the stairs. Greta urged her on with a flick of her hand. Mabel had brought her friends. The three of them coaxed Ellie down the steps and onto the pavement.

The red hatchback waited for them. Her getaway car. So close. She could escape all this, cuddle her dog, and pray that it had all been a horrible nightmare.

Harry held the back door open, and Louie jumped in. Greta circled around to the passenger seat, and Mabel tried to coax a stumbling Ellie in beside Louie. While Ellie gripped the top of the door and tried to get her legs to work, a dark SUV came screeching around the side of the hotel. It slammed on the brakes, and all four doors opened at once. Behind it, another SUV arrived, and another.

So there'd been more than one of them, Ellie noted, like she was admiring a new bloom on a bush. An aimless, absent sort of thought. The rain blurred her vision, soaked her clothing. She blinked at the vehicles, her mind fuzzy. She knew there was something weird about those SUVs. She knew they didn't belong here.

From out of the three vehicles came men and women in dark pants and bulletproof vests, some of them carrying handguns, some of them wearing what looked like tactical gear with bigger guns. They moved quickly, streaming through the door Ellie and Mabel had just exited. More of them shouted in the distance, presumably entering through the front of the hotel.

Ellie wondered if she was hallucinating, until she realized Mabel had squeaked and was clinging to her arm like it was a lifeline. So the SUVs were real, as were all these people. How 'bout that.

Three letters blazed all over, on the vests, on jackets, on the badge that a short, scary woman flashed as she stopped a foot from where they stood: FBI.

STEP FOUR: EXIT STRATEGY

CHAPTER 26

Cold numbness gave way to pain in Ellie's chest, but only after many hours. While she still existed in that frozen state, she spent the night being interviewed by the FBI. Voice monotone, she told them everything she knew. She admitted to sneaking into Jason's house, admitted to confronting Fergus. When she told them her master plan to expose Jason in front of the whole island, the agents in the room exchanged a dark look.

Agent Fernandez, the short, scary woman who'd accosted them outside the hotel, leaned her fists on the table. "That was a very foolish plan," she told Ellie.

Ellie nodded. "Yeah."

"You could have ruined a very lengthy operation with that stunt."

Of course she could have. Ellie ruined a lot of things.

Cold clung to her chest, sluicing through her veins like ice floes moving down a river. The pain hadn't arrived yet, but distantly, in some hidden corner of Ellie's mind, she knew it would show up soon.

They let her go an hour before dawn. She was on the outskirts of Carlisle, in an office building that had been unused for years, a blocky, concrete monolith that had become part of the scenery whenever she drove by. She hadn't even noticed any lights or cars outside. She had no idea when the FBI had arrived. Not that it mattered.

The rain had stopped overnight, but heavy cloud cover still blotted out all the fading stars. Helen was waiting for her outside, behind the wheel of Ellie's car. When her mother's face softened, a wrinkle appearing between her brows, Ellie felt the first pangs of hurt. She let Helen wrap strong arms around her shoulders to pull her close, melting into her mother's embrace.

The two of them had always been a bit too similar to get along. They butted heads constantly, Ellie's impulsiveness and hot temper smacking into her mother's protectiveness. Ellie had spent a long time resenting the way her mother had overcompensated for her misspent youth.

But right now, her mother's hug held all the pieces of Ellie together.

"Let's go home," Helen whispered in her daughter's hair.

Ellie nodded. When they got there, she fell into bed, only vaguely feeling the mattress depress as Louie joined her, curling his warm body against her back.

When she woke up around dinnertime, the pain finally blazed to life. It sliced into the flesh between her ribs, drawing syrupy blood. It sank into the marrow of her bones. It pulsed in Ellie's head with every heartbeat.

Hugh had lied to her. He'd held her in his arms like she meant something to him, and he'd *lied*.

She'd been stupid to trust him. Why hadn't she questioned why he was on the island? She'd accepted his line about wanting to find out about his father's family and hadn't probed any deeper. She'd known him a *week*, and she'd trusted him completely. Foolish. Utterly idiotic. She deserved to be embarrassed once more, deserved to be exposed in front of the whole island the way she had been.

Humiliation was a balm she smoothed over her skin to ease the pain of betrayal. Shame, at least, was familiar in a way that was bearable. She was used to being sneered at for her actions. She wasn't used to the bone-jarring agony of Hugh's deception.

Her body ached, so she stayed in bed and trailed her fingers through Louie's fur. Her dog put his head on her stomach and closed his eyes, not leaving her side. She slept again.

Dawn was dull and gray, as though the sun struggled to penetrate the oppression that pressed down on the island. Ellie's blinds had remained open all night, so she watched the tops of pine trees sway against the overcast sky until Louie whined beside her.

He hadn't left her side. She looked at him, his black-and-white head, his sad, soulful eyes. "Go outside," she told him. "Get Dad to take you for a walk."

Louie closed his eyes.

Ellie sighed and hauled herself up to a sitting position. Louie jumped off the bed and padded to the door, then paused and waited for her. She scowled at him. "I'm coming," she grumbled.

The effort it took to lift herself up on her feet was superhuman. Pins and needles raced down her legs, her muscles aching in protest. But she found a robe and wrapped it around herself, then led her dog down the hallway. Her father's Crocs were the closest shoes to the door, so she slipped those on and let Louie outside. He bounded out, sniffed the ground for the perfect place to pee, and finally chose a lucky fence post near the sheep pasture.

Sheep called out to each other from the far end of the field. Birds twittered. Trees whispered in the wind. Ellie tilted her head up to the silver clouds and inhaled the fresh, cool air, embracing the bite of it as it entered her lungs.

"There you are!" Claude circled around the edge of the house, carrying an empty bucket that usually held grain for the sheep. He hadn't wanted to let them graze in any of the fields far from the house since they'd discovered the milkweed, so he'd been feeding them himself. He set the bucket down and closed the distance between them, then gripped Ellie's shoulders. His eyes betrayed his worry, but he forced his lips into a smile. "You hungry?"

"Not really."

"You'll have toast," he proclaimed. He whistled, Louie came running, and the three of them went inside.

Helen and Mabel hovered in the kitchen, stealing worried glances at Ellie. Louie sat at her feet while her father cut thick slices of sourdough bread and dropped them in the toaster. Kibbles clattered against Louie's bowl as Helen filled it up, but the dog didn't move from Ellie's side. Helen moved the bowl closer, but still Louie didn't eat.

Ellie stared at the charred crescent moon in the middle of the table, her head pulsing in agony.

"It's all over the news," Mabel said in the silence, as if she were picking up the thread of a conversation that hadn't paused when Ellie entered. "They're saying the Brownlow Foundation is a sham. He's been stealing money from all the donors for years."

"Mom," Helen said. "Let's not talk about this right now."

Ellie blinked and looked at her grandmother. "Jason? What happened to him?"

"Arrested," Mabel said, dropping into her usual chair on one long side of their oval table.

It should have been a relief. It should have been vindicating. Ellie just nodded and tried not to wince as a sharp pain pierced her chest.

She didn't ask about the other man who had been there, the one who had flown to her rescue right before he'd stabbed her with a poisoned dagger. She couldn't bring herself to utter his name.

Claude placed a plate in front of her. Steam wafted from the toast, butter melting into every crevice. Ellie stared at it, and her family stared at her. Louie lifted his head and blinked at her, waiting.

She took a bite, and Louie finally went to his dog bowl to have his breakfast. He crunched his kibble, turning his head to check on her when she put her food back down on her plate. Ellie huffed, relenting. She ate the toast. It sat like a brick in her stomach.

How could she explain that this new betrayal hurt more than Jason's ever had? Her feelings made no sense. She didn't even *know* Hugh. She'd had heads of lettuce in the fridge longer than she'd known him.

Hope, she realized, was the culprit. For those few days, she'd believed that someone could love and respect her—all of her. Exactly as she was.

She was such a fucking idiot. She should have stuck to revenge.

But—hadn't she achieved exactly that? Jason had been arrested, exposed. He'd admitted all those horrible things on a live stream that was broadcast to the entire island. His fancy event had been crashed by the FBI. Ellie had her dog back.

Everything had gone exactly to plan—except it hadn't. The victory was bitter on Ellie's tongue, meaningless. What did it matter if Jason's rotten personality was finally out in the open? Who cared if she'd finally been proved right?

Ellie sure didn't.

She'd actually thought she could fix this mess herself. More evidence of her folly. She should have called a tip in to the FBI the moment she left Fergus's, got Louie, and left the island like she'd planned from the start.

She stood. "I'm going to go pack."

Three heads turned to look at her. Helen's brows arched. "Pack?"

"I'm taking the afternoon ferry," she explained.

Mabel cleared her throat. "Ellie . . ."

"Dad, do you mind calling Daphne and asking her if I can crash on her couch tonight, if the offer's still open?"

He looked like he wanted to say something else, but all that came out was "Sure, Ellie."

Ellie gave them all a jerky nod and headed for her bedroom, Louie's claws clicking on the hardwood floors as he followed.

Her suitcase was zipped up and ready to be wheeled out to Ellie's car when there was a knock on her bedroom door.

"Yeah?"

"It's me," her mother said through the closed door. "Can I come in?"

"Sure," Ellie said, setting her phone aside. She was sitting on her bed with her back leaning against the wall. Louie snoozed with his head on her calf, but he opened an eye when Helen walked in.

Helen's eyes snagged on the suitcase, then came to rest on Ellie. "All packed up?"

"Just bought my ticket," she said, lifting her phone.

The bed dipped as Helen sat on it and shimmied so she leaned on the wall beside Ellie. "You don't have to leave, honey. You know that, right?"

"I do have to leave, though. I have to get out of here."

They were silent for a while, and Ellie felt the need to address the obvious: "You were right about calling the authorities. I should have listened to you."

Helen didn't badger her, or give her a knowing look, or do anything to betray what she was thinking. She just sat on Ellie's bed and glanced around the room. Then she let out a breath. "I know how tempting it is to take the world on by yourself. I did it for years."

Ellie worried at a thread on her jeans where they were frayed in a few strategic spots around the knees. "I know, Mom. I heard the stories."

"My father was a drinker," Helen said.

Ellie froze, blinking at her mother. "Really?"

She'd never met her maternal grandfather. He'd died shortly after Daphne was born, a couple of years before Ellie arrived.

"Mm-hmm," Helen replied. Louie lifted his head and stood, then walked a few steps to settle across both their legs. "Owed money to half the people on the island, paid his debt doing odd jobs here and there. The minute he got any money in his pocket, he'd be sitting on a high stool drinking it down. Your grandmother had to pick up the slack, of course. She worked at the ferry terminal and the grocery store and anywhere else she could to put food on our table. I grew up feeling like I'd never amount to anything, and the people in those big waterfront houses loved reminding me of it too. I grew up angry, and I let it out by causing trouble. I figured if people thought I came from bad stock, why not prove them right? Then later, all that anger got funneled to other causes I began to care about. Protecting the natural beauty on the island, making sure our politicians didn't get too petty or too greedy, railing against any injustice I thought I saw."

"Is this where you tell me that being mad is never worth it, and I should try to forgive and be at peace? Being a vigilante never works, especially when you're as bad at it as I am?"

Helen took Ellie's hand and squeezed. "This island can get claustrophobic if you let it," she finally replied. "It's small-town thinking coupled with just enough isolation to make it feel like there's nowhere else to go. I understand why you snapped, Ellie. And I understand why you feel like you have to leave."

They both petted a delighted Louie, who snuffled happily under all the attention. His ears twitched while his eyes remained closed, his tail swishing gently back and forth.

Ellie let out a long breath. "I'm so embarrassed, Mom. About everything that happened with Jason. I strutted around town like I was better than my own family while I was with him. I can't believe you still welcomed me back home after how I acted. And now this. Daphne was right, you know. My plan was impulsive. I should have listened to you. And everyone saw the moment that Hugh admitted he—"

She couldn't even say it. Ellie closed her eyes, and then her mother's arms were around her. Helen whispered soothing words full of love and support, and Ellie believed only half of them.

Then Helen pulled away. "I want to show you something," she said, then got off the bed and hurried out of the room. Ellie was just about to follow her when she reappeared in the doorway, brandishing a photo album. Helen grinned. "Here we go."

Ellie eyed the album suspiciously as her mother climbed back onto the bed and let Louie settle where he liked. Then she opened the front cover of the album and laughed. "Here's your grandmother. She got in trouble during a civil rights rally that got nasty. She had the gall to wonder where I got my attitude from."

Ellie leaned forward and looked at a young Mabel mean-mugging the camera. They turned the page. There were photos of Carlisle from decades ago, when it was little more than a ferry terminal, a general store, and a few lonely houses. There was a photo of Mabel, her husband, and Helen, who looked to be five or six years old. Then Helen as a teenager, looking surly and annoyed in almost every photo, except for one at a rocky beach in Fernley National Park, where they'd caught her midlaugh as she jumped in the water.

Then came the mug shots.

Ellie stared at the photos, then at her mother. "Why did you *keep* these?"

"I wasn't going to, but Grandma insisted," Helen answered with a wry smile. "She said she wanted proof of my misdeeds for when I inevitably tried to forget about them."

Ellie arched a brow, and Helen laughed.

"Here's the one that had me being called the 'Topless Tree Hugger' for a full year," Helen said, smiling proudly, pointing to a photo of her with crimped hair, bangs that screamed the eighties, and a top that looked like scrubs. "I marched down Main Street in Carlisle to protest a logging directive from one of the big companies operating on the island, and took my shirt off when the reporters showed up. That caused a stink, I'll tell you what. Even though I had fabulous breasts in those days. Ask your father if you don't believe me!"

"Mom, stop!" Ellie couldn't help but laugh. She didn't know whether to be horrified or amused. Maybe she should be grateful she hadn't gone topless during this whole ordeal? "Why are you telling me this?"

With a sigh, Helen flipped to the last page in the album, where Ellie's mug shot had been added. A sick, gurgling feeling rose in Ellie's gut. She didn't like seeing it, didn't like being reminded of how stupid she'd been. Her smile faded, and she looked away.

"You come from a line of women who, when they see something that isn't right, aren't afraid of speaking up about it. Don't let other people's opinions of you change that, Ellie. It's the very best part of us, even when it gets us in trouble." Helen paused, sighing. "Just, you know, try not to get yourself killed. I do love you to pieces, Ellie. No matter what."

A stronger woman would have been able to claim her legacy and march into Carlisle with her head held high. Ellie couldn't. She still needed to get away. Meeting her mother's watery gaze, she spoke through a tight throat. "I have to catch the ferry, Mom. And I love you too."

Watching the ferry arrive at the terminal was a pastime Ellie had loved as a child. The precision with which the captain piloted the vessel looked like magic, bringing the huge ship in to nudge against the pier far too gently for its size. The workers were well practiced, moving with hurried efficiency as passengers waited to disembark.

Ellie watched from her car, parked in one of the long lines that would drive onto the ferry once the vessel was ready to accept them. A few drivers around her turned their engines on, but Ellie left hers off, knowing they still had long minutes to wait.

Louie sat curled in the back seat, eyes closed. That was as far as he'd allowed her to get from him since the night of the gala. Her big suitcase was in the trunk, filled with whatever she'd thrown in there earlier. Packing was a blur.

She'd lost her backpack somewhere. She'd have to get a new one.

Tiredness made her jumpy. Her mother had squeezed her tight and let her go, and her father had shed a tear as she drove off. But what choice did Ellie have? There was nothing on this island for her but bitterness and humiliation.

The pier gate opened. First, the foot passengers exited the ferry via the designated ramp. Then the cars came out, one long row at a time like a line of gleaming metal ants, until the ferry was empty. Finally, the first car in line to depart Fernley was waved forward by a man in a fluorescent-yellow vest. He had a thick beard and sun-darkened skin, and he waved the cars on, coaxing them to park as close together as possible so everyone would fit.

When Ellie drove onto the vessel and parked her car, she let out a breath. Tension loosened in her shoulders, like she'd escaped the jaws of some vicious monster and could only now take a breath. "Come on, Louie," she said, and they got out of the car. She clipped his leash on and brought him up to the top deck, finding a seat on a white-painted steel box in a forgotten corner on the starboard side. From there, Ellie could see the glittering expanse of the sea crashing against the rocks of Fernley's coastline. The air smelled of salt and the tang of metal and oil.

She let out another breath and scratched her dog's head. "We're finally going, Louie." A week later than planned, but they'd made it.

The last car drove onto the ferry, and the workers secured the gate at the stern of the ship. They'd leave within moments. The ferry's horn blasted, confirming Ellie's thought. She inhaled. Exhaled. It was almost over.

Then—"Wait!" A figure ran down the hill toward the ferry terminal, arms pumping, dark hair wild around his head. "Wait!"

Ellie pulled herself onto her feet, gripping the handrail. Hugh slowed to a stop near the end of the ferry terminal's pavement, his eyes scanning the ferry's deck. She couldn't read his expression from this distance, but she could see his chest rising and falling as he panted, could read the tension in his shoulders.

Then he lifted his gaze—and saw her.

CHAPTER 27

She couldn't just *leave*. Hugh stared at Ellie, his heart cracking.

After everything—after all they'd done together—she was just getting on the ferry and going?

No. Unacceptable. It wasn't right.

She'd listen to what he had to say; she'd understand that he hadn't meant to hurt her. She wouldn't just leave the island without even saying goodbye. That wasn't the Ellie he knew. That wasn't the woman he . . . he . . .

"Ellie!" he screamed.

The woman he knew would fight, damn it. She'd set her jaw and face him with fire in her eyes, and she'd let him know exactly what she thought of him. She'd be mad. She'd want to get even.

She wouldn't just *leave*. The Ellie he knew wouldn't run away.

"Ellie!" The wind stole his words, but he knew she'd heard him. She gripped the handrail on the deck above, her face turned toward him. Another gust of wind stuck his clothing to his front, but he didn't feel the cold. He didn't even feel the pinpricks of raindrops that battered his bare face and hands.

Hugh knew he'd messed up. He should have told her about the land, should have come clean right away. But—how? Everything had happened so fast. She'd smashed through his life and left him reeling;

he hadn't had time to sort out his emotions. He hadn't had the chance to *think*.

When he'd arrived on the island, all Hugh could think about when it came to the land was proving to himself that he wasn't like his father. The money had drawn him here, but he'd told himself he was different. He'd been focused on shoring up his own defenses to prove that he was a better person than Alexander Hartford, and he hadn't noticed what was right in front of him.

Then Ellie happened, and he'd lied by omission and justified it to himself through his own cowardice and his own pride.

Since the drama of the Brownlow Foundation Gala, he'd had most of two days to think about it, to stew in it, to regret every single minute he'd spent not telling Ellie the truth. His face hurt from the blows Jason had landed. He had a black eye and a split lip. He'd been locked up in a little room for hours while he waited for a lawyer to arrive yesterday. And when his lawyer finally did, he'd spent even more time explaining his involvement in this stinking deal to the FBI.

Thank God he'd rejected Jason's proposal. Thank God he'd emailed his lawyer about it the morning before the gala.

But it had all taken so much time, time he'd wanted to spend begging Ellie to forgive him. He was here now—and he couldn't be too late. He couldn't just watch Ellie leave the island without even speaking to him.

The ferry's engines churned the water to an angry froth as the wind picked up again. No. No—*no*. If she left, he wouldn't be able to get on another ferry for twelve hours. He'd have to go another night before he could get on the mainland—and then what?

He patted his pockets—*damn it*. He'd left his phone in his car.

Panic bit at his flesh, its venom entering his bloodstream. He couldn't let her leave, not like this.

The wind blasted again. A screech drew Hugh's attention to the faulty latch on the gate Spencer had tried to fix only a few days before. The wind swung the gate open, and Hugh saw his opportunity.

The ferry was already pulling away, but it was only a couple of feet. If he ran—if he sprinted—he could make the jump. He could—

No time to hesitate. He took off. Feet pounding the pavement, Hugh hurtled himself toward the growing gap. Spencer's words drifted through his mind from when they'd talked about people falling—or jumping—into this water. *They'd probably die in the ferry's propellers, and then we'd have a real mess on our hands.* Hugh saw himself chopped up into grisly bits of meat and blood by the giant propellers turning beneath the surface of the waves, then pushed the image out of his mind.

He'd make the jump. He had to.

The distance between him and the edge of the pier shrank as the distance between the pier and the ferry grew. He needed to run faster. He was ten feet away. Six. Three. He prepared himself to jump, his eyes on the edge of the ferry. He'd grip that little steel lip, pull himself on. He'd—

A garbled yell sounded only a moment before a body slammed into him from the side. Spencer's arms came around him like a vise, and Hugh's trajectory changed dramatically. His feet left the pavement as Spencer tackled him, the two of them careening toward the side of the pier.

They hit the side handrail, then flew over it, suspended in midair for a long moment before the water's icy chill swallowed them both. It shocked Hugh how cold the water was, how quickly it froze his muscles. He sank like a stone until survival kicked in and he started flailing.

Then a strong hand gripped his arm and hauled him to the surface, and he was met with Spencer's flashing eyes.

"What's *wrong* with you?" the other man demanded, his dark-blond hair stuck to his head.

Hugh looked over Spencer's shoulder at the departing ferry, its wake sending waves sloshing toward them even where they were sheltered behind the pier. "She's gone," he said.

Spencer frowned at him.

As they treaded water, the sound of a small engine echoed against the rocks and Lionel appeared, piloting a metal boat. He circled toward them and cut the throttle so the boat drifted beside the two men in the water. He frowned. "What the hell was that? You got a death wish or something? Surely the feds aren't that frightening."

Spencer huffed in agreement.

"Well?" Lionel prompted when Hugh didn't answer.

Hugh shook his head. "She was just going to leave, and I . . . I couldn't let that happen."

The old man let out a dry snort. "Get in before you freeze to death."

Spencer went first, climbing into the rocking boat with practiced ease. Then he braced himself on the opposite side and gestured for Hugh to follow. Hugh kicked in the water and pulled himself over the edge of the boat, tumbling gracelessly over the gunwale. He bashed his head against one of the support planks that ran crossways on the boat. Then Lionel opened the throttle, and they were circling the barnacle-crusted pier again, slicing through the lapping wake the ferry had left behind.

Lionel dropped Spencer near a ladder, and they watched him climb up the rusty rungs, water dripping down behind him.

Hugh shivered, wet clothes clinging to his body, but before he could follow Spencer up the ladder, Lionel set the boat in motion and made one big loop, pointing the boat toward the open water and the mainland beyond. He scowled at his nephew and pointed to a box at his feet. "Put a life jacket on." His tone added "you idiot" to the end of the sentence without Lionel having to voice it out loud. "There's a blanket in there too."

Hugh fumbled to unlatch the box, then slipped a life jacket on and draped a blanket over his legs. Once Lionel was far enough from shore that the sounds of cars and people had faded, he cut the boat's engine and narrowed his gaze at Hugh. "Now," he said, "you're going to tell me what the hell that was about."

Hugh met his uncle's gaze, but only for a moment. He stared at the glittering surface of the water, letting the chill of his soaked clothes sink into his skin. "She was going to leave without even talking to me."

"So you decided to get yourself chopped up by the ferry's propellers instead?"

"I could've made the jump."

Lionel snorted.

Hugh dropped his head in his hands and winced when his palm hit his bruised eye. "I panicked. I just—I couldn't watch her leave without talking to her."

"That girl's already been through too much."

Hugh's chest pinched as the boat rocked. He nodded. "I know."

They were silent for a while. A boat's engine came closer, then faded away, and their little metal dinghy rocked harder for a few moments. Then Lionel asked, "Why didn't you tell her about your father's land?"

Hugh already felt like an idiot and a dirtbag, but somehow hearing the criticism in Lionel's voice made it worse. A thousand justifications ran through his head, but in the end all he said was, "I was afraid she'd never speak to me again."

"And you agreed to help her broadcast her confrontation with Jason to the whole island. You didn't think he might use that little nugget of gold against you?"

Hugh groaned. "It all happened so fast, Lionel. I don't even know if my father was involved in the money laundering."

Lionel didn't answer. Hugh had the sense his uncle was disappointed in him, and the feeling left an awful, oily film all over his skin.

He was ashamed of himself. How would things have been different if he'd told Ellie he owned the land next door? Would she have believed him when he said he didn't want to be involved in the resort? Would she have shut him out? Would she have allowed him to see those rare glimpses of vulnerability, those pieces of her she kept well guarded?

He'd never know.

"Take me to her," Hugh begged. "Please, Lionel. I need to talk to her."

Lionel started the engine. Wind picked up and wrapped around them like an icy fist. It fluttered the ends of Lionel's silver ponytail. He stared at his nephew for a beat, reading whatever was written on Hugh's face—and pointed the prow toward the mainland.

The boat slapped the waves so hard that Hugh bounced off the seat. Over and over and over again, they cut through chill waters to try to catch the chugging ferry. Lionel knew these waters, so he took them away from the ferry's trajectory and circled back toward the docks just in time to watch the big vessel nudge its terminal. Hugh was out of the boat and flying up the ramp before Lionel had even cut the engine. He sprinted toward the ferry terminal, frustrated when he was met with a chain-link fence.

This was taking too long. Cars were beginning to disembark. Ellie would be gone within moments.

Running along the fence, he managed to find the entrance, his heart sinking when he saw cars streaming toward the road. He'd missed her. She was gone. He wouldn't get to speak to her, wouldn't get to explain. Agony lanced through his chest at the thought, until—

There! A flash of red. An old car, parked in the lot beside the terminal.

Soaked fabric clung to his body as he ran for the gate. Hugh turned into the lot just as Ellie returned from a patch of grass Louie had been using. He slowed when Ellie looked up, her eyes widening.

Louie went still beside her, his ears perking. She tightened her hold on his leash.

Hugh slowed when he was twenty feet away. His heart thumped so hard it shook his bones as the wind froze his sodden clothing. He barely felt any of it. She was still here. She was still here, and he could talk to her—

The dog sprang, breaking Ellie's hold on the leash. Louie came bounding toward him, tongue lolling, and for a moment, Hugh thought Louie was about to attack him. But the dog lifted his front paws on Hugh's legs and wagged his tail, letting out a short, happy bark. Then he dropped onto four paws, dipped his head, and sniffed at Hugh's feet—at his socks, specifically—which probably smelled horrific.

Relief swept through Hugh, turning his legs wobbly. He fell to his knees and rubbed Louie's head, keeping his eyes on Ellie's approach.

"Louie," she said through clenched teeth. "*Louie.* Get back here."

The dog turned to look at her, then shoved his snout against Hugh's neck. He licked Hugh's skin like his life depended on it.

Hugh let out a huff of a laugh, scrubbing Louie's fur. "Go back to Ellie, boy."

The dog sneezed, then turned to trot back to Ellie. She stood six feet away from Hugh, clawing at Louie's leash before winding it around her palm. She frowned at her dog, who yawned and sat, tilting his head to look at her.

Hugh stood. It was hard to speak with his heart pounding so hard, so he gulped a few times to compose himself. "Ellie," he finally managed. He wanted to touch her. Wanted to feel her skin, to wrap her in his arms.

She straightened. Louie got up again and took two steps toward Hugh, tail wagging. "Hugh," she choked out. "What are you doing here?"

That was a good question. "I needed to talk to you."

Hardness settled into every line of her face. "It's a little late for that."

"I know—I'm sorry."

She stared at him as if she expected him to say more. He tried to gather his thoughts, but they slipped away like smoke through his fingers. Purple smudges marked the space under her eyes. Her shoulders were tense, hiked up near her ears. Lines bracketed her pinched mouth as she scowled at him.

She looked like death. All he wanted to do was make her feel better.

Louie seemed to read the tension as he glanced at Ellie, then at Hugh. He let out a whine, which snapped Ellie out of her silence. "Why didn't you tell me about the land right away? You must have known when we found Spencer at the back gate. We basically drove right up to your property line."

Guilt churned in Hugh's gut, acidic and vile. He dropped his gaze. "Yeah," he admitted. "I knew. And it was confirmed the next day when I met with Jason to discuss the project."

A sharp inhale sounded, like Ellie had just been struck. Hugh closed his eyes.

When he opened them again, Ellie's gaze was shuttered. He spread his hands, begging. "I'm sorry, Ellie. You have to understand, I had no idea I would inherit this land and this business deal. I had to figure out what was going on. I didn't know who to trust."

"Right." A bitter laugh. "Because I was the crazy woman with the ugly mug shot, and Jason Brownlow was promising you a pot of gold."

"Ellie . . ."

"No, it's fine. I'm used to it."

"I didn't think that."

"I attacked you with a pair of bolt cutters, Hugh." Her voice was rough, like it had to pass through gravel on the way up her throat. "I'm well aware of what people think of me."

Louie whined again, tugging at his leash to get to Hugh. When Ellie didn't budge, he moved back over to her and nudged her leg with the side of his body. He barked once, questioning. Ellie put her hand on the dog's head in response.

Hugh took a deep breath. "Ellie, I was afraid you'd never speak to me again if I told you about the land, and the thought of that . . . I wanted to wait until I'd officially refused the deal." He wanted to say more, to explain what he'd felt about his father, but how could he? Those excuses fell flat, even in his own mind. His own pathetic daddy issues didn't justify what he'd done.

She snorted. "Uh-huh. And that just happened to coincide with getting me in bed?"

Hugh frowned. "What?"

"That's when you found your conscience again. In bed that morning. You said you had something to talk to me about. Funny how that works, huh?"

"What? No. No, Ellie, that's not how it was."

"It was, though." She let out that horrible, raspy laugh that didn't sound like her at all. "You should be proud of yourself, Hugh. I really fell for it. The whole schtick. Even that morning, when you sounded so sincere before driving away. I really thought you cared about me."

"I do. I *do*."

"If you cared, you wouldn't have lied." She spat the words, and Louie went still beside her. "You didn't care about me for a minute."

Hugh flinched. That was pretty fucking harsh. His jaw creaked as he ground his teeth. "I committed crimes for you, Ellie. You think being roped into every one of your schemes was me *not* caring about you?"

"You did that because you enjoyed the thrill." She lobbed the words at him, then opened the back door of her car to let her dog in. "That had nothing to do with me."

"That's bullshit."

"Oh, screw you."

Louie whined, then barked. He still hadn't gotten into the car.

Hugh needed to make her listen. Needed her to *understand*. He cared about her. He . . . he . . . *God*, the things he felt for this woman didn't make any sense. His heart broke in a million places, and the only thing keeping it together was his own panic. "Ellie, listen—"

"No, I've done quite enough of that to last a lifetime, and—"

Louie broke away from her and crashed into Hugh's legs. He circled between them, then sat at Hugh's feet, big brown eyes staring up at Hugh.

"Louie, get back here."

"Go to Ellie," Hugh said, nudging the dog with his calves.

Louie didn't move.

"Louie." She grabbed his collar and tried to pull the dog forward, but he wouldn't budge.

Hugh wanted to help. He was desperate to show her he cared. How could he make Ellie understand that he'd do anything, *anything*—

He toed off a shoe and pulled off a sock. "Here, Louie. You can have this if you go in the car." He brought the sock toward the open back door.

"Get your disgusting socks away from my dog," Ellie said, but Louie had gotten up and was following Hugh's dangling sock toward the car like it was a hypnotist's swinging watch.

"Good boy," Hugh said, hobbling on the pavement in one shoe and one bare foot.

"I'm not letting him keep that," Ellie warned.

Louie was beside the car's back door, eyeing the sock. Then his muscles bunched, and he lunged for the dirty, wet sock so fast Hugh stumbled back. Ellie yelled after him. Hugh grunted as his heel landed on a particularly sharp piece of gravel.

The dog took off, doing a big loop of the parking lot as Ellie chased him. Hugh's sock trailed from his mouth like a fluttering pendant flag as he zoomed around a lamppost and back toward the car. Hugh was ready to catch the dog, but Louie jumped past him and dove into the back seat of the car, curling himself around the precious, filthy treasure.

Ellie panted as she slowed to a stop, staring at her dog in the back seat. She huffed, closed the door, and glowered at Hugh. "Are you happy now?"

No, he wasn't. Not in the slightest.

Ellie circled the car, opened the driver's side door, and stood in the opening, staring at him from across the roof of her car. "You know, I felt sorry for you when you told me about your father. I actually felt real, honest sympathy for what you went through, how you grew from it. But I don't think you've grown at all. You lie and conceal. You pick and choose your truths, only admitting to them once they're exposed. Doesn't sound so different from what your father did to you."

Her words hit him like bullets, tearing through his fragile flesh. A flinch made him step back, his legs unsteady beneath him. His heel ached where the gravel had jabbed him, but it was distant, so distant from the rushing in his ears, the agony in his chest. That right there was exactly why he hadn't told her about the land.

He lowered his voice, anger burning away his guilt. "You don't know anything about me or my past, Ellie."

"That's the first honest thing you've ever said to me. Enjoy your precious piece of land. I hope you find a reputable developer to finally destroy it for you."

He watched her drive away until the chill of his wet clothes forced him to slip on his wet shoe. Lionel sat on a bench near the ferry terminal building, whittling a piece of wood. He stood as Hugh approached, eyeing Hugh's chattering teeth and blue fingernails.

Raindrops splattered on the concrete around them as the clouds darkened above. It was shaping up to be a truly awful day.

"Water's gettin' rough," Lionel noted. "There's a motel down the road. We'll go back to Fernley in the morning."

CHAPTER 28

Ellie's sister lived in a one-bedroom condo in Seattle. Ellie dropped her suitcase near the front door and looked around at Daphne's small, tidy space. It was a world away from Fernley. The living room window looked out on a brick wall that dropped down to the asphalt and concrete of a busy road below. There wasn't a bit of green anywhere, unless you counted the dying plant in the corner clinging valiantly to its single remaining leaf.

Louie entered, still clutching Hugh's revolting sock between his jaws, and started inspecting the space.

"It's not much," Daphne said after she'd hugged Ellie, "but it suits me."

"I thought you lived near the water." Ellie glanced around as Louie sniffed at the sofa. The sock dangled from his mouth, taunting her. Ellie tore her gaze away. "Where's Pete?"

Daphne shifted her gaze to the window and shrugged. "We broke up."

Shock rippled through Ellie. She stared at her sister, wide eyed. Daphne didn't meet her gaze.

Daphne was as tall as Ellie, though slightly curvier. Her brown hair was cut in a longish bob and had highlights that had grown out, as if Daphne had missed a few salon appointments. That was unlike her. Daphne's eyes were paler than Ellie's, more similar to their mother's ice-blue irises. She wore jeans and a thick cable-knit sweater of white wool to ward off the damp chill that still hadn't given way to summer.

Ellie stared at her sister and wondered how Daphne had kept her breakup a secret. Daphne, the responsible one. The one who'd left the island and gotten a steady job in accounting, who'd dated her college sweetheart since their freshman year. Daphne was the one who was supposed to exceed everyone's expectations while Ellie messed around and messed up.

"You want a beer?" Daphne asked, tucking a strand of golden-brown hair behind her ear.

Ellie shrugged. "Sure."

They sat on a secondhand sofa together, sipping beer, carefully not speaking about the fact that both their lives had crashed and burned. Louie sat on the rug nearby, guarding his beloved sock.

The sisters lapsed into silence, and Ellie thought of Hugh's laugh. The light playing in his dark hair. The weight of his arm around her waist. Her chest ached and ached and ached, but her thoughts still circled. She remembered the thunderbolt that had hit her when he'd kissed her on Jason's doorstep, the way her body had melted.

"When did you know you were in love with Pete?" Ellie asked, picking at the corner of the label on her beer bottle. She didn't know why she'd asked that. She and Daphne didn't have those sorts of conversations. But it had been asked, so Ellie let the question dangle between them.

Daphne stilled. "Is this about Jason?"

Ellie huffed. "No. I don't know if I ever really loved Jason. I thought I did, but it was . . . thin. Like an illusion of the real thing."

A hum from Daphne's throat was the only reply for long moments. Then she took a sip of beer and shrugged. "I knew right away. Pete laughed at some stupid joke I made, and that was it. Three minutes, maybe."

Three minutes. Ellie didn't know what to think about that.

"It morphed over time," Daphne continued when Ellie didn't reply. "Deepened. Changed. But yeah—that initial feeling never really went away."

"Never?" Ellie chanced a look at her sister, saw Daphne's lips flatten into a thin line.

"Not for me." Daphne leaned back on the sofa and stared at the ceiling, but her gaze was far away. "But a month ago, he came home and told me he didn't love me anymore. Completely out of the blue. So . . . yeah."

Fire burned the back of Ellie's throat. "Sorry, Daphne."

Daphne's answering laugh sounded nothing like her usual self. It crackled around the edges, flaked away to nothing. "Me too."

"Why didn't you tell Mom and Dad?"

"What, while you were going through your little crisis?"

Ellie scoffed, straightening, taking the bait. "My 'little crisis'? Is that what we're calling it?"

Daphne grinned, but it faded quickly. "I didn't want to worry Mom and Dad any more than they already were. I figured I'd let your storm pass and drop the breakup into conversation once it wasn't so raw."

"You just didn't want to give up your spot as their favorite."

"Oh, please." Daphne clicked her tongue. "Mom's favorite, maybe. *Maybe.* When you're being particularly horrible. But Dad? If he had to save one of us from a house fire, he'd choose you."

"I'm never horrible." Ellie's prim response melted into laughter. "But yeah, Dad definitely loves me more."

Daphne's lips kicked, and she shook her head. "I tried so hard to be the good, responsible, straight A daughter, and now look."

"Well, at least you've never spent the night being interviewed by the FBI."

"Not yet, anyway."

Ellie giggled. She got up and grabbed two more beers from the fridge, then dropped back on the sofa. She and Daphne had never been close, exactly. Daphne was four years older and had always acted like Ellie was an annoying fly buzzing around her head. Ellie had grown up thinking she'd never live up to the expectations Daphne had set. As they sat there, drinking a beer, Ellie realized she'd never really spent much time with her sister as an adult. It felt nice to do it now, even if everything else was a mess.

"Why were you asking about love, anyway?" Daphne twisted the top off her fresh bottle and tossed the cap onto the coffee table.

Ellie stared at the cap as it bounced once and landed on the carpet on the other side of the table. She waited for her sister to get up and tidy it right away, but Daphne just took a drink from the brown bottle. Wow. That wasn't like her *at all*. Daphne was in worse shape than she was letting on.

Daphne set the bottle down on her knee and glanced at Ellie. "So? If it wasn't Jason, who was it that broke your heart? I'll go break their legs, if it makes you feel better."

"*Good, responsible, straight A daughter*, huh?"

Daphne grinned. "Stop stalling. I told you about Pete dumping me like hot garbage. Your turn."

Ellie couldn't say his name. It was ridiculous to even feel this intensely about a man she barely knew, but Daphne had just admitted she'd fallen in love with Pete in three minutes. "It was the guy—last week—we were . . ." How could she even describe their relationship? She settled on "Lionel's nephew."

"Mom told me," Daphne said. "Hugh, right?"

"I thought he cared about me," she blurted out before her throat seized up. She swallowed bitter beer to buy herself some time, then shook her head. "I feel so stupid."

"Well," Daphne answered, "my leg-breaking offer still stands. Did you get that baseball bat back from the police after you got out of jail? Maybe we could put it to use again."

Ellie couldn't help it. She burst out laughing. It was a little louder and a little more raw than usual, but it was a laugh. Daphne grinned and touched her bottle to Ellie's, and they let their laughter subside.

"Mom showed me her mug shots before I got on the ferry," Ellie told her sister in the silence that followed. "I think it was an odd attempt to make me feel better about my own."

Daphne chuckled. "Did it work?"

"Nope."

"Maybe you just need a bit of time. You've had a rough few months."

"Hmm." Ellie sighed. The label on her new bottle came off in one piece, and she crumpled it up and tossed it onto the coffee table. "I don't know if I'll be able to show my face on the island after what happened."

"Why do you care so much about what those people think of you?" Daphne frowned at Ellie, shaking her head. "I would think you, of all people, would be able to brush off any of that judgment."

"Why me *of all people*?"

"Because you're you! You're Ellie Davis. You're a bull in a china shop. No, don't give me that look! I meant it as a compliment."

"Oh, okay, then . . . thanks?"

Daphne laughed, then grabbed the remote and flicked the TV on. They watched bad reality TV and didn't speak besides mumbled "good nights" a while later.

Louie deigned to leave his sock in a safe space behind the armchair and finally jumped up on the couch to curl up at Ellie's feet. His presence was warm and comforting, but Ellie still felt utterly lost. Though she was exhausted, it took her a long time to fall asleep.

Whatever Daphne said, charging through a china shop world and breaking everything as she went didn't feel good in the slightest.

CHAPTER 29

The first thing Hugh did when he returned to Fernley the next day was apologize to Spencer. The man had saved his life and gotten soaked in icy water for his efforts.

Spencer patted him on the shoulder and gave him a sad smile. "She's not coming back?"

"No," Hugh answered. "She isn't."

Dragging his feet up the hill toward his hotel, he inhaled the cloying scent of fresh flowers and tried to forget all the ways Ellie had marked his life.

Scoopz was open, even though it was barely ten o'clock. Rhonda looked up at him but didn't wave. He passed the street where Mickey's sat, closed and dark in the daylight. The Fernley Hotel loomed in the distance.

Carlisle had seemed vibrant and friendly when Ellie walked beside him, a new home that had accepted him with open arms. Now, he wondered how long it would be before he could leave.

There were more interviews with the authorities to sort out. There was the question of what to do with his land.

And once those things were done . . . where would he go? Could he really go back to Arizona, to the music studio that would soon be closed forever? What was left for him there—anywhere?

He could sell the land, buy the studio, and pay his mom's mortgage. Then what?

Ellie had shown him the beauty in life. She'd cracked through the hard shell of his existence and dragged him out of the dark. She'd made him laugh, surprised him at every turn. She was beautiful and vibrant and determined, even in the face of insurmountable odds.

And he'd hurt her.

He'd stayed in that safe little corner of his mind, telling himself he was being reasonable when he didn't tell her about the land. He'd explained away his guilt and fear with logical reasons that didn't mean anything in the end.

Maybe Ellie was right. Wasn't that what his father had done to him? Small decision after small decision—nothing malicious—that led to collapse. Hugh had been sensible. He'd ignored his conscience and convinced himself he was right, but he should have taken one single second to think about how his actions affected other people.

He *was* exactly like his father.

Feet stopping on the sun-warmed pavement, Hugh stared across the hotel parking lot at the revolving lobby doors.

Shame tasted like apple pie ice cream and homemade sourdough. It sounded like old records and cheek-creasing laughter shared around a kitchen table. Hugh had taken and taken and taken from Ellie and her family, and what had he given back?

He could lie to himself—like he'd lied to Ellie—and say that he'd given her his time. He'd helped her. He'd put himself at risk for her. But she was right—he'd enjoyed the thrill. He'd enjoyed her company. He hadn't broken into Jason Brownlow's house because he'd wanted to find nonexistent evidence about his father's involvement. He'd done it because he'd wanted to drink up every minute he could with her.

The only selfless thing he'd done all week was give Louie a couple of dirty socks.

Though his clothes were filthy, crusted stiff with salt and grime, Hugh couldn't bring himself to walk up to his hotel room. His feet carried him down the street and around a corner, all the way to the boarded-up window of Ellie's old business.

She had lost everything because of people like Hugh. In the end, was he any better than Jason? Her ex-fiancé had used her and tossed her aside, had tried his best to ruin her life. Sure, Jason *was* malicious. He'd gone out of his way to hurt Ellie. Hugh hadn't hurt Ellie on purpose, but the result was exactly the same. He'd coaxed Ellie out of her armor, made her feel safe, and stabbed her in the back.

"Can I help you?"

Hugh turned to see Helen Davis striding toward him, broom and bucket full of cleaning supplies in hand. She set them down next to the door and scowled at him, keys jingling as she removed them from her purse.

"I—uh, no," Hugh stammered. "I just came by because . . ."

Why had he come here?

Helen faced him, all levity and kindness gone from her expression. The woman who had been thoughtful enough to spin a mug so the handle faced him—who had made sure he had fresh coffee and eggs the morning she'd walked in on him with her daughter—was gone. In her place was a steely, uncompromising gladiator. Her chin lifted as she looked at him from head to toe and back up again, a sneer curling her lips. "I've never seen my daughter as broken as she was after that horrible gala—and I hold you responsible."

Another bullet pierced his chest. Muscles clenched against the pain, Hugh nodded. "Yes."

Her face didn't soften one bit. "You leave Ellie alone."

Hugh didn't answer. He couldn't promise that. His emotions were a churning, turbulent sea, and he knew if he agreed to leave Ellie alone forever, anger and hurt would boil over into something toxic. Instead, he gestured to the door. "Can I help you with anything in there?"

Helen harrumphed, and the keys jingled again as she brought them to the door. She held it open with her foot then narrowed her eyes at Hugh. "Don't think you can wriggle your way into my daughter's good graces by pushing a broom around."

He dropped his shoulders. "I just want to help."

She pursed her lips, then clicked her tongue and opened the door wider for him. "Just to be clear," she said when he was inside the dark space, "this isn't earning you any points with Ellie. If you think I'll go to bat for you, you're wrong. In fact, I won't tell her you were here at all."

Hugh nodded. "Understood."

Around lunchtime, Hugh and Helen locked up Ellie's office and went their separate ways. The woman hadn't thawed in the slightest, but it had still felt good to be doing something for Ellie. Hugh walked back to the hotel, detouring to grab his phone from the car. He'd left a sweatshirt in the trunk, so he popped it open—and saw Ellie's backpack.

He grabbed it and paused, feeling the thin, water-resistant material between his fingers. Not understanding why, Hugh brought the backpack up to his hotel room and set it on a chair. He stared at it for a while before showering. While he dried his hair with a white towel, he eyed the backpack some more, then tossed the damp towel on the bed and strode across the room.

He unzipped the bag. The bolt cutters were still in there, handles wrapped in red duct tape. She had twine and a little screwdriver kit. A spare hoodie. A headlamp. Her lockpicks. A bunch of items that honestly just looked like garbage.

Hugh zipped it back up, heart thumping. He left the bag where it was and grabbed some lunch.

He found himself restless and jittery, with nowhere to go. With the resort deal dead and Ellie gone, there wasn't much left in Fernley for

Hugh, except maybe his uncle, who hadn't said more than two words to him on their entire trip back to Fernley.

But Hugh needed something to do, so he jumped in his car and visited Lionel. The old man seemed surlier than he'd been that morning, which was impressive. He barely grunted in greeting when Hugh knocked on the workshop door. Hugh lingered in the shop watching Lionel work, while the other man avoided all eye contact and speech.

The message was clear: Hugh had messed up, and Lionel wanted nothing to do with him. Hugh watched Lionel work on a boat engine. Grease coated the older man's fingers, sinking into every wrinkle and crevice that lined his hands. Lionel's lips were pinched as he struggled with a stubborn bolt, but he didn't ask Hugh for help.

What was it Lionel had said about his relationship with Hugh's father? *That was pretty much the end of that.*

If Hugh was truly his father's son, he could walk away from Lionel and never look back. A switch had flipped on this island, and now he knew he was an outsider. Ellie had opened a door for him into this community, and Hugh had gone and slammed it shut on himself.

After a couple of hours of silence, Hugh left Lionel's workshop and headed back to the hotel, knowing that he should probably put his land up for sale and leave Fernley for good. He wasn't welcome here.

But he . . . couldn't leave. He found himself lying on his hotel bed, flicking through online listings of apartments in Carlisle to rent, intermittently glancing at the backpack on the chair. He looked up cars for sale on the island, then expanded his search to dealerships in Seattle. He pored over the maps of his land again and tried to decide if he could part with a chunk of it to fund his life for a while, especially considering he had a mountain of lawyer's fees and no income.

Leaving Fernley would be easier than all that, but Hugh was tired of doing the easy thing. Being angry at his father had been easy. Getting swept up in dirty business deals had been easy, until his eyes had been forced open. Even keeping the truth from Ellie had been easy.

His father had chosen the easier path. Alex had found a wealthy woman to fund his life, and he'd trimmed away all the things that held him back, like Hugh and Faye and the life they'd all shared together. But the easy path was only easy if you were a terrible person.

Hugh didn't want to be a terrible person. He didn't want to leave broken people in his wake while he smiled on a sun-kissed balcony in Greece, arms around the people he hadn't left behind.

Hugh had watched his mother make her life smaller and smaller after his father left, and now he realized he'd done the same. He'd worked in the same music studio for years, dreaming of something more without having the courage to go for it.

Then he'd met Ellie. She was made of grit and courage. She grabbed life with both hands in a way Hugh never could. She fought for what she wanted. She risked her feelings, her reputation, and her life for what she believed in.

He'd been swept up in Ellie's current, but it was only now, when he'd been tossed on the shore like a piece of flotsam, that he realized *he* was responsible for the consequences. It wasn't acceptable to hurt other people, even if you didn't mean to. He couldn't go on blaming his father for his own closed-off heart, for his careless decisions.

For once in his life, Hugh had to act. He had to *do* something.

His eyes drifted to the backpack. Hope flared in his chest, a match fizzing to life in a tiny, bright blaze. Then he got online and booked a ticket to the mainland.

CHAPTER 30

Around ten o'clock the next morning, Ellie's phone rang. She was just coming back from walking Louie, so she had to fumble with his collar and leash, doggie bags, her jacket, purse, and—*Gah! Why do I have so many things in my hands?*—finally pulled her phone out of her jacket pocket.

Hugh's name flashed on the screen. Ellie froze. She stared at the phone for a few long seconds, the vibrations traveling up her arms. Hadn't she made it very clear that she didn't want to speak to him? Hadn't she hurled awful words at him across the roof of her car before driving away?

She wanted to scream, and cry, and rage. She wanted to launch the phone out the window and watch it smash against the pavement below.

She didn't do any of those things; instead, she swiped.

"Hello?"

"Ellie." He sounded relieved. "Don't hang up. Please."

A pause. "What do you want?"

"I . . ." Hugh cleared his throat, then let out an awkward, dry chuckle. "God, this is harder than I thought it would be."

She loved his voice. It was warm and deep, and it sent little tremors spiraling down her insides. She sat down on the floor, ignoring the insistent thumping of her heart, and let Louie shift his weight so his back legs and rump were on her thighs.

"I have your backpack," Hugh rumbled, sending more tremors detonating in the pit of her stomach. "I was hoping I could return it to you."

Louie looked up, ears perking. He could hear who was on the other side of the line.

On second thought, Ellie hated Hugh's voice. It made her *feel* things. It made her body react, her brain melt, her heart squeeze. It made her dog look happy for the first time in two days.

She didn't want any of that. She just wanted to let the days meld together. She wanted to forget the previous week and a half—no, the previous six months, the previous three and a half years—had ever happened. Moving on with a new life in a new city seemed infinitely better than being reminded of all the ways she wasn't enough.

When she didn't say anything, Hugh continued: "I know you don't want to see me, but I . . ." His voice became rougher, so he cleared his throat again. He sighed. The phone rustled, like he was changing ears. "I wanted to apologize. Make it up to you. And give you your backpack."

Her stupid backpack. "I'm not coming back to Fernley anytime soon. You can just drop it at my parents' house."

"Well, I, um . . ." He let out a breathless chuckle that sounded half-embarrassed. "I'm not on the island either. I'm in the city right now."

She frowned. "What city?"

"Seattle."

She started, her head jerking back so she hit it against the wall. Wincing, she asked, "Since when?"

"Oh, um . . . an hour ago?"

What? "Why?"

There was a short pause. "I had to pick up a few things. I'm going back to Fernley on the afternoon ferry. But I figured I'd bring you your stuff, you know, since I was coming across anyway."

"Oh."

"I could meet you anywhere," he said. "Wherever is convenient for you."

She had no use for bolt cutters and lockpicks, but the backpack was pretty handy. She wouldn't mind getting it back. But that meant facing Hugh, in all his beautiful, dark-haired, muscular, rumbly-voiced glory. She was still angry at him. Louie had been depressed and moping all day yesterday, and she blamed Hugh for that too.

But the backpack could be useful. It would save her from buying a new one.

She was *so* going to regret this. "Fine."

They met near Pike Place Market. Ellie spotted Hugh as he leaned against a wall whose green paint was flaking off in chunks. He wore a charcoal-colored tee with dark jeans, and his hair was mostly covered with that beanie he'd worn when she'd bashed him in the head with her bolt cutters an eternity ago.

Damn him. He looked good, even with that yellowing bruise around his eye socket and the cut on his lip. As Ellie approached, Hugh scanned the crowd. Women and men glanced at him as they passed, and Ellie felt a stab of jealousy—or was it possession?

She shook her head to clear it, and that's when Louie caught his scent. Her dog stilled, sniffing the air, then pulled at the leash on his way to Hugh.

"Louie," she chided. "I trained you better than this. Sit."

Louie didn't look happy about it, but he sat next to her. His body trembled with excitement, his eyes steady on Hugh.

"Stand," she said, and Louie stayed by her side.

Hugh pushed himself off the wall a moment later, his face morphing from its neutral expression to something complicated. It went soft and hard at once, like Hugh couldn't quite control what was going on with his body. He cleared his throat as Ellie approached, his eyes roaming over her face like he wanted to drink up every detail.

Then he dropped down to pat Louie's head. Louie promptly ascended to dog heaven.

When Hugh reached into his pocket and said, "I've got something for you, boy," Ellie stiffened.

"If you give my dog another dirty sock, I'll never speak to you again."

Hugh looked up at her and laughed. The sun hit the broad planes of his face so perfectly, like it wanted to caress Hugh's skin as badly as Ellie did.

Wait—no. She didn't want to caress his skin. She wanted to walk away and never look back.

Hugh pulled out a treat. It was the same kind of treat Ellie had given Louie through the fence when they'd escaped Jason's house, made by a local Fernley vet who baked them herself. Ellie stared at the treat, frowning. He'd noticed the treat she'd given Louie and gone out of his way to buy it? How had he even found the right ones? He'd have had to ask someone.

Louie munched the treat in mere seconds and looked at Hugh, silently asking for more. Hugh scratched his ears and grinned, then met Ellie's gaze. "Hey," he said to her at last as he stood.

She was suddenly nervous. "Hi. You, um, have my backpack?"

He slid the bag off his shoulder and handed it over. "It was in my car."

"Right. I put it there the night we got Louie."

They were silent for a beat. Ellie stared at his shoulder because, even with his bruises, his face was too beautiful to look at. Plus, his injuries reminded Ellie that he'd gotten them while defending her.

Yeah, after he'd lied.

She gritted her teeth. "Okay, well, thanks, and—goodbye."

"You hungry?" Hugh blurted out.

"No," Ellie said, just as her stomach growled.

A slow, dangerous smile crept across Hugh's lips. He tilted his head. "Buy you a sandwich?"

She should say no. It danced on the tip of her tongue until she looked down and saw her dog wagging his tail for the first time since they'd left Hugh at the ferry terminal two days ago. Louie nudged his snout against Hugh's leg while Hugh patted him absentmindedly, his gaze firmly on Ellie's face. She could feel it like a physical touch.

She wasn't doing this because she was hungry, and she *definitely* wasn't doing it for Hugh. She was doing this purely because it made her dog happy. "Okay," she said. "One sandwich."

CHAPTER 31

Ellie ate a chicken sandwich on a bench while Hugh sat beside her, eating his own. They were quiet for a while, but it wasn't exactly uncomfortable.

Finally, mostly just to fill the silence, she asked, "Do you have any brothers and sisters?"

Hugh shook his head. "Just me and my mom growing up."

"Oh, right," she said, staring at the sandwich in her hands as she prepared to take another bite. "I knew that."

"You have one sister, right?"

She felt Hugh's gaze brush over her, but she kept her eyes on the people walking by, on her sandwich, on her dog. She nodded. "Yeah. Daphne moved away from Fernley for college, but she comes back to visit pretty regularly."

"When's your birthday?" he asked.

She finally turned to look at him, frowning. "Why?"

His eyes looked bright in this light, green specks making them look almost hazel. They glimmered as he shrugged. "I feel like I should know that by now."

She huffed, tearing her gaze away from him. "April fifth."

"Aries," he noted. "That figures."

She gaped, spinning around so her knee touched his. "Do *not* tell me that big, strong Hugh Hartford is into astrology."

"You think I'm big and strong?"

Ellie rolled her eyes.

He laughed, and it was like a blow to her chest. He wasn't allowed to have this kind of effect on her after everything he'd done.

"Nah. I dated a girl for a few months that was really into astrology. She was an Aries too, and she got really excited that I was a Libra. Something about angles and compatibility? I don't know. We didn't seem all that compatible to me." He shifted, curling his arm around the back of the bench. His arm didn't touch her back, but Ellie could sense it there, inches from her body. Hugh looked up at a passing cloud. "Maybe there's something to it, though."

Ellie sat very still, willing her pulse to quiet. The heat of Hugh's body soaked into her side, her upper back . . . all she had to do to touch him was shift a bare inch closer to him. Instead, she asked, "When's your birthday?"

"September thirtieth."

Ellie tucked that away into her memory, even though she wasn't quite sure why she'd want to remember it. She finished her sandwich slowly, telling herself she wasn't rushing because she wasn't very hungry. But when she crumpled her paper and stood, Hugh took a deep breath.

"All right," he said.

"All right," she repeated.

"I'll, um, see you around."

Her throat tightened. He probably wouldn't. "Yeah," she lied.

Hugh gave Louie one last head scratch, then waved and walked away.

After that, life went on. Louie's tail and ears dropped, and he didn't seem to enjoy his walks as much as usual, which worried Ellie. He hoarded his sock treasure like a dragon guarding its gold, curling around it every time he slept. It was truly foul, but Ellie couldn't bring herself to take it away from him to wash it.

Time marched endlessly onward, the sun rose, and Ellie had to get up. She woke up sore from sleeping on her sister's sofa, and her mind was so foggy she couldn't figure out how to work the knobs to turn on Daphne's shower. It usually took the merciless beating of scalding water over her body for a few minutes before she could think straight. She existed in a strange state of half-life in that first week, wondering what the heck was supposed to come next.

She got a waitressing job at a bar within a few days. It was luck, mostly: Daphne's friend was dating the manager, so he agreed to give Ellie a chance. She picked up every shift she could because when she worked, it was easier not to think. When she was exhausted, she could pass out without seeing Hugh's face painted on her eyelids.

One week to get to know the man, and a lifetime to recover. It didn't seem like a very good deal to Ellie, but apparently that's what she'd signed up for.

But she had to wash and feed and clothe herself. She had to pull herself together, if only so she wouldn't be a drain on Daphne's resources the way she'd been a drain on her parents'. She had to take care of Louie.

Hugh didn't call her again. Why would he? He'd returned her backpack, and now there was nothing keeping them together.

Ellie should have been happy about it, but her mood darkened as the days passed. It spiraled down, down, down with every new sunrise.

Truthfully, it was Louie who'd gotten her up those first few mornings after her last meeting with Hugh. Her dog had to be walked and let outside to do his business. She had to feed him, bathe him, pet him. He stuck by her side like glue whenever she was drowning in a black mood, dragging her back to the surface by sheer canine will.

But he wasn't happy. He didn't run as fast as he used to. He dragged his feet when they went for walks. He slept more than usual. After a couple of days, Ellie got worried enough to take him to a vet, but they said there was nothing wrong with him.

Daphne said he missed Fernley, and Ellie thought she was probably right. She missed Fernley too.

Jason's arrest and subsequent fall from grace didn't make her feel better. Wynn called one morning, when she'd been in the city for just over a week and a half, and she filled Ellie in on the news: "Fergus is cooperating with the authorities, and apparently they're throwing the book at Jason. Twenty charges and counting, Ellie. I've heard all kinds of stuff, like money laundering and embezzlement and everything. Apparently he was stealing from the charity for years. They say he could get sentenced to over a hundred years if he gets convicted of everything."

Ellie should've been jumping for joy, crowing about her successful revenge. Instead, she just stared at the brick wall outside Daphne's window and twisted her lips into a bitter smile. "White-collar crimes never get sentenced very harshly. I doubt he'll see any real consequences." These were all rumors, in any case. Who knew what would really happen to Jason? He would probably walk free. Her parents would live next door to a huge resort until they crumpled under the pressure.

"Ellie," Wynn chided. "Thanks to you, everyone saw him confess. Even if he wriggles out of the charges, the whole island will shun him."

"What, like the way they shunned him when he cheated on me? When he ran a charity promoting environmental sustainability while simultaneously planning a massive luxury development?" Ellie snorted. "Forgive me for being a pessimist, Wynn, but I just don't see it happening. No one shuns the Brownlows on Fernley."

Wynn clicked her tongue. "It's already happening! He's lost almost all his donors for the Brownlow Foundation, and the developer that signed on for the resort just announced that they were pulling out, even if the Brownlows found another location to build the resort. Sheriff Jackson has been put on leave pending an investigation because they think he was getting kickbacks from Jason all along. It's a complete mess. And it's beautiful. You did it, Ellie. You won."

Yes—but at what cost? Was it worth it to see Jason pay for his crimes when Ellie felt like her life was over?

The humiliation of her first arrest all those months ago paled in comparison to what she felt now. Even though she'd been vindicated. Even though she'd been absolved of her initial attack on Jason's car. It was worse now, because she felt so utterly stupid.

She *knew* when Hugh walked into her life that she shouldn't trust him. She'd *just* started to recover from what Jason had done, and she'd still allowed herself to open her heart up to another man. She'd practically begged him to wreck her.

She couldn't even bring herself to be mad at him anymore. They'd sat on that bench and eaten lunch together, and she'd loved every minute of it.

Stupid, stupid, stupid.

Ellie had allowed herself to dream of a life where she was valued, seen, appreciated. She'd nurtured these childish, foolish hopes that a man might actually treasure all her jagged edges. He'd lied to her and humiliated her, and all it took was twenty minutes and one sandwich for all those hopes to come to life again.

She was such a colossal idiot.

Especially when, the next day, as she was taking Louie out for his morning walk, her phone rang and Hugh's name flashed on the screen. Despite every alarm bell blaring in her head, Ellie's heart leaped. She swiped to answer before she could talk herself out of it.

"Hey," his rich voice murmured in her ear. "I'm in the city again. Bought a car, so I'm here to pick it up."

"Oh, well, congrats," Ellie said, shifting her weight from foot to foot. Did that mean he was staying on Fernley for the long term?

"I ran into your dad at his show last night, actually, and told him I was coming across to the city today." He let out a short huff that almost qualified as a chuckle. "He gave me a loaf of sourdough for you and Daphne. Insisted I bring it over."

Ellie froze. "I see."

Hugh had gone to Mickey's to see ODNT play? God, she missed that place. She missed her dad's saxophone and his massive white sneakers. She missed it all.

And wait—her dad had gone out of his way to give Hugh a homemade loaf of sourdough to bring to her? That was odd. That meant they'd talked and met up and organized it.

There was a long pause before Hugh said, "How do you feel about grabbing a coffee, and I can give you your dad's bread?"

If their first sandwich date was any indication, Ellie should hang up and run in the other direction. Spending time with Hugh only confused her more.

But when she opened her mouth, what came out was, "Sure. Meet at the same place?"

This time, they got coffee and wandered aimlessly together along the streets, down toward the water. She learned that Hugh had nearly failed out of high school until his school's music teacher took him under his wing. That's when he decided he wanted to make a career in music, but he had no interest in performing. Plus, he told her, being in the control room was its own kind of creativity.

They walked down to a park overlooking the water, and Ellie could almost see Fernley from where they stood.

"Ellie," Hugh said quietly, "I want to apologize to you. Properly, this time."

She blinked. Looked at him. Looked away. "Okay."

,"I know I hurt you. I've done a lot of thinking about what happened between us, and none of the reasons I had for keeping the truth from you were valid. I want you to know I understand that. I was wrong."

Her throat was suddenly full of rocks. She nodded.

"And when you said that about my dad—"

"That was cruel," Ellie blurted out, her voice strange and croaky. "I shouldn't have said those things. I'm sorry."

His arm brushed hers as they stood there, staring at the water. "You were right," he said. "My mom once told me that my dad wasn't malicious; he was just thoughtless. And that's how I acted with you. I'm sorry."

Nodding, Ellie brought her coffee to her lips, but the cup was already empty. She met Hugh's gaze. "Thank you for that."

"I came to Fernley thinking I could use my dad's money to somehow make him atone," he said, a bitter twist to his lips. "I felt like I might as well take what he'd given me, seeing as he hadn't given me anything else. But then I met you, and I found out what was going on with the project, and it all got muddled in my head. I was afraid you'd think I was the same kind of man as my father for accepting the inheritance, but by keeping the truth from you, I ended up acting just like him. It was cowardly of me."

"You're talking to someone who ran away from her problems because she was afraid of facing the island's rejection again," Ellie answered grimly. "If anyone's a coward, it's me."

"You're the furthest thing from a coward, Ellie." The way he looked at her then made everything inside Ellie go still. His eyes were soft, full of tenderness edged with pain. She had the urge to touch him, to trace the edge of his stubble on his cheek, but she couldn't bring herself to do it. She didn't understand what was going on between them, why she'd agreed to speak to him. She didn't understand why hearing his voice on the phone had made her feel simultaneously better and worse than she had before.

She should probably protect herself. Learn from her mistakes. Push him away and keep him out.

The moment hung between them, like the weight in the air before a thunderstorm. Gulls cried in the distance as waves crashed against the shore. Hugh parted his lips and moved infinitesimally closer, a subtle shift of his weight—

"I'd better go," Ellie said, holding her coffee cup between them like a shield.

Hugh's shoulders dropped. He tore his gaze away from hers. "Yeah," he said. "Sure."

The following week, Hugh brought her ice cream from Scoopz, nestled in a cooler full of ice. He said he'd been picking up some building supplies from the hardware store and had run into Rhonda on the way to the ferry. There was a pint of apple pie ice cream and a pint of butter pecan, which Rhonda must have told him was Ellie's usual choice.

That meant they'd talked about her. Had Hugh asked what Ellie's favorite ice cream was? Had he really "run into" Rhonda, or had he gone to Scoopz specifically for her?

The questions made hope and fear detonate in Ellie's gut, so she pushed them out of her mind.

They sat on a park bench and ate ice cream for lunch, and Ellie told him about the time she'd accidentally set fire to her fifth-grade classroom's curtains, sending black, stagnant water spraying from the sprinklers above. Hugh doubled over laughing, and she didn't feel one iota of embarrassment about her antics.

When he left an hour later, there was no strange, heavy moment between them. He just gave her a soft smile and told her to take care, then left her and Louie standing there. Ellie was oddly disappointed, but she told herself she was relieved.

The week after, Hugh had dog treats from the Fernley veterinarian to replenish Ellie's stash. Louie was overjoyed.

Ellie, if she was honest with herself, would admit that she was pretty happy about it too. And not just because of the dog treats.

CHAPTER 32

As the days passed, the rhythm of Ellie's life gained a predictable cadence. She worked, she ate, she slept, and she let Daphne drag her on torturous runs through a nearby park. At least Louie enjoyed jogging with them.

And, of course, she met with Hugh. Usually he came to Seattle once a week, sometimes twice. He always had an excuse as to why he'd come to the city, and he always brought her a token from Fernley. She looked forward to those meetings more than she wanted to admit.

She slept on her sister's couch, and the two of them avoided talking about what would happen after. Ellie and Daphne orbited around each other carefully, tentatively, testing the bounds of their new relationship. Now they weren't just sisters; they were creatures that had endured hurt and needed space and safety to recover. They understood each other more than ever before.

She stopped listening to music. Whenever she heard classic rock or old soul, it tightened her stomach so much that she nearly threw up. Now, those tunes didn't just remind her of her father. They reminded her of Hugh.

Spring ceded to summer. Sunshine beat down on all the hard concrete surfaces, and Ellie tried not to think about how beautiful Fernley would be right now.

The phone calls started in July. The first was from Gemma McMorton, who called on a Wednesday morning and asked Ellie if she'd be interested in planning a birthday party for her nephew, Cory.

Ellie frowned. "I'm not on the island," she told Gemma. "I'm sorry."

"Oh." Gemma sounded surprised. "I thought . . . well, never mind."

They hung up, and Ellie stared at her phone. That was strange.

Over the course of the week, she got a call from previous clients about a baby shower, a fiftieth birthday party, and even a small wedding reception for a couple who had eloped over the winter.

Every person who called seemed surprised and confused that Ellie wasn't on Fernley and wasn't planning on coming back.

The day she got the call about the wedding, Ellie hung up and turned to her sister. "I don't get it. Why do these people think my business is still operational?"

Daphne looked up from the stove, where she was making pasta sauce for dinner. She shrugged, a movement that looked slightly odd for some reason. Like Daphne was trying to appear more casual than she felt. "You were the only decent event planner on the island. They're probably feeling the void you left when you shut your business down."

Ellie hummed. "Yeah."

Daphne banged the wooden utensil on the side of the pot and placed it on a spoon rest next to the stove. She turned around and faced Ellie, crossing her arms. "So, I've been meaning to talk to you about something," she started. "My lease is up in October."

Ellie straightened. She glanced at the sofa, where her sheets were folded tidily, her pillow stacked on top. "I'm overstaying my welcome, aren't I?"

Daphne shook her head. "No. I was wondering if you wanted to move in together. You know. Officially. We could get a two-bedroom place; you could look for event planning jobs. I think it's time we make this a bit more permanent. You're here to stay, right?"

Why did that fill Ellie with panic?

Daphne saw it written all over Ellie's face, of course. She tilted her head, but she didn't seem surprised. If anything, Ellie thought she saw a little bit of triumph in her sister's face. "You miss the island."

Ellie grimaced. "Pathetic, isn't it?"

"No." Her sister shook her head. "You lived there your whole life. I was homesick as hell when I first left for college. I still get homesick." She gave Ellie a strange look. "How about we forget about the end of my lease. We'll reassess at the end of the summer. You can go back to Fernley if—"

"I'm not going back." The words fell from Ellie's lips with such vehemence that she snapped her mouth closed in surprise. She'd been lulled, these past weeks, into thinking that she'd moved on. But the hurt was there, lurking under the surface.

Daphne arched a brow. "Oh?"

Ellie shook her head. "I can't."

"Because of Hugh?"

"No," Ellie lied.

Daphne snorted.

Ellie scowled. "I'm serious. It has nothing to do with him. It's just . . . I can't live there anymore. I can't take the stares. The whispers. Those people will never respect me, and I'm sick of fighting for their approval. No one on that island ever wanted to see me succeed. Even when I ran my business, I'm pretty sure people only ever hired me to get into Jason's good graces."

"Ellie, you know that's not true."

"Isn't it?" Ellie let out a bitter laugh. "Who hired me to plan their baby showers and company parties? Jason's friends and coworkers."

"That's because Jason's friends and coworkers have money for fancy events, Ellie. It's not because they wanted to suck up to him. And what about all these phone calls you've been getting? Jason's bail got denied. Nobody's trying to suck up to him now."

Years-old frustration bubbled up in Ellie. "None of my success actually belonged to me." Ellie stared at the countertop. She traced the edge of it with her thumbnail, shaking her head. "I see it now, Daphne. The only reason Jason dated me was to gain access to our parents' land. The only reason people hired me for their events was to gain access to Jason. There's nobody on that island that actually cared about *me*." Her voice caught on the last words.

Because that wasn't quite true, was it? These past weeks, filled with Hugh's visits, phone calls from her parents and her grandmother, from Wynn, Daphne's help, her friendship with Lionel, Spencer's support . . .

But it still *hurt*. She met Daphne's gaze. "Even Jason's arrest—do you think anyone would think twice about him trashing my office or taking my dog if he hadn't also been stealing from everyone who donated to his stupid charity?"

"Of course they would, Ellie."

"No, Daphne. You're wrong. No one would give a damn."

"Lots of people would," she replied gently. "If you let them."

Ellie blinked at her sister, shocked. "I let people in. You're the one who hasn't even admitted to Mom and Dad that your engagement is off."

"We're not making this about me," Daphne warned. "This is about you feeling like you have to take everything on by yourself. You didn't tell anyone you were going to snoop around Jason's house. Not even Wynn."

"Wynn's ankle got messed up because of me! And I brought Hugh." Even though he basically invited himself and Ellie would have left him behind if she'd had the choice. At least at first.

Daphne went on as if Ellie hadn't spoken: "You didn't let Mom tell me until things were so stressed she let it slip by accident when I called. You didn't even want them to help you with the night of the gala. You didn't call the FBI!" Daphne narrowed her eyes. "And don't tell me everything was peachy during your relationship with Jason, Ellie. The reason your mug shot got passed around the island was because no one would have ever expected things between you to be less than perfect, because no one *knew*."

"You're saying this is my fault, then?"

"I'm saying you're a part of Fernley, Ellie. You're a part of our family."

Ellie's phone rang. They both looked at it. Mary O'Hara's name flashed on the screen.

A frown tugged at Ellie's brow. What now? "Hello?"

"Oh! Ellie! I'm *so happy* to talk to you."

Ellie grunted. She was too surprised to make words. Mary O'Hara wouldn't be happy to see Ellie if Ellie showed up at her door with a giant check for a million dollars.

"I saw the sign outside your office and was so pleased to see you were in business again! I'm planning a little celebration for this year's pie-baking contest. I'm expecting another victory, you know, and—"

"The sign?" Ellie interrupted. "What sign?"

Her sign had been destroyed by the vandal Jason had hired. She'd seen it, cracked beyond repair on a bed of broken glass.

"The one outside your office, of course. The new windows look lovely, I have to say. And the building *did* need a fresh coat of paint. I was happy to see it brightened up. Lifts the whole street right up."

Ellie's knees went weak as she gripped the counter for support. "What are you talking about? My office . . . was painted?" Why hadn't her parents mentioned that?

Ellie caught a look on Daphne's face, a look that told Ellie her sister knew what was going on and was trying to hide it. "I'll call you back," she said into the phone and hung up, then pointed the device at Daphne, her arm trembling. "What's going on?"

Daphne shrugged, the movement jerky and exaggerated. "I don't know."

"You've been acting weird. All that about your lease, about going back to Fernley . . ."

Daphne blinked, doe eyed, the picture of innocence. "I was just asking what your plans were. You can't sleep on my couch forever."

"What. Is. Going. On." She shook her phone for emphasis. "What are these phone calls about? Who painted my building?"

"I can't tell you."

Ellie reared back. "What do you mean, you can't tell me?"

"I've been sworn to secrecy."

"By *who*?"

Daphne turned back to the pot of simmering sauce and stirred it without saying a word.

"Daphne," Ellie said through clenched teeth.

"How much pasta do you want?"

"Daphne!"

"I'll put the whole box in."

"DAPHNE."

"It was Hugh, okay! Hugh did it." Daphne shook the wooden spoon as she yelled the words, sending bits of tomato sauce flying around the kitchen.

Ellie was so shocked she stumbled back and fell over a chair, landing in a heap on the ground. Louie came to investigate, taking the opportunity to lick Ellie's face as she flailed. "Ack!" she screamed, dodging Louie's kisses. She sat up, panting, and met her sister's gaze. Louie nosed her neck, then ducked down to lick her wrist.

Daphne rolled her lips inwardly.

"You're not going to tell me anything, are you?"

Lips still rolled, Daphne shook her head.

Ellie scowled and pulled out her phone. "Wynn," she said when the other woman answered. "What the heck is going on at my office?"

There was a very pointed pause that made Ellie go still. "Your office?" Wynn asked, angelic.

293

A growl rumbled through Ellie's throat.

Wynn groaned. "Ellie, don't get mad."

"Tell me what's going on," Ellie grated out.

"Hugh's been fixing your place up," Wynn admitted quietly. "Everyone's been talking about it."

Ellie was too shocked to speak. She mumbled a goodbye to Wynn, hung up, and stared at Louie as he flopped onto his side, tail gently smacking the ground. She lifted her gaze to meet her sister's. "When did you find out about this?"

"The only times I've seen you smile since you got to the city were days you met up with Hugh," Daphne said quietly. "I asked Grandma about him to see if I should get involved somehow—"

"And she obviously told you that was a ridiculous suggestion, because that would make you a nosy meddler."

"—and she told me what he was up to. It was maybe two, three weeks ago."

Ellie's gaze drifted back down to her phone. "I don't understand."

"Maybe . . ." Daphne sighed. "Maybe it's worth giving him another chance."

"He *lied* to me," Ellie protested, but it sounded weak. "He lied."

Daphne stayed silent, and Ellie ran her fingers through Louie's fur. Hugh had concealed the truth. But he'd wanted to come clean, hadn't he? And he'd visited her every week since she'd been here. And his apology had been sincere, with no qualifiers. It truly sounded like he understood what he'd done wrong.

Ellie had run away from Fernley because she'd felt humiliated. But what if those feelings were misplaced? She'd been worried about what people thought of her for as long as she could remember. That was one of the reasons she'd fallen for Jason's false charm; he'd offered her entrance into a level of society on the island she hadn't truly believed she deserved. That's why he'd been able to hurt her. Jason's rejection had been a confirmation of what Ellie had believed about herself all along.

Suddenly, Ellie understood what her mother had been trying to tell her. Yes, their family history was peppered with colorful stories. But what Helen had been trying to say was that none of them should cause shame. None of those stories affected Ellie's worth as a human, as a woman, or as a resident of Fernley.

Trust wasn't a trap; it was a *risk*. Trusting the wrong person could cause an inordinate amount of pain and anguish, as she'd learned with Jason. But trust could also open up a whole new world of feeling—of love.

If Ellie could learn to trust *herself*, she could forgive herself for her mistakes and accept herself for who she was. Mug shot and all.

The source of Ellie's humiliation—and its end—was within. Being whole, in her own heart, would allow her to move on, and ask for help, and step onto the island with her head held high.

But could she trust Hugh again? Could she let go of the fear and open her heart up once more?

"I'm scared," she admitted.

"I know," Daphne replied.

Fear wasn't serving her, though. It was keeping her in a daze, letting her stumble through the weeks until they bled together. Maybe it would be worth it to go back to Fernley, see what Hugh had done. Maybe if she had her feet on the island's soil, everything would make sense.

She petted her dog until resolve settled over her skin; then she met her sister's gaze. "I'm going to book a ferry ticket for tomorrow morning."

Daphne's lips curled. "I'll come too. Might as well tell everyone about me and Pete. They'll be all up in arms about it, and you'll have time to deal with your drama."

Ellie snorted and rolled her eyes, secretly grateful, then got online and booked a ticket.

CHAPTER 33

Wind whipped Ellie's hair as she sat in a white plastic chair on the top deck of the ferry, her eyes on the growing patch of land ahead. Her palms grew sweaty no matter how many times she wiped them on her denim shorts. Daphne dozed on a seat beside her, sunning her legs and arms.

The green smudge in the distance that was Fernley grew as the ferry chugged, stark against the blue of the water beyond. It was a beautiful day: one of those gorgeous, warm summer days that was pure magic on the island. Ellie inhaled the scent of the sea as the ferry's engine rumbled beneath her, carrying her ever closer to the shores where she'd spent her entire life.

A ding sounded over the speakers, and an automated announcement instructed drivers to return to their cars. Ellie nudged her sister. "I'm going to head down and get Louie settled."

Minutes seemed to stick together, reluctant to move on from each other. The ferry ride to Fernley was just over an hour long, but it felt like an eternity since Ellie had gotten up and showered this morning. As she moved down to her car, she almost couldn't believe she was here.

Once Louie was settled in the back seat, she sat behind the wheel of her car, leaning her head against the headrest, wondering what she'd find on Fernley. The island wasn't far from the mainland, but it felt like she had crossed into another world by leaving. She'd spent a couple of months in the city, getting swept up in a different kind of life while she found her feet again. One with more cars, fewer trees, and a lonely kind of anonymity.

Ellie never thought she'd miss the fact that everyone knew her name on the island. A couple of months ago, she'd have said that was the worst thing about living on Fernley.

But a couple of months ago, she'd been drowning in hurt and the need for revenge. She'd wanted to prove to herself and to everyone on the island that she wasn't a crazy ex-girlfriend; she'd been right about Jason all along. She'd wanted to protect her parents' land and stand up for something significant.

Now, Ellie realized, she'd been looking for a way to rebuild her self-worth. What better way than seeking the validation of the entire island?

As the ferry's horn blew and the vessel slowed, Ellie's heartbeat kicked. She couldn't see much from the vehicle deck except the top of the hill where Carlisle spilled into the adjoining forest. The asphalt of the main road from the harbor cut over the hill and disappeared over the crest, with houses and businesses lining both sides.

She knew every single one of them. She'd *missed* them.

"You okay?" Daphne asked quietly from the passenger seat.

"I know I was only gone for a couple of months, but I missed this place," Ellie answered.

Daphne smiled. "Me too."

The ferry docked, and the workers started their dance. The first row of cars disembarked in a long snake of glittering metal, then the second. Finally, Ellie's row began to move. She kneaded the steering wheel, her breaths coming in shallow pants as she struggled to stay calm.

They rolled off the ferry and onto the ramp, and Ellie let out a long exhale. She rolled down her window and inhaled the fresh, earthy, salt-laden air that smelled so familiar it made her want to cry. She drove up the hill and drank in the sight of flower baskets, pendant flags on lampposts, and brightly painted storefronts. At a red light, she saw Rhonda in the window of Scoopz. Rhonda must have sensed her gaze and looked up, smiling brightly as she waved.

Ellie was home.

It hit her like a bag of bricks. She didn't want to leave this place. She didn't want to tuck her tail between her legs and run away. She wanted to *stay*. All her friends were here. Her business was here. Her family was here.

Hugh was here.

As they drove up the hill, drawing ever closer to the road where Ellie's business sat, it became harder and harder for Ellie to take a full breath. She could feel her pulse in her fingertips, in her stomach, in her thighs. Her body thrummed with tension. What would she find? What had Hugh done?

Finally, they reached the turn. Ellie parked at the end of the street, too nervous to drive up to the building itself. She turned the car off and stared out the windshield, spying a new, bright-yellow door in the distance. She couldn't move.

Hugh had come to Seattle every week to see her. Ellie knew she was the reason he'd made all those trips; she wasn't naive. All those little tokens and presents he'd brought were thin excuses to spend time together. And she'd luxuriated in every minute of his presence, not wanting to admit that she craved it when he was gone.

Those moments with Hugh had been precious pinpricks of light in the last two months of haziness. It was like they'd mutually decided to forget about their whirlwind week and start back at the beginning. They'd gotten to know each other in a way that hadn't been possible when they were running around trying to take Jason down.

And all the while, Hugh had been fixing up her office, giving her her business back.

"Ready?" Daphne asked quietly.

Ellie huffed a breath and nodded. "Yeah," she said. "I'm ready."

Ready to face what, exactly, she wasn't sure. She knew that when she saw Hugh it would be different. Now they had their feet on Fernley. They weren't living in that strange in-between place in Seattle, where Ellie could lie to herself about why he kept showing up.

Now, when she saw Hugh, she'd have to face exactly what she felt for him.

Louie jumped out of the car when she opened the back door, his body vibrating. He could sense Ellie's mood, knew that something big was about to happen.

They walked slowly, sticking to the opposite side of the road. Ellie tried to keep her shoulders back, tried not to let her feet drag, but it was difficult. Her heart was a jackrabbit in her chest. Her stomach was a tight ball. Her hands and feet tingled. She couldn't think.

Daphne and Louie flanked her, so she couldn't run away. Not that she wanted to, not really. Ellie was done running. She stopped directly across the street from the building that had been a wreck only a few months ago.

All signs of vandalism had disappeared. The windows had been replaced with huge panes of new glass, letting in lots of light to the interior. The sign that Wynn had designed had been updated and replaced above the door. It looked like a brand-new building—a brand-new business. The whole front was freshly painted, the new yellow door cheerful and welcoming.

Ellie put a hand against her heart, completely speechless. Hugh had done this for her. Quietly, without saying a word, he'd given her her life back.

The door to Ellie's business opened.

Hugh stood in the opening wearing blue jeans and a white tee, a smudge of dirt across his chest. His brow was gleaming with sweat, as if he'd just been caught finishing up work inside.

And his eyes—his eyes were steady, serious, and they asked Ellie a thousand questions.

Her feet moved before she knew what was happening. She crashed into Hugh's chest and threw her arms around his neck. Her lips collided with his as he grunted at the impact, but it took him only a second to kiss her back with an intensity that made Ellie weak. She clung to him, her anchor in the storm.

Ellie laughed into the kiss, loving the way Hugh's hands clung to her waist, her hips, her butt. He touched her like he'd been starving, like he couldn't help himself.

They pulled apart, keeping their arms wrapped around each other. "You're back," Hugh said, voice thick.

"Yes," Ellie replied.

That's when she noticed the music. He had a little portable speaker inside, and ABBA's "Take a Chance on Me" was starting, female vocals echoing in her new office. Ellie pulled back, grinning. "I didn't know you liked ABBA."

Hugh's cheeks turned pink. He huffed a laugh, resting his forehead against Ellie's. "I've been listening to that song on repeat. Your dad thinks it's hilarious. He said ODNT's working on a cover of it in my honor for their next gig."

Ellie giggled. Hugh closed his eyes like he wanted to drink in the sound of her laughter, his breath brushing against her cheek. Ellie's fingers roamed over his neck, across his jaw, and up to his cheeks. She pulled away and flicked her gaze between his eyes, happiness igniting in every corner of her body and soul. She was beyond words.

He kissed her hungrily until Louie barked and jumped up, his front paws landing on their sides. Then Hugh dropped down and lavished Louie with the attention the dog craved while Ellie looked over her shoulder.

Daphne winked. "I'll leave you two lovebirds alone, and I'll do my best to keep the hordes away from you for an hour or two. Nothing like dropping a breakup bomb on them to keep them occupied." The hordes were their parents and grandmother, and they would indeed be shocked that Daphne and Pete had broken up. Ellie smiled gratefully, tossing her car keys at her sister, who caught them one handed and waved goodbye.

Hugh stood and tugged Ellie inside. He shut the door once Louie was inside and spun Ellie around so her back was to his front. When ABBA's song started back at the beginning, Ellie began to laugh. Hugh got his phone out of his pocket, tapped a few times, and turned the music off, laughing right along with her. Louie darted to the back of the room, sniffing every corner, investigating all the new items that had been added to Ellie's space.

A new desk had been built in the back corner, and it looked custom made. Two armchairs were positioned around a small coffee table at the front of the space, where Ellie could take client meetings. A shelf with all her old files and plans lined the left wall, with the right wall dominated by a decal of her logo and business name.

And in front of the windows, a new dog bed had a place of honor in the sunniest spot in the room. Louie found it, walked in a circle three times, and flopped down like he'd been waiting for this moment his entire life.

"Hugh," Ellie choked. "What . . . how . . ."

His cheek pressed against hers as he hugged her tight, his arms banding around her stomach. "Lionel helped."

"That must have cost a fortune."

Hugh's chuckle was warm. "You have no idea. The man could teach a master class on extortion." There was a slight pause, and when Hugh spoke again, his voice was ever so slightly hesitant. "You like it?"

Ellie nodded. "Yes. I love it. I can't believe it. After everything that happened, I never thought I'd be event planning again. But now . . ." She spun in his arms, placing her hands on either side of his face. "You have no idea what you've given me."

Lips curling, Hugh tilted his head from side to side. "It was selfish," he admitted. "I wanted you to come back to Fernley. And . . . I wanted there to be a reason for you to stay."

"Does that mean you're sticking around too?"

Hugh let out a huff, his arms tightening around her body. "I took a loan out against my land and bought the building next door. I'm going to open a music studio of my own."

Ellie's heart leaped. "Next door to here?"

Hugh's face softened. "Where else? Ellie, I'm completely in love with you. I want to be beside you, always."

Her heart cartwheeled, and she lost her balance. Hugh steadied her, smiled, and crushed his lips against hers once more. Then he lifted her up and carried her to the desk, out of sight of the big windows at the front of the room. She landed on the desk and spread her knees so Hugh could notch himself between them.

"Do you mean that?" Ellie asked quietly.

"That I'm in love with you?" His voice was deep and steady, reverberating in Ellie's limbs.

She nodded.

"Yes," he answered simply. "I love you. I want to be with you. If you'll forgive me for what I did, I'll spend my life trying to make you happy, Ellie. You're the most perfect woman I've ever known."

"I'm not perfect," she answered through a tight throat.

He grinned. "You're perfect to me."

Her breath shuddered. She closed her eyes, and tears spilled over her cheeks. "Even though I attacked you with a pair of bolt cutters?"

"Especially because you attacked me with a pair of bolt cutters," Hugh replied, the smile evident in his voice. He brushed her cheeks with his thumbs, catching her tears to wipe them away.

All her jagged edges. All her impulsivity, her fire, her schemes. He loved them all.

Ellie stood with her toes on the edge of a very tall cliff, so high up she couldn't see the bottom. Being with Hugh would be leaping off the edge and trusting that he'd catch her. Opening her heart meant risking a big fat *splat* if he didn't.

Ellie took a deep breath—and jumped.

"I love you too, Hugh. I love you so much it terrifies me."

His grin surprised her. "That's good, because I'm scared too. Maybe it means we can figure it out together."

"Yes," she croaked. Ellie let her hands smooth over Hugh's chest and shoulders the way she'd been craving for weeks. He was broad and warm and perfect. When she dipped her hands under the hem of his tee to feel his skin beneath her palms, Hugh ripped the top off one handed and tossed it aside.

They didn't speak for a while after that.

EPILOGUE

Eighteen months later

A triple celebration was in order: First, there was Ellie and Hugh's engagement. Second, ODNT had just released their first studio album, which had been recorded and produced by Hugh. Third, Daphne had officially moved back to Fernley.

Everyone gathered at Helen and Claude's. Mabel, Harry, and Greta sat queenlike on armchairs in the corner, sipping cocktails as they chattered. Wynn and Daphne were in the kitchen with Helen and Claude. Lionel sat on the sofa beside Hugh's mother, Faye, who had recently moved to Fernley to be closer to her son. She'd sold her house and, with some help from Hugh, downsized to a town house in Carlisle.

The members of ODNT and their wives were dotted around the living room, drinking and chatting. Spencer was loving on Louie in the corner, lavishing the dog with attention.

Ellie slipped under Hugh's arm and looked up at him, grinning. "Hey there, handsome."

His eyes softened as they took her in, sending her heart into overdrive. She loved when he looked at her like that. "Hi, Ellie."

Her lips curled. "Can't wait." She peeked at her left hand, where the round-cut diamond glittered, nestled in a circle of more tiny diamonds.

The band was yellow gold, complementing the golden tones of her skin. They'd designed it together at the jewelry store in Fernley the day after Hugh proposed.

"Hugh, honey," Helen called out. "Can you help us with the chairs?"

"Yep!" He planted a kiss on Ellie's forehead and ducked into the kitchen, reappearing a moment later carrying chairs, then arranging them at the long table they'd set up in the living room.

Ellie slipped across the room and sat beside Faye on the couch. "I think Hugh actually enjoys being ordered around by my mother," Ellie told her soon-to-be mother-in-law.

Faye grinned. "He always wanted to be part of a big family." She tapped Ellie's knee. "Now he is."

The past year and a half had been a dream. Ellie had opened her business and immediately been booked out six weeks in advance. She had baby showers, parties, birthdays, weddings—all manner of events for the people of Fernley. By the time the tenth person had told her that they were glad to see she was still in business, she actually believed them.

They'd come to *her*. Not for Jason. They'd hired her to plan their parties because she was a master at it—especially when things went wrong. No one could salvage a disaster like Ellie could.

Hugh had sold off a chunk of his father's land to a local who planned to keep most of the forests untouched so he could go mountain biking to his heart's content. Hugh kept five acres that neighbored Ellie's parents' place.

The FBI hadn't found any evidence of Alex's involvement in Jason's schemes. All their communication had seemed legitimate; Jason had planned on roping yet another person into his crimes. Ellie was glad of Alex's innocence, for Hugh's sake. She didn't want him to have to face any more pain where his father was concerned.

When she'd asked Hugh if he wanted to get rid of the land and start somewhere new—somewhere that wasn't haunted by his father's ghost—Hugh had smiled.

"There's no ghost," he'd told her. "My dad was flawed. He was selfish, thoughtless, and often driven by greed. But he tried to reach out to me for three years before he died, and I was the one to push him away. I've been thinking about that, about my own selfishness. I was so busy being hurt that I didn't give him a chance to right his wrongs."

"Maybe he didn't deserve that chance," Ellie had answered. They'd been standing on a cliff not far from the property line he shared with her parents, watching the waves beat the rocks below.

Hugh had wrapped his arms around her and smiled. "This land brought me here, to you. Instead of seeing it as a bribe, I've started thinking of it as a gift. And in order to accept it, I had to get honest with myself about the kind of man I want to be."

"What kind of man is that?"

"The kind who rights his wrongs," he'd said, then kissed her thoroughly.

He'd used the money from the sale of the big parcel of land to pay off the loan on his new music studio, get his business off the ground, and make sure his mother had enough money for a stable retirement on Fernley.

Ellie and Hugh rented a two-bedroom apartment in Carlisle and had dinners at Ellie's parents' house every Thursday night. Life was quiet, steady, and—above all—happy.

That morning, before the party, they'd started researching architects to design their own home on the land he'd kept for himself. Hugh seemed *very* interested to learn about shepherding from Claude, so Ellie figured he might be spending more time on her parents' property than originally anticipated. Claude was over the moon and trying to hide it.

"My son never told me how he proposed," Faye said, eyes sparkling. "Did he plan something special?"

Ellie's cheeks grew warm. She thought of that languid December morning, when they'd been tangled in their bedsheets for hours. Hugh had finally climbed out of bed and returned with two mugs of coffee, then sat on the edge of the bed wearing nothing but a loose pair of pajama pants. He handed Ellie her coffee as she sat up against the headboard, her body still buzzing from their earlier activities. Then he said, "How long do I have to wait before I can ask you to marry me?"

She'd spilled her coffee all over the sheets.

Now, she glanced at Faye and grinned. "He popped the question after bringing me coffee in bed. It was perfect."

Faye let out a soft sigh, patting Ellie's knee. "I couldn't ask for a better daughter-in-law."

Ellie's chest tightened. She peered past Faye to meet Lionel's gaze. "What about you, Lionel? Am I an acceptable niece-in-law?"

The old man reached down to grab a chip from the platter on the coffee table. He crunched down and squinted at Ellie. "You'll do," he finally said.

She laughed, then jumped when she was shushed by her grandmother. Mabel stood, eyes wide, holding the TV remote in her hands. "Look! It's all over the news!"

The chatter in the room died, and all heads turned toward the television. Mabel turned the volume way, way up in time for Ellie to hear the newscaster drone on: "The thirty-three-year-old man was sentenced to twenty-two years in prison with no chance of parole. Brownlow looked emotionless as he heard the judge hand down the sentence . . ."

Harry let out a whoop, banging her cane on the ground. "Twenty-two years, you bastard!"

Greta harrumphed, then met Ellie's gaze and gave her a subtle nod. "Good for you, girl," she said quietly. "Someone finally stood up to that family."

Ellie fell back against the cushions with a sigh. The last piece of the puzzle had fallen into place. Over the last eighteen months, she'd tried not to pay too much attention to Jason's court case and all the drama that surrounded it. There'd been so much speculation in the news and on social media that it had been easier for Ellie to avoid it completely. Jason represented a period in her life that she no longer recognized.

Hugh came to perch beside Ellie on the arm of the sofa, his hand coasting between her shoulder blades. He glanced down at her, a soft smile on her lips. "How are you feeling?"

"I'm okay," she answered. "I'm happy it's over."

Hugh had a bottle of beer in his hand, and Ellie watched as he leaned forward to grab a coaster from the stack in the middle of the table. He put the coaster down and his beer on top of it.

Ellie smiled.

"What?" Hugh asked.

"I just love you, is all."

He kissed her temple. "Back atcha."

"There's one thing I don't understand, though," Daphne said, and everyone turned to look at her, standing in the doorway of the kitchen. Well, everyone except for Lionel, who just reached for another chip from the bowl on the coffee table. Daphne frowned at the television. "Who called the FBI? How did they know about some tiny charity on a tiny island? Someone must have tipped them off ages ago."

It was a good question. Ellie tilted her head, staring at her sister across the room. It was only because she was sitting on the couch, looking in the exact right direction, that she saw the slight—almost imperceptible—pause in Lionel's movements. His fingers twitched just above the bowl of chips when Daphne asked the question, even though the rest of him didn't react at all.

Ellie stared at the old man. Evidently feeling her gaze, he turned his head and stared back. His eyes were shuttered, but Ellie had spent a lot of time with Lionel. She knew his moods. Knew when he was saying something with a wrinkle of his nose or tension in his shoulders.

At that moment, he said something with the twitch of his fingers.

"It was you," she breathed before she could stop herself.

All eyes turned to Lionel. He scowled in response.

Hugh dropped his hand from Ellie's back and straightened, staring at his uncle. "You called the FBI, Lionel? When? Why?"

"Someone had to do it," Lionel grumped.

"But . . ." Ellie was glad she was sitting, because she was so shocked that she'd definitely have fallen over. "But you hate the government. What about the OddJobs app? The IRS? You were always telling me that you didn't want those people in your business. You lie on your taxes every year, Lionel."

Lionel pursed his lips, and when the silence stretched, he finally relented. "'Bout six years ago, the Brownlow family couldn't pay their bills at my shop. All those fancy boats, beautiful cars, big houses, and I had to chase them for unpaid invoices every time they came in to get their boats' engines tuned up." He grabbed another chip and crunched down angrily. "Then, like magic, all their debts got paid. That man," he said, pointing to the television, where Jason's own mug shot was on the screen (which was, delightfully, even worse than Ellie's), "told me that now I could stop pestering him about money. Real smug-like."

"You knew something was fishy?" Ellie prompted when Lionel stopped speaking.

Lionel's hazel eyes met hers. The finger he pointed at her had engine grease staining all the whorls of his fingerprints, highlighting every line and wrinkle on his hand. "You don't steal from the people of this island. I won't bother you about nothin', and your business is your business, but you *do not* steal from Fernley. So, yeah. I called the feds. And I'd do it again if I found out some other snooty SOB was stealing from the good people that live on this island."

"I'll drink to that," Tracey said, lifting her cocktail. Sandler, her husband, grunted and touched his bottle to her glass.

Murmurs of agreement echoed around the room. Ellie leaned back on the sofa, blowing out a long breath. She met Hugh's glimmering eyes, her lips twitching in answer to his smile. He shrugged. "Can't argue with that logic."

Lionel harrumphed.

"Dinner's ready!" Claude called out. "Let's eat." He bustled over to start some soft jazz on the record player while everyone took their seats. Then, when he passed Ellie's chair, he leaned down and kissed her cheek. "Proud of you, Ellie-Belly."

Hugh slid his hand over her thigh and gave it a slight squeeze. "Love you," he whispered.

Ellie's shoulders relaxed. She grinned. "Even if I bashed you on the head with a pair of bolt cutters?"

He grabbed a dinner roll from the basket of steaming bread that Claude had just pulled out of the oven. His eyes crinkled at the line they'd repeated many times over the last eighteen months. "Especially because you bashed me on the head with a pair of bolt cutters."

Laughing, Ellie took a crusty roll from the basket and passed it down to Daphne, who was seated to her left. She looked at everyone gathered around their table and felt a rush of gratitude that in her small way, Ellie was part of what made this island so special.

This was exactly where she belonged. Right here, on Fernley Island, with her family and friends—and Hugh. It took her a week to fall in love with the man, and she hoped she never recovered.

Turn the page to see a preview of Lilian Monroe's *Conquest, Book 1 of The Four Groomsmen of the Wedpocalypse*!

CONQUEST: A FAKE FIANCÉE ROMANTIC COMEDY

The Four Groomsmen of the Wedpocalypse: Book One

CHAPTER 1

Amelia Darcy was ready to crawl out of her skin. Red ants marched through her veins, leaving burning anxiety in their wake. They traveled the length of her body in an unending loop, through every artery, vein, and capillary, around and around and around.

Because he was *late*.

Huffing in a failed attempt to clear her mounting frustration, Amelia spun on her heels and continued wearing a line through the thin red carpet of the church's narthex. The single strap of her bridesmaid dress draped strangely over her shoulder. Why had her sister chosen an asymmetrical design? At least with two straps, the feeling would be mirrored on both sides of her body, which would be acceptable. Amelia hadn't been comfortable since she put the thing on.

She wouldn't even think about the color; that would only make her anxiety worse. Earlier, when Amelia had slipped on the lilac silk garment and caught sight of herself in the mirror, she'd fully recoiled. Against her pale, desaturated skin and her pale, desaturated hair, the pastel purple shade produced a distinctly corpse-like effect. Even her eyes, which she'd always thought were her best feature, looked sunken, their pale-gray irises turning dull as worn pewter. The makeup artist had tried to glue false eyelashes on her lids, cheerily claiming they'd brighten her face right up, but then Amelia had twitched and blinked so much the whole endeavor had been aborted. So she still looked like she belonged outside in the church's graveyard instead of in the bridal party, except now with slightly irritated eyelids.

But today was Maggie's wedding day, and Amelia would wear a sparkly leotard and dance the cha-cha backward if it made her sister happy. It didn't matter what color her dress was, or how many straps it had, or if that number was one too few.

Wedding planning hadn't been fun, exactly, but Amelia had thrown herself into it. She'd made phone calls, coordinated vendors, ordered decorations, planned and attended a hellish bachelorette party, helped set up the church and the reception venue, and completed countless other tasks—all in the name of sisterly love. She'd taken her role as Maggie's maid of honor seriously.

The best man, on the other hand?

Not so much.

He hadn't shown up to the rehearsal dinner, hadn't helped with any of the preparations, and now, the only time that *actually* mattered, he was late. Two more minutes, and she'd lead the bridal progression down the aisle on her own. He could slink in whenever he arrived and watch from the back pew, for all she cared. If he showed up at all.

The strap on her shoulder slipped, so she yanked it back up. Stupid thing.

She'd strangle him when she saw him. Months—*months!*—of planning, and now the whole wedding hinged on the arrival of some mysterious best man. Nerves morphed into anger, and Amelia wanted to scream. She'd make him sorry for being so late. That was a promise. She'd strangle him with his own tie and enjoy every gruesome second of it.

Her feet stomped as she made another lap. And another. And another. Her teeth gnashed so hard a headache started pulsing near her temples.

A door creaked open behind her. Amelia whirled, only to let her shoulders drop in disappointment.

A dark-haired man poked his head out of the room where the bridal party waited. He lifted a brow. "No sign of him?"

"No." Her answer was curt. Her lips compressed, as if she could make the missing best man appear by drawing her mouth into a perfectly straight line. It didn't work.

"All right. I'll let them know." Marlon Saint James didn't seem worried about his brother's tardiness. He certainly didn't seem surprised. Even the groom hadn't worried when she'd scurried to the altar to inform him his best man was missing in action.

Emory had given her a little half smile and said, "He'll show. He's flying in this morning, probably hit traffic."

Amelia didn't share Emory's confidence. A scowl etched itself over her brow as she spun around to do another lap. She hadn't been able to get a straight answer from her sister's other bridesmaids when she asked about the best man. Sly looks and rolled eyes were the usual response to the mention of his name. Maybe a snort and a wry "You know how he is."

But she didn't know how he was. She'd never laid eyes on the man. All she knew was he was *late*.

Murmurs swelled in the church as guests grew restless. She'd wait one more minute, and then they'd start without him. She'd apologize to Maggie and Emory afterward, but really, it was—

Hinges groaned to her left. Amelia turned toward the sound, only to be struck dumb by the vision unfolding before her.

The church's arched doors split down the middle, letting in golden sunlight through the widening gap. A man stood in the center, a hand on either door, silhouetted by the sun's honeyed rays. He pushed the doors all the way open to step through them, then straightened, standing as tall and proud as a king returning from war. Or maybe a fallen angel, seeking vengeance.

Or a missing best man, finally deigning to make an appearance.

Leo Saint James stepped into the church, the sunlight limning the edges of his body in gold while casting the rest of him in black, impenetrable shadow. He looked impossibly large. For no reason at all, Amelia's heart rattled.

The doors squeaked on their way shut, and bit by bit, the best man was revealed to Amelia's hungry stare.

Because that's what was growing inside her—hunger. A ravenous ache pulsed in the very heart of her as she saw the strong lines of his face, his heavy-lidded green eyes, his softly masculine lips. There was a sort of disheveled grace to him, a quality that made him seem more than perfect. Like his appearance was a veneer her mortal gaze wasn't supposed to penetrate, his flaws purposefully chosen to make him seem simply human.

Slowly, sunlight disappeared behind heavy timber doors until a final groan and a click sounded. The best man watched her, a brow quirking at her perusal.

Suddenly she realized she'd been gaping. Her spine snapped straight. "You're late," she clipped.

His gaze didn't leave her face. "Am I?"

"And you're a mess."

Leo looked down at himself and seemed surprised to see the state of his clothes. "So I am," he muttered. "Got changed at the airport."

Edging dangerously close to mania, Amelia tried to wrangle her fleeing wits. She felt light headed and strange. He was very beautiful. But—so what?

He was also late, and that was nearly unforgivable. It was Maggie's wedding day, and nothing—especially not *him*—would ruin it. Even if this was "how he was." Whatever that meant.

Stomping toward Leo, she ignored the incessant thumping of her heart. He looked even worse—better?—up close. Rumpled. Deliciously so.

Before she could divine what they were doing, Amelia's hands rose to the bow tie hanging undone at Leo's neck. She couldn't fasten the bow until the top button of his shirt was clasped, so she clicked her tongue and pulled at his collar. He rocked forward when she yanked the fabric, letting out a short, low grunt.

From the corner of her eyes, Amelia caught the curl of his lips.

Smiling! At a time like this! Strangling him would be too kind. He deserved to be tickled to death. Or stretched out on a medieval rack and submitted to the most horrid water torture imaginable. Or . . . or . . . have every one of his long, full eyelashes plucked out.

Her fingers trembled as they dipped near the hollow of his throat to do up the button. Stubble rasped against her knuckles, and a sharp jolt of heat traveled through her middle.

"This is . . . unexpected," he said, voice dropping to a low baritone that did interesting things to Amelia's inner thighs. Amelia's inner thighs needed to get a hold of themselves. "Are you sure we should be doing this in a church? You haven't even told me your name."

Fury was a rocket launching in her chest. Explosions created a cloud of dust and debris in her veins as anger took off inside her, because he didn't even seem sorry for being unforgivably late. He was *flirting*, at a time like this! Leo Saint James, professional annoyance. Who did he think he was? Showing up at Amelia's sister's wedding, looking like a disheveled prince, then *joking* about it!

The. *Nerve.*

The man couldn't even dress himself, and he was trying to be cute with her?

"Oh, please," she hissed. "Spare me." She scowled at him, flicking her gaze upward to meet his eyes. It was a mistake. As soon as her gaze clashed with his, she saw the gleam that lived in his emerald-green irises. It promised everything dark and dirty, and Amelia wanted to let herself fall into those promises and never emerge again. Her anger was snuffed out in an instant as a wave of unfamiliar lust took over.

Strange. It wasn't like her to feel this way about men—not even the pretty ones. Flustered, yes. Anxious, definitely.

Aroused? No way.

Her body's reaction swung her back to anger, and she gripped the feeling with both fists. She was angry at him for being late. Angry at the bridal party for putting her in this position. Angry at herself for finding him attractive.

Maybe the stress of her sister's wedding was getting to her. Or it was the lack of sleep over the past six months. Her work had been intense, after all. Starting a business usually was.

A small shake of her head, and her mind felt slightly clearer. Today was her sister's wedding, and this absolute lump of a pretty boy was threatening to throw the whole thing off schedule. He needed to get himself together; then she'd hold his arm and walk down the aisle ahead of the rest of the bridal party with a smile plastered on her face. Nothing else mattered.

She tugged the collar to straighten it, then set herself to tying the bow tie. It was the same soft lilac as her dress, but against his tawny skin, the color looked rich and creamy. Of course it did. Her frown deepened, and Amelia used the moment to settle her unstable emotions. She tied the fabric carefully, straightening the corners until a perfect purple bow stared back at her.

All the while, Leo's gaze pressed like a weight. He stood very still to endure her ministrations, arms at his sides, chin lifted out of the way. But she felt it—the heaviness of his stare. He didn't have anywhere else to look but at her, she reasoned, but it still made her want to squirm.

It was no surprise that Amelia would feel put out by a beautiful man's gaze. She wasn't exactly beating men back these days. She'd been focusing on her career; she hadn't had time to date. Never mind the fact that being this close to a man made Amelia feel like she had a bird trapped in her chest and noodles for limbs. Best to avoid these sorts of situations altogether. She wasn't known for being a man-eater. More like a man-evader.

Sipping in a short little breath, she frowned at his vest. It, like the jacket and pants, was a navy so dark it was nearly black. His white shirt bunched awkwardly between his vest and pants. He'd have to retuck it.

She pointed at the offending area. "Fix this. It looks like a deflated muffin top," she blurted—and there was the other reason she hadn't had much luck with men. Words sometimes fell out of her mouth without warning, and often they weren't exactly delicate. She'd come to learn that her lack of filter wasn't an attractive trait. There were many, many data points from failed dates and awkward interactions to prove it.

But Leo didn't seem bothered. In fact, he leaned ever so slightly closer to her, so she could smell the scent of soap rising from his skin. "I was led to believe that fixing my clothing was your job," he answered, and for a moment, Amelia felt off balance. It was the velvet quality of his tone and the way his scent wrapped around her like a drugging cloud. Then she registered the laughter in his voice.

Despite herself, Amelia's eyes snapped up to his once more. He was *mocking* her. Thunder rumbled in the distance, and Amelia knew it was her temper.

She just wanted this day to go right. For Maggie. For beautiful, kind Maggie with the luminous smile. Her sister deserved this. She'd found Emory, and they'd fallen in love, and now they'd have a perfect wedding day. Amelia would make sure of it.

This was what she *did*. She identified problems, then parsed the data into something useful. Whether it was a complicated data set for a client, or a wedding venue scheduling for today's event, or ordering supplies for 70 intricate handmade centerpieces (which included 2,590 individual components, ordered from four different vendors), Amelia could sort any problem into a tidy, efficient solution.

She'd made sense of the wedding preparations, and now it would all go off without a hitch. No matter what the man before her did or said.

Leo narrowed his eyes, seeing something written on her face. What, she didn't know. Maybe he could hear the thunder just as clearly as she could. Ozone crackled in the air between them, like that breathless, heavy moment before a strike of lightning.

With a gusted breath, Leo turned, and a belt jingled. Amelia averted her gaze from his broad back, blood rising to her cheeks. It was half-humiliating, really, to be blushing at the mere sound of a belt buckle clinking. No wonder men saw her and took off running in the other direction. Middle schoolers had more poise than she did.

Leo spun around and spread his arms, a roguish grin holding up the corners of his lips. "Satisfied?"

Ugh. "Annoyed."

His smile grew, as did the trembling in Amelia's thighs.

Leo tugged his jacket sleeves and arranged his cuffs just so. He combed both hands through his hair, and the gently curled light-brown locks fell into the kind of perfect disarray that betrayed an expensive haircut.

Rings glinted on two fingers: the thumb of his right hand, and the index finger of his left. They were simple gold bands that shone in the low light of the room and drew attention to his hands. Beautiful hands for a beautiful man. He lifted his gaze to hers and arched a brow.

"Good enough," Amelia grumped, even though the more truthful statement would be *drop-dead gorgeous* or *positively edible*.

"Do I get to learn your name now?" The gleam was back in his eyes.

Nerves gripped Amelia in a tight fist. Giving him even her name was handing over more power than was wise. A man like Leo Saint James would take one look at her and crush her vulnerable heart. She felt the urge to protect herself, but Amelia was a rational being, and she knew it was only her name. He'd learn it eventually. She forced the syllables out. "Amelia."

"Amelia," he repeated, like he was sipping fine wine and detecting all kinds of hidden notes in it. Touching a hand to his chest, he said, "Leo."

"So I've heard," she said, and something undefinable flitted across his expression. His smile widened, but his eyes grew shuttered.

Amelia frowned. Odd.

No time to figure it out. She had a wedding procession to lead, and she wasn't letting Leo Saint James out of her sight for a second until Emory and Maggie were husband and wife. She reached out and grabbed Leo's wrist, tugging him toward the room where the rest of the bridal party awaited, not trusting him to follow without physical encouragement.

Then he shifted, and his hand slipped against hers. She made to pull away, but he intertwined their fingers before she had the chance to escape.

He was . . . He was *holding her hand.*

It was a shock to the system, intimate in a way she hadn't expected. That broad, warm palm pressed against hers. His long fingers curled and notched between her knuckles. The heat of it. The sheer *size* of it.

She paused halfway to the side door and stared at their joined hands. His golden tan against her pallid skin looked . . . wrong. Foreign, somehow.

It made her feel very, very hot.

Get exclusive free bonuses, including three red-hot novellas, by signing up for Lilian's reader list: www.lilianmonroe.com/FourSteps.

ABOUT THE AUTHOR

Lilian Monroe writes swoon-worthy contemporary romances with a dash of mystery, a sprinkle of suspense, and the always-satisfying happily ever after. She is the author of multiple series that go from heart-warming to heart pounding, including We Shouldn't, Unexpected, Manhattan Billionaires, and the Heart's Cove Hotties. When she's not writing, she's daydreaming about which story to tell next.

Keep up with Monroe's latest releases, freebies, and more by visiting her website, www.lilianmonroe.com.